The movement of her mouth as she spoke was mesmerizing.

It wasn't a dance he wanted from her, but something more intimate.

"What would you consider an acceptable stake in a game between us?" She nipped at her lower lip, waiting for his response.

A game between them, a wonderful exotic game. Desire lapped at Lucien the way the ocean washed over the beach. His eyes closed halfway. His attention wouldn't shift from her glorious mouth.

"A kiss," he said.

Yes. A kiss. That's what he wanted from her. That's what he needed.

At the moment, if she'd asked him to stake his entire estate against a chance to kiss her, he'd have willingly done it.

Other **AVON ROMANCES**

ALL MEN ARE ROGUES *by Sari Robins*
BELOVED HIGHLANDER *by Sara Bennett*
THE DUCHESS DIARIES *by Mia Ryan*
FOR THE FIRST TIME *by Kathryn Smith*
ONCE A SCOUNDREL *by Candice Hern*
TO TEMPT A BRIDE *by Edith Layton*
WICKEDLY YOURS *by Brenda Hiatt*

Coming Soon

NO ORDINARY GROOM *by Gayle Callen*
SEEN BY MOONLIGHT *by Kathleen Eschenburg*

And Don't Miss These
ROMANTIC TREASURES
from Avon Books

HOW TO TREAT A LADY *by Karen Hawkins*
THE PLEASURE OF HER KISS *by Linda Needham*
A WEDDING STORY *by Susan Kay Law*

DENISE HAMPTON

ALMOST PERFECT

AVON BOOKS

An Imprint of HarperCollinsPublishers

This is a work of fiction. Names, characters, places, and incidents are products of the author's imagination or are used fictitiously and are not to be construed as real. Any resemblance to actual events, locales, organizations, or persons, living or dead, is entirely coincidental.

AVON BOOKS
An Imprint of HarperCollins*Publishers*
10 East 53rd Street
New York, New York 10022-5299

Copyright © 2003 by Denise Leone
ISBN: 0-06-050911-2
www.avonromance.com

First Avon Books paperback printing: December 2003

Avon Trademark Reg. U.S. Pat. Off. and in Other Countries, Marca Registrada, Hecho en U.S.A.
HarperCollins® is a registered trademark of HarperCollins Publishers Inc.

Printed in the U.S.A.

10 9 8 7 6 5 4 3 2 1

Acknowledgments

First, I want to thank Lucia Macro for suggesting I try this new time period. Who knew the Regency could be so fun? I'd also like to thank Erika Tsang for her enthusiasm. It's priceless. Mostly, I need to thank Joan Domning, Holly Thompson (aka Holly Newman) and Allison Hentges (aka Georgina Devon). Without your assistance this book could never have been written.

Chapter 1

"**E**liza, it's come!" Cassandra Marston's call echoed through her father's empty town house. The last of their servants had left yesterday, giving up their positions with nothing more than Cassie's promise to someday pay their back wages.

Clutching the invitation to her chest, Cassie shut the door behind her, closing out the late July smoke, stench and heat that afflicted London. The sounds of the street—the clip clop of horses, the rattle of a wagon, the cries of a street vendor offering apples— dimmed.

Eight years younger than Cassie's twenty-five, her sister, Elizabeth Conningsby, bounded onto the second-floor landing, then clattered down the stairs. Like Cassie, she was dressed for traveling.

1

Still unbuttoned, Eliza's dark blue pelisse flew back behind her. She wore her most comfortable dress, one made of blue-sprigged muslin, a blue ribbon marking its high waistline.

She came to a stop beside Cassie, her golden curls bouncing and her bonnet swinging from her fingers by its ribbons. Smiling, Cassie turned the invitation in her hands to show it to her sister. Relief filled Eliza's pretty face. Her smile was glorious. Their mother, dead these past two years, had passed her beauty—golden hair, brown eyes and well-made, even features—to both her daughters. It was good that she had; their appearance was the only dowry left to either of them.

"Thank heavens for your aunt, Cassie," Eliza said, laughing and doing a little jig. "I couldn't bear the thought of starting that long ride north without being certain salvation was at hand. All we need do now is wake Father."

The drawing-room door to the right of them creaked open and Sir Roland Conningsby peered out at them, blinking sleepily. "No need to wake me," he said around a yawn. Their father had returned from his evening activities at a little after eight this morning, roused his daughters and demanded they immediately prepare to leave London, something they hadn't planned to do until later in the day. He'd then retreated to don his own unique traveling attire: a coachman's dark maroon jacket, fawn breeches and brown boots. Roland considered himself a great whip and intended to serve as their coachman on their trip to Scotland, which was fine with Cassie for it meant she didn't have to hire a driver.

He stepped out into the entry hall, scrubbing at his eyes. The settee's patterned fabric had imprinted on one side of his round face. What little hair he had left stood up around his head in a tangled white halo. Dark rings hung beneath his eyes.

"Did I hear you call out that your precious invitation had finally arrived?" he asked around another yawn, then smiled. "Just in time, I might add."

His eyes widened, then Roland glanced wildly around the sunny foyer. "Time!" he yelped, and ducked into the drawing-room, where they kept their clock.

He exploded back out into the foyer, his face ashen. "It's eleven of the clock! Didn't I tell you we had to leave before eleven?" he squawked.

"Papa," Cassie said, speaking to him as if he were a slow child, "it doesn't matter what time you want to leave. There's no going before the horses are harnessed. The Owens' stable lad had to finish his own chores before he could help us." Cassie didn't trust Roland to correctly harness their horses, not after a night's drinking, so she'd sent Eliza to beg their neighbor's servant to aid them.

"I could have done it!" Roland yelled at his eldest daughter.

Cassie stared at him. Eliza's eyes were wide and her mouth gaped. Roland had never before raised his voice to either of his children.

"Go!" he shouted. Grabbing Eliza by the arm, he pushed her toward the back of the house. She stumbled a few steps toward the stairs leading down to the house's service rooms, then pivoted back toward the foyer.

The door knocker clanged, the sound ringing through the house. Roland blanched. Cassie and Eliza shared a look, Eliza rolling her eyes in disgust. Cassie knew how she felt. She thought she'd scream if she had to listen to one more angry tradesman call them worthless while demanding they pay money they didn't have for a debt Roland had incurred.

Her father pressed a finger to his lips in warning. "We're not answering that. Run to the coach," he whispered to his daughters.

The knocker clanged again. "Conningsby, open the door," a man called, his voice as imperious as his knock.

Eliza frowned at her. Cassie shrugged. Whoever was at the door was definitely not a tradesman.

The latch rattled. The hinges creaked. The door began to open. Cassie gawked. Who would dare admit themselves to someone else's house?

"It's not locked," Roland yelped as if they ever barred their door during daylight hours.

Neville Mayne, Earl Bucksden, dressed for visiting in a long-tailed blue coat, pantaloons and a tall gray hat upon his head, opened the door. Waiting on the street behind him was his city phaeton with its spiderweb wheels, the earl's tiger, a short, ugly fellow, holding the horse's head. Lord Bucksden, smiling as if he commonly intruded without invitation, closed the door behind him and paused as any good dandy should so the women in the hall might better appreciate his beauty.

And, he was handsome. In his middle years, Lord Bucksden was fit where Roland was fat. Pomaded and brushed forward, wisps of black hair clung to his cheeks. His collar points were exalted, rising well above his jawline, while his neckcloth creased exactly so, beneath his clean-shaven, dimpled chin.

Cassie took a backward step. Although Lord Bucksden presented himself as the handsome ideal, and many gentlewomen agreed with his assessment of himself, Cassie knew better. He was no paragon. Now that she was a widow she was privy to all the darker gossip of the *ton*. One rumor said that so many highborn women had come to ruination in Bucksden's bed that the earl's bastards would one day sit at the heads of a dozen ancient families. Lord Bucksden's skill at the card table had bankrupted many, while his skill with weapons had ended the lives of three gentlemen.

"Mrs. Marston," the earl said to Cassie, sweeping his hat from his head, then fixed Eliza with his bold gaze. "Miss Conningsby."

From the corner of her eye Cassie saw her father slither into the drawing room. Coward! Roland didn't want to face the consequences of whatever had happened between him and the earl. As usual he meant to leave his womenfolk to clean up his mess.

Eliza also noticed. Shooting Cassie a worried look, she slipped into the drawing room after their father.

Cassie followed without offering Lord Bucksden so much as a greeting. An interloper, even a wellborn one, hardly warranted a welcome.

Their drawing room, with its gentle blue walls, was the only space in the house that still had all its furnishings: blue draperies, a buff carpet and the comfortable ecru settee. It reflected Lady Conningsby's long rule over this household and her iron control over her husband's purse—a control Cassie had been unable to duplicate. The value of the furnishings Cassie hadn't sold, as she tried to repay what they owed, Roland had lost at the tables. This month his club had finally stopped extending him credit, at last acknowledging that Sir Roland Conningsby could no longer cover his debts.

Roland stood with his back to the room's tall street windows, shifting from foot to foot and toying with his watch chain, fidgeting as he always did when he was feeling guilty. As his daughters entered, he opened his arms, his gesture suggesting he had protection to offer. Eliza hurried to his side. Cassie stopped in front of the large Wedgwood urn displayed on a pedestal near the hearth. She knew too well that their father had no succor to offer.

Lord Bucksden stopped beside her, again breaching all etiquette by entering their private chamber without an invitation.

"Father, why is Lord Bucksden here?" Cassie asked, ignoring the nobleman.

"Why, to collect my winnings, Mrs. Marston," the earl replied for Roland.

Roland blanched, whitening so much that Cassie thought he might swoon. "I was besotted, Bucksden. You can't possibly hold me to that ridiculous wager."

The earl cocked his head to an elegant angle. "Why shouldn't I hold you to it, Conningsby? You proposed the wager, you gambled. You lost. Now I've come to collect."

He crooked his elbow in Eliza's direction. "Miss Conningsby, if you would be so kind?"

Roland stepped between his youngest daughter and the earl. He thrust out his chest and spread his arms wide. "You cannot have her."

Cassie gasped in horrified comprehension. "What have you done?" she demanded of Roland.

Lord Bucksden shot her a sidelong glance. "What he did, Mrs. Marston, was game with me. My stake was three thousand pounds, an amount I understand would have resolved your present financial discomfort. Your father's stake was your sister as my mistress." Bucksden smiled.

Cassie's knees weakened in disbelief. This couldn't be happening. Three thousand was about a tenth of what they needed, but their father wouldn't know that. It had fallen to their mother, and Cassie after her, to tend the family's accounts.

Across the room Eliza opened her mouth as if to scream. No sound came forth. She dropped her bonnet. It bounced away from her as she sank to her knees and buried her face in her hands.

"You odious man!" Cassie cried, not certain if she

chided Lord Bucksden, her father, or all the gamblers who had conspired to complicate her life. That list included her departed husband who, despite his sweetness and charm, and his religious prattle, had proved to be a closet wastrel.

"Unnecessary vitriol, Mrs. Marston," the handsome earl retorted smoothly. "You act as though I intend your sister harm, when pleasure's my purpose. Miss Conningsby will have a far better life as my mistress than she can now expect as Sir Roland's daughter."

He smiled at the kneeling Eliza. "Sweet, beautiful creature," he crooned. "If only you weren't related to Sir Roland, your beauty might tempt some man to overlook your impoverishment and offer for you. But no gentleman could ever tolerate a marriage that connects him to your foolish, penniless sot of a sire. The only one who'll have you now is a tradesman's son, but even one so low might consider long and hard before offering. Your bloodline won't open many doors these days."

Roland's face whitened even further at this, his eyes tearing. Cassie wondered if it was the first time he'd been forced to listen to the opinion his peers and betters held of him.

Across the room Eliza sent Cassie a pleading look. The ashes of her girlhood dreams had grayed her face. A future steeped in the most horrible kind of shame made her eyes glisten.

Desperate to save her sister Cassie stepped between Lord Bucksden and the back of the room. "I don't care what you and my father wagered last night, my lord, you cannot have Eliza. Remove yourself from our house."

Steel glinted in the earl's dark eyes. When Cassie didn't move, those glints hardened into the deep and dangerous rage that had allowed him to kill men. His fists closed. It was an effective threat from a man with so powerful a form. Still, she held her ground.

He took a step toward her, his lip curling in threat. Cassie's heart failed her. She shifted to the side, out of his way, only to collide with the pedestal behind her. The urn wobbled. The invitation still clutched in her hand, she grabbed for the urn in instinctive reaction, steadying it with her hand on the handle.

Satisfaction filled Lord Bucksden's face. "Very wise of you, Mrs. Marston. Your interference could be costly to you. Defy me, and I'll see to it that you and your sister will wear nothing but rags for the remainder of your days." His warning stabbed through Cassie, all the more threatening because she knew he'd done the same to others.

"I'd rather wear rags than become your mistress," Eliza shouted, leaping to her feet. "I won't do this!"

The earl chuckled and turned to look once more on Eliza. Dark pleasure filled his gaze. "Feel free to resist with all your might, my dear Elizabeth. I like fiery women. Breaking your spirit will be the first of the many pleasures we shall share together."

He started toward Eliza, extending a graceful hand. "Come now, it's time we left."

"Cassie!" Eliza screamed, retreating to stand against the windows behind her.

Before Cassie knew what she intended, the urn was in her hands. She swung the heavy piece with all her might. It met the back of Lord Bucksden's skull with a most satisfying thud, exploding into pieces. The earl groaned and toppled, crashing against the edge of the small table standing between him and their settee. The table splintered under his weight. Lord Bucksden came to a rest on the floor among its pieces.

Silence thundered in the room, broken only by Eliza's ragged breathing. Blank astonishment filled Roland's face. Cassie stared at the fallen nobleman, trembling.

Lord Bucksden lay facedown, legs aspraddle, arms at awkward angles—a marionette whose strings had been cut. A dark stain spread out from beneath his head, dampening the carpet.

Dropping the shattered remains of the urn, Cassie took a step toward him. The rustle of her pelisse and gown was impossibly loud in the quiet. She leaned down, hoping for a closer look at the damage she'd done. Lord Bucksden's face was gray, his mouth slack. The puddle beneath his head continued to spread. His chest didn't appear to move.

"Does his heart beat?" Roland asked, his voice hoarse and low.

Edging closer, Cassie reached out for Lord Bucksden's wrist above the top of his glove. She stopped before touching his skin. What if she hadn't killed him? The thought of what the earl would do to them if he recovered from her assault spurred Cassie to lay her fingers against his wrist. She closed her eyes and concentrated. Nothing, not so much as a wayward thud under the smooth coolness of his skin.

She straightened with a start, her head swimming. "Oh help, he's dead," she whispered.

"Are you certain?" Roland asked, sounding as terrified as Cassie felt.

Ice encased Cassie, freezing her limbs, her thoughts, even the blood in her veins. "I must be. Didn't I tend to both my mother and my husband before they were laid to rest? He looks as still as either of them."

As she spoke those words Cassie's lungs ceased to work. She'd killed a man. No, she'd *murdered* an earl. She'd hang for that.

Her father caught her before she hit the floor. Wrapping his arm around her back, he brought her upright. "Now is no time to give way to the vapors, my fierce girl," he said. Fear filled his voice. "We need you clear-headed if you're going to save us."

His words brought Cassie up out of darkness, everything inside her screaming in protest. Saving them was what she'd been trying to do these past years, with no help from him. And for these past two years she'd done nothing but fail. The best she could manage was to keep the lids on the pots of boiling catastrophes that littered Roland's path. Why couldn't her father save them this time?

Eliza appeared at Cassie's side. Such gratitude filled her sister's expression that tears stung Cassie's eyes.

"A thousand thanks, Cassie. I'll never forget what you've done for me this day, not if I live forever," she said, then grabbed Cassie by the hand. "Come! We have to leave before anyone discovers what's happened."

Shaking her head, Cassie pulled her hand from Eliza's. "There's nowhere to go." Even her voice was icy, sounding as flat and frozen as a winter lake. "I've destroyed you more completely than Lord Bucksden ever could. Oh Eliza, a moment ago you were just a wastrel's daughter." Roland winced. "Now you're a murderess's sister with no prospect except a lifetime's shame after I hang."

"I'm not—" Eliza started to protest.

Cassie spoke over her. "As for escape, how? We've nothing to our names but my twenty pounds." That was all that remained of Cassie's yearly allowance from her widow's portion. "We won't keep what Aunt Philana sent to pay our expenses for the trip north. How long can we elude the Bow Street Runners with only twenty pounds?"

"But Cassie, how will the Runners find us?" Eliza asked, her tone urgent and the expression in her eyes intense. "None of our neighbors or friends know we go north to your Aunt Forster's house. They all think we're off to visit cousins in Brighton." They'd kept their destination secret to better escape Roland's creditors.

"Clever Eliza," Roland said as if Eliza were a well-trained dog. His smile sat crookedly on his lips beneath his bloodshot blue eyes. "You're right. We've got an hour or more before the earl's tiger begins to wonder what happened to his master. If we leave now I think we can elude those who pursue us."

His hopeful facade cracked. "At least for a while."

"For longer than that," Eliza retorted, determination filling her brown eyes as her jaw set. Again, she tugged on Cassie's hand. "If Papa can get us to Scotland without being detected, then we can purchase passage to America."

"America?" Cassie repeated dully.

"Not just America. Boston," Eliza urged, pulling Cassie a few steps closer to the drawing-room door, "where those cousins of Papa's live. What are their names again?"

Roland's face took light, glowing like the full moon. "Of course! Godfrey will take us in. Egad, he has no choice. He's family." He hurried to the door.

The ice in Cassie began to melt. They would go to America and begin life anew. "Once when I visited Aunt Philana, we shopped in Edinburgh," she offered. "It only took a full day to reach the city from Ettrick House. I think ships leave from Edinburgh's port all the time. Surely one will be going to America."

"At last you're sensible again," Eliza crowed, relief softening her expression.

"Wait," Roland said, stopping in the doorway and turning to look at his daughters. "Cassie says she has only twenty pounds. We'll need at least fifty each for passage to America, and more to begin a new life. We can sell the coach and horses in Edinburgh. That's only half of what we need. I need at least an hour with my solicitor. He'll let me draw two hundred pounds against my properties."

"We can't make a draw," Eliza replied with a scornful huff, crossing her arms.

"What do you mean?" Roland demanded, looking both insulted and concerned in the same instant. "Of course I can make a draw."

Her eyes wide, Cassie waved a warning at Eliza. Her sister put her hands on her hips. "You and Mama! Shame on you both for coddling him so. Now is no time to be squeamish. Tell him."

"Tell me what?" Roland asked.

Cassie drew a slow breath. Eliza was right. Their mother's control over the purse strings along with her refusal to confront their father had allowed him to remain silly and irresponsible for too long.

"Papa," Cassie said, "you can't make a draw, because you've bankrupted us."

Roland's expression flattened in surprise. "That's not possible," he protested, although with none of his usual bluff and bluster. "My properties have always provided us a good income."

"No longer," Cassie said with a shake of her head. "Do you remember mortgaging them after Mama's death?" It was something Cassie hadn't discovered until a few weeks ago, when a disreputable-looking man had tapped upon their door—a lowlife. The interview had left her feeling dirty. The man had made it clear he'd never expected Roland to make any of the payments. Instead, he'd counted on taking their properties for himself.

Roland frowned. "Did I?"

"You did, but didn't tell me. No payments were made, and now the lender forecloses. We have nothing left."

Roland's eyes hollowed. "Whatever shall we do?" he whispered, helpless as always.

Drawing a fortifying breath, Cassie launched into the explanation she'd hoped to avoid. "Eliza and I decided that I would use my . . ." she hesitated, knowing that her father didn't want to hear what came next. Eliza sent her a narrow-eyed look. Cassie plowed on.

"That I would use my skill on Aunt Philana's neighbors to generate a bit of income." Now, instead of giving them some ready cash, she'd gamble to buy their passage to America.

Disgust flickered over Roland's face. He shuddered. "You can still do that . . . thing . . . you do?"

Cassie nodded. She'd been Eliza's age when her father discovered she had an unusual gift with playing cards. He'd immediately forbidden her to game at all. She'd honored his edict until her marriage. Then, because her husband, Charles, had thought her clever for it, she'd used her odd aptitude to astound her dearest friends.

"No," Roland said. His face hardened. He drew himself up to his tallest. "No, I won't have it. No daughter of mine will court being named a sharp."

Cassie's throat tightened against an imaginary rope. Better to destroy her name than to hang. "You'll not only tolerate it, Papa, you'll thank me for it. That is, unless you'd rather I come to trial for the

earl's death. If that happens, I'll have to tell all who
listen that I killed Lord Bucksden to rescue my sister,
the daughter you offered as ante in a card game and
lost. Which shame is worse?"

Roland whitened anew at her words. In that moment, his every year showed in his face. Now that he
could no longer pretend ignorance of their situation,
his expression revealed that he knew—that he might
well have always known—what he'd done to his
family, and he was shamed by it. A lot of good that
did them now! Without a word Roland turned and
strode through the drawing-room door.

"My bonnet," Eliza cried, sprinting back across
the room to fetch her hat.

Cassie stopped just inside the drawing-room
door, waiting for Eliza to exit before her, then
stepped out. As she turned to close the door, her
gaze was drawn to Lord Bucksden's still form like
iron to lodestone.

A different sort of terror shot through her. She
hadn't used her card-playing ability since Charles's
death. What if she no longer had it? Nor had she
ever before used it to gamble. She didn't even know
if it would work when money was involved.

What if it did work? Cassie's skin crawled. To use
her skill to take coins from unsuspecting people
seemed unnatural, and left her feeling as dirty as
that interview with Papa's mortgager.

What choice did she have? They were desperate.
Without those coins she couldn't save Eliza.

Pulling the drawing-room door shut behind her,
Cassie fled to her father's coach.

* * *

Holding back the ancient coach's leather curtain, Cassie leaned out of the door's glassless opening into a misty summer afternoon. She breathed in the scents of southern Scotland: rain, damp earth, sheep and coal smoke. Here along the border between Scotland and England, the landscape alternated between long, flat plains and twisting, undulating hills. Time and countless cooking fires had stripped the low peaks of their trees, leaving only heather, prickly gorse and thick grass.

Roland snapped his whip, gave a joyous curse and drove their tired horses through a flock of complaining sheep. Inside the carriage Cassie bounced. Roland was the only one enjoying Scotland's primitive road conditions. The deeper the ruts the bluer his curses became as he immersed himself in his role as coachman.

*Baa*ing, bells ringing, the flock scattered away from their coach's wheels, leaving nothing to block Cassie's view of the rolling stretch of manicured lawn leading upward to Ettrick House. At the top of the steep slope that led from hillside to the edge of the Ettrick Water, Aunt Philana's gray stone home rose above the carefully cultivated copses of trees that dotted her estate. The house's wet slate roof gleamed like silver in the day's watery light. Three horizontal lines of rectangular windows, all decoratively capped with white triangles, marched across its face. A broad sweep of stairs led up from a gravel courtyard to a massive doorway protected by a white stone portico.

Easing back into the coach, Cassie shook Eliza out of her fitful nap. Neither of them had slept well since leaving London. " 'Liza?"

"Has something happened?" Eliza said, waking with a start. It wasn't the travails of travel that had put the new paleness in her face, framed in the brim of her bent bonnet—Eliza's hat had been damaged when she'd dropped it in their London drawing room—or laid the dark rings beneath her pretty eyes.

Cassie shook her head. "Nothing at all, darling, except that we've arrived at Ettrick House."

A touch of color returned to Eliza's cheeks. "There was no one on the road this morning?"

They'd taken turns watching the road behind them, checking for pursuers. Again Cassie shook her head. "Not a soul."

A slow smile crept across Eliza's face. New life sparked in her brown eyes. She leaned forward to throw her arms around Cassie.

"We've done it! We've reached Scotland unde-tected. Two weeks from now we'll leave for America, long before the Runners ever think to look for us here. We're safe."

"I hope so, Eliza," Cassie said, wishing she'd never swung that urn. Her stomach bucked at the thought of having taken a life, even one so vile as Lord Bucksden's. She ached at the thought of leaving the country of her birth and all she held dear. If only she'd taken a moment to think she might have found a more sensible, less violent way to escape what her father had wrought.

Smiling and looking more like herself than she had since they'd left London, Eliza took Cassie's place at the window, lifting the leather flap. A moment later she waved. Excitement raced through Cassie. She joined Eliza in the window.

The porch before Ettrick House's main door was no longer empty. A bewigged footman, wearing a blue satin coat, blue knee breeches and white stockings, stood on the top stair, waiting for their arrival. A slender woman stood at the porch's forward edge. Heedless of the damage the mist was doing to her attire, she waved at the approaching coach, using her whole arm to offer the greeting. Aunt Philana.

Leaning as far out as she dared, Cassie waved back, not caring that muck from the coach stained her sleeve. Although she and Philana weren't related by blood, their connection being through their husbands, they had fallen in love with each other at their first meeting. Their affection had persisted unabated across the years, surviving the deaths of both their spouses.

Their coach wheels crunching in the gravel, the horses snorting, Roland brought the vehicle to a halt before the stairs. A pair of hostlers, dressed in brown jackets and stained breeches, bits of straw clinging to their hats, came trotting around one corner. The footman made his dignified way down the steps, opened the coach door and helped Cassie down.

"You're here at last!" Aunt Philana called down to her former niece by marriage from the porch. Her plain lined face creased even more as she smiled. A lace cap covered her gray curls while an equally lacy shawl draped her shoulders. Philana's day dress was cut in the current high-waisted style, but made of yesteryear's fabric, a heavy gold-and-white-striped brocade.

Ignoring her aching legs and back, Cassie sprinted up the steps to wrap her arms around the smaller woman. Philana leaned back in Cassie's embrace. Welcome filled her bright blue eyes.

"I thought you'd never arrive," she said.

"It seemed like that to us, too." Cassie laughed, pleased beyond saying to be in Philana's reassuring presence. "Our axle cracked two days ago and Papa didn't think the repair would hold long enough to get us here."

"I cannot say how glad I am to see you," Philana said, blinking back tears.

She reached up and caught Cassie's face between her hands. Her palms were papery, her skin warm and her touch infinitely appreciated. The faint scent of violets emanated from her. Much to Cassie's horror, she wanted to tell her aunt the whole sordid tale of Lord Bucksden's death.

She swallowed it. She, her father and sister had all agreed that telling Philana, or borrowing from her the money they needed to escape, might lead to Philana being accused as their accomplice, when she was wholly innocent. Cassie refused to put her aunt in danger. It was bad enough that they had to come here, tainting her by the association of their presence.

"What is it, sweetheart?" Philana asked, releasing

Cassie. Her silvery brows lifted in a promise to listen.

Cassie only shook her head. "You know too well what plagues me."

Philana was the only one outside the family who knew just how desperate their straits were. It had been their financial problems that spurred the old woman to offer an open-ended invitation to the Conningsbys. Philana's eyes narrowed. She was perceptive, sometimes too perceptive for the good of those trying to hide things from her. Cassie was grateful for the distraction of Eliza and Roland's appearance beside her.

"Sir Roland," Philana said a little coldly to their father. She'd more than once written to Cassie that she could have no respect for a man who squandered his daughters' dowries and futures.

Bright color, something that might have been shame, flushed Roland's cheeks. "Lady Forster." He bowed to her, then walked swiftly toward the house's door, where he stopped. Roland had better manners than Lord Bucksden; he wouldn't enter before his hostess invited him.

Her expression warming, Philana turned her attention to Eliza, taking the girl's hands. "Who is this beauty and what happened to the darling babe I met at my nephew's wedding?"

Smiling, Eliza bobbed. "How good to see you again, Lady Forster."

"Pish," Philana said with a chiding look. "I'll have none of that. You'll call me Aunt Philana, as your sister does. Now, we'll hie ourselves inside for a moment or two while my coach is brought around. If you want your coach with you at the house party, Sir Roland, you'll need to drive it there yourself. I have only one coachman and he must handle my team," she called to Cassie's father.

"Where are we going?" Cassie asked in surprise.

Philana shot her a startled glance. "Where else, but to take up residence at Ryecroft Castle?"

"Take up residence? But I thought we were staying here for the duration of the party," Eliza said, her voice reflecting Cassie's confusion. Because Ettrick House lay less than two miles from the earl's home, the plan had been for them to reside here, then ride to Ryecroft Castle each morning and return to Aunt Philana's house every evening.

There was something sly in the smile that curved Philana's lips. "Matters have changed a little and to our benefit, I think. I met Lord Ryecroft a few days ago. He mentioned a few of his guests canceled at the last moment due to illness, and he offered us accommodations in his home for the party. I accepted on your behalf."

"But I thought the house party didn't start for another day. Why do we go now?" Cassie asked. She had looked forward to at least one day alone with Philana. It was time she needed to prepare herself for the task ahead of her.

Philana's smile dimmed into confusion. She glanced from Cassie to Eliza. "What do you mean? If we don't go this very instant we won't have time to properly prepare for tonight's ball."

"What ball?" Eliza asked.

Philana still looked confused. "Lord Ryecroft advanced the party's starting date so he could invite the entire neighborhood to a grand ball. You cannot imagine how excited the whole vale has been over the event. Didn't you read the earl's invitation?"

Cassie turned to stone. In her mind's eye she conjured up an image of Lord Ryecroft's invitation. The fine rectangle of paper imprinted with the earl's family arms lay right where she'd dropped it when she snatched up the deadly urn: at the base of the pedestal in her mother's drawing-room, not far from where Bucksden's body lay.

There it remained still, right where anyone, especially someone who might be looking for a murderess, could find it.

Chapter 2

Lucien Hollier, the only living man remaining in the long line of barons who'd ruled Graceton Castle, needed an heir, and this time he'd know for certain that his son wasn't one of Bucksden's bastards. Once he had that boy-child, Lucien intended to call out Bucksden. One of them would die.

Dressed in his black formal attire, Lucien scanned Ryecroft Castle's crowded ballroom. The room glittered from its marble floor to the candles and crystals that sparkled on the chandelier. The walls were dressed in rich red and gold leaf, the fireplace trimmed with an ornate frieze. People laughed and talked. The music swelled. The dancers, some London elegant, others Border rustic, jigged together without prejudice.

Lucien ignored the men in the room, all except for Jonathan Percy, who was making his way toward the card room accompanied by three burly squires. There was no ignoring Percy, Lucien's distant cousin and the earl of Westmorland's acknowledged by-blow. Tonight, the boy wore a bright pink-and-green waistcoat beneath a coat cut to the highest of fashion.

Instead, it was the young women, the potential wives, who held Lucien's interest. Maidens all, they shimmered and glowed in their finery, silk flowers tucked into their headbands, curling wisps of hair brushing at shoulders, their high-waisted, low-cut bodices revealing almost as much as any man liked to see. Lucien dismissed the prettiest of them; he didn't need another wife capable of attracting other men. It was the plainer women in the room he watched, assessing them one by one as if he could discern by look alone which might prove the most fertile.

"You're late, Hollier," said Adam Devanney, Earl Ryecroft, from behind Lucien. "The evening's half done."

Lucien glanced over his shoulder at his first cousin. They were as close as brothers. Adam and his siblings had been raised at Graceton Castle after the death of their mother, before Devanney's father had inherited Ryecroft's title.

At twenty-nine, four years Lucien's junior, Devanney was his father's dark and classically handsome image. His only Hollier trait, inherited from Lucien's paternal aunt, was his gray eyes. It was Lucien's fate to resemble his ancestors with his gray eyes, wavy golden-brown hair, chiseled cheekbones, and long, straight nose. As different as Devanney and Lucien were in looks, they were similar in build—both tall, broad-shouldered men.

Lucien smiled. "Hastings insisted that I couldn't make my return to society out of mourning in any state of dress less than flawless," he replied.

"Now that's a valet worth his salt," Devanney laughed. "So tell me: How hard did Hastings have to scrub to remove the stench of fish?" Lucien had spent his last two summers in isolation at his nearby fishing lodge.

"I've no skin left," Lucien retorted with a forced smile, wishing Devanney would leave off but knowing he wouldn't. His cousin was determined to do whatever it took to distract Lucien from his goal of finding a wife at this party.

"What do you do with what you catch, anyway? Don't tell me you eat it." Devanney's pretense of languid dismay rivaled anything Keane had ever produced for the stage.

Amused despite himself, Lucien let the corner of his mouth lift. "Why should I eat it when your chef pays handsomely for what I catch? Enough, to keep my lodge in beef," he finished, taunting his cousin.

Devanney huffed in disgust. "Does he? As if you needed another shilling to your name. You've more blunt than I do," he grumbled. "Ah well, I shall have to overcome my pique and pretend that I'm glad to see you out and about. A warning, cuz. If you persist, people will think you've rusticated these last two years."

"How so?" Lucien asked, a little startled.

At that moment the dance ended and the jiggers came to a halt. Rather than begin a new piece, the white-wigged, black-clothed musicians set aside their instruments to take a brief respite. The dancers wove their way back to their parties, more than a few pausing to bow to Devanney and Lucien, and receiving their show of respect in return. A moment later the sound of conversation rose to a new, thundering thrum in the big room.

Devanney again turned his attention to Lucien. His expression shifted until he looked every bit as supercilious as any society maven. "My dear Lord Graceton, it really isn't appropriate to stare at my female guests as if you mean to chew them up and spit out their bones," he warned, shaking a chiding finger.

"I was hardly staring," Lucien retorted, trying his best not to let his cousin charm him.

Devanney's pomposity dissolved, leaving Lucien staring at the most worrisome of his cousin's many faces, one of wicked enjoyment. He and Devanney shared a history of pranks between them. This ball and Lucien's return to society offered Devanney the perfect occasion for just such a trick. This was all the more true because Lucien's last prank on Devanney had been successful.

"You were indeed staring, just not at all in the right direction," his cousin replied, then took Lucien by the shoulders and turned him to look toward the back of the room. "Try that direction."

The crowd there was thinner. Lucien spied Lady Forster, a viscount's daughter who for love's sake had married down. He'd first met the old woman at the beginning of his mourning period two years ago when he purchased his fishing lodge, his private Eden, near her home. The old woman wore lavender, the color a mark of respect for her beloved, departed squire. A diamond clip held a single black ostrich feather in her steel-colored curls.

"What's notable about Lady Forster?" Lucien asked, adding to himself, *Other than to remember to stay out of her way*. Although Philana Forster was a good soul, she found far too much joy in meddling in the affairs of others for his peace of mind.

"Not her, the woman beside her. Look beyond Egremont's shoulder," Devanney said, his words directing Lucien to the back of the blue-coated colonel who stood between Lady Forster and his host.

Lucien had to shift to see the girl Devanney meant, then he wondered how he could have missed her. She was stunning, glowing as brightly as the room's candles with her golden hair and a white-on-white gown. She wore no jewelry, but her sort of beauty didn't require cold stones and gold to enhance it.

"Now, she's a prime article," Lucien acknowledged, dismissing her from his list of potential wives even more swiftly than he'd marked off the other beauties. Her vibrancy was just the sort of thing that attracted dastards like Bucksden.

As Lucien started to look away, the girl cocked her head to one side and laughed at something Egremont said. The gesture and the movement of her mouth was poignant in its familiarity, an almost painful reminder of someone else.

Colonel Egremont bowed. Lucien caught his breath and looked upon that someone, the woman to whom he'd almost given his heart.

Cassie. Six years and a simple gown of shimmering pale gray silk couldn't dim her beauty. Her hair, gathered into a beguiling tangle of curls at her nape, was still the color of sun-ripened wheat. Her fair skin was flawless, her brown eyes ringed by thick dark lashes under gentle golden brows. Her lips were just as lush and seductive as they'd been the year of her debut.

Bittersweet memories washed over Lucien. He'd been twenty-seven then, an age that now seemed impossibly young to him, and Cassie hadn't been the usual insipid debutante. For one brief crazed month of his life he'd been under the spell of her merry, impertinent personality, bewitched into believing he could tolerate a father-in-law ready to squander another man's inheritance the way Sir Roland Conningsby had already wasted his own. Lucien's delusion had ended when a giggling, drunken Sir Roland tried to trade on Lucien's interest in his daughter by begging for a little loan, one Lucien didn't doubt would never have been repaid. It was too potent an omen. Not willing to make himself a laughingstock with his peers by marrying Cassie, Lucien had reluctantly withdrawn from her circle of admirers. Good sense triumphed over a wayward heart.

Now he studied Cassie, wanting some sign that she was still the insouciant girl he'd known, only to be disappointed. Sadness clung to the curve of her mouth, while worry touched her brow. Lucien was hardly surprised. Her promising season had ended with but a single offer of marriage, from Charles Marston. Lady Forster's nephew by marriage had seemed to the world a perfect vicar and crusader against moral decay. It was all talk. Lucien had known Charles in school. Once the boy had a few drinks in him he slid off the high ground to wallow in the mire with the rest of the world's sinners, especially when the temptation being offered was gaming.

Devanney leaned closer to Lucien. Lucien started. He'd so completely lost himself in contemplation of Cassie that he'd forgotten the crowded ballroom.

"Although Miss Elizabeth Conningsby is a beauty, of the two I think her older sister is the prime article," Devanney said, his warm tone hinting that his prank somehow included Cassie.

"Only if you don't mind their kin," Lucien replied. "I tell you, there's no worse gambler than a sot, and no worse sot than one who giggles. As for her husband . . ." Lucien started, but across the room Cassie smiled and whatever else Lucien had meant to say dissolved.

The tiny lift of Cassie's lips wasn't the pretty grin he remembered; yet, hints of the clever flirt she'd been came to life in her face. Something stirred in Lucien, stretching, unwinding within him. It'd been so long since he'd felt anything but disappointment and anger that he almost didn't recognize the sensation—one of hunger for a woman's admiration, and her touch.

Devanney shot him a startled look. "Husband? We are both looking at Mrs. Cassandra Marston, aren't we? She's been widowed these past three years."

Lucien's newly awakened awareness of Cassie as a woman exploded into a full and starved life. Cassie was a widow? He looked at Devanney. "Are you certain?"

"Of course I am," his cousin replied, his brows lifting again and his mouth twisting slyly. "Rumor has it that the beauteous Mrs. Marston remained faithful throughout her marriage despite her husband's somewhat wild behavior toward the end of his life. Very proper. Very well behaved."

Lucien turned his gaze back to Cassie, and awareness of all else except her dissolved. He watched her lean toward Egremont, candlelight spilling onto the smooth, white skin of her decolletage. A tantalizing shadow appeared between her breasts. One hunger became another.

There'd been a time when pursuing and being pursued in return had been the greatest joy in his life. The thought of playing that game with a woman he had once wanted enough to consider marrying was even more alluring. What would Cassie look like stripped of her clothing, her golden hair streaming over his counterpane?

His cousin leaned a little closer. "She and her sister occupy the bedchamber directly across from yours, Hollier," he whispered. "What do you think? As you've so often told me, widows enjoy a certain freedom in society, and house parties offer so many interesting opportunities for trysts. Can you seduce the prim widow, or have you forgotten how to play the rake?"

Across the room Cassie's smile widened. Lucien threw off the ice of his past three years. It didn't matter that he knew his cousin's prank included Cassie. The challenge hung before Lucien as lush and tempting as a bunch of summer cherries.

"Come with me to meet her," Devanney urged, his voice still low and suggestive. "I'm to partner her sister for the first dance of the next set. I haven't seen Mrs. Marston on the floor for an hour or two now. I'm wagering that she'll be available. By the by, the next set begins with a waltz."

It was potent bait that Devanney dangled in front of Lucien, the way Lucien offered flies to the fish in his stream. And, just like the scaly creatures he'd spent the last months pulling out of the water, Lucien took it. His newly reawakened interest in Cassie demanded the chance to hold her close to him, guiding her through the waltz's sensual movements.

Why shouldn't he pursue her? The search for a wife didn't preclude the seduction of a widow at the same time. Why shouldn't he and Cassie fulfill the promise of pleasure that had once existed between them now that they were both free of the bonds and betrayals of matrimony?

Not waiting for Devanney, Lucien started across the ballroom, wanting that waltz more than anything he'd anticipated in the last six years.

A pleased Colonel Egremont added his name to Eliza's almost full dance card, then bowed and retreated. Cassie watched the colonel, dressed in his fine blue jacket with its scarlet trim, golden epaulettes and golden belt, leave them, torn between satisfaction and fear. The satisfaction came from the thought that although Eliza might never have her London season she'd at least have the opportunity to break a few hearts at this house party. The fear arose from the colonel's commission. Although there was nothing intimidating about the young man, Cassie had to consider him a potential enemy. If news of Bucksden's untimely death reached Scotland the soldier might well consider it his duty to take the murderess into his custody.

Laughing in excitement, Eliza leaned close to Cassie. "This night is just too superior to be borne. Why, everything about Ryecroft Castle is exquisite! I shall enjoy every moment of the next two weeks."

Cassie did her best to smile. She hadn't told Eliza or her father about the forgotten invitation, nor would she. What good would her confession do except to make them worry that the Runners were already on their way? Cassie was doing enough of that for all of them. Far better that Eliza enjoy herself.

It was a noble but isolating intention. Between looming disaster, and the noise and closeness in the ballroom, Cassie's head pounded. She opened her fan and plied it with vigor.

"You should make it your purpose to enjoy every moment," Philana commanded Eliza. "It's the duty of every beautiful young girl to wring as much gaiety from her day as she can."

Cassie let her attention slip to the ballroom's opposite end and the door that led to the earl's drawing room, where the card tables were. She longed to be there right now, hard at winning what they needed to escape England. At the same time, the thought of joining the gamesters terrified her. Because of that forgotten invitation she doubted she'd have the full two weeks to turn her twenty pounds into two hundred. Yet, if she made one mistake or won too consistently, someone would accuse her of being a sharp. The moment that accusation slipped from anyone's lips, Cassie would never again sit at a card table, and she and her family would be doomed.

"Where did Sir Roland go, Cassie?" Philana asked.

"Hmm?" Cassie's attention rose from the morass of anxiety she hid within her. "Papa? He went back to his chamber to retie his stock. He said it still didn't look right. I fear he's not tolerating his lack of a valet." She smiled at her aunt. "Thank you again for sharing your maid with us, Philana."

"Not at all. Betty enjoys the challenge and the chance to serve pretty women. My aged plainness bores her, I think," Philana replied, then glanced behind her. "Ah, good. The musicians are returning."

The men, dressed in black, their hair concealed beneath the powdered wigs that belonged to the last century, worked their way past Cassie and her relatives. Grateful for any distraction, Cassie watched them wind around the next clutch of well-dressed gentlefolk on their way back to the chairs set for them in the ballroom's corner.

"But if the dancing is to begin again, where is Eliza's next partner?" Philana asked, laughing as she caught Cassie's sister by the arm, pulling Eliza close to her. "I shan't tolerate any man abandoning you, my dear. Who is it? I shall go fetch him for you."

Eliza grinned, having fallen as completely under Philana's loving spell as Cassie. "Let me see," she replied, consulting the pretty little brass-bound dance card that Lord Ryecroft had provided for each of his female guests. "Why, it's Lord Ryecroft who has this dance. Off you go, Aunt Philana. Bring him here by his ear, with apologies to me upon his lips," she finished, shooting a laughing look from over the top of the tiny booklet only to straighten with a start, bright color flushing her cheeks.

"Oh! Lord Ryecroft. We were just speaking of you," she stammered.

Cassie glanced behind her. Her heart lifted into her throat. Standing next to the darkly handsome earl was Lucien Hollier. Pivoting, her hand at her breast, Cassie stared at Lord Graceton, the man who'd broken a foolish girl's heart.

Lucien looked even more handsome as a three-and-thirty-year-old widower than he had at twenty-seven. She didn't remember his being so tall. Cassie's head would barely reach his clean-shaven jawline. Lucien was no less fit now than he had been, judging from the way his black coat clung to the powerful span of his broad shoulders. His snowy stock was the perfect contrast to his sun-browned skin and the golden streaks summer had burned into the dark honey color of his hair. Above the rugged jut of his cheekbones the expression in his clear gray eyes was as intense as ever.

"Ladies," the earl said, bowing.

Lucien neither bowed nor spoke. He only smiled, his full attention on Cassie. Every inch of her body came to wicked life. Her pulse pounded in her ears. His charming lopsided grin hadn't changed at all.

"Why, good evening, Lord Ryecroft." Philana purred the greeting, coyly plying her fan. "And Lord Graceton. I had no idea you intended to participate in your cousin's house party."

Lord Ryecroft shot his kinsman a laughing look. "He wouldn't be here if I hadn't gone to that rustic hideaway of his and begged. I needed one more man to balance out the party."

Lucien's gaze never left Cassie. "More fool me for trying to resist him."

Cassie shivered. How could she ever have forgotten his voice? It was as smooth and deep as dark velvet.

"Lord Graceton, do you know my nieces?" Philana asked, her voice tight with repressed humor. "The one you're not looking at is Miss Elizabeth Conningsby. The one on whom your attention is so rudely fixed is Mrs. Marston."

From the corner of her eye Cassie caught Lord Ryecroft's grin. Behind her, Eliza tittered. Cassie couldn't move, not while she was drowning in Lucien's gaze.

The shift in Lucien's smile said he recognized Philana's taunt for what it was. He managed a swift glance toward Eliza. "A pleasure, Miss Conningsby," he said, then brought his attention back to Cassie. "As for Mrs. Marston, we are already acquainted."

Eliza's quiet gasp suggested an interrogation in Cassie's future. Lord Ryecroft's swift sidelong look at his cousin promised the same sort of inquiry for Lucien. Beside Cassie, Philana also shifted in surprise, her gown rustling.

"So we are, or were," Cassie replied, giving them all the explanation they craved but couldn't request. "Lord Graceton and I met during my season, eons ago."

"Eons? Does it seem that long to you?" Lucien asked, still watching her as if she were the only woman in the world.

In that instant Cassie wished she were. It would be heaven to forget for just a moment that she stood at the edge of a horrible precipice, waiting for the gentle tap that would send her tumbling to her doom. She wanted to be the carefree girl of her season, the one who'd caught the eye of a handsome, wealthy lord and dared to dream that he might offer marriage.

She told herself she shouldn't. Wanting Lucien Hollier was dangerous. She'd learned that well enough six years ago. Not that his disappearance from her side had been unexpected, considering the sort of man her father had been and still was. What she hadn't expected was that Lucien's abandonment would be the first in a string of life-changing disappointments that persisted to this day.

"If not an eon, then a lifetime at least," Cassie replied with a smile.

That made Lucien laugh, his amusement tinged with bitterness. Pleasure flared in his cool eyes. "Definitely a lifetime. Let me say that I renew our acquaintance with the greatest of pleasure, Mrs. Marston."

Lucien extended his hand. Cassie laid hers into his palm. He brushed his lips across her knuckles. Her lacy gloves were no barrier. Her senses stirred sharply, filling with longing, the wicked, wonderful and totally inappropriate longing to feel his mouth on hers and his arms around her. However wrongly, however utterly impossible, Cassie still desired Lucien Hollier with all her being.

As Lucien straightened Cassie saw the same attraction reflected in his eyes. "If you aren't otherwise occupied, would you consider joining me for the next dance?"

She hesitated. So far tonight, she'd been out on the floor twice, only to find that her impatience to get to

the card room left her incapable of enjoying the activity. Since then, she'd refused all offers under the
pretense of being Eliza's chaperone, something that
had annoyed Philana.

Across the room the musicians tuned their instruments, preparing to begin their next set. Cassie
knew the next dance was a waltz. It was a dance she
loved, cherishing it above the usual jigs and prome-
nades for the beauty of its movement.

Still, she commanded herself to refuse. Upstanding widows didn't participate in waltzes, and Cassie
needed the house party guests to see her as an upstanding widow. Nor did young women who hadn't
yet been presented to society.

Cassie's refusal stalled on her tongue. Eliza wasn't
going to be presented to society and Cassie wasn't
an upstanding widow. She was a murderess who
found Lucien's presence here and his renewed interest in her too disorienting, unnerving and incredibly
attractive to resist. To not have his arm around her
was beyond bearing.

"Don't be a fool," Philana whispered. "Tell him
yes."

It was the gentle tap Cassie had so feared. She forgot everything: propriety, her threatened repute,
that she'd killed an earl, that she needed to rescue
her family. Instead, she went tumbling over the
precipice, madly, wrongly, craving Lucien's body
close to hers.

"Yes," she said, "I would like that very much."

Chapter 3

Cassie let Lucien take her hand. With Eliza and Lord Ryecroft following, they started toward the other end of the ballroom. As they went, more than one local woman in the knots and clutches of well-dressed guests turned her feathered or flowered head to watch in disapproval. Their menfolk stroked their chins in new consideration as they eyed Cassie.

Their reaction didn't surprise Cassie. She knew their sort of folk. During her marriage to Charles she'd lived about a hundred miles south of here, on the English side of the Scots border. No matter how eager these folk were to emulate London's fashions, both in clothing and cant, they remained what they'd been born: country folk with country opinions. To them Almack's approval was no recommendation, and the waltz remained a decadent, Continental dance certain to lead to the debauching of their children.

They stopped on the area of smooth parquet flooring set aside for dancing. There were only five other couples. Cassie recognized all of them from London.

Lucien put an arm around her, then clasped her hand in his. In that moment Cassie knew the waltz's detractors were right. Although the requisite space remained between their hips she felt as if Lucien held her intimately against him.

The corners of Lucien's mouth lifted into a slight smile. "I forgot to ask. You do waltz, don't you Mrs. Marston?"

"I do." Before she'd known how impoverished they were she'd hired a dancing master to help prepare Eliza for her come out. The waltz had been one of the dances he taught, so Cassie had learned along with Eliza. They still owed the man half his fee.

"They don't approve," Lucien said, his gray eyes warm, the lift of his chin indicating the glowering guests.

The nearest violinist lifted his bow in direction. The warm voice of the viola sang out, followed by the deeper toned cello setting the dance's distinctive pace. Lucien's fingers tightened against the small of Cassie's back.

"Come then, let's show them the error of their opinion," he said, and in tune to the swelling music drew her into the glorious, graceful movements.

The years hadn't changed his ability to move

about the floor. By their first circle Cassie had forgotten that her head hurt—and the weight of the task that lay before her. All that mattered was the beauty of the music and Lucien's nearness.

She felt the heat of his hand against the small of her back. Every breath was flavored with his sandalwood scent. His gray eyes were intense. His sun-streaked hair curled lightly against the collar of his coat, tumbling forward a little so that it touched the strong line of his jaw.

Another wave of attraction washed over her, the sensation potent enough to make her shiver. The cunning lift of Lucien's lips said he noticed. His arm tightened around her ever so subtly.

He lowered his head. "Holding you this way is like a glimpse of heaven," he said, his rich voice barely audible above the music.

It was an outrageous flirt, a reminder of their shared past, when Cassie had punctured the arrogance of any man who tried to employ such flummery against her. Fighting a smile, she fixed him with her most chiding look.

"Surely, my lord, you can be more subtle than that," she said, using the same words she'd employed six years ago to tweak him.

He laughed, his face alive with delight. "You haven't changed a whit."

Would that it were true. Smiling, Cassie shook her head as they glided into another turn. "You haven't changed either."

"What liars we are," he said with a little laugh.

"May I offer my condolences on the passing of Mr. Marston?"

Sadness touched Cassie's heart, then receded. What she'd liked most about Charles was the gentle sweetness he'd always shown her in their home, and in their bed. Blinding herself to what Charles did outside their home had been a tactic she'd learned at her mother's knee, one that had failed her when she'd returned to her father's house after her husband's death.

"And, I must extend my condolences to you for your loss. It's double mine," she said. How she'd ached when she heard Lucien had wed. His wife, Dorothea Radcliffe, was exactly the sort of woman she'd expected him to choose: pretty, the third daughter of an earl and an heiress. Lady Graceton had died giving birth.

Something flashed through Lucien's eyes. He nodded, accepting her remark, then heat flickered to life in his gaze. "Now that we've addressed the niceties, what do you say we immerse ourselves in the moment? You asked if I could be more subtle." His smile was taunting. "Trust me, Mrs. Marston, I'm no longer the callow youth you remember. I can be very subtle."

Cassie read the message in his face. It was the same message he'd sent six years ago, although then he hadn't known he'd been sending it. He wanted her not as his wife, but in his bed.

If she hadn't already committed murder this might have upset her. Swinging that urn had altered everything. She had two weeks, if that long, before her life irrevocably changed. Rightly or wrongly, until her family sailed to America or the Runners came to take her, Cassie wanted Lucien's attention. She needed his pursuit to hide that she was no longer Cassandra—the upright, responsible widow who suppressed her own needs to tend to her family— but Cassie, the slayer of earls.

"You call that subtle, my lord?" she chided. "Hardly. Why, you're practically leering at me."

His eyes widened as if in innocence, but lurking behind the pretense was surprise, pleasure and desire. "I'm certain I don't know what you mean."

"If that's so, my lord, then I fear I must revise my opinion of you. The years have hopelessly dulled your intellect."

Lucien threw back his head and laughed. Cassie laughed with him, enjoying herself. The heady sensation was as seductive and alluring as the nobleman with whom she danced.

His smile roguish, Lucien lowered his head near her ear. His attraction to her enveloped her along with his scent. Cassie's body responded on its own. Three years was a long time to go without a man's touch.

"Why bother with subtlety, Mrs. Marston, when I'd much rather prefer to grab what I want." His fingers shifted against her back, making it clear what he wanted to take.

"Grabbing is frowned upon by we better sort of people, my lord." She sniffed, toying with him just as he toyed with her. "So, what do you want so badly that you must grab for it?"

His eyes sparked, recognizing that she moved their game to a new level. He answered as they made another turn by tightening his hand at the small of her back. Their hips almost touched. A thrill shot through her.

"Passion," he whispered.

"Ah yes," Cassie agreed, all innocence. "Passion is a fine thing to feel. I'm passionate about art. Why, earlier I wandered Lord Ryecroft's gallery. I vow the paintings done by his father fair stole my breath. What stirs your passion, my lord?"

Pleasure and desire filled Lucien's gray eyes at her coy question. "At this moment I find I'm passionate about the curve of your lips. No statue, no painting, no *objet d'art* has ever so deeply moved me."

As he spoke they made another turn. Lucien used the movement to again draw her closer. This time their hips brushed. Glorious heat tumbled through Cassie. She pushed herself back to a safe distance in his embrace. Lifting her hand from his shoulder, she held up a warning finger as the music reached its final crescendo.

"Retreat this moment or you'll leave me no choice but to abandon the field. Where would that leave you, but wholly unsatisfied and in need of another woman to pursue?"

Amusement and surprise flashed through his gaze, but he loosened his arm around her, then brought them to a halt as the dance ended. Keeping her hand in his he drew her fingers to the center of his chest.

"I quail at the thought," he said, shaking his head. "Madam, we have failed."

Cassie blinked. "I beg your pardon?"

"Didn't we set out in this dance to convince observers that there's no harm in the waltz?" he asked. "We failed. These yokels are right. The dance is decadent. Its movements must cause momentary madness, for nothing save lunacy could have caused me to confess my attraction to you. Tell me you won't shun me because of my honesty."

Laughing, Cassie took her hand from his and opened her fan. She peered at him over its lacy top. "You really are doing it too brown, you know."

Lucien nodded, not in the least concerned that she wasn't playing the part of a woman flattered beyond sensible thought. "I know. Forgive me. It's just that I'm enjoying this so much I'm finding it hard to stop."

Charmed, intrigued, flattered beyond sensible thought, although vaguely concerned about the strength of her reaction to him, Cassie snapped her fan shut and let it dangle from her wrist. "Enough! Take me back to my aunt."

Lucien sighed and offered his arm. "If I must."

They found Philana alone. Eliza had traded Lord Ryecroft for Colonel Egremont. Lucien released Cassie and stepped back. The distance that opened up between them felt like a chasm.

"Thank you for a most amazing dance, Mrs. Marston. Were I given the choice I'd have no one but you in my arms from this moment until eternity."

Philana gawked at the outrageous blandishment. Cassie swallowed a giggle. A smile tugged at the corners of Lucien's mouth. He bowed and excused himself.

"What was that?" Philana gasped when he was out of earshot.

"What was what?" Cassie asked blandly.

Philana almost stamped her foot. "Lord Graceton! What did he mean by what he said?"

"Oh, that." Cassie idly examined the tips of her gloved fingers. "He means that he'd very much like to attempt a seduction." Cassie glanced at Philana to gauge the effect of her words.

Her aunt's brow creased as though struggling to add sums. "What to do, what to do?" she muttered.

"There's nothing to do," Cassie replied, a little put out that Philana wasn't shocked by what she'd said.

"Of course there isn't," Philana assured her with a touch of pique in her voice. "I know you. You're far too proper to consider a liaison with Lord Graceton. More's the pity."

"Philana!" Cassie cried with all the shock she'd meant to elicit from her aunt.

Her voice was loud enough that those around them turned to see what was amiss. Philana smiled and waggled her fan at her neighbors. Not so Cassie. She again studied her fingers, waiting for their interest to wane.

Philana felt no need for such circumspection. "You misunderstand me, sweetheart," she said. "I didn't mean to suggest you should allow Lord Graceton to have his way with you, only that you take advantage of his attraction to you. Let him chase you, keeping him at arm's length. The longer you let him pursue, the greater his attraction to you will grow until he's in a proper frenzy to have you. More than one woman has found her way to the altar by this tactic."

Cassie might have gaped if her mother hadn't long ago beaten the unmannerly expression out of her. She hadn't expected Philana to be so obvious in her matchmaking, or so deluded. "Philana, Lord Graceton will never marry me."

Philana frowned. "Why not? You make a handsome couple. I watched you dance. I saw the way he smiled at you. I've arranged stranger matches than this one."

Cassie shook her head. While it was true that Philana had coordinated a number of matches that became successful marriages, she was wholly mistaken this time. Unfortunately, once Philana decided she was right about a couple she could be dogged about forcing the match to its conclusion.

"It doesn't matter what you saw, you're wrong," Cassie said, stifling a sigh. "Trust me, for I know this better than any other woman in this chamber. Lord Graceton has no marital interest in a widowed gentlewoman with an impoverished wastrel for a father." Or a woman who'd already killed one peer.

Philana's jaw set stubbornly. "And I say Lord Graceton will follow his heart, and his heart leads him to you."

"You're mad," Cassie snapped, her voice made harsh by her own bitter experience with Lucien. Six years ago he'd worn his heart on his sleeve, displaying his interest in her so boldly that Cassie had forgotten to be sensible. She'd begun to listen to her own heart's promises that he loved her.

"Trust me, Philana. Men of his rank don't wed down, no matter what their hearts may say. Please, no more matchmaking, not for me," Cassie added. "I cannot bear it now, not when I already have so much upset in my life."

Philana's jaw softened. Remorse filled her eyes. "So you do, dear. So you do," she said, then added to herself, *sotto voce*, "which is why you must marry Lord Graceton."

Cassie's head began to throb, this time in earnest. Philana wasn't going to admit defeat. Cassie pressed her fingers to her temples, trying to ease the pain.

"Ach, you poor dear. Is your head hurting again?" her aunt asked.

Cassie nodded. "I've a powder for it in my room."

"Go, take it and rest for a bit," Philana urged. "That way you'll be restored in time for the evening meal."

"Will you tell Eliza and my father where I've gone?" Cassie asked, wanting nothing more than to retreat to her bedchamber and pull the bedclothes over her head. Instead, the time had come for her to visit the card room.

With a grimace Philana said, "I forgot. Your father returned while you and Lord Graceton danced." She fell silent, twisting her hands and looking so hesitant that Cassie frowned at her.

"Is something wrong?"

Concern darkened her aunt's face. "I'm sorry, Cassie, but he slipped around the edges of the room as if he didn't want you to see him making his way into the card room." She sounded helpless and worried. "I considered stopping him, but it really isn't my place to interfere, is it?"

Worry woke, but Cassie quelled it. Her father had been different since they left London—quieter, a bit humbled. He hadn't once overindulged in drink along their route.

Most important, he didn't have any money. Did he? Concern nagged. Oh, Lord but she hoped his purse was empty.

Burying her new worry, Cassie offered Philana a reassuring smile. Whatever happened, she didn't want her aunt blaming herself. "He can do no harm."

Philana smiled in relief. "Thank heavens. Now go, take your powder."

Escaping the ballroom, Cassie made her way via the gallery to the house's residential wing and her third-storey chamber. Ryecroft Castle was actually not a castle, but a U-shaped house decorated with battlements and towers to make it look ancient. The ballroom and other public rooms were in the U, while Lord Ryecroft's guests stayed in the three-storey west wing; the service rooms were in the east wing.

The closer she got to her bedchamber the faster Cassie's feet moved, until she was nearly running. She lifted the latch, only now wishing she'd asked about keys and locks. But who locked their doors at a house party? No one.

She walked into the spacious chamber, one that easily accommodated two people. Although it was August the nights here in lowland Scotland were always damp and cool; a small fire, hardly more than embers now, burned on her chamber's efficient little hearth. A single candle, its flame jigging and dancing much like the partygoers in the ballroom, stood on a delicate washstand. The burning taper threw its golden light against the belly of the ceramic water pitcher and its matching bowl, then over the stand's edge to reveal a hint of the glorious reds and blues in the room's carpet. The pineapples atop the bed's tall posts were barely visible in the darkness, while night had turned the deep red of the bed's brocade canopy to gray.

Taking up the candle, Cassie turned to the room's wardrobe. The door creaked a little as it opened. She looked in, only to have her heart drop. Her satchel wasn't where she'd left it on the wardrobe's floor.

Panic stirred, dark and deep. She lifted the hems of her hanging gowns. She moved her shoes. The satchel still didn't appear out of the darkness.

Her heart thudding in her chest, Cassie ran to her trunk at the end of the bed even though she knew she hadn't left the satchel in it. The well-oiled hinges made no sound as the lid opened. The trunk was cavernous in the darkness, and utterly empty.

As fruitless as it was, Cassie knelt on the floor and looked beneath the bed. Lord Ryecroft had an efficient staff. There wasn't even a dust kitten.

Cassie sat back on her heels. Her hand trembled so badly that the candle extinguished. Her satchel was gone, her seed money with it. There would be no escape to America. She would hang. Eliza would be forever branded a murderess's sister, forcing her into the very poverty Bucksden had described before Cassie silenced him with her urn.

All because of her father. Cassie shot to her feet and whirled toward the door, intent on confronting her father, demanding that he return what he'd taken. She stopped herself before she reached the portal.

She couldn't confront him, and not just because good manners didn't allow daughters to scream at their wastrel, thieving fathers in public. Roland always drank at the tables and drinking made his behavior unpredictable. The last thing Cassie needed was for her besotted and outraged father to forget himself and confess to all who listened what Cassie had done in their London drawing-room.

That left Cassie no option. She sat on the end of the bed. Tears filled her eyes. As much as she hated herself for it, she wished she'd used that urn to fell her father along with Lord Bucksden.

Chapter 4

Lucien walked away from Cassie, stunned. Dear God, but marriage had only changed her for the better. During her season she'd been bold, quick with a quip or a gentle jest, but tonight!

The moment the music began, that haunted air of hers had dissipated, revealing a warm, coy, intriguing and oh-so-desirable woman. A woman who'd been his willing partner in repartee, meeting his every verbal thrust with a clever parry of her own. With each word they spoke the attraction swirling between them had heightened until it was more intoxicating than any wine.

Closing his eyes, he breathed in the memory of Cassie's rose perfume, a scent he might yesterday have scorned as commonplace. By the end of the dance he'd been ready to lick it off her skin. It was even more alluring to know that she would have allowed him to do it.

He swallowed, remembering her shudder when their hips touched. He longed for another chance to hold her in his arms, no matter what it took to put her there. Why had Devanney let her share a chamber with her sister? In the depths of the night it was far easier to tap on a woman's door and talk himself into her bed than it was to convince her to leave her chamber for his.

In the next instant Lucien was grateful that Cassie did share her chamber, for that meant he wouldn't tap on her door. Cassie Marston was dangerous, indeed. It was one thing to invite a willing widow into his bed, and quite another to be so consumed by his need that he lost sight of what was important: his next marriage, so he could make a son, then satisfy his urge to kill Lord Bucksden.

"Hollier!" Devanney called.

Turning, Lucien waited for his cousin to join him, only to smile at the number of heads that turned to watch Devanney's progress across the room. At twenty-nine, wealthy and titled, his cousin sat squarely at the center of many a mother's marital hope for her daughter.

Not that Devanney would have any of them. He was too busy searching the world for his father's paintings, seeking the one that had driven the wedge between father and son. As far as Lucien was concerned it was better that Devanney searched for paintings than return to the espionage that had

nearly cost him his life. It was also far better that Devanney took his time finding the right wife rather
than make the mistake Lucien had, and marry to suit
society's expectations.

"Egad, but how can a daughter be so different
from her sire?" Devanney asked, the single diamond
fob on his watch chain sparking as brightly as his
smile. "Conningsby's a sot and simpleton, while
Miss Conningsby makes words stand on their
heads, filling them with unexpected meanings. I've
never known a woman who refuses flattery, yet does
it so gently and with such skill that I'm flattered by
the way she punctured my conceit."

The music again swelled around them. Devanney
turned his gaze to Cassie's younger sister. Miss Conningsby presently promenaded with Egremont, the
golden trim on the colonel's short blue coat and the
girl's white dress setting them off against a backdrop of so many black-jacketed men and women in
their jewel-toned gowns.

"Everything about her takes the breath. I wager
she'll keep her husband fascinated for years." Something in Devanney's bland comment made him
sound like an old man, despairing over a life that
had passed him by.

Lucien shook his head, pitying the girl if not Devanney. It was Devanney's choice to dwell on his
past and hold himself out of life's currents, while
Miss Conningsby had no other option.

"If she ever marries," he said. "What sensible man
would offer for her, knowing that all his peers will
laugh up their sleeves, because of Sir Roland? A

shame, that. If one of Sir Roland's daughters could make a respectable match, she could lift the other up with her."

It occurred to Lucien as he spoke that he could have been that man if he'd wed Cassie years ago. His title would have given Miss Conningsby the stage her beauty deserved to make a brilliant match. But he hadn't married Cassie.

A wave of disappointment washed over him. What followed was the echo of the ache that had plagued him after he turned his back on Cassie. Would rekindling their relationship, even as an affair, result in the same pain when they again parted?

"Why didn't you tell me you knew Mrs. Marston when I mentioned her to you?" Devanney asked.

Lucien shrugged. "It had been years. I'd forgotten her until I saw her tonight."

"Not possible," Devanney shot back with a laugh. "No man forgets a beautiful woman, especially not one who looks at him the way she looks at you."

Irritation stirred in Lucien. "I forgot her," he repeated, his tone warning his cousin not to persist here.

Devanney's jaw tightened in refusal. "You were worried about being bored during the party. Will a liaison with Mrs. Marston help you pass the idle hours?"

Exasperation tore through Lucien, then he remembered Devanney's potential prank. That, along with the possibility of aching over Cassie a second time, was more than enough reason not to pursue her. "Mrs. Marston won't do at all, because I won't have her."

Devanney drew himself up as if shocked. "I don't believe you, I saw the way you smiled at her." He sounded truly aggrieved.

His cousin's determination to drive him into Cassie's arms only proved that there was some trick wrapped around Cassie's presence here. Whatever that prank was, Devanney would be unrelenting about seeing his plot through to its end. Lucien would find himself thrown into Cassie's presence time and again, even to the detriment of her repute. That wasn't right, not when Cassie had a father already more than willing to heap insults on her.

"No," Lucien said, his voice hard and his shoulders tense in refusal.

Determination disappeared as the pretense of innocence flared in Devanney's eyes. "No, what?" he asked, knowing very well what Lucien meant.

"No, you won't use her in your prank," Lucien replied with no expectation that Devanney would be deterred. Failure wasn't in his cousin's nature any more than it was in his own.

"What sort of cad do you think me? I'd never misuse an innocent as part of a jest," Devanney protested a little more strenuously than necessary.

Lucien eyed his cousin, not certain how to interpret this. Was there no prank involving Cassie, or was she a willing participant? Or perhaps the prank was ultimately innocent. It didn't matter. He wasn't playing, not when Devanney's goal was to distract him.

At an impasse, they stared at each other. Devanney's guests chatted around them. The music rose in crescendo. Couples danced, the women's gowns streaks of color brushed onto a golden night. Then Devanney slipped his fingers into his vest pocket. In nervous habit he began to open and close his watch's cover. Lucien listened in triumph to the gentle click and snap, barely audible over the noise. Devanney didn't know how to proceed in the face of Lucien's blunt refusal.

At last his cousin removed his hand from his pocket. "As you will, Hollier, but know that I think you mad to turn your back on the widow after the way she fair melted in your arms."

Devanney meant what he said, that he was willing to let the subject die for the moment. But he also meant his words as a parting thrust at Lucien. It worked. Lucien swallowed at the memory of Cassie, warm and pliant in his arms. Devanney was right; he was mad—stark, raving mad—to refuse her.

"So, will you stay here and dance, awakening the hopes of every mother in the crowd, or does the card room call to you?" his cousin asked.

Once again Lucien scanned the room, his gaze touching on the faces of the plain young women he'd thought met his requirements before the waltz. His stomach clenched, unable to bear the thought of any of them in his arms now. The search for his next wife could wait until the morrow.

"The card room calls," he replied. Aye, taking coins from some other man's purse might satisfy some of what now roiled in him.

Relief flickered across Devanney's face. "Can I impose then? Take my place as host in the card room for the next hours."

Lucien laughed at that. "I saw Percy slip in there a few moments ago. What, are you afraid he'll bankrupt your neighbors?"

Devanney shot Lucien a narrow look. "If he did I'd blame you. You perverted that devious whelp when you taught him a sharp's tricks." Jonathan Percy had briefly been Lucien's ward, during which time Lucien felt it his prerogative to teach the canny brat a bit more than a gentleman's usual skill.

"No, he's not the one who worries me," Devanney continued. "He's well-enough known around here that the only ones who'll play with him are those who can catch a sharp in the act. It's the duchess and her daughter," Devanney said, referring to the davager duchess of Carlisle, to whom he was related through his departed father. "I suppose I should warn you that Duchess Eleanor has decided you will marry Lady Barbara. She informed me of this when she invited herself to my party."

Barbara, the duchess's youngest daughter, had been trapped for years in betrothal to an ailing fiancé. Her mother had refused to allow the wedding until the man recovered, but meek Barbara, for once, stood her ground, refusing to dissolve the betrothal. The poor man's death had finally resolved the issue between mother and daughter.

"Her Grace took offense when she saw your first dance was with Mrs. Marston. She dragged Lady Barbara into the card room." Devanney offered a wry grin. "I think she means her absence from the ballroom as punishment for my failure to control you. You should have seen the look she sent me as they went."

Lucien laughed out loud. Duchess Eleanor was infamous for her snobbery, being swift to snub anyone beneath the rank of baron. She expected everyone called by the title *lord* or higher to do the same. "And, why should I throw myself into the lioness's den for you?"

"Because you and I both know there's nothing Her Grace can say or do that will convince you to marry her daughter," Devanney retorted, "or she, you. Lady Barbara assured me of this. However, she took care to tell me only when she was certain her mother wouldn't overhear. She says you will not suit. I think the matter of her betrothed has finally put a little steel in her spine."

"Good for her," Lucien said, a little amused to find his pride tweaked.

"So, will you retire to the card room?" Devanney asked. "You can both soothe Her Grace's ruffled feathers and serve as a buffer to those unfortunate squires and knights who might accidentally address her.

"Oh, by the by, I also saw Conningsby sidle into the card room not long ago. You'll need to watch him. You know what a nitwit he can be once he has a little wine in him." Devanney sighed and shook his head. "If only I could have had his daughters here without him."

The mention of Sir Roland brought Lucien's

thoughts back to Cassie and her earlier sadness. He might not choose to be her lover, but he could still be a friend, even if he made an anonymous offer of that friendship. For the duration of the party he could be Conningsby's keeper, seeing to it that the little sot didn't overspend at the tables or overindulge in his cups. It was a safe gift, one that would go far to soothe the guilt he felt over the way he'd abandoned Cassie six years ago, leaving without so much as a fare-thee-well.

Smiling, Lucien presented his leg to his cousin and made a bow flowery enough to please even Prinny. "For you, dear cousin, the stars," he said. It was a phrase from their childhood, one they'd cribbed from an amateur theatric performance.

"Ah, but I wanted the moon," Devanney replied, saying his piece in their little charade.

The music stopped. The dancers bowed to each other, then began to drift to their respective spots. Devanney gave Lucien another little salute.

"Good of you, old man. If you'll excuse me. I have a partner to claim."

After Devanney walked away, Lucien started for the drawing-room-turned-gaming-hell. It hardly looked the part with a cheery fire burning on the hearth framed by an ornate mantelpiece. Chinoiserie panels were the only decorations on the walls, which were painted a buttery yellow. At the room's far end, draperies of a pale gold had been thrown wide to reveal French doors that opened out to Devanney's garden. A pianoforte, quiet at the moment, stood close to an exterior doorway, surrounded by delicate gilded chairs. Two old women sat there, enjoying an island of peace in the midst of the ball's storm, sipping their ratafia.

The card tables stood closer to the ballroom door, eight of them with chairs for four players at each. Conningsby skulked along that end of the chamber, awaiting an invitation not likely to be extended, since the three occupied tables were already full.

Four local biddies gossiped at the farthest table, playing whist for their enjoyment rather than any monetary gain. Seated at a more central table were Duchess Eleanor and her youngest daughter, Lady Barbara. Lucien considered Barbara for a moment.

The duchess's sixth daughter, born late in Eleanor's life, wasn't a plain woman, not with her dark hair and sloe eyes, but she behaved as if she were. Then again, if Eleanor had been his mother, Lucien might also have wanted to melt into the woodwork.

It occurred to him that Barbara, with her humble attitude and defeated nature, might well make him the perfect wife. The memory of Cassie's bold repartee rushed over him. Barbara was right. She and he didn't suit.

Eleanor, wearing her famous diamonds and a green silk gown cut in a style reminiscent of the previous century, glanced at him, then almost smiled in approval. If she'd ever been a beauty, time and her disposition had robbed her of it. Her cheeks sagged and dark rings marked her eyes. Her hair was almost as white as the plume she'd pinned in it.

One of her partners, an earl's younger son, acceptable because of his bloodline, took the hand. Eleanor threw down her cards. "You cannot have taken that! Who has the ace?" she demanded in a not-so-subtle charge of cheating, one she could make only because of her rank and her sway with the ton.

Barbara bowed her head, covering her eyes with a hand. Their fourth, a beardless lord who'd just come into his father's title, leaned back in his chair to wait for Her Grace's fit to pass. He and the earl's son both nodded to Lucien in greeting, then rolled their eyes to display what they thought of Lady Eleanor's familiar complaint.

Lucien's stomach clenched. Having Eleanor as a mother-in-law would be as distasteful as shouldering the burden of Sir Roland as his father-in-law.

Jonathan Percy, Westmorland's bastard, lounged casually at the third table. A well-favored lad, thankfully resembling his mother rather than his long-faced father, Percy had matriculated from Oxford with a degree in gaming skills instead of the expected one in religion. Vibrant green stripes decorated Percy's bright pink waistcoat beneath his black coat. A dozen sparkling fobs decorated his watch chain, and his collar points reached almost to his cheekbones. His dark brown hair had been pomaded into artful curls about his face.

"I wondered how long it would be before we saw you in here, my lord," Percy called to Lucien. "Come sit with us so I can pick your pocket. In the meanwhile I'll tell you about the mare I've discovered. She'll be an asset to my father's stable." The lad had a good eye for horseflesh, and a delusion that he could augment his sorry allowance by raising and betting on his own horses.

The men playing with Percy all muttered at the invitation. The three hard-eyed local squires, well known to Lucien, were just what Devanney promised, more than capable of keeping Percy honest. Beefy men all, they weren't pleased at the thought of making room for another big man, or changing their game to accommodate a fifth player.

"Another time, Percy," Lucien said. "You have the next two weeks to try to winnow a few coins from my purse. I warn you: Attempt it at your own risk. You've a better chance of losing another month's allowance than you do of taking any of my coins."

That made Percy laugh. "We'll see who takes whose allowance."

Lucien retreated to an empty table. One of Ryecroft's bewigged footmen appeared, and supplied Lucien with all he needed to start a game, including a cup of Devanney's finest wine. Across the room Cassie's father stopped his pacing and looked longingly in Lucien's direction.

Lucien lifted his glass in invitation. "Care to join me, Conningsby?"

Sir Roland swiftly crossed the room, heated circles reddening his sagging cheeks. His ridiculous little nose almost quivered in anticipation. Coins clinked in the worn leather pouch he carried in his hand. The plebeian purse looked so out of place with Sir Roland that Lucien wondered for a moment if it truly belonged to the man. He instantly discarded the thought. Roland was first and foremost a gentleman, and as such he wouldn't stoop to steal. At least not for so few coins as that purse could contain.

"Good of you, m'lord," Sir Roland mumbled, taking his seat.

Lucien signaled for the footman to bring Conningsby a drink. The sooner Cassie's father began to imbibe, the easier it would be for Lucien to willfully lose to the man. Then, when Roland was thoroughly drunk, Lucien could return both the man and his full purse to his chamber.

"Not tonight," the little knight told the footman, waving away the wine.

Lucien blinked, startled. He'd never known Sir Roland to refuse a drink.

Sir Roland's lips twisted when he caught Lucien's look. "Not drinking tonight," he said, patting the bulge of his stomach beneath his blue vest. It was missing one of its silver buttons. "A little off my feed."

"A pity, that," Lucien replied smoothly, wondering if the wastrel was finally reforming his ways. He hoped Sir Roland's changes didn't come too late to do some good for Cassie and her sister.

Picking up the cards, Lucien shuffled, then set the mixed deck in the center of the table, offering Roland the chance to cut. "You're aware, aren't you, that Lord Ryecroft limits our winnings to twenty pounds per person per night?"

Sir Roland nodded, then cut the cards. As Lucien dealt, the smaller man shifted sideways to lounge in his chair, his legs crossed at the ankles. Setting an elbow on the table, Roland propped his head on his fist. His expression flattened. Lucien had once heard Conningsby say that he believed this posture exuded an air of merry nonchalance. To Lucien, the only thing Sir Roland's posture exuded was cavalier arrogance.

Sir Roland smirked at Lucien. "What say you, m'lord? A game of Speculation?"

So Speculate they did, playing swift hand after hand, but not for long. Less than an hour later Lucien laid down his final winning hand, gnashing his teeth in frustration. He'd done everything he could, short of exposing his cards to Sir Roland, to lose, but Conningsby played like a man who'd never before seen a deck of cards. He lost more with every hand, until all of that pouch's twenty pounds now belonged to Lucien.

Across the table a stone-cold-sober Sir Roland reeled in his chair. His face blanched until he looked as if he might faint. He giggled, but it sounded more like a sob.

"I'm done for," he said, his voice catching. The little knight came to his feet, turned without offering any show of farewell and staggered like the besotted man he wasn't out of the card room. Lucien stared at the table and the measly twenty pounds strewn across its surface, no less devastated than Sir Roland.

Lucien had done his best to serve Cassie, and he'd failed. He couldn't offer to return these coins to her father, not without offering unbearable insult. Nor could he slip them to her. Not only would the insult be just as grave, but doing something like that hinted at an intimacy that he couldn't afford and wouldn't contemplate, not with her and not at this party.

Then, what?

Chapter 5

"**C**assie, where are you?"

Eliza's gentle call startled Cassie out of her doze. Seated in the bedchamber's single wing chair, she stretched, surprised to find herself waking. She hadn't expected to sleep, not with the way her head had been throbbing.

When Philana and Eliza had come to check on her just before the evening meal began, the pain had been unbearable. Cassie had swiftly sent them away, wanting only quiet. Eliza departed reluctantly, murmuring in worry. Philana sent Betty with a potion guaranteed to ease Cassie's every pain. The concoction proved so foul that Cassie managed to down only half of it. Philana hadn't mentioned that it would make her sleepy. Had Cassie known, she'd have undressed and gone to bed before taking it. Now, her head still throbbed, the ache only a little abated, and there was a pinch in her neck from sleeping in an awkward position.

"I'm in the chair, Eliza," she said, squinting as her sister relit the candle.

"Is your head any better?" Eliza asked.

"It is," Cassie lied.

There was no sense telling the truth. Nothing Eliza said or did could ever ease what pained Cassie. Why, oh why, hadn't she done a better job of hiding her purse? She should have known her father would look for it. After all, a man who gambled away his daughter wouldn't be disturbed by committing minor thievery. Eliza had been right to chide her about coddling their father. If nothing else, tonight's long, quiet hours left Cassie knowing she wouldn't be free of her headache until she confronted him. She needed to speak her mind, no matter how improper, unmannerly or messy that outpouring might prove.

Eliza placed the flickering candle on the washstand, then made an impatient sound and put her hands on her hips. "You're still dressed! Why didn't you send for Betty to help you into bed?"

"No scolding," Cassie replied with a little laugh. "If I'd expected to fall asleep I'd have called for Betty. So is your evening finally over?"

"It is, the last dance danced now that dawn is almost upon us," Eliza replied, glowing despite the late hour. Or was that early hour? "Oh, Cassie, I'm so sorry you had to miss the rest of the ball."

"Have you seen Papa?" Cassie asked, probing to

see if Eliza had any inkling of what their father had done last night.

Eliza shook her head. "Not since before we dined. He said he wasn't feeling well and retired. It wasn't drink this time, Cassie. He seemed in control of all his senses. He really didn't look well."

Cassie sagged back into the chair in angry, hopeless defeat. That their father hadn't been drinking didn't inspire any hope, not when what Eliza described was a man who'd lost everything he'd stolen.

At the center of the room Eliza threw off concerns over their father and turned a quick circle, laughing. Cassie watched her sister become a coquette. "The music went on and on, every new dance better than the last. Lord Ryecroft was my partner twice, while Colonel Egremont escorted me three times. I think they may both be forming an affection for me."

Cassie's mouth opened to warn Eliza against letting her heart fix on either man, but before she could speak, her sister put her hands on her hips.

"Why don't I remember that you knew Lord Graceton?"

"Why should you?" Cassie replied, losing herself to the image of Lucien's charming, crooked smile and the feeling of his arms around her. "We met so long ago and our acquaintance lasted for only a few brief months. In all truth I'd forgotten him." That was another lie. A girl didn't forget her first love or her first heartbreak.

Eliza pulled off her gloves, then began to loosen her hair, putting her hairpins into her mouth as she worked. "Hmph. I can't imagine ever forgetting that man," she said from around the pins. Her hair fell, fair and curling, to the middle of her back.

Going to the dressing table, Eliza set aside the pins. "Lord Graceton's quite attractive, although not as handsome as Lord Ryecroft, and he certainly hasn't forgotten you."

Cassie's heart did the most amazing thing at Eliza's words. It was true. Lucien hadn't forgotten her and, rightly or wrongly, Cassie liked that very much.

Coming to sit on the side of the bed next to Cassie's chair, Eliza began to remove her shoes and stockings. "You do know that Philana is quite set on convincing Lord Graceton to marry you?"

Exasperation shot through Cassie; just as she had expected, Philana persisted. "Philana can intend anything she wants, but that doesn't mean what she wants will happen. A peer doesn't marry the daughter of a bankrupt sot," she said, speaking without considering that she wasn't the only daughter of a sot in the chamber.

The gaiety drained from Eliza's face. Cassie watched in remorse as her sister's expression flattened into despair.

"It doesn't matter how much any man might come to care for me, does it?" Eliza asked, her voice trembling. Tears glistened, clinging to her eyelashes. "No decent man will offer for my hand. Perhaps I should have gone with Lord Bucksden," she finished, sounding beaten and exhausted.

Cassie bolted to her feet, her hands on her hips.

"Don't you ever again say that! You shouldn't even think such a thing."

Eliza looked up at her, shaking her head. "How can I help but think about it? If I'd told him yes we wouldn't be in this horrible predicament. He's a rich man. He would have supported me. That would have given me the opportunity to support you and Papa until you found a way to restore the estate."

Kneeling before Eliza, Cassie took her sister's cold hands. "I'd rather hang than let that odious man touch so much as your sleeve."

"That's what frightens me most," Eliza said in a small, sad voice. "I don't want anything to happen to you, Cassie."

Her heart aching, Cassie forced a smile onto her lips. "Nothing will," she lied. "Now, enough of this maudlin pap. Stand up and I'll help you with your hooks."

As Eliza came to her feet, Cassie's anger at their father doubled. Her sister shouldn't even know that gentlemen supported their mistresses, much less have to regret that she hadn't accepted Lord Bucksden's scandalous proposition. Their father hadn't betrayed his daughter just once, he'd done it twice. What he'd lost tonight had doomed Eliza to a shamed and impoverished future in England, rather than a new life in America. There, she might have married a good, decent man who knew nothing of their past.

Cassie's eyes narrowed. Eliza *would* go to America. Whatever it took, she'd find a way to give her sister that new life.

By the time Eliza wore her nightdress she was almost asleep on her feet. "Turn around, Cassie, and I'll do you," she offered, yawning.

Cassie did so. "Undo my hooks, then loosen my corset so I can remove it by myself. I want to see to Papa before I retire, to be certain he isn't really ill." She didn't want to *see* their father, she wanted to cut out his heart.

"As you will," Eliza murmured. After unfastening Cassie's gown, then releasing her corset strings, Eliza slipped into bed, forgoing her prayers.

"Good night, Cassie," Eliza said.

Cassie threw a shawl over her shoulders to hide her loosened garments, saying Eliza's prayers for her, asking God to grant her sister happy dreams. Then, creeping from their room, she closed the door and started down the quiet corridor.

Dawn's rosy light, the newborn sun misty with the remains of last night's rain, slanted through the wide windows at the corridor's end. There was no one about to notice her, the house guests having just found their beds. It would be another hour before Ryecroft's servants left their own cots.

Cassie made her way down the stairs to the floor below hers. When she reached her father's bedchamber door, she neither stopped nor knocked, but turned the knob and stepped inside.

The musty room was dim, a single golden strip of light slipping through a gap in the closed draperies. Framed by the open bedcurtains, her father sprawled on the mattress, fully dressed and snoring. He cradled one wine bottle in the crook of his arm.

Another, emptied, bottle lay on the floor near her satchel at the bed's foot.

Her mouth tight, Cassie crossed the room to her missing bag. Yanking it open, she found exactly what she'd expected and dreaded. The false bottom was gone, the compartment it once concealed empty. Her outrage soaring past the point of containment, Cassie returned to the bed and gave her father's shoulder a sharp shake.

He grunted in surprise and jerked upright so swiftly that Cassie stepped back as startled as he. His hair stood straight up on his head. Snowy stubble covered his chin. Deep rings hung beneath his eyes.

"What? What?" he cried.

"What, indeed," Cassie snapped. She crossed her arms to keep from using the empty wine bottle on him the way she'd used the urn on Lord Bucksden. "You took my satchel and the coins it contained. You went into my chamber and took what I needed to save us! I want to hear you explain why you did this to Eliza and to me."

Cassie half expected him to command her out of his room. Instead, his eyes glistened with moisture. Toying with one of his waistcoat buttons, he said in a little-boy voice, "I thought if I wasn't drinking it would be different for me at the tables." His voice faded into a whisper. "I didn't expect to lose."

Anger ate Cassie alive. She cocked a brow and glanced at the empty bottle that lay on the mattress beside him.

"It's not what you think," he protested. "I refused

so much as a drop while I played. These happened afterward."

"Is the whole sum gone?" Cassie demanded.

Her father gave a tiny nod, looking anywhere but at her. Cassie flinched. Somewhere deep within her she'd hoped he might still have some of the coins.

"How could you, Father?" she pleaded, her voice quivering, her lips trembling. "You knew how important that money was. You've squandered everything that should have belonged to your daughters. I thought with our safety at stake you'd control yourself this time."

" 'Pon rep, girl, it wasn't like that," he protested. "I was trying to be your father for once."

Cassie's anger soared higher than she thought possible. "Let me understand you. To you, being my father means you steal what belongs to me, then lose it, and in losing it leave me vulnerable to the hangman's noose?"

Horror flashed over his face, hollowing his cheeks. He slumped and rubbed at his head as if it ached. No doubt it did if he'd truly emptied both of these bottles by himself.

"Egad," he whispered. "What have I done?"

Cassie frowned at him. He seemed so confounded. What piece of character did he lack that prevented him from predicting the outcome of his actions?

The corners of his mouth quivered. "If that's what you think I intended, then I cannot blame you for despising me. I don't suppose I can convince you that I truly sought to protect your reputation."

"Try," Cassie commanded.

His brow furrowed. "It's that awful ability of yours. I couldn't let you use it, not even to save us. We're not the only people with relatives in America. If someone here accuses you of being a sharp, not even the ocean will be wide enough to shield you. People write. Before long Godfrey would know. He'll throw us from his home. We'd be ruined."

"As if you haven't already ruined us by gambling away everything we own?" she snapped, her anger making her speak more harshly than any daughter should address her father.

He reached for Cassie as if begging her forgiveness. His hand dropped before he touched her. "I was only trying to protect you," he said in that small voice, utterly serious.

Then hope flared in his eyes. "Perhaps if I speak to Lord Graceton and tell him what I've done he'll give back the purse."

Cassie staggered back a step on hearing Lucien Hollier's title drop from her father's lips. "Don't you dare!" she cried.

The thought of her father revealing to Lucien what he'd done mortified her to her core. What if Lucien believed her father was again trying to profit from his reawakened interest, just as he'd attempted six years ago? Nor could she tolerate her father airing the dirty secret of their impoverishment to the man she'd once loved. What if Lucien's reawakened interest in her led him to offer financial aid? The thought of pity replacing attraction in his eyes almost made Cassie wish for the hangman's noose.

The light died from her father's eyes. He gave a tiny, strained laugh. "You're right. Wouldn't do any good, anyway. Why should he return it when he wasn't the one who did anything wrong?"

Still reeling at the thought of Lucien learning just how deep her father's decline was, Cassie lost control of her tongue. "I can't believe you gamed with Lord Graceton. Of all the men to think you could best! He's four times the card player you are."

He frowned. "Mayhap he was once, but mourning seems to have changed him. He didn't play at all well last night, missing wagers and not speculating when he should have. If I'd once had the hand for it, I could have taken all and doubled our money. I would have had enough for one passage," he finished, pleading for his daughter's understanding and forgiveness. It was something Cassie could never give him.

"What do we do now, Cassie?" he asked.

"How am I supposed to know?" she retorted sharply.

Worry darkened his expression. He again fretted his waistcoat button. "You will think of something, won't you?"

Cassie's anger flared anew. "Why must it always be me? Why can't *you* think of something? It was a mistake to come here. I don't know what I expected to accomplish by this. I'm going to bed."

Turning her back on her father, she marched back to her own bedroom, satchel in hand. After she'd donned her nightclothes, she drew aside the bedcurtains. Eliza slumbered peacefully, her hair strewn across the pillow.

The need to keep her sister safe rode Cassie hard. What if Lucien could be convinced to give back what he'd won? What if she, not her father, told him what had happened?

Cassie's stomach lurched at the thought. Last night, she and Lucien had danced as equals, unfettered by society's judgment of her and her family. They'd simply enjoyed each others' presence. Any chance that would reoccur would end the moment she mentioned money.

Climbing into bed, she pulled the counterpane to her chin. Eliza rolled onto her side, sighing in her sleep. Cassie closed her eyes, ready to embrace defeat.

Determination refused to die. She couldn't leave her precious sister alone and impoverished, vulnerable to men like Lord Bucksden.

But expose her shame to Lucien? Impossible. There had to be a way to get the money back without having to do either.

Chapter 6

❧⟨—∞⟩❧

Gambling.

Cassie started out of sleep with that word clear in her mind. If she wanted her money back from Lucien Hollier, all she had to do was win it from him. But in order to game, a player had to have something to ante. What would she offer?

The memory of Lucien's face alive with appreciation for her as they waltzed last night rushed over Cassie. Stretching herself awake, she smiled at the thought of his expression if she were to offer herself, the way her father had anted Eliza. She wouldn't, of course. She wanted both her twenty pounds *and* Lucien's respect. But what could she offer?

Wrapped in the close darkness within the bedcurtains, she frowned in thought. A dance or a stroll?

She grimaced, certain Lucien wouldn't be interested in risking money on something he could have for free. She shook her head. It was just a matter of time before she discovered it.

Filled with reborn hope, she reached to Eliza's side of the bed, searching for her sister. The mattress was empty. Startled, she threw open the curtains, only to be blinded by afternoon's bright light. She'd slept through the morning.

The room was quiet, but it looked as if a whirlwind had raced through it. The wardrobe was open, one of Eliza's dresses thrown over a door. Another lay in a careless pile on the floor. Two pairs of shoes, one of them belonging to Cassie, had been tossed out of the wardrobe. Ribbons of blue and violet were strewn across the top of their trunk. Cassie smiled. Eliza's wild touch.

Scanning the room a second time, she noticed a torn bit of paper shoved between the dressing table's mirror and its frame. Cassie crossed the room to take the note. Eliza's hand was bold and forceful, lacking any girlish curlicues.

We've gone to walk the park. I had to borrow your bonnet. Aunt Philana says there's one for you to use in her room if you're up in time to join us. Take heed! Your bonnet is much improved with that bright yellow ribbon of mine.

Cassie smiled, almost hearing Eliza's voice as her sister declared Cassie's bonnet improved. Eliza didn't hold with the notion that a widow should

shun bright colors. She'd been trying for months to
get Cassie to exchange her bonnet's dove gray ribbons for something brighter.

She went to the window and looked down into
the earl's garden. Just as Eliza had promised, the
house guests strolled about the park in twos and
threes. A small crowd had gathered near a fine lily
pond not far from the house, one of whom was Philana. There was no mistaking her bonnet; a mass of
curling gray plumes sprang from its band. Wearing
a paler shade of lavender today, Philana ambled
along the pond's shoreline a little ahead of Eliza.

Cassie recognized her sister's yellow-striped
gown and short brown jacket. Striding alongside
Eliza was a soldier with a tall, black hat trimmed in
gold braid. Colonel Egremont. His short, dark blue
jacket, the gleaming gold braid on his shoulders, his
pale blue pantaloons with their golden stripe offered
startling contrast to his black-as-night boots.

The colonel had his gloved hands folded at the
small of his back, but he leaned his head toward
Eliza. His attitude screamed of intimacy, or at least
the desire for intimacy. The possibility of Eliza's
heart being broken lent even more urgency to
Cassie's already frantic purpose. The sooner she had
her money back from Lucien, the sooner she could
get Eliza to America and into her new life.

In reaction to her thoughts, Cassie's gaze dashed
across the gentlemen on the lawn. She didn't expect
to identify Lucien, not with all the men—except the
soldiers—dressed in the same tall hats, brown-tailed
coats and fawn breeches. Yet, Cassie's gaze locked

on a lone gentleman making his way back toward the house against the tide of guests strolling deeper into the parkland.

Lucien. She wondered how she could be so certain, then decided it was the aggressive set of his shoulders and the swift, forceful way he moved. But if Lucien was reentering the house while so many guests were still strolling, she might catch him for a moment. All she needed was a little privacy in which to offer her unorthodox wager. She'd only have her precious opportunity if she were quick about dressing, and he took his time doing whatever he intended within doors. In that case what Cassie needed was Philana's maid, Betty, to tie her corset and hook her gown.

Dashing water on her face, Cassie ran a hasty brush through her hair, leaving it loose. Not eager to traipse about Ryecroft Castle in her dressing gown, even if the occupants were all out-of-doors at the moment, she went to the wardrobe and chose her garments for the day. Unlike Eliza, Cassie couldn't bear chaos. She lay her petticoat, small corset, stockings and garters in a neat row on the bed. Donning her drawers, she returned to the wardrobe to don her green-sprigged day dress, then to finally slip her bare feet into her shoes.

Throwing her shawl over her shoulders to hide her loosened attire, thus assuring at least the appearance of decency, she opened her door. And came face-to-face with Lucien.

"Oh!" she gasped, not certain which to do first:

gather up her hair, pull her shawl over her bodice to hide lack of corset, or reach behind her to hold her dress closed.

Lucien carried his hat and gloves in one hand. His honey-brown hair tumbled in careless disarray about his sun-browned face. His clear gray eyes were cool. If he noticed her dishabille, there was no sign of it in his expression.

"Good afternoon, Mrs. Marston," he said, offering a small bow.

"Is it afternoon already?" Cassie stuttered, wholly unnerved at being caught in such a state.

"It's well past noon," Lucien replied, his tone that of amiable disinterest.

Cassie stared at him. Who was this cool stranger, and what had happened to the warm man who'd waltzed with her last night? That man would have teased her for rising so late, while leering at her state of dress. Mortification tore through Cassie as she considered the only probable explanation for his change. Her father must have spoken to him even though she'd forbidden it.

She was doomed. No, she was free. She no longer had to worry about keeping Lucien's respect. That made her stomach ache.

"At breakfast this morn, your sister and Lady Forster said you ailed. I hope I find you recovered," Lucien was saying.

"I am," Cassie lied. Respect or not, how was she supposed to offer Lucien a game to win back her twenty pounds when he was so disinterested?

Lucien stepped to the door directly across from hers and put his hand on the latch. "Mrs. Marston," he said, his cold tone as distant as his expression.

Cassie reacted without thought, wanting Eliza's future. Turning her back to him, she lowered her shawl to her waist and pulled her hair to one side, then looked over her shoulder at him.

"My lord, I cannot find my maid just now. Could you fasten my hooks?" she asked, speaking so swiftly that her voice sounded thready.

Lucien froze in front of his door. Cassie watched his gaze trace the slender length of her naked back from her waist to her nape. The terrible coolness in his expression melted. Heat again burned in his icy eyes when he raised his gaze to meet hers.

Trapped in place by her need to save Eliza, Cassie burned in shame, then roasted again in a slow, knee-loosening, heat-making pleasure that came from knowing he gazed upon her naked flesh. She gave a shaken sigh.

The sound freed Lucien. "Happily," he said, a new hoarseness in his voice.

Dropping his hat and gloves next to his door, he crossed the corridor. He pulled the two sides of her gown closed across her back, his bare knuckles brushing her skin. With his touch some of Cassie's sense returned. Was she out of her mind? If she did manage to convince him to game with her he'd never accept a mere dance or stroll as her stake after this. More to the point: With each hook he fastened—hooks that Betty would have to reopen for

Cassie to dress properly—her opportunity to propose that game narrowed.

A tress of hair slipped down her back. Lucien caught it, then let it slide between his fingers. Cassie shivered, cursing herself for wanting so much more of his touch.

Oh, bother. There was no room for regret now that the milk was spilled, and naming herself an idiot wouldn't put twenty pounds in her purse. That game had already cost her more than she wanted to pay. She may as well propose it.

Never in his life had Lucien been more grateful for Devanney's nagging. If not for his cousin's harping about the idiocy of looking for a wife when he was just out of mourning, Lucien might still be in the garden. How much better to be in this corridor, his fingers brushing Cassie's naked back.

He breathed in her rosy scent. The smell ate up his resolve to avoid her from last night. Instead, his senses overflowed with her nearness, and her bareness.

Dear God, but he wanted to press his lips to her nape. He lowered his head a little, taunting himself with the prospect.

His longing only worsened as he worked the hooks at the middle of her back. Somehow, he hadn't taken Cassie as the sort of woman who went without a corset. It wasn't that unusual. A good number of society's well-bred women, including his own sister, went without one. However, none of those women inspired him to reach around and cup their unfettered breasts in his hands.

Yet another tress slid from the mass of golden hair she'd pulled over her shoulder, tumbling down the length of her back. It was more temptation than Lucien could resist. He caught it, this time bringing it to his lips, savoring its silky smoothness and the smell of roses.

"My lord, I came to Lord Ryecroft's house party anticipating the card playing. My father is unwilling to open his purse so I might wager," Cassie said.

"I beg your pardon?" Lucien asked, too far gone in desire to fully comprehend what she said.

"I said I haven't any money with which to wager." The new tension in her voice caught his attention. "Against that I wondered if you'd consider a game with me and an unconventional wager."

Some part of him registered that her question had to do with gambling and wagers. Not that he cared. All that mattered was that he had only a few hooks left to fasten and her shoulders were taut. That meant the instant he finished she'd raise her shawl and back away from him when he most definitely didn't want any space between them.

"What sort of wager did you have in mind?" he asked, more to keep her where she stood than out of any interest in her request. He finished the last hook. Just as he expected she jerked her shawl in place and pivoted, backing toward her door.

"I'd like to offer you a stroll, calling its value two pounds."

His interest more than piqued, Lucien studied her.

Light from the window at the corridor's end touched her face, marking her cheekbone and the regal lift of her brow. Her brown eyes looked as warm and rich as chocolate. Lord, but he liked the sultry way her lips curved.

"That's an expensive walk," he replied, wondering if she had anything more alluring to offer.

Disappointment danced in her eyes, then faded. "I suppose you'd say the same about a dance?"

"I think I must." The movement of her mouth as she spoke was mesmerizing. It wasn't a dance he wanted from her, but something more intimate.

"What would you consider an acceptable stake in a game between us?" She nipped at her lower lip, waiting for his response.

A game between them, a wonderful, exotic game. Desire lapped at Lucien the way the ocean washed over the beach. His eyes closed halfway. His attention wouldn't shift from her glorious mouth.

"A kiss," he said.

Yes. A kiss. That's what he wanted from her. That's what he needed. At the moment if she'd asked him to stake his entire estate against a chance to kiss her he'd have willingly done it.

"Oh," Cassie breathed, warm color staining her cheeks. She pressed a hand against her throat and stepped back again only to collide with her door. It swung open, giving Lucien a good view of a chamber strewn with feminine frippery. The chaos only made the neat line of garments on the end of the bed all the more noticeable.

His gaze caught on the corset. The memory of last

night and the waltz returned; with it came the feel of boning against his hand as he held Cassie. She didn't eschew corsets.

He glanced at her feet. They were bare inside her shoes. Of course they were, her stockings lay on the bed's end.

Then what was she doing out here in the corridor naked beneath her gown, pretending she needed his assistance to finish her toilette? What else but seducing him? Knowing that she wanted him the way he wanted her sent Lucien's longing to have her almost past containment.

"This was a mistake," Cassie said, her voice barely louder than a whisper.

Oh, no. She'd desired him enough to play temptress. He wouldn't let her courage fail her now, not with the need to again run his fingers down the length of her spine tormenting him.

"You said you wished to play cards," he crooned, playing spider to her fly. "The stake is nothing more than a single kiss. Barely improper."

Again, she nibbled at her lower lip. Dear God, but he wanted the chance to do that for himself. She shook her head. "I can't."

She started to turn toward her chamber. Lucien caught her by the hand, his fingers slipping between hers. She gave a shaken breath as their palms met. Ah, but she didn't try to extract her hand from his. It was proof that her desire for him was greater than her need to play the proper widow. He had to have that kiss, and more.

"Consider this then," he said. "I'll make you a gift

of five pounds at the beginning of our game. If at the end of our match you still have five pounds you may leave the table with that sum. If you have less than five pounds, you owe me the kiss."

She looked up at him. Why should he wait for tonight when all he need do to have his kiss was lower his head? That wouldn't be nearly as much fun as tormenting himself with the prospect of their game until the sun set.

"So be it. Tonight, in the card room, then," she said, her voice trembling.

A metallic click sounded from down the corridor. Cassie tore her hand from his and leaped into her room. Her door closed in his face.

Down the hall a servant left one of the other rooms without glancing in his direction. Lucien turned his gaze back to Cassie's door. How he longed to open it and join her.

"And after the card room, the garden, where I'll have my kiss," he whispered.

Cassie stood with her back pressed against her closed door, her heart pounding. If not for the interruption she might have given Lucien the kiss he wanted, and cheated herself of her stake in tonight's game. Even more worrisome was the realization that if he'd kissed her a moment ago, she would have happily invited him into her bedchamber and allowed the worst to happen.

Not allowed, welcomed. Cassie closed her eyes and swallowed. Not the worst, either. The best.

If Lucien's mere look was enough to destroy her

morals, what would his kiss do? Cassie desperately wanted to know, which was exactly why she didn't dare let him win tonight. No, what she had to do was to relieve him of his five pounds, deny them both the kiss they wanted, then move on to another table to win another five.

Cassie hung her head at the thought of using Lucien in this way. Why did it feel so wrong?

Chapter 7

Devanney's dining room, with its high, ornately plastered ceilings, walls covered with creamy blue-and-gold-printed linen and massive fireplace, closed in on Lucien. It wasn't that the room was decorated more formally than he liked. It was the masculine ritual of lingering at the dinner table.

The women had retreated to the drawing room to enjoy gossip and music almost an hour ago; the sounds of an etude wafted through the dining-room doorway, nothing schoolgirlish in its execution. Lucien brought his glass of port to his lips, battling his impatience. Never had an evening dragged the way this one did. It had to be nearly ten. Then again, he'd never before anticipated a game in which he would win a kiss.

Or more. Desire stirred sharply. Definitely more.

Lucien sipped again. Cassie had to know his reputation with cards. With that in mind the only reason she would have agreed to his terms was because she intended to lose. The need to again brush his fingers against Cassie's bare skin tormented him. Their card game was nothing more than pretense, a way for Cassie to justify moving from the card table to his bed.

He drained his port to its dregs, swigging it like water instead of exceedingly fine wine, then leaned back in his chair, one that looked too delicate to hold him. A white-wigged footman was instantly at his elbow, decanter in hand. Lucien let the servant refill the crystal goblet with tawny liquid as he glanced around the room.

During the day the number of Devanney's guests had swelled to more than fifty, but only twenty actually stayed at Ryecroft Castle. The locals went home for the night, not to return until the next morning for their outing to the ruins of a local abbey. That made the evening meal an intimate gathering. Too intimate.

The dining room had become Percy's stage as he told the tale of Prinny hunting on his father's estate, a tale Lucien had heard more than once. His former ward looked even more outrageous tonight, wearing a waistcoat of silver-shot blue silk sprinkled with spangles beneath his black evening attire. Lucien suspected Percy's startling attire was meant to impress Miss Conningsby and undo Egremont. Egremont and Percy were friendly competitors in all things, Egremont wanting what Percy had, Percy trying to take what Egremont had from him. Right now, their bone of contention was Cassie's beautiful sister.

Devanney, his evening attire cut with a Corinthian in mind, slouched happily in his chair at the table's head. Lucien sent his cousin a pointed look that asked if they might *please* adjourn this gathering. Devanney gave a horrified shake of his head. For good reason. Once Devanney entered the drawing room he became Duchess Eleanor's willing slave.

Devanney quirked his brow to ask Lucien why there should be any hurry. The only reply Lucien could offer was a shrug. The last thing he wanted his cousin to know was that he continued to pursue Cassie despite his refusal last night. That would only give Devanney hope for his prank.

Devanney eyed him for a moment, then grimaced in acquiescence. Relieved, Lucien turned his attention back to Percy and his story, only to have a movement near the table's end catch his eye. Sir Roland Conningsby had turned in his chair to watch the drawing-room door, a worried frown on his broad brow.

Once again, Conningsby surprised Lucien. The erstwhile sot hadn't touched his dinner wine and only toyed with his port. The little buffoon looked more downcast than Lucien thought possible.

Percy's tale finally ended as it always did, with the overweight regent tumbling off his horse. A spate of uncomfortable laughter followed. Devanney straightened in his chair.

"Your mind wanders far from hills and hunting, Hollier," he called to Lucien. "Do we bore you?"

"Not at all," Lucien replied, cursing his cousin behind his smile. Devanney might have acquiesced, but he still wanted his explanation for why Lucien was in such a hurry.

"Lord Graceton is far too polite to admit the truth, Lord Ryecroft," Percy said, his words slurring. The lad hadn't yet learned to hold his liquor; he'd consumed not only his own portion of wine and port, but what Sir Roland hadn't. "If his mind wanders it's because Prinny's foibles annoy him."

"That's enough said about that, Percy," Lucien warned.

"Lord Graceton's right. It's time to leave our regent and his preoccupations for something closer to hand," said Egremont. Even wearing his gold-trimmed regimentals, the young man seemed Percy's opposite, plain where Percy was handsome and slender where his friend had a more powerful build. Egremont's only remarkable feature was the startling blue color of his eyes. That combined with his wavy black hair saved him from being nondescript. He looked at Lucien. "My lord, might I interest you in a game of cards?"

That was the activity Lucien wanted, but not the partner he craved. The same couldn't be said of Egremont. The colonel had a score to settle, having recently lost seventy pounds to Lucien.

"I might be," Lucien said, offering the only reply polite society allowed. Egremont wouldn't be willing to let him move on to a new partner until one of them had lost the night's limit. Lucien gnashed his teeth at the thought of yet another delay before claiming Cassie's kiss.

The colonel smiled widely and rose. "Well then, my lords and good gentlemen, what do you say about joining the ladies?"

Since every man except Devanney was eager to be on to a new occupation it didn't take long for them to file from the room. Lucien, his refreshed glass of port in hand, waited for his cousin as the men made their exodus.

Devanney scowled as he joined Lucien. "Why didn't I refuse when Her Grace informed me she was coming?" he muttered.

Lucien laughed a little. "Because she's your grandfather's sister and you're a devoted nephew."

"More fool me," Devanney grumbled, walking into the drawing room.

With so few guests in residence there were only five card tables set up at one end of the room. That left more chairs available for those who preferred the amiable pastimes of music and conversation. It was Duchess Eleanor's daughter, Lady Barbara, at the piano. Her eyes were closed as her clever fingers filled the room with the grandeur of her piece. Miss Conningsby stood beside her, turning pages that Lady Barbara wasn't watching.

Cassie sat in a nearby chair, enjoying the performance. She no longer wore the demure green-sprigged dress he'd fastened this afternoon but a fashionably cut lavender gown, a breath of lacy shawl covering the mounds of her breasts that rose above her bodice. Knowing she again wore her corset tantalized rather than daunted Lucien. She could play the modest matron all she wanted, but he knew better.

A plush lilac velvet turban trimmed in gold covered her head. A few golden ringlets escaped its confinement, one curling tress trailing down the slender length of her neck. Lucien swallowed, reminded of the strands he'd caressed this afternoon. Lord, but he wanted to feel the silky smoothness of her hair against his fingers, to place a kiss upon her nape.

Impatience rose beyond all bearing. Fifteen minutes at the table with Egremont would be too long. Lucien wanted his game with Cassie, and he wanted it now.

Duchess Eleanor rose from the back of the group gathered around the piano. "About time," she called out to Devanney, her age-deepened voice interrupting the recital. "Barbara, enough of that tedious plunking. It's time to play cards."

A true musician, Lady Barbara didn't falter or stop, but new color stained her cheeks. Her chin quivered. Miss Conningsby laid a consoling hand on her shoulder. Cassie shot the duchess a disapproving glance.

"Barbara!" Eleanor trumpeted when her daughter didn't come to heel.

Annoyance flickered across Cassie's face. "A little patience, Your Grace," she said in a loud whisper. "Lady Barbara has almost reached the piece's end."

Eleanor gawked at being so boldly accosted by a mere knight's daughter. Devanney choked on a laugh. Approval swelled in Lucien. There weren't many women with courage enough to confront Eleanor. Most of them in this room trembled at the social harm the powerful duchess might do them if they dared.

"Shall we game, my lord?" Egremont prodded, then led the way to the tables.

Lucien followed, shooting yet another look over his shoulder at Cassie. She watched him in return. When their gazes met she bit her lower lip and turned in her chair.

That she couldn't keep her eyes off him only fed Lucien's desire for her. If he needed to play like an ass and lose twenty pounds to Egremont in the next fifteen minutes, so be it.

Cassie turned forward in her chair again, her heart pounding. Part of it was irritation at the duchess's rudeness, the other was Lucien. Dinner had offered her plenty of time in which to lament her sad want of sense in agreeing to that wager. With his every glance Lucien told her that it wasn't just a kiss he wanted from her—or expected from her.

That he now believed her loose was her own fault. Why hadn't she simply swallowed her pride and asked him to give back what her father had taken? Suffering his pity would have been far better than this.

Seated next to Cassie, Lady Ross leaned close. She was a nervous woman with pale brown curls and a tendency to hold her folded hands mouselike at the center of her chest. She whispered, "Well done, Mrs.

Marston. We're all so accustomed to Her Grace's rudeness that we forget to hold her to her own standard."

Seated on Cassie's other side, Philana leaned forward to look at Lady Ross. Her plume, held in her hair by its diamond-studded clip, bobbed as she nodded. "Now do you understand my excitement over my niece's visit, Margaret? Having her and her family staying with me this summer is such a boon. That house of mine has felt terribly empty since—" she broke off, tears gleaming in her eyes.

Guilt crashed down onto Cassie. She and her family weren't staying the summer. They'd be fortunate if they managed to linger the full two weeks of the party.

Lady Barbara brought her piano piece to its conclusion without further interruption. When the final sweet notes echoed into silence Eliza clapped in approval. Philana, seated next to Cassie, did the same. Others joined them.

Lady Barbara acknowledged their appreciation with a shy smile and gathered up her play book. Mr. Percy rushed to join Eliza. The dandy, one of Eliza's new admirers, leered, his face framed between his exalted collar points. "Miss Conningsby, would you consider playing for us?"

"Heavens, no," Eliza retorted with a laugh. "I should seem dross after Lady Barbara's glittering performance."

Cassie gave thanks that Eliza was no ninnyhammer. She'd never give men like Mr. Percy more credit than their due. Eliza knew that dandies like him were far too vain to let their affections expand past the tips of their own toes.

"Here now, Sir Roland." The spangled young man pulled their father closer to the piano. "You must convince your youngest to play for us."

Roland looked old and faded tonight, even in his evening attire. "You must heed her refusal, I think. Our 'Liza's fingers tend to betray her, but she's quite the thrush. Why not ask her to sing?"

Cassie eyed their father in surprise. So did Eliza. Neither of them realized he'd ever noticed Eliza's talent at singing. To the best of Cassie's knowledge, this was the first time he'd ever so much as spoken of his daughter in public.

Lord Ryecroft's younger brother, a lad of fifteen, ambled over to join them. Lady Ross's daughter, a girl about Eliza's age, followed him, bringing with her two female friends. That caught the attention of the other young men in the chamber and a group began to form.

Eliza laughed, shaking her head. "Don't ask me to sing, at least not now. I'd much rather something more active. Has anyone an idea?"

"What do you say to a stroll under the night sky?" Mr. Percy asked, offering just the sort of expedition Eliza enjoyed. "It's not every night that Scotland offers a sky clear enough to see the stars."

Excitement blossomed on Eliza's face. "Why, that sounds lovely, doesn't it?" She looked to the young people gathering around her. "If one of you has a spare neckcloth we might even play hoodman blind."

That elicited an explosion from the others, some seconding Eliza's suggestion, others offering substitute games. Dismay darkened Mr. Percy's face, suggesting that he'd hoped for a more intimate amble than the sort Eliza planned. Still, he was a good sport and joined the others in their anticipation of the adventure.

"Come with us, Aunt Philana," Eliza called. "We'll need someone objective enough to call faults when we play our game."

"Of course," Philana said.

"Might I escort you, Lady Forster?" Roland asked.

Philana blinked in surprise, but was too well mannered to refuse. "There's a capital idea, Sir Roland," she said, taking his arm.

"Will you come with us, Cassie?" Eliza stretched out a hand to her sister, forgetting in her exhilaration Cassie's purpose at this party.

"I think not," Cassie replied. Knowing of no way to remind Eliza without telling the whole room their secret, she said, "Traces of last night's headache remain and I fear the night air may exacerbate it. I don't want to miss our ride to the abbey on the morrow."

Eliza's pleasure dimmed. "Perhaps I should stay with you?"

"Of course not," Philana said swiftly, glancing from Eliza to Cassie, then to the card tables. Philana not only knew Cassie's plan to use her skill at the tables on behalf of her family, she heartily approved, even if it meant lightening the purses of her neighbors. Unlike their father, Philana didn't believe there was anything eerie or unfair about Cassie's card-playing abilities.

"Why should you stay, Eliza, when the room teems with folk?" Roland seconded. The hopeful look he sent Cassie suggested he still depended on her to solve the problem he'd created.

"Ah," Eliza said, her memory jogged by their reactions. "But of course you should stay, Cassie. However, if you change your mind later you must come into the garden and join us."

"I will," Cassie promised.

After waving them out the garden door she meandered toward the card players. Lord Ryecroft played with the duchess and Barbara at the nearest table. The duchess shot Cassie a scathing glance.

"Impudent riffraff," Lady Eleanor sniffed as Barbara laid down a card, then straightened in her chair to glare at her daughter. "Why did you play that card? You know better than to lead with trump!"

At the table to their right was a squire, a baronet and a mere gentleman. The men played their game in complete silence, their concentration so complete that Cassie read them with ease. The others might be confident in what they held, but the squire had this round. That she could tell what they held so easily was reassuring. She still owned her skill.

Lucien and Colonel Egremont sat at the farthest table, the one closest to the wall, Lucien's back to the room. Cassie stopped behind him to take a bracing breath only to have her senses fill with his scent, the heat of his body, his very presence. For an instant she lost herself in appreciation of Lucien, the man. She liked the way candlelight made his hair glow more golden than brown. The perfect fit of his coat told her that Lucien had no need of the padding some men used to look masculine.

Colonel Egremont looked up from the cards in front of him, his face radiating confused triumph. The triumph no doubt sprang from the mound of counters stacked near his hand, but Cassie had no ready explanation for his confusion. He came to his feet and bowed. "Mrs. Marston."

Lucien glanced over his shoulder. Their gazes met. Heat flared in his gray eyes. A slow, sensuous smile played across his lips.

He also rose. "Mrs. Marston."

"Where did everyone go?" Colonel Egremont asked, looking over Cassie's shoulder at the rest of the room.

Considering that the drawing room was still occupied, Cassie assumed that by everyone he meant Eliza. "A group of young people went into the garden, planning to stroll and perhaps play a game of hoodman blind," she offered.

Lucien shifted impatiently. "We play Speculation tonight, Mrs. Marston. Would you care to join us?"

"Actually, my lord, I think I've taken enough of your wealth for one night," the colonel said. "If you'll excuse me?"

Lucien's deep warm laugh sent a shiver rushing through Cassie. "Absolutely. Kind of you to leave me with a coin or two for the morrow. If you like I'll hold your winnings for you to collect later."

"Many thanks, my lord." Bowing, Colonel Egremont trotted toward the garden door.

Lucien watched him go. "Well, well. I think we've been snubbed in favor of true love."

His words stabbed through Cassie. Precious little good the colonel's affection would do Eliza. Cassie dropped into the chair he'd vacated.

Still smiling, Lucien sat, collected the cards and began to shuffle. Pleasure filled his eyes. For some reason, no doubt because she was a cynic, Cassie didn't think Lucien minded Colonel Egremont's absence at all.

"Will you have something to drink?" he asked.

She shook her head. "No, thank you, my lord. I must be at my sharpest if I'm to keep the coins you give me."

That made Lucien laugh again. "A wise decision."

He separated four pounds in notes and a pound's worth of coins from the stack near his hand and pushed them across the table to her. Cassie pulled the precious bits of paper and metal close, hoarding them like the treasure they were.

"You don't mind playing for coins instead of using counters?" His smile was both threat and promise. He didn't expect to lose his kiss.

"Of course not," she replied, a shiver coursing up her spine. She was far too susceptible to him. This match must end as soon as possible, before his charm overwhelmed her sense.

"What game shall we play?" he asked.

"Why not Speculation?" she replied, unable to

think of a game better fitted to her needs. The hands played quickly and if she raised the value of a point it could prove very lucrative in a short period of time. "What do you say to a ten shillings a point with a reckoning after ten hands?" she suggested, finding a certain symmetry to the thought of winning five hands, then losing five, to keep five pounds.

Lucien paused in mid-shuffle to look at her, his gaze lambent. "That's a little steep, even for a game as unusual as ours, Mrs. Marston. Indeed, it's so steep I might think you eager to lose."

The raw, sensual edge to his voice stirred something deep and hidden within Cassie. He was utterly convinced she meant to seduce him. She wasn't certain that she didn't want him to seduce her. Oh Lord, but she needed to put distance between them, and soon.

"That's something only the cards can determine, my lord." Cassie relaxed into her chair as best she could. "You may take the first deal."

Chapter 8

The match went well enough through the first hands. Even with Duchess Eleanor's constant complaining at the nearby table and the laughter from those guests who hadn't gone out-of-doors, Cassie had no difficulty reading Lucien's face and form. She easily sensed when to stay, when to buy cards and when to speculate. Just as she had planned, she lost a little the first game, won substantially in the next, then lost a little again, gaining, her tiny pile of coins growing. By her fifth game she had almost eight pounds, something that left Lucien frowning in surprise.

In keeping with her pattern, Cassie lost that game, returning some of what she'd earned. Then, luck happened. In each of the next two hands she drew several penalty cards, each one costing her ten shillings. She lost both of those hands, decreasing her winnings to three pounds.

What had she been thinking, setting an arbitrary end to their match? Now, to leave the table with the five pounds he'd promised her and that she so desperately needed, she'd have to win all of their remaining games. Courting an accusation as a sharp, Cassie gritted her teeth and won the next two hands, but managed to return her winnings to just four pounds, ten shillings.

The tenth and final deal belonged to her. As she shuffled she watched Lucien. He was the consummate gambler, his expression flat, his eyes revealing nothing in their depths.

Ah, but it wasn't just a man's face that exposed his thoughts. Cassie eyed the taut line of Lucien's shoulders and the way he held his right hand, working the ring he wore on his third finger. Those two aspects announced his intention to win the next hand, even if he did so by will alone.

That wasn't all she saw. The creases at the corners of his eyes screamed of suspicion, something she couldn't afford. If Lucien believed he'd been cheated he'd demand a rematch. Convention required she honor such a request. Even if she lost every hand in that match, the damage would be done. Cassie's future couldn't afford the scrutiny. She had to lose. Giving Lucien his kiss meant she remained free to gamble.

She dealt, sensing as she laid down the cards that his hand was the weaker. She lost by refusing to speculate. Across the table Lucien smiled in satisfaction, then gathered up the pot. The creases at the corners of his eyes relaxed.

"You played well," he offered as if to console.

"Good of you to say, my lord," she replied, repressing her urge to snort at his lie. She'd played that last game like a fool and he knew it, but then he thought she lost because she wanted his kiss.

Didn't she? Why shouldn't she indulge her desires? The respectable woman she'd once believed herself was dead, perishing the moment she'd swung that urn. Color seeped up into Cassie's cheeks at the thought of what she no longer needed to deny herself.

To hide her reaction she swept her precious winnings into her reticule and snapped it shut. After smoothing the sleeves of her lavender gown, she straightened her lacy shawl over her shoulders so that the knot sat at the center of her chest. As if the gossamer garment were any protection! It revealed more than it hid.

"So, when would you like to collect what I owe you?" She almost choked on the words.

One corner of his mouth quirked up. "Now would be convenient for me, Mrs. Marston."

For an instant Cassie felt as if she stood outside herself, watching her life unfold, one unbelievable, improbable event after another. If someone had told her two weeks ago that she would kill an earl, then turn her back on propriety to claim a kiss, she would have accused them of insanity.

"Where?" she asked, coming to her feet.

Heat flared in the depths of Lucien's cool eyes. Once again Cassie felt his presence reach out to envelop her. He came to his feet, pulling the sleeves of his black coat back into place, then giving his stark white waistcoat a tug. "I think we should join the others in their stargazing."

Gratitude swept through Cassie. It hadn't occurred to her until this moment that he could have made their strange wager public, exposing her to ridicule, debasing her even further than she had already debased herself. She nodded in agreement, nervous nonetheless. She glanced around the chamber, wondering if any of the others in the drawing room knew what she and Lucien were about, then started toward the garden doors, Lucien on her heels.

The duchess glared at Cassie as she neared Lord Ryecroft's table, but the earl smiled. He looked too big for the delicate chair he used. "Mrs. Marston," he said without rising, "have you already finished gaming for the night?"

"At least for the moment my lord," Cassie told him. "We thought we'd join the youngsters in their romp."

"Youngsters?" Lucien echoed with a breath of a laugh. "Speak for yourself, Mrs. Marston. I'm joining my peers."

For some reason Lucien's comment pleased Lord Ryecroft. The earl's face softened as he glanced at them. "Enjoy yourselves, children."

"If he were joining his peers, he wouldn't be going with that unmannerly commoner at his side," snapped Duchess Eleanor, turning her attention back to her hand. "It does your repute no favor to keep company with her sort, Lord Graceton."

"Madam," protested Lady Barbara, her voice barely louder than a whisper.

"That, Your Grace, is my concern, not yours," Lucien swiftly replied, offering his rebuff along with a swift bow.

Gratitude again washed over Cassie as he defended her. Still, the duchess's words stung, perhaps because her comment hit too close to the truth. It did Lucien no favor to consort with a card-sharping murderess.

Once they were out of the duchess's hearing Cassie shot Lucien a quick look. "Thank you for that," she said as they neared the garden door. "I fear I've made a terrible enemy today."

"And a good friend," Lucien said. "Lady Barbara will never forget what you did for her tonight. As for the duchess, you were doomed in her esteem when we waltzed the night of the ball. I fear she views you as a rival with her daughter for my attention and, eventually, my ring."

His words went through Cassie like a stake, revealing just how much she wished she were a rival for Lucien's ring. Fool! She'd let Philana's crackbrained notion of Lucien marrying her implant itself in her heart. The weedy, unwelcome thought had found fertile soil in Cassie's girlhood infatuation with him, swiftly setting down roots and feeding on his reborn attraction for her. She brutally tore it from her heart before it did any more damage.

"More fool the duchess for mistaking an old acquaintance for more than it is," she threw back over her shoulder as she exited. Lucien said nothing to contradict her.

Outside, the marble of the drawing-room floor gave way to brick. The porch's surface extended a comfortable distance before ending at soft sod. Strategically placed lanterns, globes of yellow in the black velvet of the night, revealed the potted trees and statuary decorating the porch. A sparkling night wrapped itself around Cassie as she breathed in the scent of roses in the earl's garden. The smell tangled with the more pervasive aromas of damp earth, wood smoke and pine.

Laughter rang in the chill air, the sound emanating a good distance from the house. Peering into the dimness, Cassie saw the pale shapes of the young explorers taking a turn about a gurgling fountain. Not certain where she was going, Cassie walked in their direction. She'd almost reached the grass when Lucien caught her by the hand. His fingers twining with hers, he gently pulled her around to face him.

Cassie gazed up at him. Night's shadows clung beneath the sharp lift of his cheekbones. Golden lantern light marked the narrow length of his nose. Once again, desire's heat radiated from him. She drew a shaken breath as his need became hers.

Saying nothing, Lucien led her to the right. An ancient marble deity appeared out of the night, its form stark white where the light touched it and feathery gray where the shadows clung. Lucien knew the grounds of his cousin's house well. Behind the statue was a small alcove cut into the house's exterior wall, the perfect place for a tryst, hidden here from both the house and the garden.

Standing with her back to the alcove's side wall, Cassie watched Lucien, her nerves twanging. Yes, she'd been a bold miss in her day, but she'd respected the limits of behavior. She'd never stepped this far over propriety's line. Now that she was here she didn't know how to behave. Did she let Lucien take her in his arms? Should she allow only their mouths to touch? What if he sought to take more than his kiss? What if *she* took the kiss, then offered him a second?

Drawing their joined hands to his heart, Lucien watched her, his eyes cloaked in shadow. "You are truly beautiful. I swear that your image haunts me, day and night."

A hint of amusement touched his voice. Did he mean his outrageous compliment to remind her of their waltz? If so, it worked. Cassie relaxed into the role she'd played that night.

"Don't squander your flattery, my lord. It's one kiss you won from me, no more." There. She'd set the parameters of the interlude for both of them.

He laughed, the sound quiet and warm. Lifting his free hand, he brushed his fingertips along the curve of her cheek. Cassie closed her eyes, savoring the sensation. After three years with no more than Eliza's occasional embrace, his caress felt like rain on parched earth. She drank it in, wondering if she might go the rest of her life without ever again knowing a man's touch.

He didn't stop at her jawline, but moved his hand downward to beneath her ear, then to the back of her neck. With his fingertips he drew a light circle at her nape. Cassie's soft turban shifted on her head, slipping out of place. She didn't care, any more than a starving man cared what sort of food he ate.

She splayed her fingers across his breast. The layers of his clothing did nothing to disguise the muscles of his chest. His heart beat against her palm, its pace faster than it should be. Cassie almost smiled, reassured to know he was as affected as she by what they did.

"One kiss," she whispered, warning him, and herself. "Take it now and be content."

Moonlight shifted across his face. He smiled and drew another circle at her nape. That won him a shiver from Cassie.

"Are you so certain you'll be satisfied with only one kiss?"

"Enough talk," Cassie said, unwilling to play the game of taunts and very much concerned over how one sort of intimacy might lead to another.

Rising onto her toes, she touched her mouth to his. His lips were soft and warm against hers, his face smooth, his skin cool in the night air. He tasted of fine port.

He drew a swift breath, then his mouth moved atop hers, his kiss deepening, demanding her response. What remained of Cassie's image of herself as an upstanding woman died.

Her shawl slid down to nestle in the crook of her elbows. She leaned against him, needing to feel all of him pressed against her. Their thighs touched, the heat of his body embracing her through her thin dress. Making a sound deep in his throat, Lucien wrapped his arms around her, pulling her even more tightly against him. When their hips met Cassie gasped against his mouth. There was no mistaking how much he wanted her.

She clasped her hands at his nape, pulling herself even closer, begrudging her corset for it stood between them like a fence. Lucien tore his mouth from hers and straightened. Cassie gave a quiet cry of protest. He couldn't end their kiss yet!

Instead, he lowered his head and pressed his lips to the mound of her breast. Cassie shook, then arched away from him, offering him more of her to kiss. The tiny sane part of her cried out in shock. What sort of woman was she?

He groaned, urging her back a step with his hands at her waist. Cassie did his bidding and found her back pressed to the wall. Lucien pressed a thigh between hers, holding her in place, then cupped her breasts through her gown and corset.

Lacking the will to stop, Cassie thrust her fingers into his hair, pressing his mouth to her breasts. He ran his fingers along the top of her bodice. Pleasure shot through her, the sensation so intense that she cried out. The sound echoed around the alcove.

Lucien instantly straightened, then once more took her mouth with his. "Sssh," he whispered, breathing the warning against her mouth when she couldn't care less if anyone heard her.

He nipped at her lower lip. His thumbs brushed

her breasts. Cassie shivered. She caught his face in her hands, then took his mouth the way he'd taken hers. Lucien groaned.

Lifting her until her toes barely touched the ground, he pressed her against the alcove wall. Their hips met. She felt the heat of his desire, then made it her own, moving her hips against his, begging for what she'd so missed in her widowhood.

"My hems are soaked!" Eliza's distant, laughing cry echoed into the alcove.

Pleasure shattered, leaving anxiety in its wake. Eliza couldn't catch her here like this. Cassie tore her mouth from Lucien's, turning her head to the side.

"Stop," she pleaded.

"Never," Lucien whispered. His lips touched her jaw, her throat.

"You must stop," Cassie insisted, even as the line of kisses he placed upon her neck sent need shivering through her. "They're coming this way."

Lucien groaned, his lips resting at the place where her neck met her shoulder. Cassie felt the rapid beat of his heart against hers. His hair brushed her throat. He lifted his mouth a bare inch from her shoulder.

"God help me, but I don't want to stop," he murmured, his breath caressing her skin.

Cassie wanted to weep. God had better help them both, because she didn't want him to stop either.

Relaxing his hold on her waist, Lucien let Cassie slide down the wall, her feet again coming to rest upon the earth. She expected him to step back. Instead, he drew her into the circle of his arms. Being held by him was so comforting, so natural despite what they had just done, that Cassie lay her head against his shoulder.

"Don't go so far ahead. We oldsters cannot keep pace," came Philana's faint call. "Come faster, Sir Roland!"

Sighing, Lucien opened his arms and backed away a step. "Your forfeit—" he cleared his throat and tried again—"I'm satisfied."

An aching laugh escaped Cassie. "Liar," she whispered.

Lucien made a sound deep in his chest. Reaching out, he caught her face in his hands and took a second kiss. The depth of his need left her knees weak.

He released her, this time backing beyond arm's length. "You're right, I'm not at all satisfied," he said, his voice low and hard. "Because of that I cannot stay."

He turned and walked away into the darkness. Cassie drew a broken breath and sagged against the wall, consumed by how deeply she wanted him. Her fingers shaking, she did her best to straighten her turban, tucking dislodged hairs back beneath the soft cap. She slapped her skirts back into decent folds, pulled her shawl up over her shoulders and left the alcove feeling as if she walked on ice.

She came around the statue just as a laughing Eliza raced onto the brick porch. Eliza slid to a halt as she saw her sister. "Oh, but you're too late, Cassie. We're just coming back within doors. We've ruined our footwear with the dew, I'm sorry to say."

"What a shame," Cassie said, walking into a circle of lantern light. How could her voice sound so normal when her insides felt like jelly?

Eliza frowned, reaching out to smooth hair off Cassie's face. "What's this? Your turban is askew and your hair's all tumbled."

Cassie gave thanks that it was only her hair that had tumbled. "Will you fix it for me, darling?"

Eliza flashed a bright smile. "You know I won't." She snatched the turban off her sister's head.

"Eliza!" Cassie protested, grabbing for her cap.

With a laugh Eliza danced away. "Didn't I tell you not to wear this silly thing in the first place? I don't know why you insist on dressing like some dowager."

Cassie lunged for her sister. Eliza dodged, squealing happily. "If you want it you must come and get it," she taunted, backing away, holding out the turban for Cassie to take.

"Give it back," Cassie demanded, even as she gave thanks for her sister. Racing around Lord Ryecroft's park would not only serve as the perfect excuse for her disarray, but would be the distraction she needed to put aside her longing for Lucien. Then she'd be free to return to the card tables and devote herself to saving her sister.

Eating himself alive for want of Cassie, Lucien circled the house to the front door, surprising the footman tending the entrance. He gave the servant a nod, then made his way to the residential wing. He couldn't face Devanney, or anyone else in the drawing room, until he once more had his body under control.

He took the stairs two at a time, then walked down the corridor to his room. He paused at his door to look at Cassie's. Knowing that she slept only yards from him did nothing for his already weakened control. As long as she shared a bed with her sister she might as well be a continent away.

Stopping in front of his door, Lucien closed his eyes. Lovesick fools and poets spoke of the earth moving beneath their feet at a lover's kiss. Lucien had considered such protestations poppycock until a few moments ago. The earth *had* moved when Cassie touched her mouth to his. His legs still trembled.

Throwing open the door, Lucien strode into his chamber. Hastings, his valet, sat in the middle of the bed—a bed more than big enough to accommodate lovemaking—with his long legs and stockinged feet folded tailor-fashion beneath him. He played solitaire. His eyes round as coins, his mouth gaping, he scrambled off the bed.

"My lord, I didn't expect you," he stammered, striving to reclaim his dignity and straighten his clothing at the same time.

"For good reason. I didn't expect to be here," Lucien said, working to make his voice gentle when he wanted to roar in frustration.

"Ah," the valet said, pursing his lips in comprehension. "I think you might need a little of the local brew. I've tasted it. Laidlaw keeps some," he said, referring to Lucien's gamekeeper at his fishing lodge. "Scots whiskey will dull anything that pains you. Lord Ryecroft's butler will happily give you some of the earl's best, but only in trade for a bottle of the French brandy hiding in Graceton's cellar."

Scots whiskey. Little did Hastings know how often Lucien had shared Jamie Laidlaw's brew these last two years. He smiled at his valet. Hastings was obtuse, but that didn't change the fact that he was a genius with more than just neckcloths.

"Ryecroft is richer by a bottle of brandy. Be quick about it, Hastings."

Chapter 9

"Another beautiful day," Devanney said, his tone taunting.

His head pounding, Lucien looked at his cousin, his hands too tight on his reins. Beneath him his tall bay gelding snorted, dancing a little in reaction. The bay was too high-strung for his own good, requiring constant attention, something Lucien didn't have in any supply this morning. Devanney stared straight ahead from the saddle of his favorite horse, as big and ugly a beast as any Lucien had ever seen.

The house party was making its way by horse and donkey to the abbey, enjoying a day perfect for such an outing. The sun stood directly overhead in a sky marred by only a few clouds. A meadow opened up before them, sprinkled with late summer flowers going to seed. Sheep grazed, still looking naked after their shearing the previous month. A distant copse of trees framed the weathered skeleton of the ancient monastery.

Both Lucien and Devanney wore brown coats, buckskin riding trousers, Hessians and tall hats upon their heads; it was the uniform required for all country outings. Only their waistcoats were different. Devanney's was a warm red, while Hastings had declared that Lucien should wear cream-colored silk.

Laughter rose from the riders to Devanney's left. Squinting against the sun's brightness, Lucien glanced at last night's stargazers. The group had swelled to twice its number with the addition of Devanney's local guests. Cassie and her sister, mounted on sprightly donkeys from Devanney's stable, rode at their center.

Cassie looked radiant this morning, dressed in a blue riding habit. A straw bonnet framed her oval face, pressing tendrils of golden hair against her brow and cheeks. The blue ribbons knotted beneath her chin complimented her complexion. Her brown eyes soft and pretty, she smiled at Lady Forster. Dear God, but he still wanted her as deeply as he had last night.

"Dare I tell you that you look the devil's own this morning?" Devanney said, sending a laughing side-long look in Lucien's direction.

"I can't imagine why," Lucien replied with no little sarcasm. He knew better than to overindulge in any spirits, much less Scots whiskey. Rather, he'd known better until Cassie's kiss left him beyond control. He vaguely recalled describing in lewd detail what had happened in the garden alcove to Hastings.

"Where did you disappear last night?" Devanney asked, probing where he had no right to pry.

"To bed," Lucien said shortly.

"An early night?" Devanney prodded again.

"An early night," Lucien agreed, doing his best to close the door on the topic.

The mere hint to mind his own business didn't stop his cousin. "Too bad you didn't join the *youngsters* in their romp. Mrs. Marston came back looking in fine fettle—for a dowager, that is." He laughed. "Even Percy raved over the escapade, although he bemoaned the state of his shoes and trousers."

"You don't intend to let this go, do you?" Lucien eyed Devanney, his hands once again tight on his reins. His gelding snorted in complaint.

Devanney grinned. "How can I, when I'm eating myself alive to know what happened? First you won't have Mrs. Marston. Twenty-four hours later you're following her out of the drawing room, grinning like a satisfied cat. Not twenty minutes later I learn that you've retired early. Meanwhile she's in the garden with the others."

The thought of Cassie enjoying herself while his desire for her ate him alive didn't sit well with Lucien. Surely their interlude hadn't affected him so much more than it did her. He looked over Devanney's shoulder at Cassie.

She had her face tilted upward to address Egre-

mont, who sat on a tall steed. The curve of her neck
and arch of her back reminded Lucien of how she'd
lifted her breasts for him to kiss. Blast it, she had to
have been as affected as he.

Stewing on the thought, Lucien turned his gaze
back to Devanney. "I'm not responsible for what
Mrs. Marston does or doesn't do."

The words came out more harshly than he intended. Lucien stifled a groan, recognizing his mistake. Now nothing would stop Devanney's prying.

His cousin chuckled, the sound low and taunting.
"Let me guess. She refused you, and in doing so inadvertently whetted your appetite for her."

His cousin was half right. Lucien's appetite for
Cassie was well whetted. If only she *had* refused
him. Instead he had to live with the knowledge that
if he'd pressed her just a little harder last night she
would have surrendered herself, body and soul,
right there in the alcove.

The thought gave Lucien pause. Why hadn't he
pressed her? After all, the whole point of pursuing
her was seduction, and she'd been his for the taking.

The sound of a galloping horse rose from behind
them. Both Lucien and Devanney turned to see who
came. It was Percy, looking more centaur than man
atop a splendid Thoroughbred mare. There was
nothing flashy about the lad this morning; Percy
was deadly serious about his horses and racing.

"Egad," Lucien said to Devanney, "has the world
ended? What's he doing up so early?" Lucien
couldn't remember ever seeing Percy about before
two in the afternoon.

Devanney shrugged. "Can you consider a man arisen when he hasn't yet seen his bed? Percy said he had business in Hawick this morning. Rather than sleep for an hour or two he chose to watch the sun rise, then rode out. That's an expensive-looking nag he rides."

So she was, but then one expected nothing less from Percy. The black mare had powerful, fluid lines, her stockinged legs owning the perfect taper of her breed. She'd make a good addition to Lord West-morland's stable. She might even make Percy some money on the course.

As always Percy couldn't resist offering his audience a show. Standing in his stirrups, coattails flying, hat cocked at a jaunty angle, he sent his new horse tearing through the ranks of Devanney's guests, whooping with joy all the way. The older men and dowagers in the party shook their heads and fingers in chastisement. The younger women bent admiring glances in Percy's direction. Not so the young men. They watched Percy's mare in envy.

"Egremont, come ride with me," Percy shouted, beckoning to his friend as he slowed his new acquisition to walk alongside Lucien's fretful bay.

Despite the thick dark rings hanging beneath his bloodshot eyes, Percy's neckcloth was fresh and his jaw devoid of what little beard he could grow. "Good morrow, my lords," he continued in congenial greeting. "What do you think of her? She's a little young, but she has heart. Why, she wanted to gallop all the way here from Hawick."

As Egremont joined them, he grinned at Percy.

"She's everything you said she'd be, Percy. Graceful lines and a pretty face. What more could a man want in a horse?"

Lucien's gaze strayed to Cassie. Graceful lines and a pretty face. What more could a man want of the woman in his bed?

Percy hid a yawn behind his hand, then frowned at Lucien. "How now, my lord. You look gray at the gills and pinched this morning."

"He overindulged last night," Devanney offered, smiling.

Lucien glared at his cousin. Just as he thought. No doubt Devanney had the news from his butler, who'd brought the whiskey.

"You?" Percy said to Lucien, then offered a commiserating nod. "Know how that goes, old man."

Then Percy noticed the ruins looming ahead of them. "Look at that! I made it just in time. We've arrived."

John Knox's faith and Cromwell's cannons had turned a once-thriving religious community into nothing but an empty stone shell. But in its destruction the building gained a lyrical beauty. Ivy softened its lichen-stained walls. Empty of the colored glass they'd once contained, the delicate pointed stone windows marched down the abbey's side.

Percy frowned at Lucien, then looked away, only to grimace and once more meet Lucien's gaze. "My lord, I hesitate to ruin your day, but I cannot in good conscience withhold what I saw in Hawick this morning. Lord Bucksden stays at the inn there."

Rage tore through Lucien at the mention of that dastard's name. His hands jerked on his reins. His bay reacted by kicking at Percy's mare.

Whinnying in surprise, the mare bucked. Percy's hat flew. Egremont's mount bolted. That only further startled the mare. Bucking and leaping, she bolted into the sedate ranks of the riders.

Shouting, Devanney's guests scattered. The mare carried a hard-pressed Percy around the altar end of the ruined church. Devanney, Egremont and Lucien followed. Everyone else guided their mounts to the far safer nave end.

By the time Percy regained control, he and his mare were halfway across the erstwhile monastery's grounds. He brought the trembling horse to a halt at the edge of the tumbling stream that cut through the ancient property. Dismounting, he stroked and murmured to the mare. Devanney and Egremont joined him after tying up their horses. Lucien guided his bay to a halt far enough from the thoroughbred that his horse could do no more harm.

He considered staying with his horse. For him, anger was a private emotion, its expression too extreme to be borne in any polite company, or near those whose opinions he valued. But the need to verify what Percy said was too great. It took every bit of his will to tame what roiled in him as he left his gelding to graze as he would and joined the others at the water's edge.

"You must be mistaken, Percy," he said. "Bucksden knows I summer in the area. He's been careful to avoid me for almost three years now."

Only Devanney knew of Lucien's desire to end Bucksden's life. However, Bucksden didn't need to know the fate Lucien intended for him to read the threat in Lucien's face the few times their paths had crossed before Dorothea's death. That had been enough to convince Bucksden he was safer at a distance from Graceton's lord.

"I'm not mistaken," Percy insisted, stroking his horse's side. "It was Bucksden, although he looks as though he boxed the watch and got the worst of it. Head's swathed in bandages and his eyes are blackened."

Lucien tried to take some satisfaction in the card cheat's injuries. He couldn't. He wanted to be the one who dealt Bucksden his wounds. And so he would as soon as he had a son to carry on his line and name.

Which he would never have, if he didn't get himself a wife.

Lucien released a disbelieving breath; by God, but Devanney's distraction was working. From the moment Cassie had exposed her naked back to him yesterday, Lucien had completely forgotten about arranging his next marriage.

Miss Conningsby strode around the end of the abbey church. She carried Percy's hat in her hand. Cassie followed her sister.

Lucien stared at Cassie and felt nothing. His attraction to her hadn't survived the depths of his hatred for Bucksden. Cassie caught his look. Color seeped into her cheeks, only to ebb almost as swiftly.

A tiny crease appeared on her brow and she hurried her pace.

"Mr. Percy, are you safe and well?" Miss Conningsby closed the distance between them.

"I am, Miss Conningsby," Percy replied, turning to show the beauty his finer side.

Laughing, Egremont stepped a little ahead of Percy to usurp his friend's pose. "His wholeness is a matter of some question. Look inside that hat and see if the idiot didn't lose his brain along with his chapeau."

Miss Conningsby smiled impishly, her brown eyes sparkling over two gentlemen competing for her affections. She stopped before them. Cassie halted a few steps behind her, watching Lucien more closely than he liked.

"Here you are, sir," Miss Conningsby said, handing Percy his hat, "none the worse for the experience. The hat, I mean."

"I'm eternally grateful, miss." Percy restored his hat to his head, tilting it a little. "Do come see what I've acquired. Have no fear. She's really the most gentle of creatures."

"She's beautiful," Miss Conningsby said, her hands caught close to her chest and her enthusiasm contrived. "But her coat is wet. Perhaps I can admire her later, when she's clean? Well, now that you have your hat, I'd like to return to the ruins. I brought my sketch book, thinking to do a little drawing. This place is gorgeous. I don't want to waste a moment with my back to it."

So saying, Elizabeth Conningsby started away from Percy and Egremont, tossing an enticing glance over her shoulder as she went. Neither young man could resist. They flew after her.

"I'll come with you," Percy announced, taking one arm.

"Would you show me your drawings?" Egremont asked, taking her other.

"I'd be delighted." Laughing, the young beauty sashayed past her sister.

Lucien waited for Cassie to follow her; instead she stood as if she'd been planted. Devanney glanced at her, then his brows lowered. He stepped to Lucien's side.

"Shall I stay or go?" he asked quietly, offering to be the ear Lucien needed to work his way out of his rage, at the same time that he tried again to use Cassie as a distraction.

If Lucien hadn't been trapped in cold anger he might have laughed. His cousin still believed Cassie held some attraction for him. She didn't, not now that he knew Bucksden was within reach. Nor was he ready to talk his way out of his rage at the earl.

"Go," he replied.

Devanney gave a nod, then strode after the giggling threesome. Once his cousin had rounded the church's corner, Lucien turned his gaze on Cassie, waiting for her to leave as well, now that they were alone and unchaperoned. He craved time and privacy to restore his control.

Instead, she held her ground, watching him in return. That tiny frown still marred her pretty brow. "Are you well?" she asked at last.

"I'm not injured," Lucien replied shortly.

"That wasn't what I meant." Cassie's tiny frown blossomed into full blown concern. "A moment ago you looked so bleak. I thought perhaps something had happened?"

A breath of a laugh escaped Lucien. Bleak wasn't the emotion he'd been feeling. Anger, for certain. Frustration, perhaps, even impatience. If only he had a brother, or a cousin who bore the Hollier name. Instead, he was the last man in the long, unbroken line of men who had held Graceton's title since the Conquest. Because of that Lucien couldn't call out Bucksden until he had a son to follow him, even though he knew he was a better man with weapons than Bucksden. A man who cheated at cards would have no compunction about cheating in a duel, not when it meant preserving his own life.

Cassie's eyes widened. She closed the distance between them. "It's your own death I see in your face," she cried softly, her eyes alive with fear for him. "Tell me. What's happened?"

Much to Lucien's surprise the whole story—that he'd almost caught Bucksden cheating at the tables, and that Bucksden, to protect himself from Lucien's accusation, had seduced the weak-willed Dorothea so any accusation Lucien made would seem petty vengeance, that Dorothea had later given birth to that poor babe who might or might not have been

Lucien's son—crowded onto his tongue. He kept his mouth closed.

His anger over the wrong done to him by Bucksden and his wife was private, his own personal hell. If he wanted to soothe his rage, then he'd speak to Devanney, who knew the tale, although he hadn't been in England at the time the events occurred. Exposing it to Cassie would be an act as intimate as the kiss they'd shared last night. How could he contemplate offering her such honesty, and exposing himself to her ridicule? She was nothing more to him than a pleasant way to pass the two weeks of this house party.

"There's nothing to tell," he said, only to hear the bleakness in his own voice. Turning his back to her, he stared down into the stream. Yellow pipe lined the banks, their tall, narrow leaves and yellow flowers shivering as water rushed over their roots. Golden coins of sunlight dropped through the overhanging branches to pierce the tumbling water. Where the light reached the streambed he could see smooth cobbles and the occasional shadow of a fish.

Fabric rustled. Cassie was leaving him. The isolation of shame again closed its lonely hand around Lucien. He fell easily into its familiar grip, having come to know it well these past three years.

To his surprise Cassie appeared at his side. She stood with her hands folded before her. Bowing her head, she watched the shimmering, shifting water.

Lucien opened his mouth to tell her to leave, only to close it without speaking. He didn't want her to go, but neither did he want her here. He waited for her to say something, knowing that the sound of her voice would break the strange spell that held him here with her. One question, even an innocent comment, and he could dismiss her.

Still, she said nothing, only stared down into the water, bearing him company. Isolation's grip shattered. As it retreated, something warm and quiet stirred deep within him, both comforting and comfortable. Tension began to drain from him.

Time ticked past, measured by the gurgle of the stream, the nearby song of the wren and cooing doves, and the distant *tap-tap* of a woodpecker. Lucien's rage continued to recede, doing so without effort on his part. One minute he smelled nothing but cold water and leaf mold, the next he savored the scent of Cassie's rose perfume. With that scent came the recollection of his mouth on her skin.

Without thought, Lucien caught Cassie by the arm, turning her toward him. She looked up into his face. Concern for him filled her brown eyes. Her loosened bonnet ribbons streamed down the front of her riding habit, marking the lift of her breasts.

"Why are you here?" he asked at last.

"Because you needed a friend."

Her answer was simple, but it revealed a truth he hadn't given enough credence until this moment. He and Cassie were friends. They had always been friends, even after he'd so rudely abandoned her all those years ago.

With rage still seething in him, he lowered his gaze to her mouth and discovered another truth. There were two ways to soothe his anger. One was to talk his way out of it with Devanney. The other would be to make love to Cassie, venting into her body what had boiled in him for so long.

The thought was so seductive that he slipped his arms around her, drawing her close. She laid her hands on his chest, pressing back from him. The heat of her palms penetrated his clothing to sear his skin.

"My lord, this isn't why I stayed," she protested softly.

"I know that," Lucien replied, speaking yet another truth. It might not be why she'd stayed, but the primal joining of their bodies was what he wanted from her now. Nothing else mattered.

He pressed tiny kisses to her mouth, her chin, her cheek, then one to the corner of her jaw beneath her ear. She sighed at that, resistance beginning to drain from her. That was all the invitation he needed.

Lucien took her mouth with his, demanding she become the woman of the alcove. Her lips softened beneath his onslaught. He pulled her closer still. Her bonnet tumbled from her head, hitting the ground near her feet. With it went a pair of big combs. Her hair uncurled from its knot, spilling down her back in a glorious golden mass. Lucien thrust his fingers into its thickness, savoring its softness.

Shivering, Cassie turned her head to the side. "Let me go," she whispered. "You must let me go, my lord."

He didn't want to release her. He wanted to lay her onto the sod, cover her with his body, then love her until he no longer remembered anything except her.

Anything but Cassie? He froze. Damn Devanney! His distraction *was* working.

Lucien's arms opened. Cassie stumbled back a step, as eager to escape him as he was to let her go. Stooping, she snatched up her fallen combs and bonnet, then disappeared into the foliage along the stream's bank. When she reappeared her hair was once again neatly confined beneath her bonnet. She stopped a few yards from him, well out of arm's reach. It was her turn to look bleak.

"It shames me to know that I've lost your good opinion," she said, her voice so low he barely heard her over the stream.

She turned and strode away from him. Lucien watched her disappear around the church's corner. A new emptiness opened up within him.

If she thought she was the only one who paid a price for that kiss they'd shared last night, then she was wrong. Their kiss had shattered their previous ease with each other. His life would be poorer for that.

Closing his eyes, Lucien drove all thoughts of Cassie from within him. Simmering rage, born on the day Bucksden had seduced his wife, once more closed its hand around Lucien. He sank back into its familiar embrace. There would be no more distractions.

Distraught, Cassie made her way around the corner of the ruined church as quickly as she could. She now knew exactly what happened to women who strayed too far from propriety's boundaries. Never again would she banter with Lucien the way she had at the waltz, because he would never again respect any limit she placed on him. Instead, he'd see her every gesture as an invitation to join her in bed. What grieved her most was that despite the way their previous involvement had ended, she did con-sider—had considered—Lucien a friend. The desire they'd unleashed between them last night had ended that.

"Cassie!" Philana caught her by the arm. "Didn't you hear me calling you?"

Cassie blinked herself back into awareness, only to realize she'd walked the whole length of the church without noticing. She glanced around her. Beneath the arching canopy of broken stone vaulting over their heads, Lord Ryecroft's guests strolled the church's length in twos and threes, their footsteps muffled by the grassy carpet beneath their feet. Lady Ross's young son climbed into an empty window and struck a pose. Animated conversation echoed from the altar end of the ruin. Dressed in high-waisted riding habits in shades of green and blue, Eliza and her newfound female friends sketched from their seats on a crumbling length of gray wall dotted with tiny, star-bright daisies. Standing be-hind them were the party's young bucks, busily complimenting the women they wooed on their art-work.

"What's happened?" Philana asked.

The spray of gray feathers decorating the old woman's bonnet rippled in the day's gentle breeze.

Her riding habit was a deep green, a color that suited her and made her blue eyes seem brighter—and sharper, as if she could pluck out with her gaze what Cassie preferred to keep hidden.

Feeling as lonely as Lucien had looked a few moments ago, Cassie shook her head. "Nothing worthy of your worry, Philana."

That was God's own truth. No upright woman could have any pity for her. Lucien's behavior this morning was exactly what she deserved, considering what she'd done with him yesterday.

The worry on Philana's face shifted into pique. "What you do to put off your father won't work on me," she scolded, then her gaze shifted onto something beyond Cassie's shoulder.

The irritation cleared from Philana's face. "Now that's a pleasant sight for these old eyes."

Cassie glanced behind her to see Lucien striding into the church. Despite all that was wrong between them she still reacted to his presence. How could she not? His buckskin riding trousers displayed his powerful thighs, his brown coat the breadth of his shoulders. He looked more privateer than titled nobleman, what with his roughhewn features, lightly curling hair and his sun-browned skin.

Cassie looked back at Philana, determined to end her aunt's meddling. "Lord Graceton tells me that Duchess Eleanor expects him to wed Lady Barbara."

"No!" Philana cried, her eyebrows flying high. "He cannot seriously entertain such a notion. Why, the two of them couldn't be less suited. Their union would be the same disaster his first marriage was, although not for the same reasons. At least Lady Barbara's not the brainless idiot Lady Dorothea was."

Cassie didn't know how great an idiot Lucien's wife had been, except that her name had been one of those scandalously linked with Lord Bucksden. By the time a widowed Cassie had returned to London, Lady Graceton had retired *enceinte* to Lucien's estate, where she and her child later died. By then the gossips had moved on to the next scandal du jour.

"I tell you, Cassie, Lord Graceton is meant for you," Philana was saying. "Everyone here can see it. Why, a dozen people have told me what a handsome couple the two of you make."

Cassie sagged, unable to bear her aunt's persistence on this most painful subject. "Enough, Philana," she pleaded. "Every time you speak of this my concentration flags. If I can't concentrate, then I cannot win what I need to sustain my family," she lied.

Philana's face softened. She pulled her niece into her embrace. Cassie relaxed against her aunt, finding the warmth of Philana's body as comforting as her familiar violet water scent. Only the little dignity Cassie had left to her kept her from burying her face against Philana's shoulder and sobbing like a babe.

"Tell me," Philana crooned. "Tell your auntie what makes you fret so."

The dangerous desire to spill all the horrors of the past weeks washed over Cassie. She dare not. Doing so compromised Philana's safety. Cassie pulled free of her aunt's embrace and took a step to the side.

Confusion and hurt tangled in Philana's expression. That she'd hurt Philana tore Cassie to bits.

"I can't tell you," she said, desolate that this was the only explanation she could offer. "Please don't ask me why I can't. Instead, say you love me still."

The hurt faded from Philana's eyes. She cupped Cassie's face in her papery palms. "On that point you need have no worries. You will always be beloved by me."

She lowered her hands, her expression firming. "Forgive me, but against your distress I must repeat my offer. Let me name you and your sister my heirs."

When Philana first made the offer Cassie had been both awed and terrified. She'd refused then, just as she would refuse now. "You are good beyond what I deserve, Philana," she said, grateful that Roland had chosen to remain behind and couldn't hear this discussion. "You know I cannot accept. I couldn't bear it if my father squandered your fortune the way he did ours. You cannot know how it feels to open your door to find some man saying he holds the mortgage on your home and is foreclosing."

Philana made a gentle, distressed sound. "How I ached for you when I read that in your letter."

She once more wrapped her arm about her niece, smiling, the light in her blue eyes radiating affection. "I think that things may be changing for you, though. The Roland of this house party isn't the man I met at your wedding, or at Charles's funeral. Is it possible he's at last learned his lesson?"

The image of her satchel, stripped of every pence

she had to her name, rose before Cassie's inner eye. She shook her head. "Don't trust him, Philana," she said harshly. "No matter what he says or does, don't trust him."

"I must take your direction on that point," Philana said, "since you know him better than I. Now, what do you say we go encourage the servants to lay out our picnic?"

Her suggestion had nothing to do with food. Rather Philana was offering the promise Cassie so wanted. She would no longer press Cassie about what bothered her, or attempt further matchmaking between Lucien and Cassie, even though she might remain convinced of their suitability as a couple.

Cassie leaned her head against Philana's shoulder. "What would I do without you?" she asked, her voice trembling, her heart breaking.

If she did manage to win enough money to buy passage to America, how would she ever survive leaving Philana, especially knowing the hurt she'd do her in going? If she failed to win enough money, how would she ever bear the look on Philana's face when she learned her niece was a murderess?

Chapter 10

"Pardon, Sir Roland," asked Squire Kerr, "but would you be looking for a game tonight?" His thick Scottish accent tortured his request, suggesting he'd been born and raised here on the Border. The squire, a great bear of a man with a lantern jaw and graying hair, kept his voice low, not wanting to disturb Eliza as she sang, accompanied by Lady Barbara on the piano. No London pretense for him; he closed his neckcloth with a simple knot, and his leathery skin and callused hands suggested years working out-of-doors.

Cassie narrowly eyed him, wondering if he approached Roland because her father was such a poor player. The squire and his two companions had been her gaming partners last night after the stargazing expedition, which may have been why he wasn't inviting her to his table. The three men knew each other well, and Cassie had used their familiarity to her advantage, letting her winnings rise to fifteen pounds before giving them back most of what she'd taken. When she'd retired from the drawing room it was with a total of more than ten pounds in her reticule.

Longing washed over Roland's face, but he didn't shift out of his morose slump. Although not a hair on his head or crease in his neckcloth was out of place, he still managed to look untidy. He shook his head. "Can't. I'm listening to my daughter sing. Demmed fine voice she's got."

Roland laid a hand on Cassie's arm. "Perhaps my elder daughter will prove a good substitute? She's a fair player."

The squire's bushy brows wriggled in surprise at a refusal from a man once eager to sit at anyone's table, but he nodded. "What do you say, Mrs. Marston? My partners tonight are set on Cassino, and we'd like a fourth."

Cassie came to her feet, smiling. "I'd love to join you, squire. Lead the way."

Following the big man across the room, Cassie marshaled her energy. The emotional upset at the abbey this afternoon had left her feeling unbalanced when she needed to be at her sharpest. Given the ease with which she'd won from these men last night, tonight could prove equally as profitable. The prospect of putting more than twenty pounds in her reticule was alluring indeed.

Squire Kerr stopped at the table at the back of the room. Cassie's heart sank to her toes. Colonel Egremont, dressed tonight in his more formal regimental coat, came to his feet. Lucien shifted in his chair to look over his shoulder at her, then came to his feet in polite recognition of her presence.

No longer was Lucien the privateer of this morning, but an icy, powerful nobleman. The black of his formal attire and the stark whiteness of his carefully creased stock were as daunting as any armor. Tonight's waistcoat, the same pale gray color of his eyes, had more life to it than did his flat gaze. It wasn't hard to read the message in his eyes, not after this morning. To him she was a tart unworthy of his regard in polite society.

Anger flickered in Cassie. That didn't mean he wouldn't enjoy another game with a kiss, or worse, as a stake. For just an instant she considered demurring, then discarded the idea as rank idiocy. All that could matter to her from now until the end of the house party was winning. She couldn't afford to be picky about her partners since the duchess wouldn't have her at Lord Ryecroft's table. The only other card players in the room were another foursome, with no room for her.

"Have you come to join us, Mrs. Marston?" the colonel asked.

"I have indeed," Cassie replied, hiding her discomfort behind a smile as the squire pulled out the chair next to Lucien for her.

She sat, only to immediately wish she had the colonel's chair. Despite his disdain, Lucien's presence enveloped her, sending her already rattled nerves skittering out of control.

Cassie planted her elbows on the table. She told herself that she wouldn't lose. She just wouldn't.

"I take the rest of the hands," Cassie Marston announced, laying out the king of spades. "I think that brings me to twenty-one," she added, without looking up from the table.

Outrage seared Lucien. "So they are," he agreed coolly as Cassie again took the most points in their hand.

They counted their cards. Cassie had indeed reached the points necessary to win the game. His jaw tight, Lucien watched her claim more coins from him. He couldn't remember ever losing so much in such a short period of time, and certainly not to a woman. By God, but she was up almost to the house limit of twenty pounds after only an hour's play! Losses like this happened to Sir Roland, not to him.

Cassie drew her winnings closer, then nervously pushed a ringlet behind her ear, disturbing her coiffure. She wore no cap tonight. Instead, curling golden tendrils framed her face while the rest was drawn back into a wild knot at her nape. Her high-waisted gown was a pretty blue with long sleeves and a bodice far more conservatively cut than the previous night's gown.

Lucien gave thanks for Percy and the news of Bucksden's presence at Hawick. If not for Lucien's still-simmering rage over the news he might have remained blinded by his lust for Cassie. In that case

he might have considered her dress's higher neck-
line tonight as an attempt to restore the respectability she'd lamented at the ruins. Now that his desire
for her had passed, Lucien saw Cassie for what she
was: a sharp.

Cassino was a game that required a deal of luck,
according to some. Lucien knew they were wrong.
To win at Cassino a player needed to know when to
build, when to capture and strong nerves. Lucien
had better nerves than most men, but apparently not
better than Cassie's. Her play was too perfect. She
built lines that no one else could match.

She had to be cheating. He just couldn't identify
how she was doing it.

"I had no idea you were so skilled a player, Mrs.
Marston," Egremont said, his expression flat. Lucien
cocked a brow at the young man. So, Egremont also
suspected that Cassie manipulated the cards.

"I know. I can't believe my luck," she said, sounding more chagrined than pleased by her good fortune. "I've never won like this. It can't last much
longer."

As she spoke she sent a distraught glance in Lucien's direction. That only fed his welling suspi-
cions. She knew he doubted her luck, something no
innocent would have noticed. Nor would an innocent have worried over a run of luck. Men who believed fortune simply happened gloated, crowed
and boasted when they unexpectedly won.

Not so card sharps. A good sharp was subtle and
careful, picking his marks with care. Such a trickster
never made an overt show of winning. That's what

confused Lucien about Cassie. She was winning so obviously and with such consistency that it looked as though she meant to pick their purses.

Laughter exploded from a group across the room, where a noisy game of charades proceeded. Egremont came to his feet and bowed. "If you'll excuse me? Mrs. Marston, your sister and her team are in dire need of my assistance. I've never seen such lackluster guesses in my life."

Cassie blanched. She folded her hands in her lap. "But I've never won like this before," she repeated, her words sounding like a plea for understanding.

Across from her Squire Kerr grinned, revealing a missing right eyetooth. "That's two nights in a row for you, eh, Mrs. Marston? It looks like you'll get to keep all your winnings tonight instead of having to give it back the way you did last night."

The gathering clouds of Lucien's suspicion congealed into a thunderstorm. Blast it, she *was* a sharp, albeit a strangely careless one. Her greed tonight had gotten out of hand, that's all.

Anger at the way she used Devanney's party for her nefarious scheme stirred, dark and deep, straining to share the space he'd given his rage at Bucksden. Then Lucien realized the full meaning of what she was doing. By God, it wasn't just Devanney's party she used, but him!

Hadn't she made a fool of him, standing in the corridor with her naked back, tantalizing his desire for her, using his lust to take him for five pounds? Not quite five pounds. She'd given him that kiss.

His mouth tightened as he remembered the depth

of his lust for her last night. She'd had to lose to him. If she hadn't, he would never have let her leave the table.

Against that, he found a different meaning in the pattern of her wins and losses last night, especially the way she'd lost that last hand. He hadn't won that kiss. She'd given it to him, no doubt considering it a small price to pay to take his money, counting on his lust to blind him.

Lucien's outrage grew. In the garden she'd counted on his friendship and his honor to prevent him from pressing their kiss to its ultimate conclusion. How she must have exulted when he retreated all the way to his bedchamber. With him gone she could practice her filthy trade without worrying about his scrutiny.

Seething, Lucien hooked a casual elbow over his chair's delicate back. She'd picked the wrong man to use this time. He'd expose her for what she was, here and now.

"Congratulations on a stupendous run of luck, Mrs. Marston," he said, his tone jovial. He glanced at the squire. "Is she doing as well tonight as she did last night, Kerr?"

"Better," the big man said. "When all was said and done last night I'd only lost a little less than two pounds, but it was a near thing. At one point she had all but a shilling of my nightly purse limit."

Cassie's brow creased. Her smile sat crookedly on her lips. "That only shows how swiftly and completely luck can change."

"Too bad I don't have that shilling tonight,"

Squire Kerr said without concern. Bracing his hands on the table, he came to his feet. "I'm done for. If you'll excuse me?"

"No, wait," Cassie protested, reaching out as if to stop him.

She looked frantic. As well she should. Lucien curled the corner of his mouth in scorn. She was too late to stop the squire or to prevent her exposure.

Lucien leaned forward, his forearms braced on the table. He bared his teeth in a smile. "Mrs. Marston, I find myself intrigued by your card playing. Did you acquire this skill of yours during your marriage? I have distinct memories of you refusing all card play six years ago."

"Of course I played cards six years ago," Cassie replied, swallowing, blaming Lucien to the depths of her soul for this catastrophe.

It really was all his fault. His nearness left her addled beyond cohesive thought. With her conscious mind despairing over the loss of his respect and her body reveling in his scent and the memory of his mouth upon her skin, there'd been nothing to check her unusual skill from expressing itself to the utmost. And, express itself it had, joyously winning every hand without care or concern.

Even after she'd noticed what she was doing she couldn't stop it. No matter how she tried to lose, she continued to win. It was time to quit, before things got any worse. As if they could!

"If you'll excuse me, my lord," she said scooping her godforsaken winnings closer to her.

Lucien caught her by the wrist. "No."

"No, what?" she asked, looking into his face, her heart breaking. She'd thought losing his respect destroyed her. She was wrong. Having him think she was a card sharp was even worse.

His expression darkened until he looked as dangerous as Lord Bucksden. "No, I won't excuse you. I want the chance to win back some of what you've taken from me."

It was no request. If she didn't agree, Lucien would publicly accuse her of being a sharp. That couldn't happen. Cassie needed to be able to play cards. Thirty pounds wasn't enough to save her family. But how could she stop him?

As Cassie strove for some way to avoid his threat, someone tapped on her shoulder. She glanced behind her. It was Eliza. If not for the pink ribbon at her waist, she would have looked like a specter. She was as pale as her white dress.

Cassie forgot the peril Lucien presented. She wrenched her arm from his hold and shot to her feet. "What is it?" she asked, pulling Eliza close.

Trembling like a leaf, her eyes alive with fear, Eliza put her mouth near Cassie's ear and breathed, "Mr. Percy and Colonel Egremont were talking just now. Mr. Percy saw Lord Bucksden in the city of Hawick, no more than thirty miles from here."

The earth shifted beneath Cassie's feet, so great was her relief. The earl wasn't dead. She wasn't going to hang.

Terror followed. A living Lord Bucksden was far more dangerous than a dead earl. He'd come for them with revenge burning in his heart. She didn't know why he hadn't already appeared at Ryecroft Castle's door, but he soon would. They had to leave England this very night! But how? All she had was thirty pounds.

Lucien came slowly to his feet, his hands braced on the table. His face was hard, his gray eyes as cold as winter. He leaned toward her.

"Sit down, Mrs. Marston. You *will* give me the chance to win back what you took from me."

Anger tore through Cassie's panic. Arrogant nobleman! He was trying to intimidate her into letting him destroy her.

Well, Lord Graceton was too late. Her repute was already dead. Before long the whole world would know it.

The constraints of good behavior and concern for her repute that had held Cassie prisoner for all her life shattered. In its place came a rush of confidence and the perfect solution to her dilemma. With her repute already destroyed, then it didn't matter what happened tonight. She needed two hundred pounds. Lord Graceton wanted to prove to himself that she was a sharp. Amazingly enough, it would cost him exactly two hundred pounds to do it.

She almost smiled. He'd make his accusation, but he'd never prove it. He couldn't. She'd never once had a card up her sleeve.

"Go," Cassie whispered in Eliza's ear, giving her sister a reassuring squeeze. "Tell Papa what you told me. Also tell him that I'll have all we need by night's end. Go back to your game and let no one suspect that anything is amiss."

Admiration, gratitude and relief filled Eliza's gaze. She nodded, then started back to her new friends. Cassie moved around the table to stand behind the chair across from Lucien.

"You can't have your rematch, my lord. I've won my nightly limit," she said.

Uncertainty flickered behind the outrage in Lucien's eyes. Cassie wanted to gloat. He'd noticed her change from worried widow to confident cardswoman, but didn't know what to make of it. He was at her mercy. She lifted her chin, challenging him, nay, daring him to do his worst. Whatever that was, it couldn't be worse than what Lord Bucksden planned for her.

"Devanney," Lucien called to Lord Ryecroft.

Their host sprawled in his chair across from the duchess, his long legs stretched comfortably out before him. He peered over the fanned cards in his hand. "No need to shout, Hollier," he drawled. "I'm right here."

"Release Mrs. Marston and me from your nightly limit," Lucien demanded.

A smile played at the corners of Lord Ryecroft's lips. His brows lifted in satisfaction. Cassie took in the message he sent without effort. Lord Ryecroft liked the fact that Lucien was angry at her. Her outrage soared. Was she the pawn of every nobleman in England?

"I excuse both you and Mrs. Marston from any limits on your wagers," the earl said, then looked at Duchess Eleanor. "It's your play, Your Grace."

A menacing smile bent Lucien's lips. "What do

you say, Mrs. Marston? Piquet, this time, at a pound a point?"

Cassie was almost insulted at the way he dangled the amount before her like bait, offering her his pocket to pick. Pulling out the chair, she sat, picked up the deck, and began to remove the smaller cards. "That's acceptable, but I think we need to sweeten the pot a little. Twenty pounds goes to the one who wins the first *partie*."

Cassie looked up at him, feeling more powerful and in control than she had in her entire twenty-five years of life. "Tell me, my lord, do you intend to play on your feet?"

Lucien gnashed his teeth as Cassie ended their *partie*, smiling. "That brings me to a hundred and eighty pounds, my lord. Too rich for your blood yet? Or, should I say for Lord Ryecroft's treasury?"

Her little jibe only fed his slow-burning rage. Lucien had needed to borrow coins from Devanney to cover his wagers, since she wasn't willing to play for chits.

"We play until I know how you're doing this," he retorted. She'd rue the day she made a fool of him.

Cassie plastered an innocent expression on her face. "I'm certain I don't know what you mean, my lord."

The taunt had a rapier's point. Lucien slammed his fist on the table. "Blast it, how in the hell are you doing it!" he shouted.

Every head in the drawing room turned in their

direction. Devanney laid down his cards and came to his feet, shrugging his shoulders to straighten his black coat. "Is something amiss, Hollier?" he asked.

Duchess Eleanor sniffed, the single white plume decorating her gold turban quivering with disdain. She snatched her shawl over her shoulders with one hand, holding her cards close to her chest with the other. "Lord Ryecroft, don't you dare leave this table," she warned. "We're in the midst of a game."

"Is this your prank?" Lucien demanded of his cousin. "Did you arrange for her to do this to me?"

Devanney frowned in what looked like honest confusion. "Do what?"

"She's a sharp," Lucien snapped, only to regret his accusation in the next instant. Once again, he spoke before he had proof. Without proof his accusation meant nothing. How could there be no proof, when she was richer by a hundred and eighty pounds of his money?

Cassie recognized his mistake. He saw that in the tiny, smug lift of her lips. "I am not," she cried, sounding like the hapless, impoverished, helpless widow she should have been. "Lord Ryecroft, I beg you. Come and see for yourself that I'm doing nothing untoward."

Devanney left his game to join them. The rest of the guests also moved in their direction, their interest piqued. That was, all save Duchess Eleanor.

Folding her cards, the noblewoman turned in her chair. The golden color of her dress and turban made her look sallow and accentuated the dark rings beneath her eyes. But then, who saw the dress or the woman, when she wore a king's ransom in diamonds around her neck?

The duchess eyed Lucien in impatience. "Here's what comes of associating with riffraff, my lord," she told him. "They lack all sensibility and honor. Let your losses to that hoyden be a lesson that you should never again mingle."

If Eleanor thought her snobbery did anything but further repulse him from a union with poor Barbara she was wrong.

Their expressions hard, Squire Kerr, Percy and Egremont were at the head of the crowd gathered around the table. The beautiful Miss Conningsby pushed past them, followed by Philana Forster. The old woman looked dour and steely in her usual gray attire.

Cassie looked up at her sister. Their affection was palpable. "Will you go check on Papa, Eliza? He looked quite ill when he left the room a little while ago," Cassie asked gently. For a moment the girl looked ready to argue, then she nodded reluctantly and made her way out of the crowd around them.

"What happens here, Cassie?" Lady Forster demanded. Her wrinkled brow furrowed deeper as she looked from Lucien to her niece by marriage.

"Lord Graceton cannot comprehend how I continue to best him at cards," Cassie—Cassie the Sharp—said.

The old woman's face cleared. She glanced at those around them, then looked at Lucien. Amusement filled her sharp, blue eyes.

"Ah, I can understand how you might feel like that, my lord. Unnerved me, too, the first time she did it to me."

Lucien almost gawked. Philana Forster was in on this trick! All the proof he needed was the sly look in the old woman's eyes.

"Of course," Lady Forster continued, "I had sense enough to quit rather than throw good coins after bad, once I realized I was outmatched."

Lucien's outrage roared skyward. Blast it, he wasn't outmatched!

Devanney lay a hand on his shoulder as if to calm or console. Or gloat. "I'm here, Mrs. Marston," he said, "but I'm not certain what use I'll be to you."

"I put my repute in your hands, Lord Ryecroft," Cassie told him, her soft brown eyes wide. She touched a hand to her breast, the gesture delicate and feminine. "I know Lord Graceton is very angry about my winning, but I vow to you on my sister's life that I'm not in any way manipulating the cards. I pray, watch our play and judge accordingly."

Then, holding up her hands, Cassie displayed her long sleeves. "Please, if anyone sees the outline of a card, say so. Better yet, extract it from my sleeve," she challenged. No one commented or accepted her dare.

"Now, Lord Graceton, what would you like to wager?" Cassie asked him, all the smugness gone from her expression.

If Lucien weren't convinced that she was cheating he might have thought he saw regret in her eyes. He reminded himself that nothing about her was honest or real.

"One final *partie* of Piquet, one hundred eighty pounds, winner takes all," he said and watched in satisfaction as concern flickered in her brown eyes.

She didn't want to risk what she'd already taken from him, which was more edge than Lucien thought to have. He hoped that in her determination to keep what she'd already won she might grow careless.

"You'll play for my chit, Mrs. Marston?" Devanney asked her.

The concern in Cassie's eyes deepened. She glanced around, taking in the faces of her witnesses and nipping at her lower lip in hesitation. It was cold comfort to Lucien that it wasn't just his chit she didn't trust. The only sound in the room was the hiss and pop of the fire as everyone waited on her response.

"As you will," she agreed at last.

"Deal, Mrs. Marston," Percy commanded, shifting to stand behind Cassie. Although Percy again wore his vibrant pink-and-green waistcoat, the proud dandy had given way to serious gamester.

Cassie shuffled. The cards rattled. Someone coughed. Percy's shoes scraped against the wooden floor as he shifted to better see her hands.

She dealt and Lucien picked up his cards. Play proceeded. He took the most points in the first hand and repeated his success in the second hand. He eyed Cassie in disbelief. She was sorely mistaken if she thought sending him over the Rubicon and losing all would convince these men she wasn't cheating. He needn't have worried. She took the most points in all the remaining hands, leaving him with less than a hundred at the end of the partie.

Lucien tossed his cards onto the table. "Well? How is she doing it?" he demanded of Devanney and Percy. His words echoed into the room's tense silence.

Both men shook their heads. Percy shrugged. "My lord, what can I say? Every card dealt stayed in her hand until she played it. Nothing changed. She simply outplayed you."

"All I saw was remarkable play," Devanney seconded. "Hollier, you're outmatched."

Lady Forster smiled in triumph. "Didn't I tell you?"

"Well done, Mrs. Marston," cried Lady Barbara, looking surprisingly pretty as she smiled. She began to clap. The other young ladies followed her lead, laughing and applauding one of their own sex besting a man.

Squire Kerr looked relieved, as did his companions from last night. Their pride was intact; they hadn't been played for fools. Egremont held onto his suspicion.

"Are you certain, Percy?" he asked.

"There's no question of it," Percy replied, sending Lucien another helpless smile.

"Nay!" Lucien whispered in disbelief, having sense enough to keep his reaction to himself.

His pride ached enough that he closed his fist against it. He stared at Cassie Marston, knowing both Percy and Devanney were wrong. She was doing something. No one played like she did.

Behind Lucien, Devanney breathed out a relieved sigh, then gave Lucien's a shoulder a pat. "Now you know what it's like to play with *you*, Hollier," he said, repaying with words the many times Lucien had lightened his purse. "I fear you've met your match in our Mrs. Marston."

The only one unaffected by Cassie's victory was Cassie. No smile touched her lips. Nor was there a sign of gloating in her eyes.

She came to her feet in a graceful movement. "Many thanks for serving as my witness, Lord Rye-croft," she said. "Now if I might make one further request. The only thing I have commodious enough in which to carry this," the lift of her hand indicated the coins and notes that represented half her winnings, "is a satchel in my chamber. My sister is there. If you could send someone to fetch it for me?"

"But of course, Mrs. Marston," Devanney said. Every inch the congenial host, he indicated for a footman to do as she needed. "And, I apologize again giving you mostly coins. We've no use for wads of the flimsy here at Ryecroft. The locals won't take them for their payment, preferring old-fashioned silver instead."

Still stewing in disbelief, and utterly certain that he'd been taken—that they'd all been taken—Lucien remained at the table. When the satchel arrived he watched Cassie fill it with her winnings—his coins. She closed the bag over the top of his money and shot him a single short look.

He thought he saw regret in her eyes. If so, he didn't want it. Instead, he took satisfaction in knowing that by exposing her skill, or whatever it was, he'd ended any chance that Cassie Marston could ever again use it against another honest man. Once the tale of this night made its rounds through society she wouldn't sit at another card table at anyone's affair. If she wanted to strip men of coins she'd have to seek out with the young swells in the gaming hells, men who deserved to be parted from their fortunes. Doing that wouldn't restore the respectability she'd pretended to lament earlier today.

Cassie gave her filled satchel back to the footman to carry to her chamber, then offered Devanney a deep curtsy. "Again, my lord, you have my gratitude for your assistance."

"The pleasure was all mine, Mrs. Marston," Devanney said, daring to continue savoring his cousin's comeuppance.

Cassie then turned and offered Lucien the same sign of respect. "Lord Graceton, I cannot explain my skill. If it's any consolation to you, my father wishes it didn't exist."

A pretty speech, but meaningless. Lucien made her no response. She sighed, all expression leaving her face. Even then she remained the prettiest woman in the room. How could something so lovely prove to be dross beneath the surface?

"I'm exhausted, my lord," she said to Devanney. "If you'll excuse me?"

"I'll come with you, dear," Philana Forster said.

"Good night, Mrs. Marston," Devanney said, laughter still filling his voice. "Lady Forster."

Lucien's eyes narrowed. Damn Devanney. He had no right to enjoy this so much.

Chapter 11

It was just as well that they were fleeing to America. Cassie left the drawing room, knowing her connection to the class of people she considered her own had been irrevocably severed. Oh, they might clap and laud her tonight, but Duchess Eleanor would see to it that everyone who was anyone knew what Cassie had done. Soon, there wouldn't be a member of the *ton* who wouldn't consider her beneath their notice. They'd agree with the duchess that she was riffraff.

Cassie started up the stairs to the bedchambers, the footman carrying her newly won wealth a flight ahead of her. Philana followed so closely behind that Cassie could hear her aunt's angry breathing. Philana had been glowering from the moment they left the drawing room.

Her aunt's upset only made Cassie's spirits sag all
the worse. The time had come to tell Philana everything. It was a chore she didn't much want to face.

In the corridor candles ensconced in mirrored
holders threw their light down onto the runner that
covered the floor, driving the skulking shadows
against the baseboards and ornate crown molding.
The night-blackened arch of the window loomed at
the corridor's end. The good weather of the morning
had given way to Scotland's usual rain, droplets pat-
tering against the glass.

Ahead of them light streamed out of Cassie's open
chamber door. The footman exited, his gold-
trimmed, blue satin coat and breeches shining in the
light. The stark white of his powdered wig framed a
freckled face. He passed Cassie and Philana without
offering so much as a glance. When he was gone Philana caught Cassie by the elbow, stopping her just
outside her door.

"What were you thinking?" she demanded. "I
thought you intended to be subtle at the tables. And
for heaven's sake, what made you decide to use
Lord Graceton of all men? You had to know that a
gamester like him would never accept your skill for
what it is. Almost four hundred pounds will serve
you well for now, but you'll never again use that
skill of yours. Not in any decent establishment."

Cassie wondered what most upset her aunt: Did
Philana despise her for becoming the center of unwanted attention, or was she angry because she'd
never achieve that match between Cassie and Grace-

ton's lord? Cassie's betraying heart dared to ache at that thought. She cursed herself for wanting what she could never have had even if she hadn't picked Lucien's pocket.

"I know that," Cassie replied, her mouth twisting sadly. "But then, I won't ever again be playing cards in England."

"You surely won't," Philana retorted, lifting a finger to scold. She caught herself, frowning. "What do you mean, never again in England?"

Cassie only took Philana by the arm and led her into the bedchamber. Eliza had a branch of candles set on the washstand, the tapers offering light enough to reveal the richness of the blue-and-red bedcurtains as well as the deep mahogany color of the bedposts. Her golden hair glowed as brightly as the flame as she leaned over Cassie's trunk. She straightened as they entered, holding a stack of nightgowns clutched close to her breast.

Philana's eyes widened as she took in the trunk, the clothes folded on the bed's end, and Eliza's waiting satchel, in which she'd carry a change of clothes and her overnight needs.

"Cassie, what's happening?"

Cassie closed the door and led Philana to the small chair. "Sit and I'll tell you."

Eliza hurried to stand alongside Cassie, still holding the nightclothes, fiddling with a length of lace that trimmed a garment's sleeve. Fear hid in the dark hollows beneath her eyes. "Cassie, he's come after us so swiftly. How did he find us?"

Cassie offered her a half-hearted smiled. "He has the invitation. I dropped it when I picked up the urn," she said.

"What urn?" Philana demanded, her gaze as steely as her gray gown. "*Who's* come after you? Why are you packing?"

Eliza turned to her. "Aunt Philana, Papa did a terrible thing before we left London to come here. He staked me in a game of cards with Lord Bucksden. If he'd won he would have gained three thousand pounds. Unfortunately, he lost, which meant I was to become the earl's mistress."

"He did *what*?" Philana fairly levitated from her chair, so great was her outrage. Her face flushed bright red. "Why, that base dastard! How *dare* he use his daughter in such a foul way!"

Eliza spoke over Philana. "The only thing that stopped the earl from either taking me, or fulfilling his threat to drive us into the poorhouse, was Cassie. She hit him with our Wedgwood urn. We thought she'd killed him."

Philana collapsed back into the chair, gasping for air. She looked as gray in this instant as she'd been red in the last. She stared at Cassie.

"You didn't," she gasped. "Kill him, I mean."

"He looked dead when we left him on our drawing-room floor," Cassie replied in a tiny voice. The sound of the urn exploding against Lord Bucksden's head reverberated out of her memory. Her stomach gave a sick buck.

"Not dead enough," Eliza said, her voice hard beyond her years. "Tonight I overheard Squire Kerr and Colonel Egremont laughing as Mr. Percy described having seen the earl in Hawick with his head bandaged and his eyes blackened."

Eliza's bravado faded. Fear flashed in her eyes. "Oh Cassie, Lord Bucksden must be in a frenzy to avenge himself on us." As if she couldn't bear to think about this Eliza whirled, hurrying back to the trunk and her packing.

"My stars, but this tale is as tragic as anything I've seen on the stage," Philana said. Frowning, she jerked her shawl around her shoulders. "All I can say is that it's a shame you failed, Cassie. If ever there's a man who deserves murdering it's Lord Bucksden."

"At the time it seemed that way to me as well," Cassie murmured. "I'm only grateful that he hasn't yet knocked on Lord Ryecroft's door and demanded that Papa fulfill his wager. For the life of me I cannot understand why he hasn't. Perhaps he waits for his injuries to heal, not wanting to make a spectacle of himself?"

Her comment teased a breath of laughter from Philana. "I think we need look no further for your reason than Lord Graceton. Three years ago Lady Graceton let Lord Bucksden into her bed, something Lord Graceton didn't accept with the grace that some husbands do. The rumors say that he intends to call out Lord Bucksden when next they meet. If your attack rendered the earl at all unsure of his dueling skills, then I can understand his wanting to keep his distance. He only duels when he's certain of his chance to win."

A tiny sound escaped Cassie. She dropped to sit on the end of the bed. What irony. While Lucien had been trying to destroy her tonight, he had also unwillingly shielded her from Lord Bucksden.

Philana leaned forward, her hands on her knees. "Why didn't you tell me this when you first arrived?" Hurt filled her voice and her gaze.

"How could I?" Cassie replied, taking Philana's hands. "I thought Lord Bucksden was dead and it would be the Bow Street Runners who'd come chasing us. I didn't want them accusing you of knowingly harboring a murderess."

Philana nodded slowly, accepting that as a sensible excuse. "So you leave tonight. Where is it you go? And why do you think Lord Bucksden can no longer hurt you once you are there?"

"To America," Cassie answered.

With a sharp intake of breath Philana tore her hands from Cassie's. She blanched, looking every one of her years. "America!" she cried in an old woman's voice, falling back into the chair's embrace. "Why not Italy?"

"Because Papa has cousins in the American city of Boston," Eliza offered when Cassie didn't reply.

All Cassie wanted was to crawl beneath her bedclothes, close her eyes and sleep forever. "What choice have we? We must put as much distance as possible between us and what happened here," she finally said. "Lord Bucksden no longer comes just to claim what he won from Papa, although I don't doubt he still wants Eliza. He'll be wanting to ruin us even more completely than Papa has already done. We must depart before he learns that you are our patron, Philana. I won't have the earl harming you because you protect us."

Philana drew a shattered breath. Tears gleamed in her eyes. The corners of her lips tried to lift. "That's my sweet Cassie, always thinking of another. Whatever shall I do without your visits? With you in America our letters will be far less frequent, I fear."

Already missing Philana, Cassie did her best to smile. "I cannot bear it," she replied, feeling as desolate and lonely as Philana looked.

There was a tap on the door. Her nerves on edge, Cassie started. Eliza answered it. Their father, his neckcloth untied and waistcoat buttons undone, stepped inside, closing the door after him. His expression was resolute, something that Cassie had never before seen on his face.

Philana exploded from her chair, her fists clenched and her face alive in outrage. "How *dare* you show your face here, sir!" she almost shouted. Both Eliza and Cassie hushed her.

"I won't be silenced," she snapped. "This man isn't fit to live. He certainly isn't fit to be any woman's father."

There was no sign of anger on their father's round face. Neither was there shame. He glanced at his children when they again tried to silence Philana.

"Don't stop her, girls. Lady Forster is exactly right," he said in calm acceptance of her judgment. "I am fit for nothing. I never have been. I certainly don't deserve daughters as good as either of you. If it's any consolation, Lady Forster, know that I hate myself more than you can ever do."

That stole Philana's steam. Huffing into silence, she settled for crossing her arms and glaring at him. He looked at Cassie.

"How much did you come away with?" he asked.

"One eighty in coin, plus a promise from Lord Ryecroft for another one eighty. I fear I emptied Ryecroft's treasury of their ready cash," Cassie replied with a crooked smile. The confidence that had buoyed her throughout the contest with Lucien drained from her.

Her father beamed. " 'Pon rep, Cassie! You did better than I ever thought. Would that we had time enough to give Lord Ryecroft a chance to redeem his chit. It would be nice to go with something extra in our purses. But then, we'll have the coach and horses to sell in Edinburgh before we set sail. Old as that coach is, it's still worth something." He nodded to himself. He'd inherited their vehicle from his father. "The horses are good, solid beasts. That'll be something."

Eliza frowned at him. "Don't we have time to wait for Lord Ryecroft to pay us? Aunt Philana says Lord Bucksden won't come to Ryecroft Castle as long as Lord Graceton is here. I'm sure he could send someone to his bank on the morrow."

"Who knows if they'll have enough in coin at any bank?" he retorted. "And we can't take notes. There's a lot of folk who don't trust 'em. No, we can't afford to wait. We leave tonight when the house grows quiet. By dawn we'll be well on our way to Edinburgh, with no one here the wiser as to which direction we went."

Cassie hadn't thought about making a secret of their leaving, but it made sense. The less information they left behind them, the harder it would be for Bucksden to locate them.

"But that cannot work," Eliza protested. "We need servants to carry down our trunks, and grooms to harness our horses."

Philana opened her arms. Her face filled with her need to save the nieces she loved from the clutches of a debauched and dangerous earl. "I have a way to make your departure both obvious and secret at the same instant, Sir Roland."

With a fond but pained smile Philana looked at Cassie. "Shame on you, you hussy. Your display of prowess at the card table has made me terribly ill and no longer able to face my neighbors. I must immediately take you and your family back to Ettrick House."

Roland's eyes narrowed. His pudgy jaw firmed. "Here now, I won't have you talking to my daughter that way. She can't help what she does at the card table."

Philana laughed, the sound harsh and not at all amused. "Too late, Sir Roland. No matter what you do or say, you'll never be a father to these girls."

She laid a hand on Cassie's shoulder. "I shall send a note with my apologies and explanation to Lord

Ryecroft just before we leave. Everyone will know exactly where you've gone, or at least they'll think they know."

"No," Cassie protested. "That will only lead Lord Bucksden to you, seeking us. I don't want him hurting you."

Philana embraced her. "Darling, you're giving that awful scoundrel more credit than is his due, even as evil as he is. If you're not at Ettrick House with me he can have no power over me, just as he had no power over you or Eliza until your father gave it to him. I'll be safe, but I cannot rest easily until I know you're safe as well. Now pack, darling, pack. The sooner we leave, the sooner you can be on your way to safety."

Although Lucien had retired with the rest of Devanney's guests several hours ago, he was too angry to sleep. He paced his chamber, dressed only in his nightshirt and dressing gown. With every step he felt more of a fool. It didn't help that both Percy and Egremont had chuckled behind their hands at him for the rest of the evening. That beautiful little cheat had tarnished his repute.

He stopped at the window, looking out over a landscape that had been carefully sculpted into idyllic beauty. The scattering clouds were rags, wrung dry of last night's rain. They blushed at the first touch of the sun. White fingers of mist snaked up from the river at the end of Devanney's park land, threading through the artfully arranged copses. A hunting hawk or perhaps a sated owl soared over the treetops, scattering the smaller birds. Peacocks howled and strutted in the cross-shaped herb garden below Lucien's window, welcoming the dawning day as they eyed the moist ground for unwary insects.

Leaning his forehead against the cool glass, Lucien strove to tame what boiled in him, something he'd been trying to do since he reached his bedchamber. It wasn't possible. All he could think about was that every man and woman in the room had watched Cassie best him at cards, and not one of them had seen anything untoward.

He knew better. She was a liar and a cheat who had used him for a fool. He wouldn't be satisfied until he knew how she'd done it.

Closing his eyes, the unwanted memory of Cassie in the garden alcove returned to taunt him. Even knowing what she was, his senses stirred. He wouldn't be satisfied until he'd had her in his bed and discovered if her lovemaking fulfilled the promise of her kiss.

That he could still want her after what she'd done to him was akin to tonguing a sore tooth. One touch too many, and frustration and aching pride, already a noxious stew within him, finally exploded beyond his control. He strode back across the room, but this time he didn't stop himself. Opening the door, he stepped barefooted into the corridor.

The newborn sun warmed the window at the hallway's end, bringing out the vibrant blues, greens and reds of the corridor's long runner. Two long steps took him to Cassie's door. He put his hand on the lever, only stopping himself at the last second from opening it without knocking. To barge into her chamber might make him seem a bounder attacking an innocent woman, when a good number of Devanney's guests already wondered if he was a poor loser. He wasn't—both he and God knew it—although the two of them might be the only ones who did.

Gritting his teeth, he rapped on Cassie's door. There was no answer. He tapped again, louder this time. Again, no answer. This time when he knocked the sound echoed down the still hallway.

The door to the right of Cassie's creaked open. Lucien recognized Lady Barbara's maid. The girl blinked against the brightness in the corridor. She was dressed, but her hair was loose beneath her voluminous ruffled cap.

"Oh, I thought you were knocking on our door," the maid said when she saw him. "You'll not have an answer from them ladies, my lord. They left last night. I was just coming up to bed when I met their trunks coming down the stairs." Having said her piece, she pulled the door gently closed behind her.

Lucien thrust open Cassie's door. No longer was the room strewn with female frippery. Instead the floor was clean and the wardrobe doors were closed. The coverlet hadn't been disturbed and only ashes filled the hearth.

So, she hadn't been as secure in her deception last night as her confidence suggested. If she ran, it was because she believed he'd soon discern she'd cheated. Grinning in exultation, Lucien whirled on his heel and strode down the quiet hallways of Ryecroft Castle to Devanney's bedchamber. He entered his cousin's private room without knocking, startling Devanney's valet. The man was already dressed and laying out his master's carefully pressed neckcloths.

"My lord." The servant offered a swift bow, showing no surprise at Lucien's unexpected appearance. Their valets were accustomed to the casual relationship between their masters.

Devanney liked opulence. Even with the draperies closed his room glowed, from the plasterwork moldings decorated with gold leaf to the silk wall covering, done in a pattern of willow and rose. The settee at the bed's foot was covered in golden brocade. On the ceiling, cherubs peered down from behind clouds or played tag in an artificial sky. One solitary winged babe had retreated to the room's corner to relieve himself. Although the chubby creature had his back turned to those who might want to spy on him, Adam Devanney—the artist, not the earl—had painted him winking over his shoulder at his audience.

Lucien strode to the bed and threw back the green-and-gold bedcurtains. Devanney, his dark hair tousled, lay with his back to Lucien, lost in his dreams. Still reveling in the confirmation that Cassie had hoodwinked everyone but him, Lucien sat on the bed. Leaning over, he put his mouth near Devanney's ear.

"Oh, my lord, your prowess makes me weep with joy," he whispered in falsetto, running his finger up his cousin's arm.

Jolted out of sleep, Devanney came upright with a start. He groaned when he saw Lucien, then dropped back onto the mattress. "Blast you, Lucien. Watson, what the hell are you thinking, letting this bleater in here at this hour?"

Watson didn't bother answering. Lucien only grinned at Devanney's attempt to prick his pride. "I'm no bleater. Our little sharp has flown the coop. She took my money and her family, fleeing to avoid questions she didn't care to answer."

Devanney scrubbed his hands through his hair and yawned. "No, she didn't. Lady Forster took her away. It seems the old woman didn't much care for last night's exhibition. Just before we retired last night she sent me a note begging my pardon, saying that she and the Conningsbys would have to excuse themselves from the remainder of the house party."

"And you call me the bleater?" Lucien protested in outrage. "You're the one being gulled. I tell you, Cassandra Marston is running to escape her eventual exposure."

"If that's so, then why didn't she demand I redeem the hundred and eighty pounds I owed her on your behalf?" Devanney asked. "Not that I could have done it last night."

Lucien frowned. "She didn't collect?"

"Not a farthing." Devanney rolled onto his side, facing Lucien. "If you think she went for any other reason, then go to Ettrick House and ask her." He pulled the bedclothes over his head. "Either way, go away and let me sleep," he said, his command muffled.

Wanting to roar at the way his cousin blinded himself to Cassie's obvious guilt, Lucien came to his feet. "I have a hundred pounds that says she won't be at Ettrick House when I get there." Even slipping past his clenched teeth his words thundered in the quiet room.

Devanney threw back the bedclothes, squinting at Lucien in the room's brightening dimness. There was just enough light for Lucien to see a gambler's gleam come to life in Devanney's eyes. "Make it one hundred eighty. If she's at Ettrick House to greet you, then it's double you owe me. If she's gone as you contend, then you owe me nothing."

Lucien grinned. "Not good enough. If she's there I owe you three hundred and sixty. And that's what you'll owe *me* if she's fled to parts unknown."

"You heard that, Watson?" Devanney called.

"I did, my lord," the valet called back.

"Well, what are you waiting for?" a laughing Devanney asked Lucien. "Go to Ettrick House and settle the wager."

Chapter 12

Barely two hours later, Lucien rode past the stables at Ettrick House, then drew his horse to a halt before Philana Forster's door. The morning was misty, but the sun was warm enough to tease tendrils of steam from the house's roof as the slate tiles dried. A breeze drove the wisps upward until they became part of the thicker plumes of smoke rising from the house's chimneys. Yet moist, the house's gray stone walls looked almost blue against Classical white trim around the windows and doors. A few of the dozen or so gardeners looked up as Lucien mounted the stairs. The rest were hard at their morning chores, some clipping bushes into fanciful shapes, others spading up beds. Other than that, the house appeared to slumber, something Lucien wouldn't be doing until after he'd confronted Cassie.

A bewigged footman opened the door at his knock. The young man's coppery red eyebrows were startling under his powdered hairpiece. It took Lucien a moment to recognize the lad; he was a relative of Lucien's housekeeper at his lodge. The boy's flat expression, required of his position, clung precariously to his face. No doubt he wished to tell this unexpected caller to return at a more decent hour.

"Lord Graceton, calling on Lady Forster and Mrs. Marston," Lucien said, handing the man his card.

The footman led Lucien into a comfortable drawing room, then disappeared. Lucien eyed the chamber in approval. Unlike Devanney's more formal décor, this room looked as if someone actually lived in it. The walls were covered in creamy printed linen fabric and ancestral portraits. More recent, and more personal, miniatures crowded the tops of two small, inlaid chests at either side of the door. A pair of spectacles and a basket of needlework sat on the cushioned window seat of the room's bay window. A cat lay curled in the basket. Knickknacks lined the cornice that framed the window. The view through the glass was of the short, green plain that led down from the house to a tumbling river, the Ettrick Water; Ettrick House nestled against the thrusting, folding hills that ran almost the width of southern Scotland.

Lucien paced, his impatience growing with every breath. Ten minutes became twenty, then thirty. He told himself it was a good sign that Lady Forster's butler hadn't appeared to refuse him, or asked him to return later. At last he heard a woman's footsteps in the hall. Utterly certain it wasn't Cassie Marston, Lucien turned.

When the door opened he grinned in triumph. It was Lady Forster. That old Philana had dressed hastily, there was no doubt. Her blue- and gold-striped day dress hung crookedly on her elderly frame, the bodice concealed beneath a swathing shawl. Her uncoiffed hair was covered by a voluminous lace-trimmed cap.

"Lord Graceton," she said, managing a curtsy. "To what do I owe this unexpected honor?"

Lucien saw no reason for pretense, not when Philana Forster's behavior last night suggested she was a conspirator in the farce. "Tell me where she's gone and don't waste my time by pretending that she's sleeping upstairs. I rode past your carriage house. The Conningsbys' coach wasn't there."

That knocked the beginnings of dissembly right off the old woman's face. Exasperation flashed in her blue eyes, only to disappear as swiftly as it'd come. She crossed the room, sat on the window seat, then stroked the sleeping cat.

"Why do you chase her?" she asked after a moment, knowing without explanation who it was he wanted.

"Because she runs," Lucien retorted. "She's no innocent, madam, and you know it. If Cassandra Marston flees it's because she expects me to discern how she did what she did last night. She doesn't want to be anywhere near me when I discover it. I, on the other hand, want very much to return her to

Ryecroft Castle, where she will admit to everyone there that she is a sharp."

"So it's your pride that drives you?" Lady Forster asked, studying him as if weighing something she saw within him. "You cannot bear that a woman bested you at cards?"

Lucien's eyes narrowed. "You misjudge me, madam. I will happily lose to either man or woman as long as my loss is a fair one. I will not tolerate being cheated."

"And you're certain she cheated you?" the old woman asked.

"Completely," he told her, once more feeling the power of vindication.

Her jaw tightened. "But if it could be shown to you that she did nothing untoward, you would accept it?"

"*If* is the appropriate word, my lady," Lucien snorted.

"But would you accept it if her innocence could be proved to you?" Lady Forster insisted.

"Of course," he snapped, annoyed at yet another person treating him as if he were a poor loser.

Taking no affront at his harsh tone, Philana tapped her forefinger against her lips, her expression contemplative. A moment later her face cleared. Her wrinkles shifted until she almost looked as if she were smiling.

"The Conningsbys ride the road to Edinburgh, on their way to purchase passage away from England."

Lucien laughed aloud. Here it was, proof that what Cassie had done last night wasn't the outcome of natural talent. Better than that, he'd just won himself a tidy sum from Devanney. Now all he had to do was catch Cassie Marston.

"Have a wonderful morning, Lady Forster," he said, bowing.

Turning on his heel, Lucien walked to the door. It would be wise to detour to his fishing lodge, which lay only a mile or so from here and not too far off the Edinburgh road. It wasn't just Cassie who fled, but her father, sister and whatever servants they had with them. He didn't wish to confront them alone and unprepared. He'd have his lodge's gamekeeper, Jamie Laidlaw, at his side before he stopped the Conningsbys.

"Push, Eliza!" Cassie exhorted.

"I *am* pushing," a cranky, exhausted Eliza snapped, her shoulder braced against the two trunks lashed to the coach's back luggage rack. It wasn't the first time on this short journey that they'd taken their places here, their sturdy, short boots sinking almost to their tops in the muddy road.

In the box and once more dressed as a coachman, their father snapped the whip. The exhausted horses snorted and strained. Together, Cassie and Eliza shoved. The wheels slid and shifted, spewing muck as they turned.

Pushing with what little might she had left, Cassie glanced skyward, frantic. It had to be nearly ten in the morning, and they'd managed only sixteen miles, passing through the village of Selkirk. At this rate they'd be in Edinburgh sometime next week. That was, if they ever reached the city. Not long ago Roland had called down from his coachman's perch that he could see a pair of men riding in their direction. For all Cassie knew, they might be men out and about on their own business, but what if they weren't?

The unwieldy and overburdened vehicle began to move. Cassie pushed harder, leaning her whole body against the trunks. The front wheels caught on the lip of the ruts they'd carved in the soft road. Again, her father snapped the whip. The horses whinnied.

There was a loud crack. The wheel at Cassie's right tilted to the side, disconnected from the coach. Unbalanced, the vehicle roared back down into its ruts. The ropes holding the trunks jerked, then one snapped.

"Cassie!" Eliza screamed, scrambling out of harm's way.

Cassie wasn't fast enough. The vehicle toppled, landing with a thundering crash. The trunks tumbled down. One nicked her knee, driving her to the ground. The other landed atop her foot as she hit the grassy verge. Stars danced before her eyes. She jerked on her trapped foot, only to bite back a shriek at the pain in her knee.

At the front of the fallen coach the horses screamed and thrashed in their traces. Her father rose to his hands and knees from where he'd landed in the grassy sod. "That demmed axle. I knew the repair was no good," he shouted, then leaped to Cassie's side to lift the trunk off her foot. She yelped as her ankle began to throb in time to her knee.

Calm purpose filled Roland's round face, making him look more commanding than she'd ever seen him. "I have to see to the horses. Eliza, come help your sister to her feet," he called, then raced to the horses.

Flinching, Cassie rolled onto her back. Overhead the morning's clear sky had given way to a sullen layer of clouds that had already once spat rain at them. A sodden breeze ruffled the grasses and bent the broad white heads of Queen Anne's lace on the verge.

She sat up and gingerly moved her leg. Tears, having as much to do with failure as with pain, filled her eyes. She'd gambled everything on this escape, and now all was lost. If Lord Bucksden was behind them, he'd soon have Eliza.

Eliza came to help her rise. "Are you all right?"

"I think so," Cassie replied, swallowing.

"Move your foot," her father called back to them as he stroked the nose of the lead horse. Where that beast went the others were content to follow. They grew steadily calmer. "If it's broken it'll snap and hurt like the . . . well, terribly."

Cassie did as she was bid. Nothing snapped or popped. She set her foot on the earth. When she shifted some weight onto it pain streaked through her leg from her tiniest toe to her knee. She lifted the foot.

"I don't feel anything that I shouldn't," she reported, her voice trembling, "but I cannot walk on it."

"No need to walk," her father said, coming back to join them. Purpose and confidence firmed the cut of his jaw. "We ride the horses from here, taking only our satchels."

Eliza made a despairing sound at the thought of abandoning her few belongings. Cassie knew how her sister felt. Mud had spattered her from near the raised waistline of her fashionable pelisse to the garment's sweeping hemline. No doubt the dress she wore beneath the coat was equally ruined. The thought of immigrating with nothing but a single change of clothing and their personal effects was daunting indeed.

"Cheer up." Roland smiled at his daughters. He climbed into the side of the fallen coach, the mud-splattered tails of his maroon jacket falling soddenly against his leather breeches. "We'll use what we get from the sale of the horses to replace some of what we leave here."

"Can you still see the riders?" Cassie asked.

"Eh?" Standing atop the coach's side, Roland turned to look behind them. Their position atop the hill gave him a clear view of the road in either direction. "They come steadily on, but I don't think it's the earl. Didn't you say Mr. Percy reported Bucksden's head was bandaged?" he asked Eliza.

"He did," Eliza replied. "He said the earl's whole head was swathed so thickly that he couldn't wear his hat."

"That's what I thought." Their father lowered himself into the coach with more agility than Cassie had ever suspected he owned. "The two men behind us both wear their hats. There's not a speck of white to obscure their faces. We have about a quarter hour before they reach us. Perhaps we should just let them catch us. We might ask for aid?" His voice echoed oddly out of the fallen vehicle.

"No," Cassie said. "What if those men serve Lord Bucksden?"

Roland threw their four satchels up onto the side of the coach. Clambering back out, he collected the ropes that had secured their trunks. He wound one of them through the handles of two satchels, making saddlebags of them. Having never seen her father do anything useful, Cassie watched in amazement. When he finished with the remaining pair of satchels he went to unharness their horses.

Cassie again tried to put weight on her foot, but the pain was almost sickening in its intensity. "Help me to the side of the coach," she said, laying an arm over Eliza's shoulder.

Hobbling was worse than she expected. Her good foot kept slipping in the muck, which caused her to put too much pressure on the injured one. She was panting and trembling by the time she leaned against the coach.

Their father brought the first horse around. "Cassie, climb onto the coach. From there it would be an easy step to settle on his back."

"Eliza first," Cassie said, still wincing at the

throbbing. It didn't help to imagine having to bend her leg as she rode without saddle or stirrup for support.

Eliza climbed onto the coach with ease, then sat astride the horse, aghast at the way her skirts hiked past her knees. Roland brought the second horse around for Cassie.

"Now you, girl," he commanded.

Cassie set her injured foot on the front axle brace to thrust upward. Pain shot up her leg. She changed feet and tried again, but her injured ankle refused to hold her. It was impossible.

"I can't," she cried.

"You have to do it, Cassie," Eliza said, terrified for her. "The men are close enough that I can almost see their faces. We have to go."

Frantically, Cassie tried again. Roland grabbed her by the waist and lifted her until she sat on the edge of the coach, then he brought the horse to stand against the vehicle. Cassie bent her knee to swing her injured foot over the horse. The pain was so intense that stars circled in her vision.

"I can't," she cried again. "Even if I could get my leg over his back I cannot bend my knee enough to sit astride."

Reaching down, she touched Roland on the shoulder. "Mount, Papa. It's up to you now. Take Eliza and the money. Go without me."

"No, Cassie!" Eliza cried in protest.

"I will not!" her father retorted. "If those men work for Bucksden, they'll—"

"What if they don't work for Lord Bucksden?" Cassie interrupted, caring for nothing at this moment but Eliza's safety. Philana was right. Cassie had been giving Lord Bucksden credit for more power than he owned. As long as she denied him Eliza there was little he could do to hurt her. "That's a risk I can afford to take, but not one that Eliza can bear. She's the one Lord Bucksden wants, the one the earl has some right to claim."

"But, Cassie . . ." Eliza started to protest.

Cassie silenced her with a lift of her hand. "I won't hear it. What can Lord Bucksden do to me? I have no repute left to tarnish, nor can I be any more impoverished than I already am. No, if those men are from Bucksden, then they'll swiftly ride on after you once they realize I'm not the one they want. All the more reason for you to go as swiftly as you can."

When Eliza again tried to object Cassie said, "Buy my passage to America, Eliza, then send a note to Philana's house with the line and schedule. As soon as I can, I'll follow you to Boston."

It was a plausible fantasy. Cassie counted on it to convince her father and sister to leave. "Go this very moment," she told them again, her voice filled with every ounce of command she owned.

Tears filled Eliza's eyes. She kicked her heels into the big horse's side. The horse trotted away from the coach.

Roland shook his head. "Would that I had never seen a deck of cards," he said, then stepped up onto the coach's forward wheel, doing what Cassie couldn't, mounting the horse. He laid his makeshift saddlebags over its shoulders and followed Eliza, leading the other two coach horses.

Chapter 13

Still seated on the side of the coach, Cassie watched her family disappear, devastated. How would Eliza ever remain safe without her? How could Cassie protect herself without her family? If the men about to come upon her were from the earl she was in terrible trouble.

And if they weren't? Then perhaps they could help her. She needed somewhere to hide until her knee and ankle were healed enough to permit riding, or until she discovered some other way to reach Edinburgh.

It couldn't be Ettrick House, not when it was only a matter of time before Lord Bucksden appeared on Philana's doorstep. Lucien's presence at the house party might keep the earl away from Ryecroft Cas-

tle, but Lord Bucksden would surely poll Lord Ryecroft's local guests, seeking information about the
Conningsbys. He'd get an earful after today's end.
By then everyone attending the house party would
know what had happened in the card room last
night, and that the Conningsbys had returned with
Philana to Ettrick House.

What Cassie needed was a place to hide where she
wasn't known, and where she wouldn't need to pay
for food or lodging. Cassie sighed. What she needed
was a miracle.

The answer came in a flash. What she needed was
to be anyone except Cassie Marston, one of the
women sought by Lord Bucksden.

Not so long ago a tale circulated in London about
a soldier who'd taken a blow to the head and lost all
memory of his life before that blow. Cassie looked at
the toppled coach beneath her, kicking her good heel
against its bottom. It wouldn't take much to convince anyone finding her here that she'd hit her head
and lost her memory. As long as the coming men
weren't Lord Bucksden's servants, her tale would
surely win their pity. All she need do after that was
convince them to take her to some sympathetic
householder who would extend hospitality, expecting nothing in return until she regained her lost
memory.

The thought of using people's goodness against
them made Cassie feel as dirty as her mud-stained
pelisse. Right or wrong, it was her only choice.
Swiveling, she gingerly lowered herself through the
square opening in the side door, thankful that the

coach's central opening had never contained glass as the side windows had. Jagged shards were all that remained of those panes.

Cassie eased her feet down the length of the bench seat until she landed gently on the opposite door frame. Her weight strained the door beneath her. Mud oozed through its unglazed opening, the muck spilling onto Cassie's boots.

Hobbling back a step, she eyed the seat, calculating how she might have landed if she'd been in the coach when it fell. It took a moment to arrange herself accordingly and still another moment to feel comfortable in the position. She tried tucking her hands beneath her head as if she slept, but decided that despite the comfort it was an unlikely position. Instead, she arranged her hands in front of her breast, backs down and fingers curled into the palms. That was better: a position conveying feminine helplessness and fragile vulnerability.

Closing her eyes, Cassie tried to relax, only to have her straw bonnet crunch in her ear as she breathed. She sat up and tossed the hat across the coach as if she hadn't been wearing it at the time the coach toppled. Then, pulling out a few pins, she used her fingers to muss her hair. Looking appropriately disheveled, she settled back into her chosen position.

That was better. She looked every inch the damsel in distress, and just in time. Horses whickered as the men rode onto the hill's crest.

"What this?" asked one man, the lilt of Scotland in his voice.

"Conningsby's coach," Lucien answered.

Cassie's eyes flew open. Lucien? Hope tore through her, only to die a terrible death. There was only one reason for him to follow her. Her secretive departure from Ryecroft Castle last night must have confirmed to him that she was a cheat. He didn't know she had any other reason to run. But how did he know she was on the Edinburgh road?

Exasperation ate at Cassie. Philana and her meddling! She'd told Lucien how to find them.

With Philana's few incautious words she'd destroyed Cassie's elaborate plan to protect her. Cassie sighed. At least she wouldn't have to misuse the kindness of strangers. Lucien already knew who she was and he wasn't likely to take her anywhere except back to Philana's house, willy nilly.

If the thought of putting Philana in danger was terrifying, the thought of a trip back to Ettrick House in Lucien's custody made Cassie's heart ache. He'd spend the journey demanding she reveal how she'd beaten him last night. Even if Cassie told him the whole truth, confessing to her strange skill, he'd never believe her. All he wanted was her admission that she was a sharp. Nothing else would satisfy him.

Suddenly, pretending she couldn't remember anything seemed even more attractive. If she couldn't remember Lucien, then she wouldn't have to discuss last night with him, no matter how determined he might be to make her talk. Cassie relaxed back into her helpless posture and closed her eyes.

*   *   *

"More fool them tha' travels our roads in such a vehicle." Jamie Laidlaw laughed harshly, surveying the toppled, horseless coach. His green eyes sparkled in amusement beneath a dark fringe of his hair.

Lucien had to agree. Such an accident wasn't uncommon for heavy coaches on Scotland's uncertain roads. He dismounted and walked toward the fallen vehicle.

"Ye shouldna waste yer time, m'lord. The coach horses are gone. No doubt they've ridden on, na' wanting to meet you," Jamie called after him. As always Jamie, who was Lucien's gamekeeper, spoke with none of the servility that he should have employed when addressing one of England's peers.

In all truth Jamie was more the doer of odd jobs and errands at Lucien's lodge, as well as husband to its housekeeper, than he was caretaker or gamekeeper. His familiarity toward Lucien had evolved over the previous summer as he played the role of Lucien's drinking companion and storyteller. Jamie and Maggie were the only servants Lucien kept at the lodge. He sometimes even eschewed Hastings, depending on his mood. Jamie enjoyed his title, however, and lived up to it in his dress: a short-crowned hat, decorated with a buckle that he must have gotten from his grandfather; a serviceable brown coat, patched waistcoat, leather knee breeches, thick stockings and heavy boots.

"It's my time to waste," Lucien replied to Jamie, toeing one of the trunks lying on the road.

What clue to Cassie's trick had he, Percy and Egremont all missed last night? It had to be something obvious. Not only were the Conningsbys fleeing like the devil was on their tail, their haste was so urgent that they left their possessions behind as they went.

He stopped at the coach's side, glanced inside, and then froze. Cassie lay in a lifeless heap at the bottom of the vehicle. The hem of her lavender pelisse was filthy with mud, her golden hair, torn from its usual careful confinement, was in wild disarray.

"Jamie!" he shouted, then leaped up onto the side of the coach.

Tossing aside his hat, Lucien lowered himself through the window and dropped to a crouch beside Cassie. The coach rocked a little in reaction to his landing. Mud oozed into the interior, touching Cassie's hand. Her fingers moved. Her eyelids flickered.

Relief tore through him. She wasn't dead, only unconscious. What was he doing? He'd indulge in no pity for a cheat, not even a beautiful, injured one.

"Aye, m'lord," Jamie said, leaning into the window above Lucien. Pity cut creases into his lean cheeks. "Ach, the poor, wee creature. They left her here, hurt and alone."

"She wasn't alone for long, was she?" Lucien retorted, torn between agreeing with Jamie—what sort of man left his unconscious daughter alone on the road?—and the certainty that the Conningsbys had known someone followed them. Both Lucien and Jamie had seen Sir Roland look back at them not long ago.

Cassie groaned, tried to move, then gasped, stiffening as if in pain. Her eyes opened, their usual golden-brown color darkened to almost black. Sighing, she looked up at him.

Something deep within Lucien stirred. Despite what he felt about how Cassie had misused him last night, he still desired her. But then, for the past six years all the women who'd caught his eye and piqued his lust had looked like Cassie, with alabaster skin, a short, straight nose and wide-set eyes beneath gently arching golden brows. His gaze came to rest on her mouth. The lush thrust of her lower lip promised passion while the vulnerable angel bow of her upper lip begged for his kiss.

She studied his face in return, her look a caress. Then, a strange blankness came over her expression. She frowned.

"Who are you?" she asked, her voice tremulous. Her frown deepened. "Who am I?"

Her words destroyed all Lucien's compassion, leaving plenty of room for outrage. Just what sort of fool did she take him for? Lucien had seen stunned men taken from the boxing ring at his London gymnasium. Those hit hard enough to temporarily lose their memories had blank faces and glazed eyes. Their questions were frightened and frantic as they fought to wrench the missing answers from their uncooperative brains. She had none of those symptoms. This was but another of her nefarious attempts to use him.

The means to give her her comeuppance rushed

over Lucien, the idea both stunning in its brilliance and ultimately satisfying. Best of all, it would expose her to the world for the cheat and liar she was. Mustering every ounce of acting ability he had, Lucien crooned, "Why, my dear, how can you not recognize me? I'm your husband."

Her husband?! Cassie shoved herself up to sitting, staring at Lucien. He wasn't her husband. He knew it, she knew it. So did the man watching them through the coach's upturned window, according to the startled sound he made.

Shocked words of denial leaped to her lips. Triumph blazed in Lucien's steely eyes. In that moment he looked every bit as dangerous as Lord Bucksden. No, he looked like a man willing to step outside society's conventions to have what he wanted, and what he wanted was her complete destruction.

Cassie swallowed her protest, avoiding his waiting trap by a bare breath. If she denied their supposed union, then she couldn't have lost her memory. The moment she erred and revealed her amnesia was a lie, Lucien would use her extravagant falsehood to validate all the terrible things he believed about her. As if anything could make Lucien think her any worse. It was time to tell the truth.

Tired, hurt and defeated, Cassie opened her mouth, only to hesitate as the most outrageous thought unfolded in her. What she needed was a hiding place and someone to protect her from Lord Bucksden until she could reach Edinburgh. Accord-

ing to Philana, Lucien kept some sort of lodge near
Ettrick House. Where better for her to hide than with
her new *husband*, Lucien, whom Lord Bucksden
feared?

"You're my husband? she asked uncertainly. She
not only played her trump card and called Lucien's
bluff, but upped the ante in this new game of theirs.
"Try as I might, I cannot say I've ever before seen
you in my life."

Astonishment shot through Lucien's gray eyes.
Triumph drained from him as the trap he'd laid for
her closed around him instead. His eyes narrowed,
his jaw tightened.

He'd just realized that unless she admitted she
didn't have amnesia he couldn't retreat. Doing so
meant he had to admit to his own lie, and that he
wouldn't do, not when it turned him into the same
cheat he accused her of being. Nor was she going to
give him a chance to retreat. Cassie wasn't sure if she
should laugh or worry.

She looked up at the rustic watching them. The
man's gaze was intent, an air of amusement clinging
to the dour lines of his chiseled face. Perhaps it was
the game playing going on here, but Cassie had no
trouble reading his face and form. He was enjoying
their acting better than any Punch and Judy he'd
ever seen.

"Tell me, sir," she asked him, placing a hand on
Lucien's arm. "Is this man truly my husband?"

A worried crease appeared between the rustic's
brows. He glanced at Lucien. Whatever he saw in his
master's face reassured him.

"So he's told me, madam. Ye'll not be knowing me as we've na' met until this very moment," he replied. The rustic took care to tiptoe carefully around his lie.

That left Lucien no choice but to play his next card. "Oh, my poor darling," he crooned. "Look how my inattention has hurt you. Why did I agree that you should travel to Edinburgh on your own?"

Cassie barely stopped herself from rolling her eyes. Oh, she was on her own all right, without maid, companion, coachman, or even horses. Had she really suffered from amnesia, she might well have been asking some very pointed questions of Lucien about the sort of husband he was.

"Would that I remembered you," she said. "Perhaps I'll regain my memory when you take me home."

Outrage flashed through Lucien's gaze as he lost yet another round to Cassie. "Open the door, Jamie, and I'll lift her up to you," he growled.

"Aye, m'lord," Jamie replied, then disappeared.

The coach door squeaked open, displaying a larger panel of the sky to Cassie's view. Lucien slipped his arms beneath her. As Cassie's injured leg bent over his forearm pain shot through her. She gasped and struggled against him. His eyes narrowed and his arms tightened around her to hold her against him.

"No, stop," she pleaded. "My leg hurts when it bends."

"Let me see," Lucien snapped.

He set her down, her back braced in a corner, her

legs stretched across the top of the downward-facing door. Treating her with the familiarity of a husband toward his wife, he lifted the mud-stained hems of her attire nearly to her thighs.

Cassie surveyed her injured leg in dismay. Above her white stocking and pink-and-green-embroidered garter her knee was swollen, the skin already darkening to the blue-black of a bruise. Her ankle didn't look as puffy as she expected, although it throbbed against the top of her short boot.

"Ach, ye poor, wee creature," Jamie said, reappearing above the coach.

"Egad, no wonder it hurts when you bend it," Lucien said, new gentleness in his voice. "How did it happen?"

Cassie opened her mouth to tell him that the trunk fell on her, only to swallow her explanation at the sly look in his gray eyes. This was a trap and the opening wager on their next hand.

"I don't know," Cassie replied, doing her best to sound like a woman who'd lost her every recall. "My ankle throbs as well."

"All the more reason to get you home as soon as I can, darling," Lucien said, threat still lingering in his voice.

Darling. What would it be liked to hear him honestly call her that? Lucien slid his arms more carefully beneath her this time. Cassie wound her hands together behind his nape. As he lifted her she breathed in his scents—sandalwood, damp breeze and horse. His warmth enveloped her, tantalizing and comforting all at once.

He came upright in the fallen coach's open doorway, rising into the day's dim light, and sat Cassie on the coach's side. His eyes narrowed as he gently tucked a strand of her tumbled hair back behind her ear. Although it was a gesture in which a husband might indulge, it was also a threat. With his touch Lucien hinted that if she pushed this game to its logical conclusion he might well demand his *husbandly* rights.

Not certain how to respond, Cassie eyed him for a moment, only to lose herself in appreciation. Did Lucien know how exceptional he looked in the blue, long-tailed coat, buff waistcoat and buckskin trousers he wore this morning? How she liked the look of his rugged features and the way the rising breeze tousled his honey-colored hair.

Would Lucien truly press her into his bed? The certainty that he would never force her rose from the depths of Cassie's soul. If he'd been that sort of man he would never have left her in the garden when she'd all but begged him to use her.

What would it be like to be Lucien's *wife*, if even for only as long as it took her injuries to heal and to guarantee Eliza's safety? That notion, born from the seed that Philana had so capably planted in Cassie the night of the ball—the seed Cassie had been so certain she'd killed—sent out new shoots. Twisting like a vine, it twined itself around her heart, resisting her efforts to tear it out. Instead, it promised that even the pretense of marriage to Lucien would be better than the unending barren, impoverished widowhood Cassie expected to endure.

She sighed. She might play the role of Lucien's wife for the moment, but she'd never be his cherished love or the woman Lucien honored above all others by offering his marriage vow. She'd best not forget that over the coming days.

Chapter 14

Under a glowering ceiling of clouds another gust of sodden wind tugged at Lucien's hat. Raindrops pattered on his back. The breeze smelled as wild and vast as the almost treeless sweep and roll of the Scottish landscape around him.

He looked down at Cassie, dozing fitfully against his shoulder as she sat sideways in front of him in his saddle. It wasn't an easy ride for her. He'd used his waistcoat to bind her injured knee to keep it from bending, then braced her leg on his thigh. Her bonnet lay in her lap, the hat's brim too wide for their intimate position.

Her hair, smelling of rainwater and rose, brushed his jaw. Her breast pressed against his chest, her hip against his open thighs. Three days ago her nearness might have left him wild with wanting her. Today, Lucien kept as tight a rein on his reaction to her as he did on his gelding.

How could the woman he'd known and respected six years ago have changed so much? For the second time in twenty-four hours Cassie was getting the best of him and again doing it in front of a witness. He glanced at Jamie.

Riding alongside his employer, the servant squinted back at Lucien, one eye closed. Confusion and amusement filled the harsh lines of his face. A moment later Jamie shook his head and chuckled, the sound no more than a breath.

Finding himself yet again the butt of someone's amusement sent Lucien's simmering anger soaring anew. His gelding, already unhappy about carrying Cassie's additional weight, pranced in protest. The movement jostled Cassie's knee.

Gasping, she jolted out of her nap, straightening between Lucien's arms and grabbing for her leg. Her breasts pressed on his upper arm. Lucien squeezed his eyes shut as sensations shot through him. Blast the conniving little sharp! Blast himself. How could he still want her, knowing that she used him?

She had to be using him. Why else would she persist in the pretense of amnesia when they both knew there was nothing wrong with her memory? A tiny voice rose from deep within him. If he didn't want Cassie to use him, all he had to do was take her to Philana Forster's house, then ride away without a backward look.

Every ounce of Lucien's pride roared in refusal. He wouldn't let her go until she admitted to being a sharp and a liar, thereby restoring his dignity.

Cassie sagged back against him, her face pale. "Can we stop for a little?" she asked, her voice thready.

"My lodge isn't much farther," he replied, then added in bitter afterthought, "darling."

Blast, blast, blast. Taking her to his lodge meant violating the sanctuary he'd made of the place. In the two years he'd owned the house, not even Devanney had visited.

Philana Forster's house. Again, Lucien's jaw tightened in refusal. Why hadn't Cassie folded when he named himself her husband?

"How far?" she begged.

"You can see it now. Look there, to the west," he told her; another spate of rain tapped at his back.

Cassie turned her head in the direction he indicated, then sagged back against him. "Not so far," she said in deep relief, leaning back against his shoulder, her head tilted up, her eyes closed.

That she could remain so relaxed when she was completely at his mercy bothered Lucien. Perhaps she believed him too honorable to fulfill his threat. In that she was wrong. He'd give her until nightfall to admit the truth. If she didn't, he'd join her in bed and demand she play the role of his *wife*.

The corners of Lucien's mouth tightened. Not even this new Cassie would go that far to avoid confessing. Once she realized that he meant to take her unless she admitted to everything, she'd crumble. Only then would he return her to Philana Forster.

It wasn't long before Lucien and Jamie were drawing their horses to a halt in front of his lodge, which was in truth a Border pele tower. A sort of fortified farmhouse, the square structure was built of stone and stood three storeys tall and a good forty feet wide. It nestled in the embrace of the rugged hills at the point where they gave way to the long plain that stretched down to the Ettrick Water.

Behind the tower, the stream Lucien fished had cut a narrow, snaking gorge into the hills, one deep enough that it took a good climb down to reach the water's edge. In wilder times men from this side of the border had raided the other, bringing their stolen English cattle and sheep to graze the banks of the hidden stream, watching over their ill-gotten gains from the tower.

Except for the apple orchard outside his door and a good-sized copse planted north of the tower by the previous owner, there were no trees. Instead, the hills that rose some three or four hundred feet above his tower's roof wore an emerald cloak of rough heather, bracken and grass, nothing taller than his knees.

Jamie dismounted, then hesitated. "Shall I take the cart and bring back yer lady's trunks, m'lord?"

"First, go within and warn Maggie that I and my *wife*," Lucien's tongue stumbled over the word, "intend to spend the night here."

Jamie choked back a chuckle. He trotted to the

tower, entering and leaving the door open behind him. The savory smell of baking bread and roasting meat flowed out of the tower kitchen. Lucien's stomach reacted; he hadn't eaten yet today, but this was Maggie and Jamie's dinner, not his. Lucien hadn't expected to return to the tower tonight, and Maggie used the kitchen as she pleased.

"Maggie, his lordship comes, bringin' his wife with him." Jamie's amused announcement echoed out to Lucien.

He clenched his teeth, dismounted, then turned and held his arms up to Cassie. She slid into his embrace. He lowered her until her feet met the earth. She gasped, then clutched at his arm to hold herself erect.

"Pins and needles," she said, looking up at him, a rueful smile twisting her lips. Her voice was barely louder than a whisper. New trepidation filled her expression.

Confidence rushed through Lucien. It was about time. All he need to do was press her a little, pretending to want congress with his wife. She'd be singing of her sins in an instant.

A hint of disappointment swirled through him. Once she'd confessed, he'd have to retreat, forgoing all thought of lovemaking. That he could still want Cassie in his bed, knowing all the wrong she'd done him only exasperated him.

"Let me carry you in, darling," he said, pasting a smile on his face and sweeping her up into his arms.

He carried her through the door and directly into the kitchen. As always, the room's comfort and clutter closed about Lucien, welcoming him home. The walls were white plaster, the ceiling wooden and crossed by thick, age-darkened beams.

To call the chamber crowded didn't do it justice. The scullery consisted of a pump and two stone sinks against the back wall. A narrow wooden cupboard stood to Lucien's left. At the center of the room was a thick, scarred table, its surface littered with whatever bowls, knifes and other cooking implements Maggie had been using. More dangled from hooks driven into the table's thick sides. Pans hung on the walls along with bigger implements, ricers, sieves and choppers and such. A number of small cheeses hung in net bags. Bunches of herbs dangled from the beams. A cheery blaze burned in the round brick-trimmed mouth of the fireplace set in the wall to the right of the door. The oven was a smaller opening high on the hearth's plaster face.

The air was warm, fragrant and moist; Maggie had water boiling at one side of the hearth. A good sized piece of meat roasted on the other, sizzling and spitting as it cooked, more than enough for four. Two smaller pots sat at the front of the hearth, their lids chattering. The smell of stewing apples rose from one of them.

Jamie and tall, narrow Maggie stood in front of the two small doors leading to the tower's tiny pantry and just as small dairy. A youth of no more than twenty and as tall and thin as Maggie stood beside her. The lad shared Maggie's coppery hair, long nose, thin lips and pale, freckled skin. Lucien recognized him as one of Maggie's nephews.

"My lord." The boy bowed to Lucien, then swiftly disappeared through the door into the gray afternoon.

As he left, Maggie fixed Lucien with her sharpest gaze. Framed by her ruddy lashes her green eyes narrowed. One faint, red brow lifted. Maggie wore her Sunday dress and her best lace-trimmed cap, something that startled Lucien. She'd taken care to roll up her sleeves and cover her finery with her well-used apron.

He waited. Servant or not, Maggie was her own person; if she considered Lucien's returning with a "wife" to be ill considered, she'd say so. Lucien supposed it was his fault she spoke as she willed to him. He'd spent too much of his required mourning period closeted in the intimacy of this tower with only Hastings, Maggie and Jamie as his attendants.

A moment later Maggie turned her pointed gaze to Cassie, staring as if her look could penetrate the little sharp's heart. But rather than show scorn, Maggie's face softened in consideration. She gave a single nod, as if something of import had been decided, then bobbed.

"Lady Graceton," she said to Cassie, then looked at Lucien. "I see ye've found her, m'lord."

"I have," Lucien replied, not certain why Maggie supported his bluff, but grateful that she did.

"She's injured," he added. "I'll take her up to her chamber. Fetch fuel for her hearth and come see what you can do for her leg."

"Aye, ye do that m'lord, take her to her chamber. I'll be na' a moment 'fore I come after you."

Frowning in surprise, Lucien turned toward the stairs. What in the world had gotten into the woman?

Lady Graceton. The title pierced Cassie like a knife driven all the way to her core. Why had that woman called her Lady Graceton, even though she had to know that Cassie wasn't Lucien's wife, or his lady?

Cassie looked at the green-and-gray world framed in the kitchen's open door. Beyond these humble walls she was vulnerable to Lord Bucksden. Inside, she was at Lucien's mercy, her position all the more precarious if his servants supported him in his ruse.

Now was the moment to speak the truth, admitting to everything Lucien wanted to hear. Once she'd done that she could demand that he return her to Philana's house. She opened her mouth. No words came.

Now! It had to be now, before he took her to *her* chamber. Still, not a single word left Cassie's mouth.

Turning, Lucien carried her toward one corner of the kitchen. Cassie looked over his shoulder at the tall, thin, redheaded woman. The woman smiled at her, her expression filled with approval, as if she were congratulating Cassie on a job well done. Cassie frowned in confusion.

"Have a care," Lucien said sharply as he slid sideways into a narrow, spiraling staircase, "sit as straight as you can or you'll hit your head."

It was a good thing he warned her. The plastered

wall of the stairwell closed around them, pressing
them close. The only sounds were their breathing
and the echoing scrape of Lucien's boots against the
stone steps. With her arms around his neck Cassie
felt the beat of his heart against her own.

Lucien paused on the second-storey landing to re-
settle her in his arms. That gave Cassie a glimpse of a
large room, a hall of sorts. Like the kitchen it had a
wooden, beamed ceiling and white plastered walls,
the expanse decorated with portraits. A pretty blue-
and-green carpet covered its wooden floor. A pair of
blue settees stood before the empty fireplace against
the far wall. The hearth was nearly as wide as the
room and so deep that it contained a pair of benches.

Lucien continued up to the next landing, which
opened up into a stark, spacious bedchamber. Here,
the sharply pitched ceiling was the underside of the
roof, support beams crisscrossing in the open air.
White wainscoting trimmed with a simple molding
decorated the lower portion of the plastered walls.
The fireplace stood on the stair wall.

There wasn't much in the way of furnishings. A
well-worn carpet covered the scarred wooden floor.
A washstand and a chair stood next to the bed, while
a chest and single small dresser offered storage. The
bed, although constructed of fine mahogany, was as
lacking in decoration as the walls. Only the barest of
yellow fringe trimmed its solid red counterpane.

Another door stood in the wall across from the
landing. Lucien carried Cassie to it, taking her past a
wide window that offered a spectacular view of a
long plain and a distant river. Behind the door was

yet another bedchamber, nearly the twin of the first right down to the window, except that the bed was bigger and the counterpane done in glorious blues and golds. The hearth in the far wall was empty, but the room's chill had less to do with the lack of a fire than with the sense that the room hadn't been used in a long time.

Lucien set Cassie on the edge of the bed, then dropped onto one knee before her. After removing his hat and gloves, he lifted her hems to reveal her waistcoat-bound knee, then began to unwind her makeshift bandage.

As he worked Cassie looked at the door behind him and the other bedchamber. Lucien's bedroom. He would sleep between her and the stairs, or rather between her and escape.

That is, if he didn't fulfill his threat and try to sleep *with* her. The longing to be Lucien's wife stirred, more powerfully this time, but not his amnesiac bride. She didn't want to properly protest that he wait for her to remember him before he demanded his husbandly rights. Cassie wanted Lucien Hollier in her life, her bed and her body, now.

Cassie recoiled from the thought, shocked at herself. This game of theirs had gone too far. She opened her mouth to tell Lucien what he wanted to hear, only to have Eliza's image rise before her mind's eye. In Cassie's mental picture, her sister was trapped in a similar bedchamber with Lord Bucksden.

That thought was too horrible to bear. Cassie

swallowed her confession. Whatever it took, Eliza had to reach safety.

Lucien pulled his waistcoat off Cassie's leg, dropping the muddy garment onto the floor. The binding had not only kept her knee from bending too much, but eased the throbbing. As it began again to pulse she eyed it with critical concern.

"I think the swelling's worse and it's darkened much more," she said, speaking more to herself than him.

Lucien sat back on his heel, then gently lifted her leg, bending her knee a little. She flinched as pain shot through her. It wasn't as bad as she expected. He let go of her foot, then glanced up at her.

"I dare say it'll look even worse by the morrow. Maggie may have something to ease the bruising and take down the swelling."

There was no expression on his face or in his eyes. She might as well have been an injured horse.

"Thank you, my lord," she replied, feeling more alone than she'd ever known possible.

His gray eyes grew as cold as the room. "Lucien."

"I beg your pardon?" Cassie asked, startled.

"My wife calls me Lucien," he said, that angry, challenging edge to his voice.

An Eliza destroyed by Lord Bucksden's lust swam before Cassie's inner eye. "Do I?" she asked blankly. "And, what do you call me?"

He blinked as if surprised by her return challenge, then determination flared to life in his eyes. Reaching up, he ran his fingers down the curve of her cheek. Cassie's heart twisted. He'd offered her the same caress in Lord Ryecroft's garden, but then it had been filled with affection. Now, all his fingers against her skin conveyed was threat.

"I have called you Cassie," he answered grudgingly.

She stared at him, flabbergasted. The comfortable way he pronounced her pet name suggested that he had, indeed, been referring to her as Cassie in his mind, instead of Mrs. Marston or even Cassandra. Only the people who loved her called her Cassie.

As if speaking her name freed something within him, Lucien's expression softened. In that instant he became the man who'd stolen her heart six years ago, the same man who'd claimed her kiss in the garden two nights past. This was the husband Cassie wanted, a friend with whom she could laugh and tease, a man who cared enough for her not to leave her injured and alone on a deserted road. A lover who respected her enough to retreat when she told him no.

Without thought Cassie reached out to claim that man, wanting him more than she dreamed possible. She lay her hand on his shoulder. The ice melted from Lucien's gaze. This time when his fingers came to rest against her cheek all the affection Cassie craved filled his touch.

Footsteps rapped sharply across the floor of Lucien's bedchamber. Lucien snatched back his hand and came to his feet, his eyes once again as hard as ice. Maggie bustled in and hurried to the hearth, carrying an armload of wood.

"Maggie, when you've seen to my wife"—again Lucien stumbled over the word, no doubt despising it as much as Cassie did at the moment—"I'll be wanting dinner. You've enough for the four of us?"

"Aye, m'lord," Maggie replied without turning to look at him as she placed wood and kindling in the hearth. "Will you and your lady dine together in the hall?"

The thought of dining across a table from Lucien made Cassie cringe. He glanced at her, his expression flat. "I doubt she can manage the stairs."

Cassie took his words to heart. If she'd been his true wife he would have carried her down to his hall just as he'd carried her up here. But she wasn't his wife, and he would never be the husband she'd dreamed about six years ago.

"It's just as well that I eat in my chamber tonight," Cassie said. "I fear I'm exhausted."

"As you will, m'lady," the Scotswoman replied without looking up from her chore.

Lucien turned on his heel and crossed into his own bedchamber, closing the door behind him. Maggie opened the flue and brought the fire to life, then came to Cassie, brushing nonexistent dust from her gown. Without a word of introduction or any show of deference she knelt and examined Cassie's injured knee, moving it much as Lucien had. Again, Cassie flinched.

"Na' more than a wrench, despite the pretty colors," Maggie pronounced a moment later. "I've a liniment that should help."

She looked up into Cassie's face. Approval,

amusement and deep pleasure all flashed in her green eyes. "I'd offer ye a bath, but the tub canna come up yon wee stairs and ye canna come down to the kitchen, na' without aid, and it doesna' appear as his lordship wishes to offer ye that aid. What say ye to a bucket of water, soap and a towel?"

"Yes, thank you," Cassie said, wanting very much to be free of mud.

"So, ye've no memory at all?" Maggie asked, her expression flattening into the anonymity of a servant.

"None at all," Cassie replied, then being a fraud got the better of her. The words she couldn't speak to Lucien exploded past her lips. "How can you be so kind to me when you have to know—"

Maggie put a hasty finger against Cassie's lips to stop her. "Na' more, my lady. There's much ye canna ken about this wee drama of yers. My husband says ye were found on the road in a fallen coach and that ye've na' any recall of yer own good husband—tha's all that matters t'me. Now, here's a bit fer ye to chew on. Two summers and a good part of last spring and autumn has Lord Graceton spent in this house, serving his mourning period as if he truly grieved, when I think he canna have been much pained by his wife's passing. In that time he's na' brought man nor woman here. Until ye."

She gave special emphasis to this as if there was some import to Cassie's arrival here in Lucien's custody. Cassie knew better. The only reason Lucien brought her here is that he wanted to twist the truth out of her before he had to admit he'd lied to her. The competition raging between them would continue only until Cassie was certain Eliza was safe.

"Now, we'll say na' more of that, my lady," Maggie said, the honorific rolling far more easily off her tongue than the word *wife* did from Lucien's. "I'll fetch ye water and yer liniment."

Chapter 15

Cassie awoke with a start. Her heart pounding, she fought her way free of a dream in which she again swung that urn at Lord Bucksden. She stared into the darkness, lost for an instant in the deep shadows and silvery half light around her. Embers snapped and popped, the wind howled. Rain rattled at windowpanes. The dwelling creaked and groaned in the stillness of night.

And she was utterly nude beneath the bedclothes.

The day rushed back over her, the toppled coach, Eliza's departure on horseback, Lucien and her supposedly missing memory. Missing memory, indeed. The only thing Cassie couldn't remember was falling asleep in this bed.

She recalled washing, then Maggie taking away

her muddy clothing, promising to bring up Cassie's nightgown when Jamie returned with her belongings. Cassie had then yawned her way into the meal Maggie brought, dining upright in bed, coddling her leg. After that, there was nothing.

Sighing, she slid deeper into her bedclothes. Her knee twinged, but not as badly as it had earlier. She'd never before slept unclad. It was a sensuous feeling, smooth cotton against her skin.

She rolled carefully onto her opposite side. A thick unnatural shape loomed, framed in the open doorway. Cassie gave a startled, wordless cry.

"You were moaning in your sleep," Lucien said.

"Oh, it's you," she gasped. Separating his form from the enclosing night, she discerned the grayer tones of his flesh and hair from the darkness that must be his bedrobe.

"Who else would be in your bedchamber except your husband?" he retorted, but this time the bitterness in his voice wasn't aimed just at her.

The reminder of how Lord Bucksden had hurt him brought Cassie completely awake. "Who else, indeed," she murmured. "I'm sorry if I disturbed you."

"I wasn't yet asleep."

Lucien came to her bedside. That his footfalls made no sound said his feet were bare. He sat beside her, his weight making the bed dip.

As always happened when they were close, the heat of his body reached out to her, his sandalwood scent taunting. Cassie looked up at him, picking out his features. There was nothing tousled about his appearance. He hadn't been sleeping.

No, he'd been waiting. Her heartbeat lifted to a nervous pace. He was going to do it. He was going to force her to choose between protecting her heart and body from him or protecting Eliza.

It was her turn to bluff, only she had nothing in her hand, or rather on her body, that could support her ruse. "What time is it?" she asked, stalling.

"Late. Very late. Long past time to be abed," Lucien said, then leaned down and brushed his lips against her cheek.

There it was, his threat. He moved his mouth, touching his lips to hers. It was a dry kiss, lacking any trace of the passion he'd shown her in the garden.

Cassie didn't know whether to exult or cry. He didn't expect her to let him into her bed or her body. He expected her to fold before his bluff, his *husbandly* demand, and give him his confession.

If not for her dream and her fear of being vulnerable to Lord Bucksden, she might have done it. At least, that was the excuse she gave herself for persisting in her ruse. "Then you should go to bed," she told him.

Consternation wafted from him. She'd again upped the ante in their game when they both knew her hand was no match for his. "I intend to," he replied, his lips hovering over her ear, his breath caressing her skin.

Cassie shivered. "But isn't your bed in the other room?" she asked, demanding that he show his hand.

"Yes, but I've decided to sleep in here tonight," he murmured, now nuzzling her ear.

Cassie again shivered. Not even knowing how angry Lucien was with her could stop her from wanting him. Every inch of her body came to life, demanding that she invite Lucien to join her. It was to stop herself, not him, that she spewed the awful nonsense she'd practiced during this morning's interminable ride.

"Please, Lucien," she said, his given name coming less fluidly from her lips than her pet name had come from his. "Wait a few days or perhaps a week. Surely by then I'll have regained my memory and you'll no longer be a stranger to me."

There wasn't an ounce of sincerity in a single syllable. Damnation. Cassie closed her eyes. Why couldn't she be one of those women who found a wife's duty distasteful?

"How can you say we're strangers?" Lucien whispered against her throat. "We're husband and wife."

Something wicked stirred deep in Cassie. Why should she worry about what she and Lucien did here tonight? She'd be gone to America soon enough. As for carrying his child, she was probably barren. She'd been two years married without so much as a flicker of life in her womb.

With that, what little remained of her barriers disintegrated. Sighing in resignation and trembling in anticipation, Cassie turned her head to the side, craving Lucien's kiss against her nape. He released a startled breath, his mouth again hovering a bare

inch from her skin. A shiver flew down her spine.
Lord, but she was worse than a wanton if all it took
to set her senses on fire was the idea of his kiss.

What in God's hell was she doing? Lucien reared
back from her. She wasn't supposed to agree to let
him into her bed, she was supposed to confess to being a sharp. Why wasn't she folding, now that he'd
called her bluff?

She made a quiet sound and turned her head to
look up at him. The gentle curve of her cheek and
the line of her nose glowed pale white in the night.
Her eyes glinted.

Slowly, she drew her arms out from beneath the
bedclothes. What remained of rational thought in
Lucien died. Not so much as a scrap of fabric covered her arms. She was naked beneath the linens.

Reaching up, she brushed her fingers across his
chin, then traced the outline of his lips. Without
thought Lucien turned his head to kiss her fingertips. Her caress moved on across his cheek until she
gently combed her fingers into his hair.

He closed his eyes, lost in sensation. When she
traced the outline of his ear he laid his hand on her
wrist and stroked the naked length of her arm. Then,
cupping her cheek in his palm, he leaned down to
brush his mouth across hers. She gave a tiny gasp at
his play and caught his mouth with hers. Her lips
softened, begging him to kiss her the way he'd done
in the garden.

Unfettered by thought or purpose, Lucien's need
for her, six years denied, exploded into an inferno of

wanting. He buried his hands in her hair and gave her what she requested. His mouth moved across hers, his kiss filled with every ounce of desire she'd awakened in him. She made a tiny sound. Wrapping her arms around him, she pulled herself against him, rising off the mattress just far enough that she exposed her back to Lucien.

It was an invitation he couldn't resist, not after the interlude in Ryecroft Castle's corridor. He stroked the length of her spine, bringing his hand to a stop against the curve of her hip. Her skin felt every bit as wondrous as he'd imagined.

He kissed her cheek, her ear, then down her neck until he nuzzled at her nape as she'd begged him to do a moment ago. She moaned, arching against him in taunting pantomime of the joining they both craved.

Lucien shook, wanting to feel her breasts against his chest. No, he wanted to feel every inch of her skin touching his. Releasing her, he dropped his bedrobe. It was all he wore. None of his clothing was here.

Catching the corner of the coverlet, he started to pull back the bedclothes. Cassie gasped and put a hand at the top of her chest to hold the bedclothes in place.

"Don't," she cried softly.

Anger sliced through what already raged in him. The devil take her! She was again trying to use his desire against him. Not this time. He reached for the coverlet again. This time she only slid to the side a little as if making room for him.

"It's only that I barely know you," she whispered.

It wasn't the shrill protest Lucien expected, but of late none of Cassie's responses had been what he expected. No matter her reason, for six years she'd haunted his dreams and his desires. He needed to see her.

He tossed aside the bedclothes. She made a small sound but didn't try to shield her body from his view. Lucien breathed out in appreciation.

It wasn't dark enough to conceal her. Shadows clung to the hollow in her throat and the valley between her breasts, marking her navel and concealing the temptation that hid in the triangle of hair between her thighs. He traced the slender curve of her waist from her ribs to the gentle flare of her hips. She caught his hand, twining her fingers with his, then pulling up the coverlet until most of her was again covered.

"This is wrong," she whispered. Honesty rang in her voice.

Everything in Lucien howled in protest. She was going to confess! She couldn't do it now, not when he'd never wanted a woman as much as he wanted her.

"How can it be wrong, when we are man and wife?" he argued quietly. With those words he tossed aside the last remnants of the honorable man he'd once believed himself. Better a lie than to lose Cassie now.

"Are we?" she pleaded.

Lucien's need flared even higher. She wanted to

be persuaded to give herself to him as deeply as he wanted her pliant beneath him. Lifting the bed-clothes, he joined her in the bed. The linens were warm, smelling of fresh air, Maggie's liniment and Cassie.

Lying on his side, bracing himself on his forearm, he nestled against her. His thigh pressed to hers, his ready shaft touching the gentle curve of her belly. Rather than recoil, she shifted even closer. Lost in sensation, Lucien closed his eyes.

"Of course we're married," he said. "We've been wed these past six years."

His eyes opened. Why had he said six years when any number would have served? He sighed in resig-nation. He'd been a fool not to wed Cassie six years ago. Damn his arrogance. He'd discarded the clever, charming woman he wanted because she had a de-graded father and no fortune to instead wed a feck-less tart with blue blood and nearly as much money as he had.

"Have they been happy years?" Cassie whis-pered, running her hand across his chest, boldly ac-quainting herself with his body.

Her touch robbed Lucien of his voice, but not his need to explore her the way she was discovering him. He drew his fingers up from her hip to her waist, coming to a stop beneath her breast. Her hand against his chest stilled. He traced the circumference of her breast with a finger.

"Have we been happy?" she whispered again, her voice hoarse and trembling.

"Deliriously," he replied. *Delirious* was the perfect word for how he felt at the moment.

As he again kissed her he brushed his thumb across her breast's peak. Cassie cried out, thrusting as boldly into his caress as she'd done in the garden. The sound of her pleasure drove his own higher.

Lucien touched his lips to her breast, doing what her corset had prevented in Devanney's garden. Again she cried out, threading her fingers into his hair to hold his mouth where it was. Lucien groaned as need for her blazed past any hope of containment. He suckled like a babe, listening to the sounds of her pleasure while lost in his own.

When he could bear it no longer he took her mouth with his, then slid his fingers over the curve of her abdomen until he stroked her netherlips. She jerked against him in welcome response to his caress, as ready and eager as he. Then, she was pushing back from him, easing across the mattress away from him. Beyond control, Lucien followed her, pulling her beneath him, breathing out in satisfaction as her legs opened to him. She braced her hands against his shoulders to keep him from lying full atop her.

"But do we love each other?" she demanded, breathless with the same need driving him past sanity.

Kneeling above her, Lucien caught her hands in his. Twining his fingers with hers, he again lowered himself atop her, pressing the backs of her hands against the mattress so she could resist him no longer. He savored the feeling of her beneath him and the sensation of his shaft brushing the entrance to her womb.

With her hands trapped in his, he pressed a kiss to her lips, then another, and another until she made a greedy sound, wanting something more substantial. He smiled.

"Do we love each other? Yes, with all our hearts," he breathed against her lips. "Come, Cassie. Love me."

Of course she loved him. She'd never stopped loving him. Seduced by Lucien's sweet lies, Cassie relaxed into their pretense of a marriage and happily cradled his body atop hers.

His thighs were between hers. Her breasts flattened gloriously against the powerful expanse of his chest. She could feel the strength of his arms against her, even if his grip was gentle as he held her hands. His kiss told her how desperately he needed her.

Lifting her hips, she took his shaft into her. He gasped in quiet surprise, then thrust more deeply. The first hints of the joy Cassie had learned to cherish between husband and wife rippled over her.

Three years was a long time between joys. Wanting the sensations she knew he could make in her, she arched against him, trying to goad him into faster motion. Instead, his next thrust was slow and deliberate. Despite that, another ripple of pleasure hit her. Cassie gasped in surprise. That had never before happened.

She tugged on her trapped hands, needing to touch him. At the same time she tried to lift her legs, knowing her calves atop his thighs could make her pleasure even better. Pain sliced through her as she bent her knee. She gasped and stiffened in reaction.

He instantly stopped moving and raised himself on his forearms. "I've hurt you," he said, his deep voice thick with need. He released her hands.

"No, I've hurt me." She waited for him to move within her again. When he didn't she caught his face in her hands and lifted her head to press her mouth to his.

"Don't stop. Whatever you do, don't stop," she pleaded against his lips.

With a laughing groan, Lucien took her mouth with his, then began to move in earnest. Cassie clasped her arms around him and let him carry her into that gentle rush of joy. It came, leaving her panting and crying out, but he still moved within her.

New pressure woke within her, stunning in its intensity and promising a depth of joy she hadn't imagined possible. That pressure demanded she move. Greedy for what it promised Cassie cried out against his mouth, then clutched his arms and thrust up against him, driving him deeply within her.

He gasped, his movements quickened. His breathing grew ragged. That pressure in Cassie grew beyond all toleration. She writhed beneath him, hurting her knee and not caring that she did. All that mattered was the wave after wave of joy that crashed over her.

Shouting, Lucien rose above her and drove himself into her one last time. She swore she felt his seed enter her. Her world shattered in a wondrous explosion of pleasure.

Panting, Lucien came to rest atop her, then rolled to the side, taking her with him as he went. Breathless and cradled in his embrace, Cassie lay her head against his shoulder. Her eyes closed. At peace, feeling loved, cherished and protected, she let herself drift.

Lucien cradled Cassie close as she dropped back into her dreams. Stunned by what had just happened between them, he watched the sky through the window. Maggie hadn't closed the drapes when she'd come to retrieve Cassie's dinner tray. Every so often the scudding clouds would part to show him a fecund moon.

God help him, but the earth had again moved. Not moved, exploded. Closing his eyes, he bent his head against Cassie's and pulled her closer still.

She sighed in her sleep, her hand slipping off his arm to nestle between them. Despite the depths of his satisfaction, the feeling of her body against his stirred Lucien's desires anew. How could one woman be so different from all the others he'd bedded?

Lucien breathed out in disappointment. She couldn't be. It was that ridiculous game of theirs.

From the moment she agreed to play cards for a kiss everything had changed. He'd never felt so alive. When their game ended, as it surely must, so would his attraction to her.

Would it? The memory of what it had cost him to part from Cassie six years ago filled him. It had hurt to leave her then, when all he'd known of her was the pleasure of her presence. What would it be like to part from her now that he knew the pleasure of her presence in his bed?

He ought to take that as a warning. He ought to leave her now, riding hellbent back to Ryecroft Castle and Devanney. In the morning Jamie could take Cassie back to Philana Forster's home.

Instead, Lucien pulled the bedclothes around them, then reached up to rearrange the pillows. Cassie made a quiet sound and rolled over, turning her back to him. He fit his body against hers and closed his eyes. For as long as Cassie had "amnesia" he would remain her husband.

Chapter 16

Morning was streaming through the window unhindered by the sheerest of draperies when Cassie awoke, the sun spilling a diamond-shaped pattern of light onto the worn floorboards. The brilliant blue sky outside the glass was marred with only a few towering white clouds. A beautiful dawn, at least for the moment.

Inside the room the air was warm. Someone had stoked the fire; flames leaped and danced on the hearth. Behind her, Cassie felt Lucien's weight and warmth. The regular sound of his breathing said he slept.

She smiled, surprised at how pleased she was that he hadn't retreated to his own chamber. This was especially so since she remained unclothed. If sleeping unclothed was a novel experience for her, sleeping unclothed with a man who wasn't her husband, despite this little game they played, was beyond belief and more than a little wicked. What startled her most was that she could feel so comfortable nude in Lucien's presence.

She rolled over to face him. Her knee twinged, but not nearly as badly as it had last night. He had his back to her. The bedclothes were pushed to his waist.

Cassie's smile widened as she eyed the breadth of his bare back. The need to touch him filled her. She hesitated, stopped by her inner monitor's warning. Touching him wasn't appropriate.

She gave a tiny snort of disbelief. There was no societal mandate to cover this situation. Certainly, pretending to be a nobleman's wife while behaving as his mistress had never been a subject of any of her mother's many lectures on manners and feminine behavior. And after last night's lovemaking, Cassie's shattering pleasure and Lucien's shouts, it really was too late to retreat to the role of demure widow.

Putting her hand on his arm she measured the breadth of his shoulder with her palm, savoring the strength cloaked by his smooth skin. She paused at his nape to comb her fingers into his hair. She liked the way the strands curled lightly around her fingers almost as much as she liked her temporary freedom to touch him as she willed.

He made a sound, then stretched, arching his back and thrusting his elbow high as he pulled a fist into the curve of his neck. Cassie admired the play of muscles in his arm and across his back. New desire stirred from the embers of last night's passion.

Then he rolled over to face her and she forgot to breathe. Here was the Lucien she'd loved six years ago, the Lucien she still loved. All of yesterday's anger was gone. His eyes were so warm they were almost blue.

He smiled and her heart melted. Needing to imprint his image in her memory for all time, she touched her fingers to his temple. Following the straight line of his brow to his nose, she marked his nose's narrow length to his lips. There, she traced the outline of his mouth.

He caught her hand, touched a kiss to her fingertips, and pressed her palm against his heart. Loving him all over again, Cassie moved her fingers against the springy hair that covered his flesh there.

Amusement and pleasure flared to life in Lucien's gray eyes. He rolled onto his back, inviting her to touch him as she would. Cassie accepted, easing closer and coming up onto one elbow to better enjoy her task.

Starting with her hand on his far shoulder, she drew her palm over his chest, mapping its masculine swell and fall. Then she moved her hand downward across the flat expanse of his stomach. With her fingertip she marked the narrow path of hair that led to the part of him most male. Her hand stopped where the counterpane blocked her path.

With a quiet laugh Lucien threw back the bedclothes, exposing all of him to her touch. Embarrassment and excitement tangled in Cassie as she eyed the strong length of his legs. Her gaze fixed on his stirring shaft, curiosity getting the better of her. Although Charles had touched her he'd never wanted Cassie to touch him in return, something that led Cassie to believe she could hurt him.

"Don't ever stop," Lucien murmured, pleasure and laughter filling his voice as he echoed the words she'd said to him last night.

Wanting to please him, but nibbling her lip in hesitation, Cassie followed that line of hair until she almost reached his groin. There her caress stopped. She froze, torn between wanting to touch him and the certainty that she was worse than a tart because of what she wanted.

At last she looked at him. "I don't know how," she whispered, offering him no more explanation than that.

Lucien released a long, slow breath. Desire's heat burned in the skin along his cheekbones. His eyelids lowered as he took her hand. Placing her palm on his shaft, he curled her fingers around it, then drew her hand downward.

Cassie watched in wonderment as his skin slid beneath her hand in the most intriguing way. The sensation was surprising, almost silken. When he released his guiding hand, freeing Cassie to do as she willed, she stroked him again, this time shifting her hand a little.

Lucien's quiet sound of pleasure at her play stirred an answering throb in her. That touching him could excite her as much as it did him had stunning implications, implications Cassie was more than willing to explore. Again she stroked him, anticipating his reaction and her own.

He shifted beneath her caress, his hands flattening into the mattress as if to say that she could do as she willed with his body. Cassie's breath caught at that. Within her she felt the beginnings of her own warmth and wetness.

Freed of all restraint she set to pleasing them both, watching Lucien as she toyed with him. His eyes closed. A tiny crease marked the spot between his brows. After a moment he drew a shaking breath, then his hips shifted a little.

Cassie smiled, knowing the meaning behind that motion, at least in herself. She definitely wasn't hurting him. Remembering the joy she'd taken last night from his slow, deliberate thrusts, she practiced the same thing on him, stroking his shaft from root to tip and back.

He groaned. His eyes opened. "Kiss me," he demanded, his voice low and hoarse.

Cassie touched her mouth to his, her hair falling around them to enclose them in a golden curtain. He threaded his fingers into her hair to hold her mouth against his, then closed his other hand around her breast. Cassie shivered at his caress, the desire to take him within her growing with every breath. As her need expanded so did her inventiveness in the way she moved her hand on him.

Lucien gasped against her mouth and arched sharply beneath her. One instant Cassie was leaning above him, the next she fell back onto the mattress with a laugh, Lucien atop her. Her laugh dissolved into a glorious gasp as he thrust himself into her. He braced himself above her on his hands, the desire in his gaze searing her. His jaw tightened as he fought for control.

Smiling, Cassie shifted beneath him, taunting him.

He took a sharp breath. "Stop that," he growled.

"I thought you said I wasn't to stop." She laughed, running her hands over his chest, stroking her palms over his nipples.

He shuddered at her play, then collapsed atop her, taking her mouth with his as he thrust into her. It was Cassie's turn to arch beneath him. That startling tension from last night again unfolded. Crying out, wanting the joy she knew lurked within it, she again thrust up against him.

Lucien half laughed, half gasped against her mouth. "You have to stop. You're driving me mad with wanting you," he said between kisses.

"I can't stop," Cassie whispered, arching beneath him again, barely aware that she was speaking. All that mattered was that wondrous tension and her pursuit of pleasure. She clutched him, digging her fingers into his back, then raised her good leg until her calf rested over his buttock.

"Lord, don't stop," he said, giving himself over to the serious pursuit of ecstasy.

They found it together, Cassie's world once more shattering in joy as Lucien again cried out in release. That she could again drive him to sound only added to Cassie's enjoyment. When he relaxed atop her she held him close, feeling his heart beating against her own. He buried his head in the curve of her neck, the new growth of his beard prickling as he kissed her nape. She shivered at his play and felt him smile against her skin.

Laughing, she threw her arms around him, holding him close. As she filled her heart with him she willed this moment to continue for all time. Reality nibbled at that thought.

This would end, it had to and it wouldn't be pleasant when it did. She shoved that thought to the back of her brain, storing it for some other, more distant time. All that mattered now was Lucien and this magical place.

Rising onto his elbow, Lucien kissed her, then sat up. "Come, my sweet, it's time to begin our day."

Lucien left Cassie to pursue his own ablutions, taking his bedrobe and closing the door behind him as he went. Shortly after that, Maggie appeared, bearing stacks of clothing from the trunk Cassie shared with Eliza. Reality took another bite from Cassie's fantasy as she watched Maggie unwittingly store Eliza's clothing in the room's small dresser.

Where was Eliza now? Had she reached Edinburgh safely? Fear shot through Cassie. If she hadn't, Cassie might never know what became of her.

Maggie didn't give Cassie long to brood over her sister. Looking far less dour this morning than she had yesterday, the woman bustled back up from the kitchen with hot water and Cassie's own soap, promising a true bath come the morrow. Her tone was filled with the certainty that Cassie would be here on the morrow and all the morrows that followed—when nothing of the sort was possible.

Once Cassie had washed, Maggie examined her knee and smilingly pronounced it well on the way to healing. She applied more liniment, then bound it with such skill that there was almost no pain when Cassie hobbled. After that, Maggie helped her dress, waiting patiently as her *lady* agonized over her attire.

Whatever did a woman wear to join her temporary husband at the breakfast table after they'd shared a night of unmitigated passion? What Cassie finally chose wasn't one of her newest dresses, if the clothing she'd bought just prior to her mother's death could be called new, but a favorite, a white dress printed with a light blue check. She wondered if she chose it because it dated from her marriage to Charles and reflected a certain wifeliness. She filled its bodice opening with a net fichu embroidered with tiny flowers, laughing inwardly at herself as she did so. She was making another stab at respectability when that state was now far beyond her reach.

And then there was her hair. About half her hairpins remained in the fallen coach, and Eliza had been using Cassie's bigger combs when they parted. Maggie had no extra to share.

Cassie did her best, twisting her hair into a tight

knot, then using what pins she had left to try and hold it in place. Strands kept escaping, the knot sliding to one side or the other. At last, she donned a lacy cap to confine it.

Reality took another bite from fantasy as Cassie remembered Eliza laughingly scorning the cap as too old for her youthful sister. As satisfied with her appearance as she could be, Cassie shooed Maggie ahead of her, refusing the housekeeper's aid as she hobbled slowly down the stairs under her own power.

She entered the second-storey hall and paused, lost in pleasant surprise. The room occupied the full width and breadth of this strange tower-house. The light streaming through the broad window on its south wall made the aged floorboards glow golden and the plastered walls gleam, while the colors in the carpet looked jewel bright. What Cassie hadn't seen yesterday was that it served as both drawing room and dining room. As much as she admired the elaborately carved gate-legged table with its six chairs, the pretty blue sofas with their delicate curves, their matching tables, the little chests, her trip down the spiraling stairs left her with questions about how these things had come to be in this chamber.

Lucien, already at the table, came to his feet at her entry, smiling in welcome. Although he'd shaved, he still wore yesterday's attire without his waistcoat, which was no doubt creased beyond repair after serving as her bandage. His neckcloth was fresh, its knot a simpler version of the one he usually wore.

Reality nipped off yet another piece of this fantasy. Of course Lucien wore yesterday's clothing. His attire and his valet were still at Ryecroft Castle.

"Look at you walk on your own feet," Lucien said, coming out from behind the table to take her arm, supporting her for the remainder of her trip to the table. Cassie leaned against him, loving his nearness, but she had to laugh.

"No doubt your back is grateful for my improvement. What a chore carrying me must have been." She took her chair.

"I can't say that any part of me minded holding you close," he lied as he sat beside her. His mouth lifted into that charming lopsided grin she liked so much. Fantasy regained all the ground it had lost while she dressed.

The table was set for two, the breakfast laid upon it comprising a surprising array of food. Lucien had his beef, but there were also steaming oatmeal, fried ham, boiled eggs, breads and jams. Maggie appeared with the teapot, took two teacups from the massive cupboard behind the table, and then retreated down the stairs. Her haste almost screamed of a desire to leave her lord and lady to their own devices.

Cassie eyed the cupboard. "I must ask, since I've no recall," she said, reminding him of their game. "I can understand bringing the beds up the stairs, for they come apart. But, how did these things come to be in here?" The sweep of her hand indicated the room's furnishings.

He cocked an eyebrow at her, looking vaguely

smug. "When I"—he caught himself—"*we* acquired this place, it had only narrow slits for windows. Not surprising, given the tower's somewhat violent purpose in times past. We decided it needed more light, so we had the architect cut this window, as well as the ones in the bedrooms. Before the glass was installed we used a crane on the roof to lift the furnishings to window level, then the workmen brought them in and set them in place. Need I say there won't be any redecorating?" he finished in amusement.

But of course that's what he'd done. Cassie had seen the same sort of crane used in London's warehouses and some of the city's narrower homes. She hadn't expected to see it here in the hinterlands, any more than she would have expected Lucien to own such an odd little house.

"What do we do here?" She sipped at her tea, comfortable in their game for the moment.

"We indulge ourselves in privacy," Lucien replied, cutting a piece of meat.

"Do we?" Cassie murmured, intrigued, watching him eat and wondering if he knew what he'd revealed to her. "Do we do anything here other than hide?"

He shot her a sharp sidelong look. "We fish in our stream, which runs behind the house."

Cassie made a face at that. Early in her marriage when she was yet committed to being a good country wife she'd once followed Charles to the local stream. The fishing part had been enjoyable enough, but then she'd caught something. Charles had insisted she be a true fisherman, or woman as the case was. She had to remove her own fish from her hook. Just thinking about that day was enough to make her stomach turn.

"I hope I don't," she said.

Amusement again flared in Lucien's eyes. "You most certainly do. You're a better sport than I am."

Cassie sent him a narrow-eyed look. Lucien's taunting smile dared her to spar with him. That brought back the joy of their waltz. Reality retreated, leaving her once again completely swathed in their fantasy.

"Well, it's a shame I don't remember, because it's not often a wife outdoes her husband. And, more's the shame that my knee will keep me away from the stream for such a long time," she said, meeting his feint with one of her own.

Lucien's face blossomed in pleasure. "I wouldn't dream of denying you. We'll go today. I can carry you on my back."

Cassie nodded. "What a wondrous husband you are to me, willing to serve as my pack mule. I cannot thank you enough, my love." The endearment slipped off her tongue, both unexpected and startlingly sincere in its intent.

Something flashed in Lucien's eyes. He leaned near and before Cassie realized what he intended, pressed a kiss to her nape. His effort won him a gasp and a shiver. He smiled against her neck, then put his mouth over her ear.

"I far prefer it when you carry me," he whispered.

Cassie stifled her laugh. So did she. God help her, but so did she.

"Lucien, darling, I'd do anything for you, but I hardly think I could carry you all the way down to that stream and the fish we both so love," she retorted, purposefully misunderstanding him.

Amusement rumbled deep in his chest. He straightened. "Eat your breakfast. There's something I want to show you."

She wasn't ready to quit sparring. "Really? I cannot imagine there's anything left to see that you haven't already shown me this morning."

Lucien's eyes closed. He bowed his head. Cassie frowned, wondering if she'd gone too far.

In the next instant he threw down his fork and knife, then shoved his chair away from the table. Before she knew what he intended he'd snatched her around the waist and dragged her onto his lap. She squealed, her tea sloshing, then settled in his arms.

"What are you doing?" she cried, both amused and stirred. He wanted her again. She could feel it.

Desire's warmth burned in Lucien's gray eyes. His smile was almost a leer.

"What else, but answering your challenge. Shall we go see if there's anything I haven't yet shown you? Consider if you will, the idea of my bearing your weight instead of you bearing mine."

She caught her breath as his words awoke a vivid image. Until this moment she'd never considered such a thing. That she might be the one to control their pleasure left her awash in a wanton rush of need.

"Touché," she breathed against the skin of his throat. After touching her lips to the spot where his jaw met his neck, she leaned away from him and sent him her most innocent look.

"What a shame I've lost my memory and can't remember you ever bearing my weight, save, of course, for when you carried me yesterday after my accident. Do I often call upon you to do that sort of thing?" she asked.

"All the time," he assured her, then leaned down until his lips brushed hers as he spoke. "I'm feeling particularly capable this morn. Perhaps we should retreat immediately and attempt it? Who knows, but it might just jog your broken memories."

Lucien's kiss left Cassie breathless with longing to rush back up to her bedchamber and turn his suggestion into a reality. Rather than indulge her he retrieved his utensils and began to cut a piece of his beef.

"What are you doing?" she protested as he reached around her and lifted the bite to his mouth.

"Eating," he replied when he'd swallowed. "I think I'll need all my strength today." He began to cut another piece.

"If you want to eat shouldn't I move back to my own chair?" Cassie demanded, not really wanting to move. "This is hardly an efficient way to consume a meal."

"On the contrary," he replied, then offered her the piece he'd just cut. "This way two can eat as efficiently as one."

Cassie fought her smile. She opened her mouth. He dropped the meat into it and began to cut himself another piece as if he truly believed what he said.

Suppressing a laugh, she reached for a slice of bread, slathered it with butter and jam, then broke off a corner and offered it to him. A smile filled his eyes as he accepted the bite.

"What did I tell you? Nothing but efficiency in this household," he announced.

So their breakfast continued, she fed him bread and jam while he offered her his beef. When they left the table, long after the tea was ice cold and the oatmeal had hardened almost to stone, Cassie's stomach was full but the rest of her insisted it was starving.

"Now, come with me," Lucien said, taking her arm and leading her to the stairwell.

Chapter 17

Cassie started up the stairs ahead of Lucien. He let her take the time her knee needed. She paused when she reached the landing that led to their bedchamber. When had she come to think of it as theirs?

"Not here," Lucien said with a laugh, and stepped past her.

Much to her disappointment, he continued up the stairs to the trap door in the roof. He threw open the small door, revealing a square of August sky. The wind whistled down into the stairwell, tugging at Cassie's cap and making her hems flutter.

"What are we doing?" she asked.

"Going onto the roof," he replied as if that were a commonplace destination.

Lucien must have seen the doubt in her face. He smiled. "It's not as strange as it sounds. You'll see."

Climbing the last steps, he disappeared through the door. Not as sanguine about this as he, Cassie followed, one hand on her cap to keep the wind from taking it. When she could look through the opening she saw Lucien standing in a tiny path between the slope of the rising roof and the top of the house's forward wall, which extended above the roof to the height of his knees. Lucien offered his hand to steady her as she joined him, then closed the trap door.

The wind pressed Cassie's dress and petticoat to her legs. Her cap strained at her hand. Wisps of hair escaped its confinement to snake about her face.

Turning her, Lucien pointed to a set of tiny steps leading up to a seat that jutted out from the house's stone chimney. "That's where we're going."

With Lucien right behind her, his guiding hand on her elbow, Cassie started toward the seat. Rather than slate tiles the narrow path she followed was covered in stone rough enough to offer good footing. She glanced over the roof's edge to the ground. Her stomach danced at the drop even though the low wall protected her. She settled thankfully onto the seat. The bulk of the chimney sheltered her from the wind while the warmth of the fires burning in the house radiated from the stones behind her.

"Why is there a seat here?" she asked, astounded.

"Quite a trick, eh?" Lucien looked smug at her surprise. "Jamie tells me that during less peaceful times in the past, the Scots and the English spent their days stealing from one another. If a man wanted to keep kin and kine safe, he needed someone on watch. Thus the seat."

He waved her to her feet. "If I sit first we can share it."

Cassie stood, forgetting to hold her cap. The wind snatched it, sending the lacy thing swirling out of her reach. It soared, its ribbons streaming behind it like the tails on a kite. Her few pins slipped and her hair unraveled to writhe around her.

"My cap," she cried.

Lucien grabbed her as if he feared she intended to leap after it. "Let it go," he said, pulling her down to sit between his legs. "We're private here. You don't need it."

It was the sort of thing a husband might say to his wife. Still acting the part of her mate, he ran his fingers through her tumbled hair, carefully gathering it into a tail before draping it in front of her shoulder. Once her hair was out of the way, he wrapped his arms around her, then pulled her back against his chest.

"Look at that. There are days when I vow I can see all the way to England," he said.

"Can we really?" Somehow Cassie had thought England more distant. She scanned the long valley and the rise of the hills at its opposite end.

Lucien laughed, his amusement rumbling against her back. "No, it's just a fancy of mine. I like the look of the land here. There's something secretive in the way the hills jut and turn, streams and hidden valleys in their folds. It's not at all settled and predictable like the landscape around Graceton Castle. When I look out over this I'm reminded that I'm only a man in God's eye, something Lord Graceton has a tendency to forget."

Leaning back against him, Cassie turned her head away from the view he so admired to watch him instead. It was the second time he'd offered her something deeply personal about himself. He glanced at her and smiled, the expression warm and intimate, even loving.

Not wanting to disturb the tenor of the moment, she once more turned her gaze out over the plain before them. Here and there she could see flashes of movement and color, people going about their daily chores. A hunting hawk soared. Clouds trundled overhead, forming and reforming in the sky above them.

The vastness of the land's lift and roll did indeed make her feel small. Her gaze caught on a hill that stood about half as tall as the ones behind Lucien's tower. It dominated the head of the valley, the river curling around its foot. Something stood against its side, square and gray. She squinted. It was a house, a large one.

"What's that?" she asked, pointing.

He looked where she indicated. "Nothing important," he said and caught her chin to turn her face away from it.

Too late. Cassie recognized Ettrick House. With that, reality began to gulp up fantasy.

Had Eliza yet reached Edinburgh? If she had, then she would have sent her message to Cassie, directing it to Philana. That would be Philana's first inkling that Cassie had separated from her family and that Eliza didn't know where she was.

Cassie's heart twisted at the thought of Philana, frantic, wondering where Cassie was and what sort of harm had come to her. How could she selfishly remain here with Lucien, indulging in sin, when Philana might be eating her heart with worry? She had to send a message.

No, it wasn't a message she needed to send to Philana, but herself. She needed to leave Lucien.

Cassie relaxed into Lucien's embrace, her eyes closed. The beat of his heart against her back pleaded with her not to go. Only here in his arms, it seemed to say, would she be safe.

And desired. And loved.

Her eyes opened. Last night he'd asked her to love him. At the time she'd thought it nothing more than words spewed in the heat of passion. She knew from Charles that a man would promise anything in the moments before he achieved his own release.

Once more turning her head against Lucien's shoulder, she studied his profile. His features were almost as rugged as the landscape. His gray gaze was intent as he watched the distant hills, but there was something peaceful in his expression. It was a startling change from the anger of yesterday and even more startling after the bleakness she'd seen in his face at the abbey.

What if his words of last night had been the first of

these unknowing revelations of his? That he might truly love her only made Cassie all the more desperate to stay.

Eliza may not yet have reached Edinburgh. Or, even if she had, she may not have yet sent a message to Philana. After all, Roland had their horses to sell. It might take him days to arrange their passage to America. Eliza wouldn't write until she was certain of the ship and sailing dates. Surely Cassie could stay for one day, for one more night.

"Lucien, tell me about our marriage," she asked, her voice shaking as she fought to hold onto their shared pretense.

Blast it all. Why hadn't he remembered that Ettrick House could be seen from this vantage point? Lucien tightened his arms around Cassie, battling to keep reality at bay the same way she must be.

He rested his chin on her shoulder. "What is there to say? We met during your season. I wooed you. You married me."

"Why did you woo me?" she asked, her voice softening.

She didn't ask that just because she wanted him to restore their fantasy. She wanted an explanation for why he'd ceased to pursue her six years ago. It was no more than she deserved and something he should have given her at the time of his retreat. Bittersweet feelings welled.

"I have to admit that your beauty first drew me." He paused to touch a kiss to her cheek, then added,

"You remain just as beautiful, despite your many years."

He meant it as a gentle jab, aimed at her for the role of dowager she'd tried to play at Devanney's party. The corner of her mouth lifted. She shot him a sidelong glance, her brown eyes warm and filled with affection for him.

"Kind of you to say," she murmured.

"Not kind, truthful," Lucien replied, wanting her affection as much now as he had six years ago. He moved a hand to cup her breast despite the barrier of her corset. She caught her breath and shifted into his caress. Pleasure and something else roared through him, stunning in its power and leaving him astounded by his change since yesterday.

Where was his anger at the Cassie who'd used him at the card table? To what corner had his determination to expose her fled? Mostly, he wanted to know how he could be certain that she would offer no further betrayals.

That was the problem. He couldn't be certain. Which Cassie did he hold in his arms? Was she the manipulating card sharp, a woman who would surely use him for her own ends? Or was she the Cassie who'd kissed him in the garden, a woman driven by her passions and the needs of her body? He wanted to believe that their repartee at the breakfast table this morning proved that something remained of the bold but upright Cassie he'd known six years ago.

"And it was for my great beauty that you married me?" she asked, aiming dry amusement at herself.

"No, it was your wit," he said, speaking the truth. It was her wit that had bound him to her side until her father's request for a loan. "No one has ever made me laugh the way you do, Cassie."

She looked at him. In her gaze he saw that she accepted what he'd said as the truth, the reason for his attraction, both then and now. But despite his professed attraction he hadn't married her. He expected recrimination, but instead her dark eyes were soft with acceptance and understanding. She knew why he hadn't offered for her hand, and forgave him for it.

Would that he could forgive himself for abandoning her and their affection. Lucien sighed and again turned his gaze to the distant horizon. Like today's clear air, time's passage offered new perspective. He didn't like what he saw of the man he'd been when he first met Cassie. It wasn't what Sir Roland had done that caused Lucien to reject marriage to her, although he still recoiled at the thought of a connection to her father. If he'd been willing to take the time, he could have devised a way to control the little wastrel.

He hadn't been willing. Rather his pride hadn't been willing. Six years ago he'd turned his back on her because he gave more weight to the opinions of his peers than his own heart. The irony pierced him to the core. Rather than wed the *unworthy* woman he wanted, he'd arranged a match with a woman who was his supposed peer. And instead of happiness in the union, he'd found himself saddled with a feather-brained woman-child who'd disliked him as much as he disliked her. There was something sad in knowing he hadn't liked his wife enough to care whom she bedded, only that her actions didn't reflect badly on him.

In the end the result had left him the butt of his peers' jests, the very fate he'd thought to avoid by rejecting Cassie. What sort of fool did that make him? Lucien closed his eyes. What sort of fool considered trading a noble tart for a card sharp whose wanton presence here was no less immoral than his wife's behavior?

Cassie stirred in his embrace, leaning her head back against his shoulder. Lucien opened his eyes to find her watching him. A small frown marred her brow as if she sensed his black thoughts.

"So, was our wedding a great event?" she asked, taking her turn in this game of theirs.

"No," he said, more than willing to spin a tale for both their benefits if it meant turning his back on a stingingly bitter reality, even for just a few minutes. "It was a small, intimate affair, just our families. I didn't want to share you with anyone."

Amusement sparked in her eyes. "Really. And I didn't object, demanding something more grand and hundreds of guests?"

He laughed. "You did, but I held firm. In the end you said you loved me too much to risk losing my affection over the size of our cake."

"That sounds like me," she agreed, the wind making wisps of hair dance around her face. "I should want to cherish your affection for me above all else."

Her words made his heart shift oddly in his chest. In that instant he found himself wanting to cherish her affection for all his days. He battled that misbegotten desire with every bit of strength he owned, only now recognizing the danger in this game of theirs. Perhaps things would have been different if he'd married her six years ago, but that time had come and gone. He was no longer the Lucien who'd courted her while she was most surely Cassie, the sharp and liar, the woman who'd used him to her advantage at Devanney's house party two days ago.

He reminded himself that her family had abandoned her on the road yesterday. Roland couldn't have known who it was following them. That meant he'd been confident in Cassie's ability to protect herself by whatever means necessary. Hadn't she proved herself adept with her ploy of amnesia, albeit much to Lucien's pleasure?

No, the only place he could be Cassie's husband was in this fantasy of theirs. His heart, beaten but not destroyed, protested. It insisted he was wrong about Cassie, that she was still the woman he'd loved.

Loved? The word caught Lucien by surprise. If that's where his thoughts bent, then it was past time to end this game and return Cassie to Philana Forster.

But how could he let her go before he knew what it was like to bear her weight upon him in bed?

Blast it. Blast her. Blast him. Rightly or wrongly, he wasn't ready to let her go. He wanted to spend the day holding her, then another night making love to her until neither one of them could remember who they were.

He lowered his head to touch his lips to the place where her neck met her shoulder. There was pleasure in her sigh. Staring out at the landscape, she leaned her head to the side, offering him more to kiss.

Another day. Another night. That would have to be enough. Once the dawn came on the morrow he'd do what he must and put an end to their game.

Cassie tilted her head to the side as Lucien kissed her, her heart aching. She felt his battle to hold onto their pretense in the way his arms tightened around her. He wasn't yet ready to let her go any more than she was ready to leave him.

But when the moment for revelation came she knew he'd let her go, doing so without hesitation, just as he'd done six years ago, no matter how greatly he regretted not having offered for her then. It was stunning how much the thought of losing Lucien a second time hurt. How was it possible that she could have such depth of feeling for him, when he'd only been back in her life for a few days?

"It's a sad thing when a woman must ask her husband about her particulars," Cassie said, striving to conceal what ached in her.

"Is there more you'd like to know?" he asked, eager to return to their game and ignore what stood as clearly before them as Ettrick House across the valley.

Cassie looked up into his face, her fantasy torn to shreds by reality's wind. Staying here with him was risking more than she could afford to wager. It was time to retreat to Philana's house and find some other way to avoid Lord Bucksden.

"What is it?" Lucien asked, his brows lifted. The same pain that tortured her lurked in his gaze. There was some comfort in knowing that he wasn't succeeding at distraction any more than she was.

Cassie sighed. She had to leave, but she couldn't go while he still believed she was a card sharp. She only hoped that one revelation didn't lead to another. How in the world could she ever explain what her father had done without provoking Lucien's eternal disgust?

"There's nothing left for you to tell me," she said, "but there's something I must tell you."

The pain in his gaze flared. His gray eyes chilled until they were icy again. "Not yet," he started to protest.

She touched her fingertips to his lips to stop him. Even knowing he would eventually abandon her again didn't stop Cassie from loving Lucien more than she ever dreamed possible.

"Yes, now. Will you play cards with me?"

Chapter 18

"And you don't want to buy that hand?" Lucien asked from his seat at the head of the bed, pointing to the tiny pile of cards, the third hand, that lay between them near the center of the bed. He wore only his shirt and buckskin breeches, having removed his coat and pulled off his boots. His long legs were stretched out before him, ankles crossed.

"No," Cassie replied, feeling far less comfortable than he looked. She sat sideways at the foot of the bed, her back against the footboard, her uninjured leg curled beneath her.

Lucien had insisted on holding their card game behind her bedroom's closed door. Cassie suspected this had to do with pride. He didn't want either of his servants to come upon them as she bested him at cards again and again.

"Why not?" Lucien demanded as intensely as the first time he'd asked that question, eight rounds of Speculation ago.

"Because there's no trump in it," Cassie replied with worried certainty. If the tightness of his expression was any indication, then repetition wasn't improving his disposition. He hadn't taken this demonstration well from the start.

Lucien turned over the third hand between them, revealing all three of its cards. Just as she'd said, there was no trump in it. He looked at her, confusion and disbelief darkening his brow.

"How can you know that?" he demanded again.

Miserable, all Cassie could do was shrug. "I just know," she whispered.

Frowning, he crossed his arms and leaned back against the headboard. "And what's in my hand?"

Again Cassie shrugged, wishing with all her heart she'd allowed their fantasy to persist a little longer. She wanted the Lucien who'd smiled at her this morning. This was the Lucien who'd been so angry at her that he'd followed her from Ryecroft Castle, determined to wreak vengeance.

"The only trump you've got is the exposed card," she replied, her voice shaking.

Lucien reached to the three cards next to his hip, one up, two down. Moving the upper card, he flipped over the lower two and huffed in disbelief. There was no other trump in his hand.

"What's in yours?" His eyes were steely, his voice hard.

"One trump," she said. She turned them over to show him.

"A draw," he announced, then again shook his head. "How can you do this?"

Her misery growing, Cassie stared at her over-turned cards. "I don't know how to explain it to you any better than I already have. I just know. There's only one thing that I can explain. My skill's sharper when I'm near you."

"I beg your pardon?" There was a trace of outrage in his voice. His brows were high on his forehead, his eyes wide in surprise.

Cassie cursed herself for an idiot. He no doubt thought she blamed him. It was too late to retract her comment.

"Something's different when I'm close to you. That's what happened the other night when we were playing with Colonel Egremont and Squire Kerr. I sat next to you and—"

She stopped, then tried again, seeking some way to make sense of what had happened that night when there was nothing sensible about it. "All I could think of was you, how upset you'd been at the abbey, and what had happened. While I was busy thinking of you I wasn't paying attention to what happened at the table. I didn't notice I was win-ning," she said, her voice trailing into a whisper. "Even after I noticed I couldn't stop myself."

To her surprise his expression softened. His laugh

was a bare breath. Some of the Lucien she loved returned.

"I've noticed that about you. You have trouble stopping once you've set yourself on a particular course. Not that I find the trait totally disagreeable," he added. The corner of his mouth lifted, the returning warmth in his eyes reminding her of this morning.

Embarrassment burned in Cassie's cheeks. Wicked and wrong as it was, she longed to once more make use of this bed the way they had already twice done. She could hardly credit herself for such a fool. As if again holding Lucien in her arms and against her body would change anything. After this demonstration ended he'd return her to Philana's house and abandon her without a backward glance.

The softness faded from his expression. "Before that night you had better control over this skill? That means you really did lose to me on purpose on the first night."

Cassie wanted to melt through the mattress and hide beneath the bed. "I did. I had no choice. You were so certain your abilities at the table outmatched mine that I had to lose. If I'd forced you to give up that kiss you would have challenged my abilities just as you did the second time we played. I needed your five pounds and I couldn't afford a rematch," she told him. "You were going to demand it. I could see it in the way your eyes creased and the tightness of your jaw."

His expression hardened again. "So all you originally wanted from me was access to my purse?"

Shamed that he would equate her with some London whore, Cassie buried her face in her hands. This was awful and so much more complicated than she expected. The mattress shifted as he left his end of the bed to join her. She jerked in surprise when he stroked her back.

"I beg your pardon," Lucien said, withdrawing his caress. "That was uncalled for on my part. Only by lying to myself can I pretend you didn't want to give me my kiss as much as I wanted to take it from you."

Cassie dared to look up at him. Harshness lingered in his expression, but some of the man who'd asked her to love him last night peered at her from behind his angry mask.

She sighed. "Know that it cost me dearly to take those coins from you. Because of what I did in the corridor outside our rooms, because of that kiss in the garden, I lost your respect."

Confusion flashed in his gaze. He reached up to push a loose tress behind her ear. "If keeping my respect was so important to you, then why did you do any of it?"

Ah, but he didn't contradict her to say she still owned his respect. How could he, after what they'd done here these last hours? She fought her hurt. He'd asked for an explanation. After all that had happened he deserved one, but this wasn't going to be nearly as easy as explaining her skill to him.

She started at the beginning. "It's a long story. Aunt Philana arranged for me and my family to attend Lord Ryecroft's house party because there would be gambling. Philana wanted to give me a chance to use my skill for profit at the tables, something I'd never before done," she added.

Lucien's eyes chilled. The harshness returned to his face. Cassie's heart quirked. She plowed hastily on, trying to explain if not excuse herself.

"Philana warned me that I could only use my skill if I agreed to take less than the nightly limit. Not that I would have done any differently. I wouldn't have considered attempting it at all if not for my father." Sighing, she stopped, having reached the point where her confession became horribly sordid.

"Did Lady Forster tell my cousin about you and your skill?" Lucien demanded.

His question surprised Cassie. "I don't know. I can imagine Philana admitting as much, not wanting to misuse Lord Ryecroft's hospitality."

The corners of Lucien's mouth quivered. "Of course she told him. Why else would he point you out to me on the night of the ball? That bleater. He wanted me at the card table with you, hoping you'd do to me just what you did. Oh, he'll pay dearly for this one. I don't know when or how I'll manage it, but he'll pay."

It was Cassie's turn for confusion. Lucien's brows quirked. There was new easiness in his expression and posture.

"My cousin and I have a history of pranks," he explained. "I'm wagering that you and this skill of yours are Devanney's latest trick against me. So if you came to my cousin's house party expecting to win a small fortune, why didn't Lady Forster give you something to use as a stake? Why arrange a game between us for that kiss?"

"She didn't give me anything because I arrived at Ryecroft Castle with coins of my own," Cassie said, then let words fall from her lips before she lost the courage to speak them. "It was my purse you took from my father on the party's first night."

When the words were out Cassie again wanted to melt through the mattress and curl up beneath the bed. It was hard to believe there was anything left to stir her shame, not after all she'd done these past weeks. Telling Lucien that her father was not just a wastrel but a thief proved there was.

If admitting this much was so awful, what would it feel like to tell Lucien that her father had used Eliza as the ante in a game with Bucksden? Cassie's soul writhed at the thought.

Pity for Cassie surged through Lucien. He watched her blush fade and misery again darken her eyes. She sighed, then turned her gaze to the counterpane, her hair falling forward to hide her face from his view.

Lucien resisted his urge to take her into his arms. It had cost her dearly to tell him what her father had done. One touch, one misguided word of sympathy, the offer of so much as a farthing to aid her, and he'd destroy what little dignity she had left.

Nor did he need any more explanation to understand why Cassie needed to gamble at Devanney's party. It was enough to know her sire was Roland Conningsby, a man who had stolen more from his daughter than just her purse. Hadn't Roland squandered both his daughters' inheritance?

Cassie's explanation left Lucien with more questions than it answered. Premier among them was who this woman seated beside him might be. Lucien no longer believed she was Cassie the Sharp, but he now wondered how well he'd known the Cassie of six years ago.

And why, if her plan had been to win a little each night, accumulating a tidy sum over the duration of the party, had she taken him for three hundred and sixty pounds, all in one sitting? She had to have known that making such a show of her skill would end her chance of ever again using her abilities to aid her family.

"This thing you do with cards, you've always been able to do it?" he asked, still struggling to make sense of her odd ability.

She nodded without looking up, her face yet cloaked by her hair. Suspicion nagged at Lucien. He caught her chin and turned her face up toward his, wondering if she was hiding something from him.

Tears of shame glistened in her eyes. Suspicion died. He couldn't bear her pain. Lucien drew her against his side, his arm around her. She sat tensely next to him as if she'd rather he not hold her.

"But, how do you do it? Help me understand," he asked again, only to watch helplessness fill Cassie's gaze. She wasn't being evasive. She truly didn't know how to answer his question.

He reframed it. "Do you stare at the backs of the cards and know what they are?"

She gave a tiny negative shake of her head. "Usually I only sense the strength or weakness of a hand." Her voice was soft. "Sometimes, as when I played with Squire Kerr and his companions after you left me in the garden, the other players are so intent on their hands that they almost tell me what they hold. I see it in the set of their jaws and shoulders, in the way they arrange their hands or lift their eyebrows. Or in their odd gestures."

She took his hand and touched the golden signet ring he wore on his third finger. "When you think your hand isn't strong enough you twist your ring."

"I don't," Lucien retorted, piqued that she would think him so careless a gambler. "It won't even go all the way around my finger."

To prove his point he closed his hand and tried to turn the ring. The raised face hit his smallest finger. For it to go any farther he'd have to open his fingers. He knew better than to make so obvious a nervous gesture at the card table.

She offered a tiny smile. "But it does shift. You move it back and forth with your thumb."

Frowning, Lucien drew his thumb across the back of his ring, only to find a spot worn smooth on the band. As he touched the ring there it twisted, striking his little finger. Without thought he shifted it back in place, doing it by moving his smallest finger. The motion had a familiar feel, one of long habit, like an unconscious gesture often made.

Comprehension drove the breath from Lucien.

Cassie wasn't doing anything eerie or untoward, at least not in assessing the players at a table. Reading an opponent was a skill every card player worth his salt ought to own. The only difference with Cassie was that she seemed to be doing it better than anyone Lucien had ever met.

"How did you know there was trump in those hands?" he demanded.

She grimaced a little, one shoulder rising as she again struggled to explain herself to him.

"Tell me step by step," Lucien suggested. "Don't assess, just talk."

Cassie nodded, then frowned in concentration. "Well, with this last hand we were nearly through the deck and all but three spades had been played. So when spades came up trump for that last hand I knew there could only be two more. Once I know what cards I need to find, my mind begins to suggest where things might be. Sometimes, as when we gamed with the squire and the colonel, all I actually sense is when to play with abandon and when I shouldn't wager."

Relief and amusement welled in Lucien, the pair of emotions tangling and growing until he had to laugh. He pulled Cassie closer to him. She pressed her hands against his chest, trying to keep her distance.

"Why are you laughing?" she demanded, straining to free herself.

He let her go. She immediately slipped off the bed to stand at its side. Still chuckling, Lucien followed her, sitting on the bed's edge and looking up at her.

"I'm laughing because I find myself well and truly humbled. You're no sharp," he told her. "Devanney and Percy were right. All you did the other night was outplay me. You have my deepest apology."

Astonishment and relief flashed in Cassie's eyes. Some of the tension drained from her. "Thank you," she replied, "but I still hope I never again face a match like that one with you, Colonel Egremont and Squire Kerr. I really couldn't stop winning, no matter how hard I tried."

Something warm awoke deep in Lucien. He came to his feet. She took a backward step, again maintaining a decent distance between them. That only made Lucien smile.

"So my nearness drives you to distraction, does it?" he asked.

Heat flared in Cassie's cheeks, not shame this time. She took another backward step. "I think I've fed your conceit enough for one day."

Her insistence on keeping him at arm's length spurred the rest of Lucien's questions. "If you aren't a sharp, then why did you flee Ryecroft after our match? Running only convinced me you'd done something you didn't wish to explain. You should have stayed on at the party, playing every night, keeping your winnings modest. Not even Duchess Eleanor could have done you any harm with so many witnesses all observing you and finding nothing amiss. Your combined winnings would have given you a tidy sum."

Cassie smiled nervously. She clasped her hands

before her. "I couldn't bear the thought of you glowering at me every night. What if I lost everything because of your glares?"

Everything about her screamed of falsehoods. That only brought Lucien back to the lie that had resulted in them sharing this bedchamber. "Why, when I found you, did you tell me you didn't know who you were?"

She wrung her hands. Her brow pinched. Reluctance filled the lines of her body. He knew the moment she decided she had to give him the truth. Her brown eyes began to glisten.

"Because I'm a coward. I knew how angry you were with me and that you'd demand I explain my skill. I didn't think you'd believe the truth. It seemed easier not to be who I was, and not to remember what had happened between us."

Lucien nodded, accepting her excuse. If not for the past night and their game of marriage he wouldn't have believed she was anything but Cassie the Sharp.

"I still don't understand why you ran from Devanney after he'd offered you his protection. You *did* realize that's what he'd done when he declared he saw no cheating at our the table?" Devanney had no choice but to shield Cassie, especially if he'd put her in the position of being accused of wrongdoing in the first place.

"Nor can I comprehend why your family abandoned you," Lucien continued. That wasn't exactly true. He could understand her father leaving her, but not her sister. He wouldn't soon forget the look of affection they'd shared when Cassie sent Elizabeth from Devanney's drawing room.

Cassie gave a quiet cry and turned her back on him. Surprised at her reaction, Lucien joined her. She looked up at him, mortification filling her face.

"I cannot bear to tell you. It's so horrible," she whispered.

Lucien gave a breath of a laugh. As if anything could be worse than his own story. He waited, curiosity prodding him.

At last, Cassie drew a shattered breath. "Just before we were to leave London to come north Lord Bucksden tapped on our door. He'd come to claim my sister. My father had wagered Eliza in a card game the previous night and lost her. Before Lord Bucksden could take Eliza I hit the earl with our urn and knocked him senseless," she finished in a rush.

Rage exploded in Lucien at the mention of that dastard's name, his anger no less powerful or devastating than when Percy mentioned Bucksden at the abbey. Instantly, he turned away, not wanting Cassie to see him lose control. Moving to the window, he stared unseeing over the stark landscape as he battled his emotions.

Cassie and her sister had been right to run. That Bucksden risked a duel by coming into Lucien's reach said he wouldn't stop until he'd wreaked vengeance on the woman who'd humiliated him. Outrage grew, expanding to include Roland Conningsby.

What sort of son of a bitch gambled away a woman under his protection? What sort of father left his daughter on the road when the man who wanted to do her harm might have been chasing them? The thought of what might have happened to Cassie if the man following her had been the earl drove Lucien's emotions beyond any constraint.

His fists clenched. His heart contracted in fear for Cassie. He wanted to pound his fists against the wall and scream to high heaven that Bucksden had to die.

But why wait for Bucksden to make an attempt to hurt Cassie? Lucien already had just cause to challenge the man, and the earl was at hand. All he needed was a second, and that he had in Devanney.

Lucien turned toward the door, ready to ride hell-bent for Ryecroft Castle and his cousin, only to freeze as his imagination provided the many ways Bucksden could inflict pain on an unprotected Cassie. Blast, but this house was too isolated. He couldn't leave Cassie here with only Jamie and Maggie to stand between her and Bucksden's wrath.

If she couldn't stay here, then he had to take her with him to Devanney. Lucien once more looked out the window, this time seeing the vast expanse of land before him. Impossible! He only had two horses, his and Jamie's. The thought of the two of them meeting Bucksden in the open between here and Ryecroft Castle was problematic. Bucksden wouldn't be traveling alone; he never did.

What, then? Lucien closed his eyes, trying to think, only to be suffused with fear for Cassie all over again. Blast it all. He wouldn't have the control he craved until he knew Cassie was safe, but he couldn't make Cassie safe without calling men here to protect her, and that meant exposing the wrong they'd done here to their unforgiving world.

Chapter 19

Cassie flinched as Lucien turned his back to her. All the joy of this morning dissolved into painful irony. He was disgusted by her story. Who wouldn't be? Once again, her father's debauched behavior had driven Lucien from her. A fantasy marriage was the only union she'd ever have with him.

She couldn't say Lucien's reaction surprised her, not after all the wrongs she'd done him—seducing him into gambling with her, taking his money, pretending amnesia—and now telling him just how low her father had fallen. That didn't stop a part of her from pining for the Lucien of that morning. She blinked back tears. She hadn't begged him for explanations the last time he'd rejected her and she wouldn't do it now. Nor would she cry over losing him, at least not in front of him.

Bereft, she let the rest of her explanation fall from her lips. "Eliza overheard Mr. Percy say he'd seen Lord Bucksden staying nearby. That's why I accepted your challenge to play. I needed enough to buy three passages to America. Then the carriage fell and I hurt my knee and couldn't mount the horse. So I sent Eliza on to Edinburgh ahead of me, knowing that of the two of us Lord Bucksden can do her the greater harm. Then, there you were. I used you, Lucien. I could think of no place safer to hide from Lord Bucksden than with you."

Lucien didn't shift from his tense stance at the window. His hands remained clenched at his side. His shoulders were taut. He said nothing.

Cassie's grief grew. It was done. Their "marriage" was revealed for the pretense it was; the affection he'd shown her today proved to be nothing but a sham.

The sounds of women's voices raised in argument echoed up from the kitchen. Cassie's heart filled her throat. She turned toward the closed bedroom door. Footsteps rang in the stairwell.

"Hie, ye'll come back down here," Maggie shouted. "Ye've no right t'intrude."

"I have every right. Lord Graceton has kidnapped my niece," Philana shouted back.

Cassie gasped. Throwing open the bedchamber door, she hobbled to the landing, then started down the steps just as her aunt came around the last turn of the spiral stair. Philana wore sensible green cotton beneath a summer pelisse made of linen. The plumes on her bonnet fair quivered in outrage as indignation blazed in her blue eyes. Her eyes narrowed and one eyebrow rose as she took in Cassie's loosened hair.

"It's not what you think, Philana," Cassie cried, reaching behind her to frantically roll her hair into a knot, one that couldn't hold. Her pins remained on the roof where they'd fallen when the wind had taken her cap.

"It no longer matters what I think, does it?" Philana retorted, her voice harsh. Her gaze slipped over Cassie's shoulder. "I expected better of you, Lord Graceton."

Cassie whirled to find Lucien on the landing. His expression was as frigid as his gaze. Then she saw him the way Philana must, dressed in his shirt sleeves and stockinged feet. He looked like a man who'd done, well, what they'd done.

Why hadn't he stayed in the bedroom? Cassie could have pretended to Philana that he wasn't in the house. Then again, why should Lucien hide? It wouldn't be the end of his world when the tale of their interlude spread.

He stared at Philana for a moment. Some of the ice thawed from his face. Cassie swore she saw relief flicker through his eyes.

His reaction was like a knife to the chest. He was glad Philana had found them. He was ready to be free of her.

"You're the one who sent me after her, Lady Forster," he replied, his deep voice lacking all inflection. "After that you cannot pretend surprise to find us together now. You obviously knew she was here. Or is it by magic you happen to come here to claim her?"

Cassie wanted to melt into a puddle on the stone floor as she understood. Philana and her misguided matchmaking! Not even the threat facing Eliza had stopped her aunt from trying one last time to bring Cassie and Lucien together. Only this time Philana had succeeded, no doubt beyond all her expectations.

"It's the future, not the past at issue now," Philana retorted, then shook a chiding finger at him. "How dare you make a captive of my injured niece. You *will* call at Ettrick House in two hours time to make this right." Subtle triumph filled her voice.

Cassie's mortification consumed her as Philana threatened Lucien with forced marriage. Now Lucien would believe Cassie a tawdry tart who'd laid a sexual trap for him. If there'd been any hope left that Lucien would ever again be the tender man she'd been with on the roof, or for them to have the marriage he'd described to her, it was dead.

Having delivered her ultimatum, Philana turned her attention to Cassie. "You'll come with me this instant," she commanded, then started down the steps.

Cassie did as she was told, leaving Lucien without a backward glance. There was no need. The Lucien she'd known wasn't the nobleman who stood behind her.

Maggie waited in the kitchen, glaring knives at

Philana. After Maggie handed Cassie her bonnet and pelisse, cleaned of yesterday's mud, Cassie followed Philana out of the house. Again the wind caught her, molding her garments to her body and toying with her still-loosened hair. Waiting in the courtyard was a fine carriage drawn by four horses. Its canvas top had been lowered so its passengers might enjoy the warmth of this fine August day. A pair of footmen waited at its back, while a coachman held the horses. Jamie stood at the carriage's door, ready to help them into the vehicle.

As Philana accepted Jamie's hand, Cassie threw her pelisse over one shoulder and donned her bonnet, stuffing her hair into it. The kitchen door rattled as it opened.

Cassie told herself not to do it, but like Lot's wife, the urge was irresistible. She looked behind her. Her breath caught. Lucien stood in the opening, shrugging into his coat, his boots once more on his feet. He wore no hat; the wind shifted the honeyed strands of his hair around his face.

Despite all the wrong they'd done between them and his new coldness, Cassie's body reacted to his presence. Her admiration for him was deeper now that she was so well acquainted with the pleasure they could make between them. The longing to once again feel his arms around her tangled with the shame of the wrong that they'd done, what Philana had done, what Roland had done.

Watching her in return, Lucien stepped out of the door. Although there was no change in his flat, frozen expression, something in his posture spoke to her. In that instant Cassie fooled herself into believing that he loved her the same way she loved him, idiot that she was. She let her momentary delusion convince her that he intended to ask her to marry him and make right what they'd done wrong.

Lucien's gaze shifted from her to the carriage. He gave an approving nod, then turned. Without so much as a promising gesture in her direction, he started for the tiny paddock behind the house, where his and Jamie's horses grazed.

Cassie's last remaining hope of a union with Lucien shattered like her mother's urn. Cassie turned her back on him, telling herself she was more than ready to be done with Lord Graceton, his anger, his fantasies and this strange little tower house of his.

Jamie helped her into the carriage. Cassie joined Philana on the forward facing seat, her pelisse across her lap. Nearness to her meddling aunt woke an anger strong enough to drive off her pain. Cassie indulged herself in the emotion, content for the moment to blame Philana for all that had happened.

"There's no call to look s'glum, Mrs. Marston. Some of us here will dearly miss ye," Jamie told Cassie as he closed the carriage door.

"Jamie, where's my saddle?" Lucien shouted from the paddock.

"Coming, m'lord," Jamie shouted, offering Cassie a cheerful grin before sprinting to help his employer.

The coachman climbed onto his perch and gave the reins a sharp snap. The carriage jerked into motion. Cassie slid on the seat. Her pelisse tumbled onto the carriage floor. She left it there.

With every nerve on edge she waited for her aunt's first disparaging word. She'd open fire in return, venting all her well-deserved indignation onto Philana for what she'd helped to orchestrate. However, Philana refused to cooperate. She kept her head turned away from Cassie, watched the passing landscape and acted as if nothing were amiss.

The carriage bumped along over rut, hole and mound. The faint track leading away from the tower house was boggy, the bright green sod peeled back by wheel and hoof to reveal the rich, black velvet of the underlying earth. Hunched on his perch, the coachman had his hat pulled down around his ears to prevent the wind from taking it. His coattails, hanging over the back of his seat, fluttered. The horses' manes and tails flew like pennants. Cassie's bonnet ribbons streamed.

Still, Philana persisted in her silence. Cassie could bear it no longer. "How could you send Lord Graceton chasing after us? How could you continue trying to force this match after I'd asked you not to?" she demanded.

"How could I not send him after you? You and your sister were in dire need of a protector. I'll not apologize for what I did. Wasn't he there to take care of you after you were injured?" Philana calmly replied, still staring straight ahead.

That left Cassie looking at her profile from the tip of her nose to her chin. The rest of her face was hidden by her bonnet's wide brim. The corner of Philana's mouth lifted. It was half of a tiny, triumphant smile.

Cassie made a sound that mingled disbelief and frustration. "I could have done with a little less caretaking."

Philana turned her head to look at Cassie. That triumph of hers filled both corners of her mouth and radiated from her blue eyes. "Is that so? Would you care to tell me the sort of excess you experienced?"

"I don't care to tell you anything." Cassie crossed her arms and turned her head so her own bonnet's brim blocked Philana's view of her face.

"A shame, that. I'd love to hear the details," her aunt replied, not at all perturbed by Cassie's retort.

"Not bloody likely," Cassie whispered to herself. The profanity should have relieved her outrage. It didn't work. "You sent him after me," she charged, despising herself when her voice quivered. "You hoped that Lucien would—" She caught herself before she confessed more than she wanted Philana to know.

"Lucien, is he?" her aunt murmured, that triumph now filling her voice as well as her smile and eyes. "And what, pray tell, might I have hoped would happen while you were in his custody?"

Cassie marshaled her defenses. "More than he did, which was to rescue me from a fallen coach and treat my injuries."

Philana laughed. "Oh come now, I'm not so simple as that. Consider this, Cassie. A confession on your part will go far to encourage Lord Graceton in the direction he must go."

"I won't marry him," Cassie said in blunt and

painful refusal. The union Philana proposed wasn't a marriage, but a prison. Cassie would rather die in shame than face a cold, resentful Lucien for all the days of her life.

Philana turned her head so she could again look at Cassie. Concern folded her brow and dimmed that awful confidence of hers. "Of course you'll marry him. You must. You spent the night with him. There's no choice left to either of you."

"There is a choice," Cassie said. "I can live out the rest of my life as a tart."

Shock flattened Philana's expression. "Don't even jest about that, Cassie!"

"If that's my only escape from marriage to Lord Graceton, so be it," Cassie snapped back. The words came out more harshly than she intended. She added, more gently, "I won't marry him, because he doesn't want to marry me."

"Doesn't want you?" her aunt retorted in disbelief. "Why, the man fair eats you with his eyes every time he looks at you."

Cassie rubbed at her head as it began to ache. "That's a different sort of wanting, Philana, and you know it."

"You can lie to yourself all you want, child. I know better," her aunt persisted. "You'll see. He'll be at our doorstep this afternoon, ready to offer his proposal."

With Philana's words Cassie's indignation collapsed, its fiery warmth abandoning her the same way that Lucien had now twice done. She turned her attention into her lap and her clasped hands. Her fingers were bare. Maggie had forgotten to give her her gloves.

"He won't, Philana," Cassie said, appalled. Her voice no longer merely quivered, it was into a full tremble. She wouldn't cry over him, she just wouldn't. She swallowed the lump in her throat. "He didn't offer for me six years ago, and he won't offer for me now."

Philana caught her by the arm, pulling her around on the seat until they faced each other. Her blue eyes sharp, the old woman studied Cassie. The folds on her brow deepened as her confidence began to lag.

"You're serious, Cassie. You really don't believe he'll offer marriage. How can you be so certain about what he plans now or what he planned in the past? Cards you know. I'm not convinced that you read men's hearts nearly as well."

Cassie closed her eyes, returning in her memory to the tower house's roof. In her imagination she again felt Lucien's arms around her and heard his gentle voice as he told her the tale of their "marriage," how her beauty had attracted him, how she had accepted his proposal and given way to his desire for a simple marriage ceremony. He'd spun the scenario out of his heart and the well of his regrets. He'd wanted to marry her six years ago; she knew that as surely as she knew she loved him. That is, Lucien had wanted their marriage, until common sense, and Sir Roland Conningsby, had intervened.

"I can be certain because he told me," Cassie replied, opening her eyes and clutching the front of her gown as if her grip would prevent her heart from hurting any more than it already did.

Philana shook her head, looking worried indeed. "You're wrong. You have to be."

"Why, because you will it to be otherwise?" Cassie returned. "Well, not even your will is enough to usurp the wrong my father did me, both six years ago and last week. According to Charles, it was my father who drove Lord Graceton from my side. He tried to profit off Lord Graceton's affection for me by asking for a loan. Charles was present at the club that night and overheard their conversation."

Charles, who had been the least of Cassie's suitors at the time, had related the story to her with no little triumph. It was a small cruelty, but one she'd later forgiven. Charles had been desperately in love with her and thrilled at the opportunity to dispense with a serious rival.

"Think about it, Philana. If Lord Graceton turned his back on me because he didn't care to deal with my father six years ago, how much more willing could he be to deal with him now? Just before you arrived I was telling Lord Graceton about Eliza and Lord Bucksden." The pain of losing Lucien a second time again sliced through Cassie. "You saw him, Philana. Did the man who met you on the landing look at all pleased about being trapped into marriage by your ploy?"

The furrow in Philana's brow grew deeper. There was nothing left of her confidence or her triumph.

"Could I really be so wrong?" she murmured,

then horror flashed in her eyes. "Oh Lord, what have I done to you?"

Her aunt's reaction only brought the reality of Cassie's ruination home to her, and how she'd brought it all onto herself. "Nothing, Philana," she gasped, "you did nothing. If there's blame for anything that's happened it lies solely at my own feet. Nor should you worry over me. I won't be here long enough to suffer for what I've done. If Eliza hasn't already sent you a message from Edinburgh, she will do so soon. She was to inform me of sailing dates for my trip to America."

"Oh," Philana said, the tiny word fraught with consternation.

Terror for her sister shot through Cassie. "Philana, what is it? Has something happened to Eliza?"

Philana waved away Cassie's panic. "Nothing at all. She's safe, just not in Edinburgh."

"Not in Edinburgh? Then where?" Cassie demanded, forgetting everything else in her worry over her sister.

Philana fiddled with her gloves, resettling them onto her hands. "At Ettrick House."

"She's *what*!" Cassie cried. "Is she mad? She cannot be there. Lord Bucksden must have learned by now that we were visiting you."

The tears Cassie had refused to shed on Lucien's behalf now filled her eyes. This couldn't be happening, not to her and not to Eliza. How could her sister have squandered what little edge she had over the earl? God help them, but they were once again within Lord Bucksden's reach.

Philana put a soothing hand on Cassie's arm. "Cassie, darling, don't fret. She's safe, surrounded by my entire household. The earl is an awful, immoral man, but he's hardly likely to burn down my house to reach her. Nor should you be upset with Eliza. It was love for you that brought her back to me. She told me yesterday that she and your father continued on until her conscience could bear it no longer, then returned for you, only to find nothing left of you but your hairpins. They didn't know that it was Lord Graceton who'd taken you, so they rushed to Ettrick House, pleading that we search the neighborhood for you. That's when Rob, here," she pointed to one of the footman riding behind her, "returned from his visit to Mrs. Laidlaw, Lord Graceton's housekeeper. That's how I knew where you were and that you were safe with Lord Graceton."

Cassie buried her face in her hands. Only she *hadn't* been safe with Lucien.

"Oh, Philana," she cried. "If only I'd killed the earl and stayed in London to face justice. A public trial and death by hanging would have been so much easier to endure."

Chapter 20

With the crunch of gravel, Philana's carriage came to a halt before the sweeping steps that led to her home's front door. Maggie's nephew hopped down from his perch to aid them. As Cassie exited the carriage her hair slid from the confinement of her bonnet, again spilling around her. She tore off her useless hat, lifted her skirts and started up the steps, battling her need to scold Eliza for returning and wracking her brain for another way to save her sister.

The front door opened before she reached it. Philana's butler, Robson, small and balding, dressed in black, stepped out onto the porch. Nervous furrows lined his naked brow. He offered Cassie a little bow. They knew each other well enough from Cassie's visits over the years.

Behind Robson were two burly men. They
stopped just in front of the doorway, inadvertently
blocking Cassie's access to the house. One was a
footman, wearing his glossy satin attire and powdered wig. The other looked to be a man better acquainted with the out-of-doors, a gardener or a
parker. His shirt was undyed linen, his brown jacket
was patched, his knee breeches made of leather,
while his boots were meant for tromping through
mud. An untidy nest of hair escaped his well-worn
hat.

Robson nervously clasped his hands before him.
"Lady Forster, it happened just as you said it might,"
he called down to Philana as she mounted the stairs
behind Cassie. "He came shortly after you departed
as if he'd been waiting for you to leave."

That froze Cassie's feet to the porch floor. She
knew without doubt who *he* was. Lord Bucksden
had found them.

Robson's expression was one of guarded worry. "I
did as you instructed, my lady, informing him that I
believed you'd gone to Ryecroft Castle to participate
in the house party and didn't expect you until this
evening. He was none too pleased to hear that and
even less pleased when I refused to let him wait for
your return. Alex, here," Robson indicated the
roughhewn outdoorsman, "says that he's retreated
for the moment to the inn in the village," he said.
"The earl and the two ruffians who ride with him are
presently taking a meal there. My lady, he may well
have set a lad or someone to watch the track. That
means he'll soon know that you are returned." Rob-

son paused, shaking his head in concern. "You've misjudged him, my lady. He won't be put off by any means. I think it will take force to prevent him from entering when he returns."

Panic shot through Cassie at the thought of having to physically battle Bucksden in order to save Eliza. She forgot about scolding her sister. She needed Eliza safe in her arms.

Her heart pounding, Cassie pushed past the men, thrusting into Ettrick House's entry hall, a long, narrow chamber that occupied the middle third of the square house's length. White marble floor tiles inset with tiny black squares and fluted half columns gave the impression of an ancient temple.

"Eliza?" she cried as the others followed her inside the house.

"Cassie!" her sister called back and thrust her head out of the doorway to Philana's drawing room to the right of the entryway.

Eliza's face was blotchy and her eyes reddened. Affection tugged at Cassie's heart. Eliza wore her blue sprigged dress, the garment surprisingly unwrinkled considering how Eliza had stuffed it into her satchel. Despite the tribulations in Eliza's life at the moment she was still girl enough not to neglect a single item of her attire. She'd even taken the time to tie a wide blue ribbon around her head to hold back her hair.

Roland leaned out from behind his daughter. He looked wretched, the skin on his face sallow and sagging. Deep, dark circles marked his blue eyes.

His hair looked uncombed and he wore no coat over his maroon waistcoat and shirt. The only coat he'd taken with him from the coach was the jacket of his driving attire. That wasn't an appropriate garment for a gentleman to wear in Philana's house.

When Eliza saw Cassie she forgot decorum and raced into the entry hall. Cassie dropped her bonnet and held out her arms. Eliza embraced her with a half laugh, half sob.

"God be praised," she breathed into Cassie's shoulder. "You're safe. I've been dying by increments, imagining you friendless and injured, or worse."

"We'll want tea and sherry in the drawing room, Robson," Philana requested. "Alex, go to the storeroom over the stable. I believe that's where we stored Squire Forster's hunting weapons after his passing."

"No," Cassie whispered in horror, clasping Eliza even closer to her.

Where a moment ago Robson had worried over hurting an earl, he now grinned. "You heard her, Alex," he said, herding both men ahead of him in the direction of the service chambers. "We're to arm ourselves."

Cassie caught Philana by the arm. "You cannot shoot at Lord Bucksden. Dear God, but what if he's killed? Your servants will hang for it."

Philana snorted. "You speak as if any of those old weapons will fire. Even if they could they're useless without gunpowder and shot, and we keep none of that in this house, although I dare say I could put my hands on it if I were to ask any of my tenants." She paused as if considering, then shook her head. "No, we don't need it, not if my only purpose is to give Lord Bucksden pause. This is my house. If I refuse to admit him, then he will not come in."

Eliza straightened in Cassie's embrace, her arm tightening around her sister. "I hope you don't depend on any pretense of manners to stop Lord Bucksden," she said, her voice quavering.

Philana blinked in surprise. "I beg your pardon?"

"What Eliza means is that you cannot depend on Lord Bucksden to act like a gentleman," Cassie replied, her voice sounding thready to her own ears. "When we didn't answer the door in London he opened it himself and walked in as if it were his residence, not ours."

Philana whirled, strode to her door and shot the bolt. Iron rang against iron as the bar hit the plate. "Go," she commanded both Cassie and Eliza. "Into the drawing room with both of you. I'll see that the rest of the doors are bolted."

Cassie and Eliza made their way to the drawing room, Eliza clinging to her older sister like a limpet. Roland backed out of the doorway as they entered, taking a stance next to one of the room's small, inlaid chests. Cassie breathed in the warmth and security that had always permeated Philana's drawing room. She loved the cozy chamber, having spent many a happy hour in its embrace.

Nothing had changed in here for all the years

Cassie had known Philana, except for the increasing number of Philana's mementos—seashells, the odd dried nosegay, bits of ancient statuary and glass collected from her trips to Italy—that lined the tops of the door and window frames. The wall covering was the same creamy linen printed with a faint red design. The same portraits and miniatures, Philana's many august ancestors and some of Squire Forster's not so renown progenitors, decorated the walls and sat upon the chests. Mrs. C, Philana's cat, sat on the cushioned bay window seat. She meowed in recognition, calling to Cassie as she always did.

With her arm still around Eliza, Cassie started for the window and the cat. Her sister gave a quiet gasp and pulled free of Cassie's arm. "Not there," she whispered, sounding frantic.

"Eliza, you cannot truly be afraid of being seen, not from here," Cassie protested. "First of all, Lord Bucksden already knows you're in the house. Why else would he demand entry while Philana was gone, except to separate you from your protector? Secondly, we're a storey above the ground. We'll see him long before he sees us."

As far as Cassie was concerned it was far better to know when Lord Bucksden arrived than to sit in nervous ignorance, awaiting a tap on the door. The color and life drained from Eliza's face. She backed away from Cassie, wringing her hands.

"I don't want to see him. Cassie, you didn't hear him. When Robson refused to let him wait he cursed and threatened Philana's destruction and poor Robson's life." Tears began to again trail down Eliza's cheeks. "What am I to do, Cassie? Tell me what's right."

Horror ate up all the pleasure Cassie had taken in this chamber. Eliza wanted permission to give herself to Bucksden! Fear for her sister drove the chastising words Cassie had forestalled from her mouth.

"Why didn't you continue on to Edinburgh? If you had, you wouldn't be here, contemplating how best to answer that question."

"I had to come back. I couldn't bear to go on without you," Eliza protested, then swiped at her eyes with the back of her hand. "Excuse me. I need a fresh handkerchief," she whispered, and hurried from the room.

Cassie wanted to kick herself. As if Eliza didn't have enough worries at the moment. Here she was, making it worse.

"For shame, Cassie," Roland chided, his voice stern as he stepped out of his quiet corner to confront his eldest daughter.

Anger tore through Cassie. "How dare you speak so to me," she said, letting her outrage act as a barrier to fear. "You abdicated any right to act as my father the moment you joined Lord Bucksden at that gaming table."

"I dare because Eliza doesn't deserve your harshness," he replied, sounding nothing at all like the Roland Cassie knew. "If you must blame someone for what happens here today, blame me. I brought Eliza back here. She was so distraught at the thought of you alone and unprotected on the road that I feared she'd fall ill from worry."

"Are you mad?" Cassie cried. "Far better that Eliza ailed in some distant and protected inn than to have you return here into Bucksden's very arms."

The little color remaining in her father's face disappeared. He looked ancient, but not frail. He didn't cringe. Nor did he fidget, not with his waistcoat buttons, not with his watch chain, not even tapping his foot.

"I've already accepted your disgust as my due, but save your tirade for another day," Roland retorted. "Our only concern now is your safety, and Eliza's.

Cassie chaffed at being in the unusual position of enduring her father's rightful scorn. "Until this morning the safest place for Eliza was on a ship bound for America. Why did you give way to her? Eliza's still a child. You are her father. You should have taken her to Edinburgh."

"You're so certain of that?" It wasn't a question as much as another chide. Roland shook his head. "If you are, then it's proof that you haven't been thinking clearly of late. I saw the reality of it once Eliza and I were alone on the track. What would have happened to us if we'd come upon Lord Bucksden?"

"But he didn't know where we were yesterday," Cassie protested.

Roland crossed the room to catch his eldest daughter by the arms. "You're still not thinking, Cassie. Not even if we go all the way to America will fleeing Lord Bucksden resolve the wrong I've done.

We must confront him. We must find a way to end this, with you safe from Lord Bucksden's ire and Eliza free of his claim."

Glaring at him, Cassie wrenched free. She wasn't certain she liked this new father of hers. What right did he have to tell her what to do? Guiding their family had been her job these last two years since her mother's death.

"Only a few days ago you were begging me to concoct any sort of scheme to save us. Now here you are complaining about the one I created." That she'd paid for the scheme with her pride made it doubly hard to consider that she might have been wrong to propose it. "If you don't like my ideas, come up with one of your own," she continued, only to be disgusted at herself. She sounded peevish. That was beneath her, even in their present situation.

Shaking his head, Roland stepped back from her, his arms crossed. His expression hardened with new determination. "I do have some ideas, but nothing I'm ready to share with you. Now, tell me what happened after we parted. Lady Forster said Lord Graceton was the man following us and that footman of hers said you were with him as of yesterday afternoon. Where were you, and did Lord Graceton do you any wrong?"

His question drove the breath from Cassie, half because she hadn't expected her father to care what had become of her and half because his question brought back all the pain of Lucien's second abandonment. "I spent the night at Lord Graceton's fishing lodge. By morning I again had movement in my knee." She framed her reply to sound as if she'd spent the night doing nothing more than recuperating.

"Did he do you any wrong?" Roland insisted, sounding very much like a concerned father, when until today he'd been anything but that.

Cassie opened her mouth to lie to him only to discover that she couldn't. She wanted to remember what little joy she'd taken in that interlude. Even to speak obliquely about the events was to make them seem tawdry. Nor did she want to share any of what happened with her sire, now that there seemed to be two of him to distrust. The father she'd long known might well use the knowledge of Lucien's supposed misbehavior to extort money from a new, rich source. As for the man who stood before her at present, Cassie very much feared he intended to add his voice to Philana's in demanding marriage.

She shook her head. "Now is no time for that, Papa. Our efforts are better spent devising a new way to escape Lord Bucksden."

"Or, a way to deter him until we can remove you and Eliza from harm's way," Philana added, sweeping into the room. She removed her bonnet, setting it on the chest by the door, then unbuttoned her gray pelisse. "Do you know anything about guns, Sir Roland?"

Roland nodded. "I do."

"Good, then could you assist my servants? They presently assemble Squire Forster's weapons in the kitchen. While I'm certain Alex is more than competent I'd like to know that the result won't win Lord Bucksden's laughter rather than his trepidation." Philana's tone was that of a woman discussing the condition of her garden rather than the defense of her embattled house guests.

"But of course," Roland said.

He turned a final, narrow-eyed look on Cassie, his expression saying that her answer hadn't distracted him, then he left the drawing room. Cassie waited until he'd closed the door before she gave way to her panic. She threw herself into her aunt's arms.

"Philana, what are we going to do? Bucksden will be back and I cannot believe he'll be deterred by guns that don't fire."

Philana offered her a quick hug, then set Cassie back from her. "What you're going to do is go upstairs and soothe your sister," she said. "I heard her crying when I passed the stairs. As for me, I'm going to write a note to my neighbors, begging their assistance."

"No!" Cassie cried. "How will you explain to them why you have to resist Lord Bucksden? You can't, not without ruining Eliza for all time. What if such a show of force thwarts him and he chooses to wreak his vengeance by spilling the tale before so many eager ears?"

Philana huffed and crossed her arms, eyeing Cassie in disgust. "This is what happens when certain folk allow those ninnyhammers who reign at Almacks to do their thinking for them: Otherwise sensible people become convinced that facades and appearances are more important than reality. Why should what your father did with Lord Bucksden affect Eliza in any way?"

Pain shot through Cassie. "How can you say that to me after I just told you how my father's behavior drove Lord Graceton from me?"

"Lord Graceton is but one man, Cassie," Philana replied with a shake of her head. "And I say more fool him if he cannot rise above his prejudice to do the bidding of his heart. May he continue to rot in his loneliness." Having cursed Lucien, Philana crossed the room to the delicate little desk in the corner.

"You're right to think that Eliza won't be courted by earls and dukes should this tale spread. However, that can't be hardship to her," she called over her shoulder to Cassie, opening the desk's front. "I doubt Eliza ever expected to make such a brilliant match. There are other worthy men. Why, judging from the whirlwind that made Eliza its center at the house party, I'd warrant there are at least five eligible men in this neighborhood alone who'd happily look past Sir Roland's behavior to have her."

Cassie stared at her aunt's back, stunned and wanting desperately to believe. Could rescuing Eliza from Lord Bucksden really be as simple as exposing the truth of what he and Roland had done? Everything in her recoiled at the thought of people laughing at them from behind their hands—or worse, forbidding their daughters from having anything to do with the Conningsby girls. Perhaps Philana was right. Perhaps all would be forgotten when the next scandal broke.

"Of course, you'd have to allow me to provide Eliza a dowry," Philana added.

Cassie's hopes crashed. Of course it wasn't as simple as Philana made it sound. Her aunt's solution was almost the same one she'd applied to Cassie and Lucien, except instead of trapping a husband for Eliza she meant to buy one. A purchased husband could be no better than a trapped and seething Lucien.

Robson opened the door. "Tea, my lady," he announced as a footman carried the service into the chamber.

"Thank you, Robson," Philana said, her back still to the room. "Be a dear, Cassie, and go fetch Eliza. She could use a bit of something to steady her nerves. I gave her the blue room."

Feeling lost and hopeless, Cassie did as Philana bid, climbing the house's central stair to the second storey. Ettrick House was a big square with a central stairway. That meant landings stretched the depth of the house. On the second storey that gave Cassie access to four doorways, two on either side of the stairwell. The door to Eliza's bedroom was ajar. It creaked a little as Cassie pushed it aside to enter.

Philana's blue room was in fact blue and white. Below the chair rail the wood paneling had been painted white. Framed Chinese panels, their dark blue design painted on white silk, covered the paler blue wall above the railing. Sun streamed in through a wide, deepset window, its open shutters painted white, while the draperies were the color of the sky. The creamy carpet was woven with a dark blue pattern and the little dressing table of pale wood had a top of lapis lazuli. Even the air in the close room was blue, filled with the faint scent of lavender, in which all Philana's linens were stored.

Eliza, dressed in blue and white, lay on the bed, staring up at the pale blue brocade canopy above her. Cassie glanced down at herself. She was also in blue and white. They might as well have been part of the room's furnishings.

"You're right. I shouldn't have begged Papa to come back for you," Eliza said, still staring above her and sounding miserable. She shifted her clenched fingers around the ball of her sodden handkerchief.

"No, I'm wrong," Cassie replied with a sigh, then came to sit beside Eliza on the bed. The mattress supports creaked. "We should never have parted. As for you I won't have you contemplate for an instant sacrificing yourself to save us. It's no longer just a matter of satisfying Papa's debt, you know."

Eliza drew a steadying breath, then rolled onto her side to put her head in Cassie's lap. "I know," she whispered, then laughed. It sounded more like a hiccough. "Until he came to the door I'd been picturing myself as quite the tragic heroine, giving up my freedom to save you."

Her words teased a quiet laugh from Cassie. Hadn't she thought herself that same heroine as Lucien carried her to his lodge? How easy it had been to cloak her heart's own longing to hold him close in sanctimonious trappings.

"Sometimes you're too pure for this mundane plane," she told Eliza, brushing a few wayward golden hairs from her sister's forehead. "It's enough to know you'd give your life for me, sweetheart. I don't need you to actually do it."

"He frightened me, Cassie," Eliza whispered. New tears glistened in her eyes.

"Can't we turn back time?" she begged softly. "I want to return to Ryecroft Castle. I want to dance and laugh, and eat wondrous meals. I want Mr. Percy and Colonel Egremont to pretend to fight over me."

She turned her head in Cassie's lap to look up at her. "That will all end for me now, won't it?"

Still wanting to save her sister more than anything, Cassie lifted Eliza to embrace her, avoiding the question at the same time. Eliza lay her head on Cassie's shoulder.

"If only you'd been at that card table with Lord Bucksden, Cassie. You wouldn't have lost that game," she whispered.

Then, wiping her face with her handkerchief, she pushed free of Cassie's hold to touch a strand of her sister's loosened hair and gave a watery smile. "Good heavens, look at you all atangle. Come to the dressing table and I'll make something a little neater of this for you."

Cassie hesitated, having experienced Eliza's handiwork in the past.

"Please, it will give me something to do," Eliza pleaded.

Chapter 21

Mud-spattered and sweat-stained, Lucien drew his foaming mount to a halt before Ryecroft Castle's main doorway. His rage hadn't abated in spite of his reckless ride. At least he knew Cassie was safe, if only for the moment. Thank God for that meddling old woman and her three servants. That had to have been manpower enough to make Buckden cautious about approaching them during their short ride to Ettrick House. He hoped.

Dismounting, he climbed the few steps to the front door and threw it open without knocking. The startled footman staggered back from him, gawking, his face framed by his wig's powdered curls. "My lord?"

"Where is he?" Lucien demanded. It took all his will not to bellow.

The footman blinked rapidly as if trying to make sense of the question. "I believe Lord Ryecroft is still in his chamber, my lord," the servant stuttered.

Of course Devanney was still in his chamber. It wasn't yet noon and his cousin hadn't had the pleasure of being caressed awake just after dawn. Remembering this morning brought with it another reminder, one of how much it would hurt to lose Cassie, and how much more it would hurt if he somehow lost her to Bucksden's violence.

"See to my horse," Lucien commanded, then strode into Devanney's home, spewing muck with every step as he made his way to the stairs leading to the residential wing.

Lady Barbara and the duchess were just descending. Dressed this morning in a cream gown with a narrow red stripe, Eleanor had left off her ostentatious diamonds to make do with rubies at her throat, breast, wrist and fingers. She even wore a gaudy ornament of the same blood-colored stones on her pink turban; it was a dragonfly rising out of a great spray of gems. The insect, set on a tiny spring, quivered and danced with her every movement.

Barbara, descending ahead of her mother, wore blushing pink, the color complementing her dark hair and eyes. She sucked in her breath when she saw Lucien, then pressed herself to the banister to let him pass. Her worried gaze never left his face.

Not so Eleanor. The duchess stood her ground, expecting Lucien to stand aside. Incapable of playing the game of pleasantries at the moment, he merely shifted on the step to push past her, giving her a sidelong glance as he went.

Eleanor's eyes widened in outrage. She turned on the stairs to face him. "What sort of arrogance is this, my lord? Going about filthy and half dressed, showing no respect to your betters? Didn't you learn anything from your first brush with scandal three years ago? I suppose not, or you wouldn't now be sniffing after riffraff. I hope you'll take a lesson from the catastrophe your inattention to class has caused."

Lucien froze as the noblewoman again denigrated Cassie. Rage exploded beyond any hope of containment. He turned to face the disdainful duchess, who still stood on the step below him.

Lady Barbara gasped. She slipped down another step, grabbing her mother's arm as she went. "Come, madam," she whispered, "let him be."

Eleanor shook free of her daughter's grasp. "We aren't going anywhere until Lord Graceton awards me the show of respect that is my due," she trumpeted.

"And what sort of respect do you believe your due, Your Grace?" Lucien demanded. His words almost cut his tongue as they left it.

Eleanor's eyes narrowed. Her chin lifted. "I am a duchess. You will bow to me."

Sneering, Lucien bent slightly, offering her the barest show of respect possible. "This I do in honor of your station, but not you."

Eleanor's jaw dropped in astonishment. Bright color washed her face. Not so Barbara. She blanched and again tugged on her mother's arm.

"He's bowed, madam. Come," she urged. "Let's be on to breakfast."

"I will not!" Eleanor almost shouted. "He will beg my pardon, or I vow I'll—"

"You'll what?" Lucien snarled. "Destroy my repute? Didn't you just tell me it was too late for that? Nor will I beg your pardon for speaking the truth. Your Grace, you are a sorry excuse for a woman. You demand respect from those around you, giving them nothing but your scorn and rudeness in return. How one such as you wrought such sweetness in a daughter is beyond my comprehension."

Eleanor jerked as if he'd struck her. The color left her face, leaving her looking grayed and old. Her mouth opened and closed, but no sound emanated.

"Lucien!" Devanney bellowed, using his cousin's given name, an intimacy they'd given up when they went off to school, leaving behind boyhood notions to become men.

Lucien turned his back on the duchess. Adam Devanney stood on the second-storey landing, looking every inch the country gentleman in his brown waistcoat, fawn trousers and sturdy shoes. His shirt collar lay open, yet awaiting his neckcloth. His cuffs still lacked their closing studs.

"I need a second, Devanney," Lucien said, climbing the last few stairs to join him.

Rather than reply, his cousin caught him by the arm. Devanney's grip was tight enough to bruise. "Pardon, Your Grace," he said to the still-gaping Eleanor. "My cousin isn't himself at the moment. If you'll excuse?"

Devanney gave the duchess no chance to respond, only dragged Lucien the few steps it took to reach his bedchamber, then shoved him through the doorway. Growling, Lucien whirled on his cousin. Devanney gave him another shove, driving him deeper into the room.

"Out, Watson," he shouted at his valet.

Watson beat a hasty retreat, slamming the door behind him. Yet another of Devanney's shoves propelled Lucien into the center of the room. Lucien's boot heel caught on the edge of the carpet. Stumbling a little, he pivoted, only to be blinded by midmorning light reflecting off the many gilded and silken surfaces in the room.

"What the hell was that, Lucien?" Devanney demanded angrily, standing between Lucien and the door. "You don't come into my house and insult my family, no matter how much Eleanor might have deserved that speech of yours."

Lucien's anger soared to new heights as Devanney again spoke to him as if he were a child. "A second, Adam," he retorted, using Devanney's given name in return. "Either you'll serve me or you won't. Answer now. If you refuse, I mean to go to Percy."

Devanney threw his arms wide in frustration. "For what duel? What are you talking about?"

"I mean to kill Bucksden," Lucien replied, cold satisfaction washing over him.

It couldn't happen soon enough. Rapiers. He wanted to feel the blade enter Bucksden's flesh. He wanted the warmth of the earl's blood on his hands and to feel the man shudder as he perished beneath Lucien's death blow.

"My second, Adam," he said again. It was a command, not a request. Percy would serve, but not as well as Devanney.

Devanney's eyes narrowed, his fists clenched. "Talk to me, Lucien. Tell me how you met Bucksden and what happened to put you on course for this duel. What happened to your need for a son to carry on your name?"

The instant his cousin spoke the words, Lucien's heritage wrapped itself around him like a rope. He had no right to risk his life before he'd done his duty to Graceton's line. Siring a son to follow him was the only unmitigatable requirement of his title.

As duty bound Lucien's hands and restricted his ability to protect the woman he loved, he threw back his head. "I don't care about my godforsaken title. Bucksden dies today before he has a chance to hurt Cassie," he shouted.

Raising his voice was the wrong thing to do. Some of what boiled in him eased. That left room for calmer thoughts. Damn Adam. He was going to talk him out of this, when a duel to the death was the only way to make Cassie safe.

"Sit and tell me everything," his cousin commanded, giving Lucien another push, this time toward the settee at the end of his bed.

Lucien collided with the cushioned bench, then sidestepped it. "I've waited three years to do this,

Adam. I'm done waiting. If you don't wish to be my second, so be it. Let me leave so I may ask elsewhere."

He took a step toward the door. Devanney shifted to block his path and lifted his fists, a boxer's stance. "If you want to leave you'll have to knock me senseless. That will be no mean feat, even for you. Think about it, Lucien. What if battling me leaves you too injured to face Bucksden? Ten minutes. The earl won't disappear. Now, tell me what's happened or hit me!"

For one insane moment Lucien closed his fists, considering the latter option. He reined in the urge. Devanney knew very well that once Lucien began to strike out he'd regain control of what raged in him.

"This is the thanks I get for risking my life to drag you, half dead, out of France?" Lucien snarled, attacking with words since he didn't dare use his fists.

His cousin's expression froze. "A low blow, cuz, inexcusable even when you're like this. I didn't ask you to come for me, or to force Lord Candlestone to release me from his service, any more than I asked for the burden of this godbedamned title I have to wear."

Regret tore a great hole in Lucien's anger. He hadn't meant to hurt his cousin. What had been solid and unmovable in the previous moment dissolved, turning into smoke and slipping through his fingers. Damn Adam. He was going to win, whether by action or by speech, when Lucien wanted to remain blindingly angry until Bucksden was dead and Cassie was safe.

"No more distractions. I have to meet Bucksden, Devanney," Lucien said, only to realize all was already lost if he'd reverted to using his cousin's family name.

"They're not my distractions, they're yours," Devanney snarled back, dropping his fists.

Lucien took a step toward him and the door behind him. Devanney knew him well enough not to hit him. Instead, he gave Lucien another, far gentler shove, sending him again toward the settee.

"Listen to me, Hollier, you pigheaded idiot," he growled. "If you truly considered the wrong Bucksden did you as heinous as you protest, then you'd have called him out three years ago. You didn't. You might be able to fool yourself, but you can't fool me. All you ever expected to accomplish with your threat was to keep Bucksden worried and on edge. Now, damn you, tell me what's changed!" he roared.

The truth in Devanney's words drove Lucien down onto the settee. The last of his rage evaporated, leaving only fear for Cassie in its wake. He didn't know how to protect Cassie except to kill Bucksden. But killing Bucksden meant risking his own life, a luxury tradition wouldn't allow him.

"Bucksden must die. He intends to harm Mrs. Marston and her sister," Lucien said, shaken by the thought of his life ending and never again waking in a bed next to Cassie.

Across the room Devanney exhaled in noisy relief. The tension drained from his shoulders. His hands opened, then he scrubbed his fingers through his hair, destroying the results of Watson's careful combing.

"Better," he said, coming to stand in front of Lucien. "Now the rest of it. Why would Bucksden want to harm Mrs. Marston or her sister?"

Lucien laughed, the sound short and harsh. "Imagine this if you will, Devanney," he said. "Bucksden, the arrogant, cold slayer of men, felled by a slender little beauty armed only with pottery."

Devanney cocked his head, waiting for more explanation than that. When he didn't get it right away, he dropped to sit next to Lucien on the settee. Lucien offered him a wry smile. Now that his anger was ebbing he could afford to indulge himself in perverse pleasure as he imagined the scene.

"Mrs. Marston knocked the earl senseless with an urn when he threatened her sister. Don't ask me for the why of it. That's a tale that only she has the right to tell."

Devanney released another long, slow breath. He leaned forward, his forearms braced on his knees. "Well now, that's quite a scenario. You're right to think Mrs. Marston and Miss Conningsby in danger. Bucksden's pride must be writhing. That he's come so far to find them suggests he has no intention of stopping until he's avenged himself upon them."

"Which is why he has to die," Lucien said, forcing himself to lean back into the settee's corner and giving thanks that he and his cousin understood each other so well. That Lucien had come here rather than allow rage to send him to Hawick to find Bucksden was proof of that. He couldn't afford to face Bucksden in a duel while raging. A single breach of the rigid rules that governed such meetings made the difference between murder and the deadly satisfaction of honor.

Devanney nodded. "Huh. I can see how you'd come to that conclusion. Let me ponder this for a moment."

Lucien was content to let his cousin think, and to ponder the situation along with him. There had to be a better way to resolve this debacle. Cassie needed to be safe, while Lucien needed to spend the rest of a long life enjoying her touch.

After a silent moment Devanney shot him a smiling, sidelong look. "May I assume that it was Mrs. Marston who kept you from returning last night?"

"You may," Lucien replied with a half smile.

Devanney tsked and shook his head. "Poor Hastings. He was almost beside himself at the thought of you without fresh clothing. I had to command him to remain here when he wanted to rush off to that lodge of yours, certain that was where you'd gone."

Lucien laughed at that, feeling easy in his own skin again. He and Devanney did, indeed, know each other well. He put an elbow on the settee's arm and bent his smuggest look upon his cousin.

"By the by, you owe me the full three sixty. She was on the road to Edinburgh when I found her."

"No!" Devanney sat up in surprise. "I vow to you, Lucien. I saw nothing untoward in her play the other night."

Lucien laughed. "Of course you saw nothing wrong. You and Percy were right. Mrs. Marston simply outplayed me."

Devanney's brows lowered. He looked like a man who feared he was about to be taken, but didn't know how to stop it. "Then how can I owe you the full amount?"

Lucien grinned. "Because, my dear Devanney, Mrs. Marston's status as a sharp was never a condition of our wager. It was only if I found her anywhere but at Ettrick House. The three sixty is no more than my rightful due after this prank of yours. You knew from the start she was no sharp."

Rather than complain that Lucien had cheated him, a slow smile played across Devanney's mouth. "I knew nothing of the sort. I didn't even know she played cards."

Lucien eyed his cousin. This wasn't the way their pranks worked. Once the victim uncovered the trick, the prankster had to confess to arranging it.

"Then, if it wasn't to see me humbled at the tables, why did you direct me toward her at the ball?"

Devanney's gray eyes filled with satisfaction. He shifted on the settee, stretching his long legs out before him and bracing one arm on its back. "Marriage, my dear cousin. Your marriage."

Devanney let Lucien stew in curiosity for a moment before he offered the rest of his explanation. "Philana Forster called on me the moment she heard that you'd agreed to attend my party, begging that I include her nieces—and Conningsby." He rolled his eyes at that. "You can imagine my reaction. I had enough to handle in my sweet Aunt Eleanor without adding Sir Roland to the brew."

"But you didn't refuse her?" Lucien asked.

Devanney offered a rueful grin. "Of course I did. To no avail. That woman has more persistence than Sisyphus. At last I told her I'd only extend my invitation to her nieces if I liked her reason for insisting that they be included. You'll never guess what she related to me."

Lucien grinned. God bless that meddling old woman. "That her elder niece was the perfect wife for me. All she needed was the opportunity to bring us together."

Watching astonishment blossom on Devanney's face was worth the trouble Lucien had bought himself by making mincemeat of Eleanor. "How did you know?" Devanney demanded.

"Because when Lady Forster came to claim her 'kidnapped' niece"—Lucien shot a glance at Devanney's pretty little cloisonné clock on the mantelpiece—"a half hour ago she demanded that I appear at Ettrick House in two hours' time, to offer Cassandra Marston the protection of marriage."

His confession drove Devanney back against the settee with enough force to make the seat jerk even with the two of them sitting in it. "Kidnapped?" he gasped.

"Kidnapped," Lucien replied with a shrug as if it was part of his daily routine: rise, bathe, don his attire, kidnap Cassie.

When Devanney continued to stare, Lucien smiled. "I didn't realize that's what I was doing at the time. When I found Mrs. Marston on the road, their coach had fallen and she was alone with a wrenched knee, having been abandoned by her family. Fearing my anger, she pretended amnesia. So, I claimed to be her husband."

Both appalled and amused, Devanney relaxed back into the settee's corner. "Madness. What were you thinking?"

Lucien's smile widened as he understood now what he hadn't let himself see at the time. Nothing had changed in the six years of his separation from Cassie. He'd wanted to be her husband then, and he still wanted to be her husband now.

"I was thinking that if I were her brother or her cousin I wouldn't be able to demand my husbandly rights—in order to force her into confessing that she was a sharp," he said.

"Egad," Devanney said weakly, his eyes wide. "Did you?"

"Force a confession?" Lucien asked, purposefully misunderstanding his cousin. "How, when there was nothing for her to confess?"

Devanney's eyes narrowed in reproach.

Lucien laughed. "Anything else is none of your concern."

The realization of what Lucien had done left Devanney shaking his head like a man befuddled. "All this because I let that old woman bring her nieces to my party, hoping to tweak you a bit. A thousand pardons, Hollier. I only thought this would be my best prank ever. I had no idea it would actually result in your being forced to the altar. You won't let her do it to you, will you? Good God, you'll have Sir Roland as your father-by-marriage."

"What if I told you I was going to do it?" Lucien asked, studying the toes of his muddy boots.

"I'd say I didn't believe you," Devanney retorted with enough harshness that Lucien looked up at him.

Concern filled his cousin's eyes. "Lucien, if you think the gossips were unrelenting after Dorothea . . ." he warned, shaking his head.

"A shame you didn't catch me before I tore your sweet Aunt Eleanor limb from limb," Lucien said with a laugh. "She'll do her best to see me completely ruined with the *ton*."

"You don't sound particularly put out about it," Devanney replied.

"Why should I be?" Lucien shrugged again. "Let them say what they please. I hope they enjoy this as much as I do. It's worse melodrama than any London play I've ever seen—what with a card-sharping beauty, a noble kidnapper, illicit lovemaking, a bankrupt knight, both financially and morally, a humiliated earl, and a forced and degraded marriage."

The concern melted from Devanney's expression. The corners of his mouth lifted. "You love her."

"I do," Lucien agreed, "and I won't give her up, which brings me back to Bucksden. What's your conclusion? Is there another way to stop him outside of a duel?"

"You could marry her," Devanney suggested. "Once she and her sister have your protection, Bucksden won't dare to touch them."

"You know better," Lucien said with a sigh. He

straightened on the settee and ran his fingers through his hair. In his haste to reach Ryecroft Castle he'd forgotten his hat and gloves. His hair was windblown and tangled. If his face was as mud-spattered as his shirt and boots, then Eleanor had been right to chide. He must look a disgrace.

He braced his forearms on his knees and looked at Devanney. "If I don't find a way to permanently end his threat, doing it now, Bucksden will only be encouraged to repeat what he did to poor Dorothea three years ago when he feared I meant to expose him as a card cheat. I don't want him slinking away to plot some sly vengeance. I won't live my life always looking over my shoulder and worrying about what nastiness he has in store for me, or for Cassie. No, this must end, here and now."

Devanney frowned. "A duel cannot serve you, then. It isn't a mere scratch to satisfy outraged honor that you want to deal him, but a death wound. According to Percy, Mrs. Marston did him some injury. That leaves you with a conundrum, Hollier. You don't have time to let his injuries heal, but if you kill him while he's injured you risk forfeiture and exile."

Exile. The word rang in Lucien, only it wasn't his own banishment he contemplated. "You're brilliant, Devanney," he said with a laugh. "Exile is the perfect solution."

Surprise shot through Devanney's eyes, then his mouth tightened. "Your exile won't last long. If you dare to leave me alone in this country, I vow I'll come after you with blood in my eyes," he snapped back, half serious.

"Not me, you twit. Bucksden," Lucien retorted. "What is it he can do that might result in his exile?"

Devanney laughed quietly. "He could kill you in a duel," he said, his suggestion winning him a chiding look from Lucien. "Well then, what if you tried again to prove he cheated at cards? That would be the end of him. But that won't work either. He'd never agree to play with you, and even if he did he wouldn't do anything untoward. A shame you couldn't prove what he did three years ago," he added in after-thought.

With Devanney's words the perfect solution came spinning up from inside Lucien. He stifled his laugh. A duel fought with a deck of cards. It really was too perfect—that is, if he could get Cassie to agree.

"I have an idea," he said, "but I'll wait to share it with you until I've spoken with Cassie—Mrs. Marston," he amended, catching himself. He vowed to himself that nothing would change the intimacy they'd shared, even if he had to insert the demand that she sleep unclothed into their wedding vows.

He came to his feet, once again feeling in control of his emotions and his destiny, which was why he'd come to Devanney in the first place. "Well then, I'll change and be off to Ettrick House." As urgent as his need was to stand between Cassie and Bucksden he wouldn't make her a proposal of marriage looking less than respectable. That would dishonor Cassie and the affection he felt for her.

"I'm coming," Devanney said, his tone suggesting it would do Lucien no good to protest.

"What of your party?" Lucien asked.

Devanney grinned. "You're out of your mind if you think I'll stay here and listen to Eleanor complain about you. Go. Make yourself decent while I change into riding attire. You can tell me all about this idea of yours on the way."

Chapter 22

⌒◯◯⌒

The occasional fallen leaf skittered over the grassy avenue. The pines lining the way to Ettrick House sighed. The wind tugged at Lucien's hat and pushed at his back as if urging him to greater speed. More speed would have pleased Percy's thoroughbred mare; Lucien had borrowed the horse, not wanting to wind his own bay. She kicked up her heels and begged for a chance to run. It took effort to keep her at a sustainable pace.

"Hollier," Devanney said in warning as he rode alongside Lucien. Devanney was no longer a study in brown and Lucien was no longer muddy. Instead, they wore similar blue riding jackets, fawn breeches and black boots.

At Lucien's glance Devanney pointed to where

the avenue gave way to gravel, less than a quarter mile ahead of them. It was an impossible tableau. Four men stood on Ettrick House's raised porch, Sir Roland Conningsby at their forefront. All of them were armed—two with pistols, one with a sporting gun, and Sir Roland holding an ancient military musket. Conningsby held his weapon as if he were familiar with it. Lucien supposed he might be. Before he'd pickled his brains Sir Roland must have trained at arms in his youth. It was something all gentlemen did.

Their weapons were aimed at the three men standing with their horses at the base of the porch stairs. Of those three, two were servants, dressed in unremarkable garments. Bucksden, on the other hand, was unmistakable, even from the back.

It wasn't just the earl's form that identified him. Bucksden, although not as tall as either Lucien or Devanney, was a powerfully built man; it was his physical prowess that kept most men from confronting him. Nor was it Bucksden's attire, although he tended to rival Percy in his regard for fashion. His overcoat, an unnecessary affectation on so warm a day, was fashionably caped. Beneath its hem his perfectly polished Hessians gleamed in day's light. No, it was Bucksden's strange headgear that distinguished him. Instead of a hat he wore a swathing, bulky white bandage wrapped around his head.

Lucien wanted to groan. He was too late. He'd needed to speak to Cassie before they confronted Bucksden. She had to understand as Devanney already did that there could be no show of affection from her toward him until they dispensed with the nobleman's threat. One hint of a connection between Cassie and Graceton's lord, and Bucksden would smell the trap Lucien wanted to set.

Had intended to set. Hadn't yet set and now couldn't. Lucien gnashed his teeth in frustration.

"Now what?" Devanney asked.

"What else can we do? Let's see if Conningsby really intends to kill Bucksden," Lucien replied, then gave the mare her head. She made good use of her freedom, leaping into a happy gallop. Devanney did his best to keep pace, kicking the ugly creature he rode into a canter.

"Leave, Bucksden. What you want you'll never have from me," Sir Roland's shout echoed. The knight didn't sound like his usual silly self.

"You fool, you have no choice," Bucksden shouted in return, the sound of his anger as identifiable as his form. Neither he nor his companions had yet noticed that others approached, but two of the men on the porch looked Lucien's way.

"You're a man of honor. You agreed. What's done is done. Now, bring Miss Conningsby to me." The earl reminded Roland of their wager at the top of his lungs. "And Mrs. Marston as well!"

Heat stirred in the ashes of Lucien's rage. Bucksden would die before he laid a finger on Cassie.

Rather than fold before the earl's demand Sir Roland stepped to the edge of the porch and pointed his musket at Bucksden. "You want them? You'll have to come through me first."

Bucksden laughed at that and pulled something

from his coat pocket. He extended his arm. Metal glinted. Smoke puffed with a sharp report. The horses standing near the porch whinnied and danced.

Sir Roland screamed and fell back, dropping his weapon. The musket shattered as it hit the porch floor, the stock falling over the edge. Two of Lady Forster's guardians shuffled back a few steps. The other one, maybe braver than the rest, knelt at Sir Roland's side.

Lucien pulled the mare to a huffing, snorting halt. Bucksden and his servants turned. It didn't surprise Lucien to see that the earl's servants weren't the sort one took to Almacks or St. James Palace. The one holding the horses had been a frequent visitor to a boxing ring, or so said the flattened bridge of his fleshy nose. The taller had short hair and a lean, hungry face, the look of London's tougher neighborhoods clinging to every sharp line of his form.

Dismounting and keeping a tight hold on the mare's reins, Lucien faced Bucksden. The earl eyed him in return, his expression impassive—Or rather, Lucien assumed it was dispassion. It was hard to tell, what with the damage Cassie's urn had wreaked.

Although Bucksden was impeccably dressed in riding attire, a dark blue coat, buff breeches, boots and a white waistcoat heavily embroidered with gold, he was no longer the handsome man over whom so many women swooned, at least not at the moment. Both his eyes were blackened, the bruising beginning to fade to a hideous shade of yellow. Not

all the damage would fade. The skin at one corner of
his right eye had torn. A doctor's needle had drawn
together the edges of what would become a small
but ragged scar, not disfiguring unless you were a
man who prized his appearance above all else. As
for the earl's once-perfect nose, it now had the same
bend that afflicted his servant's more bulbous pro-
boscis.

Lucien eyed the bandage on Bucksden's head,
wondering what further damage hid beneath it,
then noticed that black hair curled out from beneath
the gauzy binding only on one side of the earl's
head. Bucksden's head was shaved on one side.

No wonder the earl was here, raging. He had
nothing else to do. It would be a long while before he
was again presentable to society.

As Devanney brought his horse to a halt and dismounted, Lucien bowed to the injured earl. "Good
heavens, my lord, what in the world happened to
you? Did you take a turn in the ring with Gentleman
Jim?" he asked, pretending ignorance.

Bucksden's lips tightened until his mouth was a
narrow slash across his face. "Something like that,"
he replied, evading an explanation he didn't want to
give and avoiding Lucien's questions.

On the porch Sir Roland grunted and rose to sitting. He clutched a hand to his shoulder where
blood soaked the fabric of his shirt beneath his fingers. The servant crouched at the knight's side was a
rustic who looked as much bear as human, but his
calm expression and knowledgeable touch suggested he was familiar with wounds.

"Sir Roland, are you badly injured?" Lucien asked, amazed that the little man remained conscious, although he wasn't surprised Roland yet lived. While Lucien didn't put murder beyond Bucksden, the earl was too good a shot and too smart to commit murder in the light of day and before witnesses.

"I'll live," the knight grunted, sounding disappointed at the prospect. Lucien wondered what had happened to the feckless giggler Sir Roland had been.

Bucksden made an irritable sound. "Of course he will. It's naught but a flesh wound. Take that as a warning, Conningsby. I don't care for men pointing weapons at me." He tossed his spent pistol to the hungry Londoner, who caught it handily and put it in his coat pocket.

"I can't say I know any man who does," Lucien agreed, scrambling for some new way, any way short of his own death in a duel, to end Bucksden's threat against Cassie and her sister. He jerked his head at Devanney, suggesting that his cousin make his way up to the porch. Devanney let his eyes widen as if in fear, hardly a credible response from a seasoned spy, then did as he was bid, his footsteps crunching in the gravel.

As Devanney went to the porch Lucien looked at Lord Bucksden, playing the part of the astonished visitor who simply happened upon this scene. "But why was he pointing a musket at you in the first place?"

"It's a private matter, Lord Graceton," said Sir Roland, startling Lucien. He'd expected that protest to come from Bucksden.

The earl tried to lift his brows, only to flinch when the movement tugged at his stitches. "I must respect Sir Roland's wishes in this regard," he said.

As Devanney climbed the stairs to the porch the two men near the door turned in his direction. Although they didn't point their weapons at him, Devanney held out his arms in a gesture of peace and smiled. "Easy, my good lads. Will you kindly inform Lady Forster that Lord Graceton and Lord Ryecroft have come to call?"

"I hope you get a better reception from the old woman than I have, my lords. Good day," Bucksden said as he prepared to retreat.

Lucien's fists clenched in frustration. Bucksden couldn't leave, not yet. Their confrontation had to begin and end here and now. It was unbearable to think that Bucksden's threat might hang over Cassie, and him.

Stalling, Lucien said, "Dare I mention I was surprised to hear you were in the neighborhood, Lord Bucksden? Our paths so rarely cross."

Bucksden turned, pebbles scraping beneath his boots. He looked back at Lucien, the wind shifting the hair beneath one side of his bandage. He tried to narrow his eyes, only to flinch again.

The bolt on Lady Forster's door opened. Percy's high-strung mare took offense to the noise, tossing her head and trying to back away from the porch.

Moving to hold her by the bridle, Lucien watched Cassie exit. Two of Lady Forster's men retreated into the house, closing the door behind them.

Lucien's heart filled with the sight of Cassie. She still wore the very proper blue-and-white dress of this morning with a lacy fichu filling its bodice, but her hair was no longer unbound. Instead, it had been done in a series of intricate twists and was so tightly pinned in place the wind could gain no foothold. All in all, she looked even lovelier than she had at breakfast. Ah, but she didn't look half as lovely as she had at dawn.

Anger followed pleasure. God take Bucksden and Conningsby! He ought to kill them both for the wrong they'd done the woman he loved. He caught himself. He could afford neither anger nor pleasure if he wanted to keep Cassie safe. He banished any hint of expression from his face.

Blast it all. Why couldn't he and Devanney have arrived ten minutes earlier? Then he would have had the chance to explain all to Cassie, including why she must challenge the earl to a card game. But what he'd most needed to tell her was to make no show of greeting him.

She went to her father. "Papa?"

Roland clumsily worked his way onto his knees, then rose to his feet, keeping his hand clamped over the seeping wound on his shoulder. "Go back inside, Cassie," the little man commanded, sounding not at all like himself.

Rather than do his bidding, Cassie looked from Devanney to Bucksden, then her gaze shifted to Lucien. Rather than cry out in joy at his presence, something Lucien's heart would have been glad to hear, a breath of a frown marred her pretty brow. She watched him, her gaze both wary and expectant.

Lucien ached as he understood. She'd watched him the same way in the courtyard of his lodge, wanting proof that his affection for her hadn't changed. He'd tried his best to give her what she'd needed then, but his anger had been too overwhelming to permit it. Now, when he was ready to tell her everything she wanted to hear, he didn't dare extend so much as an encouraging look.

Cassie studied Lucien, praying for some indication from him that he'd come to offer her marriage. That's what Philana had crowed when she recognized it was Lucien riding up the avenue on Mr. Percy's horse accompanied by Lord Ryecroft. How Philana had exulted over the two men appearing at exactly the right moment. Something to do with fate. How Cassie's foolish heart had swelled with misguided hope.

Lucien might look the well-dressed beau dressed in his riding attire, but he hadn't come here as a suitor. It was disinterest, not love, she read in his expression. He watched her as if he didn't even know her, which explained Lord Ryecroft's presence at Lucien's side for this visit. It wasn't marriage they came to propose, but some settlement that would free Lucien from Philana's abhorrent threat of forced wedlock.

Reminding herself that she'd come out to do something other than break her heart anew over Lucien, Cassie again looked at Lord Bucksden and again confronted the damage that she and her urn had wrought on the earl's face. She didn't wonder that he raged, even threatening assault charges. She didn't credit his threat. The earl was too proud a man to tolerate anyone knowing what she'd done to him. No, he had some fate other than a trial and imprisonment in mind for her. She didn't care to imagine what it might be.

Lord Bucksden's lips lifted into a tight, satisfied smile. "Well now, here you are, Mrs. Marston. I see you're more sensible than your sire. Go back inside and fetch your sister. It's time we were on our way." Threat lay heavy in his tone.

Her father made a worried sound. "Didn't you hear me, Cassie? I told you to go back inside."

Cassie looked at her father. He wore no hat and his white hair danced around his head in the wind. Just now his skin was as pale as his hair—even his lips. His blood-sodden sleeve clung to his arm.

"You're the one who should go in," she replied softly. "You're hurt." A flicker of gratitude for him woke in her. No matter what her father had done wrong in the past he'd come out here intent on stopping Lord Bucksden. That was more than he'd attempted in London when the earl had first come to claim Eliza.

"It's nothing," her father retorted, then urged again: "Go."

Lord Ryecroft crossed the porch to stand at Cassie's side. Unlike his noble cousin the expression on the tall earl's handsome face was warm, even sympathetic. He offered a small smile, filling the movement of his mouth with the promise of protection. Then he looked down at the men below the porch floor.

"Heavens, Bucksden," he drawled, "I fear I'm all adither in confusion. Can you make it clear for me? Why would you come to Lady Forster's house armed, and is it one or both of Conningsby's daughters you want to take against their father's will? Lastly, why ever would you want to take either of them? I must warn you. I won't stand for Mrs. Marston and her sister leaving my party. It would make a shambles of the event. Too many men," he finished with a shudder, as if an unbalanced ratio between the sexes at his party was a fate worse than death.

"Stay out of this, Ryecroft," Lord Bucksden warned, his voice flat.

"But how can I?" Lord Ryecroft protested. "Mrs. Marston and Miss Conningsby are integral to my party. If they leave, then what ever shall we do about our little play? Both have parts in it, and their absence would put an end to our little drama when I'm just beginning to enjoy it. I fear the show cannot go on without them."

Cassie frowned. What did he mean, play?

"What sort of help are you?" Roland snarled in Lord Ryecroft's direction, startling Cassie. "All you care about is your party, not protecting my daughters." Pivoting, he snatched Alex's unloaded pistol from the big man's belt and pointed the useless weapon at Lord Bucksden. His arm quivered, the muzzle of the pistol dancing along with it. "Here and now, my lord. If you want them, take them from me," he demanded.

Cassie gasped in understanding. Her father's solution to their dilemma was to provoke Lord Bucksden to do murder. *His* murder.

"Put the pistol down, Sir Roland," Lord Ryecroft said gently, leaning over to catch the older man's shivering arm. "Even if Lord Bucksden has another pistol, I seriously doubt he intends to accommodate you."

Making a desperate sound, Roland yanked free of Lord Ryecroft's grip. The effort unbalanced him. He staggered forward, too close to the edge of the porch.

"No, he has to shoot me! This is all my fault. God help me, I was drunk. I don't even remember making the wager. All I recall is those two blighters of his," he aimed the trembling pistol at Lord Bucksden's servants, "dropping me off at my step, telling me to prepare to give up my daughter when the earl came for her at eleven."

Lord Ryecroft lunged for Roland, moving more quickly than Cassie thought possible for so indolent a man. He wrenched the pistol from Roland's bloody fingers, pulling the knight back from the porch's edge. Roland cried out, fighting to free himself.

"I beg your pardon, Sir Roland, but I cannot let you do that," Lord Ryecroft said, releasing him.

Roland's knees gave way. This time Alex caught him, steadying him on his feet. "No," Roland whispered in defeat, his face ashen, his eyes swimming.

"Take Sir Roland into the house and see to that injury," Lord Ryecroft commanded Philana's parker, then waited as Alex half dragged Roland to the door. It creaked open to admit them, then shut again.

"Now my thoughts truly swim, Bucksden," Lord Ryecroft continued. "Did I hear Conningsby aright? You and he gambled over the possession of an innocent girl?" he said, a touch of disgust in his voice. "By God, but that's cheeky, even for you."

"You heard Conningsby. This is none of your concern, Ryecroft," Lord Bucksden retorted. His tone might have been casual—any other man would have been shouting in outrage at such a slur—but the earl's pretense of calm didn't mean that he wasn't seething. The depth of his irritation showed in the way he turned his neck against the binding of his collar and neckcloth.

"Having heard Conningsby's confession, I think we're obligated to question," Lucien said, speaking as if he didn't already know what Sir Roland had done. That made Cassie glance at him, wondering. There was nothing for her to see except Lucien's expressionless face.

"No matter what Conningsby says, he made the wager, on that you have my word. Should that not be enough for you"—Lord Bucksden sent a burning sidelong look at Lucien—"then know that the wager was witnessed and registered at our club. For the record, I didn't suggest the terms. Conningsby freely offered his daughter to me when I mentioned that I'd seen her on the street and admired her."

It was Eliza's unwitting solution to their dilemma—another card game, this one between Cassie and Lord Bucksden—that Cassie had brought with her onto the porch. Because of that she found herself watching the earl as if he sat across a card table from her. His bluff was written in the aggressive jut of his jaw and the faint narrowing of his eyes. Roland hadn't offered him Eliza.

That didn't mean Roland hadn't agreed to put Eliza on the table, especially if he'd been drunk at the time. But he hadn't gone into the game planning to use Eliza as ante, the way Cassie now meant to do.

That Cassie could read Lord Bucksden so easily gave her the confidence she'd lacked a moment ago. This was going to work. She'd defeated Lucien at cards. Surely, she could also defeat Lord Bucksden.

Buoyed, she stepped closer to the porch's edge. "My lord, perhaps you can understand why we resist you, given my father's insistence that he doesn't remember making the wager," she said, seeing no need to mention that she'd only heard Roland's confession this very moment. "I'd like to offer you a way to resolve the whole matter, once and for all.

Consider a second game, one between you and me. Possession of Eliza will be on the table. If I win, you must release any and all claims to her. If I lose, you may do with her as you wish."

Chapter 23

Beside Cassie, Lord Ryecroft sucked in a startled breath. For an instant Lord Bucksden looked almost horrified, then all expression left his face. As for Lucien's reaction to her challenge, Cassie had no clue. He was bent behind Mr. Percy's horse, doing something with the girth's buckle.

Anger sparked. That arrogant, useless, selfish nobleman! What did she need with a man who fiddled with riding gear at the very moment she risked her sister's future? Lucien was unworthy of her, not the other way around. Let him offer his settlement. She'd throw it back in his face, even if that meant living out her life in the direst of poverty.

Lord Bucksden thrust his hands into his overcoat pockets in an unwitting show of resentment. It wasn't because he didn't like that Lucien and Lord Ryecroft now knew the terms of his wager with her father. While Lord Bucksden might not like the tale of wagering over Eliza spreading, it would hardly hang over his head like that sword over Damocles. This was a man who had more than once ridden the crest of scandal and paid no price for what he did. No, he was upset because Lucien and Lord Ryecroft had witnessed her challenge. That had given his fellow noblemen the right to involve themselves in the settling of Eliza's fate.

Lord Bucksden brow furrowed as deeply as his injuries allowed. A gust of wind toyed with what black hair escaped his bandage and swirled his overcoat's hem around his boots. One of his servants spat. The other shifted impatiently. Mr. Percy's horse stamped and tossed her head, trying to escape Lucien's grip on her bridle. Vicious pleasure filled the earl's eyes.

"I see no reason to risk my possession of Miss Conningsby in another game. My wager with Sir Roland was recorded and witnessed. I won. Your sister is rightfully mine, a fact to which Lord Graceton and Lord Ryecroft must stand as witness. Bring her to me, Mrs. Marston. Now."

Panic shot through Cassie. Having two noble witnesses to her challenge wasn't going to help. Instead, Lord Bucksden would use their respect for the strict code that ruled wagers to prize Eliza out of Philana's house.

"I don't think we can stand aside and let you take Miss Conningsby," Lucien replied, his voice harsh.

Relief almost weakened Cassie's knees. Whatever Lucien thought of her, he wasn't going to turn his back and let this happen. Cassie looked at him, ready to forgive him much, only to have gratitude crash into disgust at herself. Lucien was glaring daggers at Lord Bucksden while Lord Bucksden returned the sentiment in full. How could she have forgotten their shared history? Lucien didn't care a whit about Eliza. All he wanted was a way to hurt Lord Bucksden.

"You have no choice in the matter," Bucksden snapped. "The wager's registered. It is legitimate."

"So you say," Lucien snarled, "but how can we know that, unless we make a trip to London to see the register?"

The intimation that he might be lying made Lord Bucksden rise onto the balls of his feet in preparation for attack. In the next instant his heels flattened back onto the ground. Cassie read the earl in surprise. Lord Bucksden thought Lucien was arranging a trap for him.

Her disgust grew. The earl couldn't be more wrong. Lucien didn't care what happened to her or her sister. If he did, then he'd have been up here on the porch and at her side as his cousin was.

"But Hollier, why should anyone have to ride to London for anything?" Lord Ryecroft asked, his handsome face alight as if in inspiration. "We can resolve everything here in no longer than an hour's time. It's all so easy, Bucksden," he said to his fellow earl, his voice alive with boyish enthusiasm. "Accept Mrs. Marston's challenge. Once the two of you have played, there can be no question as to who placed what wager and who won. Once you've taken the match, we'll have no choice but to let you leave unhindered with Miss Conningsby."

"Why should I play a second game when I've already won the first?" Lord Bucksden demanded.

"You seemed in such a hurry to claim Miss Conningsby. Now that the wager has been placed in doubt, we'd be doing less than our duty if we allowed you to take her until a man rides to London and back to verify that all is as you say it is. Not that we don't believe you," Lord Ryecroft qualified, holding out his hands, the quintessential peacemaker. "It's just that she's a young thing. Who knows what might happen between now and then? Play the game and be done with it, as Mrs. Marston says, once and for all," he persisted.

Confidence roared back through Cassie. It took all her will not to press her hand to her chest to calm her racing heart. Thank God for Lord Ryecroft. How could Lord Bucksden refuse now, when the proposal so obviously served him?

Lord Bucksden shot another wary glance around him, still expecting a trap. He looked to his servants. The taller one gave a half shrug.

"Devanney, I cannot agree to this unless I know Miss Conningsby is a willing participant," Lucien said as Mr. Percy's horse again sidled and fought his hold on her bridle.

As he sought to calm the horse Lucien's gaze flickered in Cassie's direction. Fool that she was, Cassie thought she saw softness in his eyes.

"Well, Mrs. Marston?" Lucien asked irritably. "Invite Miss Conningsby to join us."

Cassie huffed. What a lovesick fool she was, putting expressions on the face of a man who didn't want her. She turned toward the door. Young Rob, Lucien's housekeeper's nephew, peered out at her through the crack between door and jamb. At her nod he moved aside and Eliza stepped out, looking pale and frightened but calm, then Rob closed the door behind her. She swept forward to join Cassie. Only the tightness of her joined hands revealed how terrified she was.

"This is worse than anything I imagined," she whispered to Cassie, then offered a brief curtsy to the gathered peers. "My lords, I am willing to abide by the terms of this wager."

Lord Bucksden's attention locked onto Eliza's face. Lust heated his expression. Then his gaze drifted downward in lewd appraisal of Eliza's form. Cassie choked back her scorn. She should have realized that bringing Eliza out here would change things.

"A few hands of cards," Lord Ryecroft said, his tone light as if it weren't the rest of Eliza's life being decided by this match, "and all is resolved."

Lord Bucksden frowned at his fellow earl. "You would vow to uphold the terms of the wager?"

"Absolutely," Lord Ryecroft answered without hesitation. "You win, and Miss Conningsby leaves with you. Mrs. Marston and her father must swear not to attempt to reclaim her. If Mrs. Marston wins, you must swear to give up all claim to Miss Conningsby, making no further attempt to take her from her family."

"Graceton as well?" the earl snarled, shooting a burning glance at Lucien.

"I would so vow," Lucien replied.

"There is one thing, however," Lord Ryecroft said, tapping his chin with his forefinger. "It's such an odd wager. I think for everyone's security it would be best if the game were played before as many witnesses as possible. I can think of no better place to stage it at the moment than Ryecroft Castle, what with all my guests presently in residence. Now, I know you cannot like this, Miss Conningsby," the handsome man said, offering Eliza a quick smile, "but there's no reason to announce the terms of the wager. The other witnesses only need know that the ante on the table is of a personal nature."

This time it wasn't suspicion but embarrassment that plagued Lord Bucksden. He took a backward step. "I prefer not to make a public appearance at the moment."

Lord Ryecroft dismissed Lord Bucksden's bruises with a wave of his hand. "I know you've done your best to be circumspect since you arrived, but when an injured earl appears in one of the local villages it doesn't take long for news to spread. Everyone at my party already knows about your—how shall we say?—temporary disfiguration?" A tiny smile lifted the corners of his mouth. "Tut Bucksden, it's too late to be shy. Rather than hide, strut boldly into my door and tell them all about your experience in the boxing ring. Anything else will free people to fabricate their own explanations for your injuries. How the rumors already run!"

Lord Bucksden's chin jerked up in insulted reaction. Beside Cassie, Eliza turned her laugh into a cough. Cassie bit her lip to keep from smiling. How cleverly Lord Ryecroft used words to drive Lord Bucksden where he wanted him. Either Lord Bucksden agreed to play their game at Ryecroft Castle, or he would seem a coward.

Scowling, Lord Bucksden again looked at Eliza. "Who attends this party of yours, Ryecroft?" he asked, watching her.

"There are a number of locals whose names will mean nothing to you," Lord Ryecroft replied, "but you'll know Percy from the tables, I think. And perhaps Colonel Egremont, Sussex's nephew?"

Lord Bucksden gave a brusque nod at that, his gaze still fixed on Eliza. The intensity of his look drove Eliza to shift subtly to the side, half hiding behind Cassie. Cassie stifled her urge to clasp her sister in her arms. It was pointless to try and protect her now.

"Oh, and there's my great aunt, of course," Lord Ryecroft added as if in afterthought. Cassie doubted anyone could ever forget Eleanor.

Lord Bucksden looked surprised. "The duchess of Carlisle attends?"

"Lord, but how *could* I have forgotten how well

you and Her Grace know each other?" Lord Ryecroft shook his head. "The two of you have often been companions at the table in London, haven't you? I dare say she'll be pleased to see you, even bruised as you are. She's lamented the lack of quality at my party."

Lord Bucksden looked from Cassie to Eliza.

Cassie watched as Lord Bucksden's shoulders first tensed in consideration, then relaxed in satisfaction. She read him with ease. He was not only utterly certain that he would win, he intended to enjoy besting her and walking away with her sister, knowing the pain it would cause her.

No, it was more than that. What most intrigued the earl about this match were the witnesses. As much as Lord Bucksden desired Eliza, what he wanted more was to take her from Cassie, doing it in front of witnesses who, if they but knew what was happening before their eyes, might have tried to stop him.

She knew it was wrong, but Cassie hoped the earl hadn't heard about her game with Lucien from any of the locals he might have interviewed. As much as Lord Bucksden craved hurting her, she craved his angry astonishment when he realized he faced a capable player. She hoarded the image of him raging, beaten for a second time by a woman he dismissed as beneath him.

Lord Bucksden bowed. "My lords, I accept Mrs. Marston's challenge and am willing to join her at Ryecroft Castle for this game."

"There's one last thing," Lucien said, no inflection in his voice. "I think it only fair that Lord Bucksden be warned. Mrs. Marston is a more than capable cardswoman."

Cassie's precious image of the defeated and raging earl exploded. Her anger at Lucien roared into an inferno. What sort of cad *was* he? She'd taken his point well enough at the tower when he turned his back on her. He didn't have to actively try to hurt her.

Lucien's warning gave Lord Bucksden pause. He frowned up at her as if he thought he could gauge the level of her skill by studying her face. Cassie offered him what Eliza called their ninnyhammer expression, one that combined the batting of eyelashes over expressionless eyes while curving the mouth into a simpering smile.

It worked. The earl shot a burning look at Lucien, every line of his body saying he believed Lucien gave the warning only to shake his confidence. "When shall we meet?" Lord Bucksden demanded of the master of Ryecroft Castle.

"Why, now, of course," Ryecroft replied, looking every inch the congenial host. "This card game will be the perfect diversion for my guests and just as dramatic as any play, I think. If Lady Forster doesn't mind sending a man ahead to warn my household what to expect, we can all ride over together. That is agreeable to you, Mrs. Marston, isn't it?"

"Of course," Cassie replied, surprised that she sounded so calm when fire filled her lungs.

Taking her sister's arm she started for the house. Lucien wasn't content to simply abandon her this time. He wanted to completely destroy her and Eliza. Well, he'd tried his best and failed. Now it was her turn to act. She intended to come out the victor over both these insufferable, conceited noblemen.

Chapter 24

❦❦

"**W**ell, that's it. We're here," Philana announced grimly, speaking for the first time in nearly an hour as, wheels crunching, the carriage trundled past the gurgling fountain that marked the beginning of Ryecroft Castle's drive.

Once again wearing her green summer pelisse atop her day dress, Philana sat in the carriage's forward-facing seat, the gray plumes on her bonnet waving in the stiff breeze. Cassie and Eliza sat across from her; they hadn't wanted to watch the men riding ahead of them.

Roland hadn't come with them, although not by choice. He'd pleaded, promising that his injury was nothing more than a scrape. But even Eliza, who was no nurse, could see he was far more gravely affected

by his wound than he would admit. It was Philana
who finally convinced him to stay, arguing that appearing at Ryecroft Castle with a bloody shoulder
wouldn't serve Eliza's cause. They'd left him sobbing in the drawing room.

Cassie turned on the seat to look at the house. It
wasn't that she disbelieved Philana, it was the sense
of unreality that held her in its grip. She had to con-
firm for herself that what was happening wasn't
some awful dream.

Ryecroft Castle was a massive, three-storey U-
shaped structure of reddish stone. Grand windows,
glass gleaming in the sun, marked its walls, even on
the servants' wing. Useless crenellations marched
across the house's roof line. From behind that toothy
façade rose a fanciful forest of chimneys, each one
different from the others. Some spiraled, others
stair-stepped, and still others looked like pots. The
wind swept through them, turning humdrum
smoke into snapping gray pennants.

Her gaze shifted to the men riding ahead of the
carriage. What a strange parade they made. Lord
Bucksden led the way, he and his two servants now
just disappearing between the house's twin wings.
Lord Ryecroft and Lucien rode about a half dozen
yards behind the bandaged earl, which meant they
hadn't yet reached the outermost edge of the building. Lucien looked marvelous atop Mr. Percy's beautiful horse, far better than his more handsome
cousin looked on the bulky beast he rode.

What was she doing?! Cassie wrenched around on
the carriage seat. Her lavender pelisse slipped off

her lap; it was too warm to wear and, considering
what she faced, she didn't care if she arrived covered
with road dust. She let the garment lie on the carriage floor as she carefully stoked her anger at Lucien, reminding herself of all the wrongs he'd done
her. She needed it. Anger was all she had to keep
anxiety at bay.

The journey here had given her plenty of time to
recall the way luck had shaped her first game with
Lucien. It wasn't going to happen again. It couldn't.

The carriage entered the cavernous embrace of the
house's arms. The snort of the horses echoed around
them. Eliza made a tiny desperate sound.

Unlike Cassie, who was too warm, Eliza huddled
in her blue pelisse, clutching it close to her. On her
head was Philana's spare bonnet, although it didn't
look its old self. The need to be busy had plagued
Eliza terribly while they'd waited for Lord Bucksden's reappearance, so she and Philana had
searched Ettrick House for something to remake the
bonnet. They came up with a pretty violet ribbon
embroidered with pink and yellow flowers. That,
and a pair of blue ribbon rosettes had replaced the
bonnet's former black plumes and ribbons. The corner of Cassie's mouth twisted upward in a reluctant
smile. If the end of this card game left Eliza facing
her doom, then she meant to confront it in her own
particular style.

Eliza made another sound. Her shoulders
hunched. Her head bent.

Cassie put an arm around her sister, pulling her
closer. "What is it, dearest?"

"I think I'm going to be ill," Eliza whispered and clutched her midsection.

"Didn't I warn you not to sit in that seat? It always makes me ill," Philana said sharply, anger and tears mingling in her eyes.

Cassie sent Philana an irritated look, then stroked a hand down Eliza's back. "No you're not, darling. All will be well. You'll see," she soothed, wishing there was someone to soothe her.

This time she didn't need to work to stoke her anger. Damn all men and their exaggerated ideas of honor! Where was the honor in gambling over the possession of a woman? Rather than agree to this game, both Lucien and Lord Ryecroft should have found a way to deny Lord Bucksden's claim on Eliza. Let them play their foolish games. She'd save her sister, be damned if she didn't.

As Cassie straightened she met Philana's gaze. Her aunt looked as angry as she felt. "You won't lose," she commanded her niece.

"Of course not," Cassie replied without hesitation, buoyed by her anger.

Far too soon the carriage stopped before the mansion's door. Lord Bucksden's disreputable-looking servants were just remounting to ride their horses back around the building to the stables. Philana descended first, making her exit from their vehicle as proudly as any queen. Cassie sent Eliza down next, then followed. The butler met them inside the door, taking their outerwear and bonnets.

Lord Ryecroft's entry hall was Palladian in style, its floor and walls all creamy marble. A long bas relief panel faced the doorway, depicting men in togas around a table. Cassie hadn't yet been able to discern what it was they were supposed to be doing at that table. The ceiling two storeys overhead repeated this motif. Ovals of plaster flowers encircled more bas relief. On them, toga-clad men—some at war, others studying and still others lifting their hands and opening their mouths to offer the world some stunning profundity—were trapped forever in plaster.

The hall ran the length of this part of the house, rather like a gallery. The doors that opened up off of it gave access to most of the public rooms. A footman stood to one side of the drawing-room door. Conversation echoed from the opening, reverberating oddly into the entry hall, the sibilance magnified by the marbled surfaces.

Glancing over her shoulder to see that Cassie and Eliza followed, Philana marched to the drawing room. The *tap-tap* of her shoes and the rustling of her gown filled the entry hall. Eliza and Cassie followed, joining Philana in the doorway.

The room was crowded, what with all fifty house party attendees in the chamber. Every one of the twenty-odd chairs arranged in a semicircle around the single card table at the room's center was filled. The rest of the guests stood, sipping tea or something stronger served by the footmen slipping through their midst. It made for an elegant tableau, the men in blue, brown or dark green long-tailed coats and black pantaloons, the women wearing dresses in every color of the rainbow—some solid colors, some sprigged, some striped. The matrons among them all had their heads covered with lacy or beribboned caps or turbans. As always, only two men stood out. Mr. Percy wore a vibrant green brocade waistcoat beneath a coat of deep blue, while Colonel Egremont, seated next to him in the circle of chairs, proved the dandy's foil in his regimentals, his pale blue trousers with their golden stripe down the leg, his blue jacket with its scarlet trim. His golden epaulettes and cording glimmered as they caught the sunlight streaming in through the wall of french doors across the room.

Not all the people in the room were interested in the forthcoming game. Eliza's friends had retreated to the settee, relocated for the moment near the piano. Three ladies, including Lord Ryecroft's young sister and Lady Barbara, occupied the seat. A pair of lads perched on its arms, while a few more hung over its back as they conversed with the ladies. Three more girls sat on the floor beside it, chatting to each other.

"May I join them?" Eliza breathed, almost pleading.

"Only if you wish me luck," Cassie whispered in return.

Eliza's giggle was quiet and desperate. "Luck, luck and more luck," she said, and then, with a quivering smile to Philana, started toward her friends.

The only one in the room who paid Eliza any heed, proof that the terms of the wager were still secret, was Lord Bucksden. He sat facing the door, having taken the chair at the far side of the room's sole table. He'd shed his overcoat. With his bruises, his bandaged head and his riding attire he looked out of place in the refined elegance of the room. Not so Duchess Eleanor, who stood behind him. Even though her white dress with its narrow red stripe did her complexion no favors, the garment was the perfect backdrop for her rubies.

Philana made a sound. Cassie glanced at her. "I really despise that man," Philana muttered to Cassie. "I'm going to make Colonel Egremont or Mr. Percy give me a chair so I can better watch you win. And you will win," she commanded, then left Cassie alone in the doorway.

Cassie contemplated the only remaining empty chair at the card table. Its back faced the door. Lord Ryecroft and Lucien occupied the other two chairs at the table. Like Lord Bucksden they still wore riding attire, and although they'd shucked their hats and gloves, they looked out of place among the elegant witnesses. The two men had pushed their chairs far enough from the table to indicate they weren't players.

Although she told herself not to do it Cassie's gaze caught and clung on Lucien. His chair was turned so its back half faced the door. He sprawled in it, his arms crossed over his chest in impatience. He watched Lord Bucksden.

She waited for anger to spike. Instead, a part of her sighed, once more admiring the curl of Lucien's sun-streaked hair against his snowy shirt collar. All too well she remembered the feel of her hands against his flesh that morning. Only this morning? It felt like forever ago.

"Ah, here she is at last," someone whispered. Cassie thought it might have been Squire Kerr. Fabric rustled. The quiet thrum of conversation dropped into silence, even in the youngsters' corner.

Cassie's heart pounded in her ears as she started into the room. Lady Ross reached out to touch her sleeve, offering a reassuring squeeze and a smile before again clasping her hands at her bosom. Squire Kerr nodded, his brows lifted in encouragement. His wife, a quiet woman, gave a friendly waggle of her fingers. Another man winked, his expression conveying that, however strange this match might be, he expected her to take the day.

Cassie stopped behind her chair. Lord Ryecroft almost sprang to his feet. Lord Bucksden rose more slowly, watching her the way a hawk watches a mouse. Lucien rose last, almost reluctantly, then turned to look at her.

Cassie wasn't certain if she should cry or laugh. It happened again. His presence reached out to embrace her. Despite the hurt he'd done her and her anger at him, her body still reacted to him.

Their gazes caught and held. His gray eyes were clear, untouched by any emotion. He crossed his arms, then the fingers of his exposed hand moved, drawing her attention to them and his signet ring. It flashed a little as he moved it on his finger just as she'd shown him that morning.

Startled, she dropped to sit in her chair, still staring at his hand. He moved the ring again. She glanced up at him, not certain what to make of this, or if she should make anything of it at all.

His eyebrows quirked upward, but before she could read anything into that gesture he dropped back into his chair, shifting once again so he sat with his shoulder to her. All she could see of his face was the rugged jut of his cheekbone and the line of his carefully sculpted sideburn where his hair didn't cover it.

Confusion tore through Cassie's carefully contrived anger, then shredded her confidence. Her unwanted awareness of Lucien spiraled. Why was he doing this to her? What was he doing to her? Whispering, the house guests closed in behind her, rustling and shifting as they sought to see the table.

"Humph," said Duchess Eleanor. "I shall never understand men. As if it weren't bad enough to damage your pretty face in the boxing ring, my dear earl," she said to Lord Bucksden, laying a friendly hand on his shoulder, "now you intend to game with riffraff. At least *you* have an excuse, my lord. Your brains are likely addled from your injuries." She shot a raging look at Lucien, leaving Cassie wondering what he'd done to earn the duchess's wrath.

Not finished complaining, Eleanor looked at her great-nephew. "Ryecroft, I still cannot comprehend why such haste was needed in arranging a card game. It's shameful, I tell you. Men dressed for riding in a drawing room! In my day we never countenanced such a thing. Isn't that so?" she demanded of the watching ladies, most of whom were quick to nod whether or not they agreed with the duchess.

Lord Ryecroft, his dark hair windblown, leaned back in his chair until it balanced on two legs and smiled up at his great-aunt. "I know, darling. Very improper," he said as if commiserating. "We shall just have to muddle through and pray that this sort of situation never again arises, shan't we?"

Eleanor shook her head in exasperation, the ruby insect pinned to her gold and red turban dancing in reaction. "Why can't we know what the wager is?" she complained. "It's hardly right that we're asked to witness this game when we're ignorant of its purpose. Then again, I suppose I shouldn't be surprised, not with that one," she did all but point like a fishwife at Cassie, "at the other end of the table."

Calculation and concern flashed through Lord Bucksden's eyes. He glanced at Lucien, the set of his shoulders saying he once more sensed a potential trap. Then he looked up at the duchess. "Why do you say that, Your Grace?"

Eleanor lifted her chin in dismissal at the same time she aimed the weight of her irritation at Cassie. "Because everything about that commoner is improper."

Cassie almost laughed. The duchess had no idea how true her words were. Beside her, Lucien made a sound, then he sat back in his chair, tilting it a little.

Lord Ryecroft leaned forward, once again moving so swiftly that he startled Cassie. He smiled and motioned to the waiting footman, who provided a deck of cards. "Well, now that we're all here, will you both agree to a partie of Piquet, winner takes all?"

Lord Bucksden was raging. Not that anyone but Cassie would have known it. He sat very quietly in his chair, no expression on his face. He didn't tap his fingers, his toe, or even move a ring on his finger. Instead, he blinked. Not rapidly, but slowly and with such precision that it wasn't natural. Every so often he craned his neck, as if trying to escape his binding neckcloth.

"She's quite the player, isn't she?" Squire Kerr whispered in admiration, his accent so thick it took a moment for Cassie to decipher his comment. Like many of those watching, he'd lost himself to the tension of the game, moving closer with each hand until he almost leaned over Cassie's shoulder. Hardly anyone sat in the chairs any longer, including Philana. Two hands ago she'd come to murmur her regrets in Cassie's ear, saying she needed air, then left the chamber. She hadn't yet returned.

"That's an understatement," Mr. Percy replied, standing between the seated Lord Ryecroft and Colonel Egremont. The dandy grinned. "Look at her hold her own against Bucksden!"

"I did warn Lord Bucksden of her skill," Lucien said, his voice harsh and low.

That won him Lord Bucksden's first burning glance of the game. The earl instantly turned his attention back to the cards he shuffled. He returned to his involuntary blinking.

Cassie glanced at Lucien. He hadn't moved since

the *partie* began, but like Lord Bucksden he revealed his emotions in his body. So much tension filled the lines of his shoulders and legs that he seemed ready to explode into motion at any instant. Cassie hoped he wouldn't move, at least not until this game ended.

It was happening again: Lucien's nearness and her confusion over what she felt for him feeding her skill. She could practically read Lord Bucksden's hand through the backs of his cards, knowing almost before he did what he'd discard and what he'd keep. The edge had served her well. As they began their sixth and final hand of the *partie*, Cassie had a total of eighty-seven points, while Lord Bucksden had accumulated only seventy-three.

The earl began to deal. Cassie bit her lip and watched her cards slide to a halt before her. She left them where they lay until the last one was dealt, then cupped her hand over them and sent a prayer heavenward, asking for a *Pique*. That was only possible if the cards she'd been dealt had a point value of thirty or more. The reward for achieving a pique was to double thirty to sixty. Sixty points would give her an edge that Lord Bucksden couldn't possibly beat.

She picked up her hand. There was no pique, but she had potential in clubs. She chose her five discards, set them aside, then lay her hand atop the eight cards that made up the talon from which she'd replace what she'd just thrown. The sad certainty that there was nothing higher than a jack in that tiny stack flowed through her. Praying she was wrong, she took her five, looked at them, then begged for death.

All she had in her hand was a *quint* in clubs, a series of five, and a *quartorze*, four queens. And she'd discarded all the defensive cards she needed to block Lord Bucksden's play. If—and that was a great *if*— Lord Bucksden didn't have more points than she did, the total point value of her hand was twenty-nine.

Lord Bucksden held his cards close to his chest, as he'd done all night. He didn't like anyone staring into his hand, and the press of Lord Ryecroft's guests bothered him. He'd complained until the duchess finally demanded that Lord Ryecroft order his guests to move back from her precious earl. Even the duchess had retreated, taking a chair not far from his side and only daring to glance toward his hand from time to time.

Whether he held his cards close to his chest or at arms' length, Cassie had no trouble reading his hand. He had spades, of that she was certain, because she had none except her queen. But how many did he have?

She waited for him to show her the answer. Confidence began to radiate from him. Its intensity told her all she didn't want to know. He had all the spades except her queen.

Then the corners of his mouth relaxed. He had better than seven spades. He had three more face cards, perhaps kings or aces, and most likely three of them. That left his last two cards small—eights or sevens.

Her heart broke into a thousand pieces. She'd lost. He had more points in his hand than she did, which meant she would gain nothing in the declaration.

He'd decimate her as they played. Desperate and doomed, she watched Lord Bucksden, waiting for him to set aside his two small cards and replacing them with two from the talon's remaining three cards.

Instead, he chose three to discard. Surprise tore through Cassie's despair. What was he doing? He'd broken his *septieme*, his series of seven. It wasn't worth trying to draw his fourth high card for his *quartorze*. Nor would he get it, not in that talon.

He lifted his discards out of his hand. Eleanor peered over his shoulder to see what it was he threw even though the knowledge did her little good—not when she couldn't see what he kept in his hand. The duchess watched, hoping for a glimpse of the new cards he drew, then leaned back into her chair.

Lord Bucksden stared at his hand for a moment, rearranged the cards, then squared them into a stack in his palm. He then used his free hand to push away his discard pile. It was the earl's one nervous table habit, and he did it with every hand. Cassie hadn't yet discerned the meaning behind his seemingly fussy need to move his discards.

Once the cards he'd thrown were pushed to the side, the earl shifted his cards from one hand to the other and pushed them around a bit as he re-fanned them. "Declarations?" he asked Cassie, looking at her from above his hand. Confidence still wafted from him.

She frowned at him, undone by her own weak hand and his strange behavior. "Point of five," she said.

"Not good," he returned with a shake of his head. "Point of seven."

Cassie's breath stopped in her lungs. Stunned, all she could do was shake her head. He couldn't have a point of seven. There were only eight cards in the suit. She had one and he'd thrown away one in his discard. All he had was six.

He frowned at her. "Mrs. Marston?"

Lucien shifted in his chair to look at her. Cassie strained to make her voice work. Nothing happened. She wanted to grab Lucien by his lapels and scream about what the earl was doing. Instead, all she could do was gape at him.

As if Lucien heard the words she couldn't speak, vicious pleasure came to life in his expression. Cassie's breath rushed back into her lungs. Lucien believed Lord Bucksden had just cheated. His confirmation of what she'd seen freed her locked tongue.

She looked back at the earl. "You can't have a point of seven," she gasped. "You threw a spade."

Her charge rang in the tense room. Someone gasped. Others began to mutter. Mr. Percy's eyes jerked wide. His hand went to his stomach as if it hurt him. Colonel Egremont's gaze narrowed in blazing anger.

Near Lord Bucksden, the duchess's face paled until she was almost as white as her dress. She pressed a hand to her breast. The earl's face could have been carved from ice.

"You're wrong," he growled, then tilted his hand away from his chest so all could see. He carefully fanned his cards so all the spades were exposed while keeping the rest of his cards tucked behind them, hidden from view. "There are seven here. Only an idiot would throw a spade when he has seven in his hand."

"I'm not wrong," Cassie insisted. "You dealt yourself seven spades, then you threw the smallest one, hoping to replace it with a high card to make a *quartorze*."

The earl started as she revealed to him exactly what he'd done. His surprise vanished beneath rage's cloak. He roared to his feet and turned toward Lucien.

"God take you, Graceton! I knew I shouldn't have agreed to this. You set a sharp on me. These cards are marked. No more! My original wager is legitimate. It will stand!" His words thundered in the quiet room.

Lucien rose to meet him, every line of his body tense. Creases appeared at the corners of his eyes. His mouth was tight.

"Mrs. Marston isn't the sharp in this room. Every man here will attest to that. What she just did to you at this table she did to me two nights ago."

"She did indeed," Lord Ryecroft agreed, his hands folded behind his head as he leaned back in his chair. Although his pose was casual, there was a subdued tension to his form that hinted at an anger as deep as Lucien's. "More to the point, how can you accuse Lord Graceton of trapping you, when it was he who warned you about Mrs. Marston's skill? No one forced you to disregard his warning," he finished with a shrug.

"Lord Graceton speaks the truth. Mrs. Marston is no sharp. We all saw that the other night," Squire Kerr seconded. Other men in the room echoed him.

"We did indeed," called Lady Barbara as she pushed past the squire, then worked her way around the table to her mother's side.

Eliza followed Lady Barbara, only to stop beside Cassie's chair. She looked at Cassie, desperate hope filling her face. The only response Cassie could give her was to grab her hand and hold on for dear life. No cheater was going to take her sister.

Lord Bucksden's control collapsed. He gaped openly at those around him. Mr. Percy slammed his fist against the table.

"If Mrs. Marston says you discarded that seven, then you did it," he almost shouted, his handsome face dark. "If we're looking for sharps in this room, then I think we must look in your direction."

Cassie took a terrified breath. She'd better be right. Mr. Percy had just risked his life on what she'd alleged.

"Do you dare!" Lord Bucksden roared, pivoting to face the younger man, his cards still in his hands. As he turned his back the duchess leaned over to take his discards.

"I do," Mr. Percy said, bowing. "Name your weapon, my lord. I am at your convenience."

Across from Cassie, Eleanor held up the earl's thrown cards. There were only two, not three cards. The duchess closed her eyes and bowed her head. Lady Barbara leaned over her shoulder, whispering. Eleanor shook her head, then sent a hard-edged look at Cassie, as if she couldn't bear the thought of having to support a commoner's claim over that of a noble. She came slowly to her feet.

"And, what of me, my lord? Will you call me out as well when I also name you a cheat?" she asked, her age-deepened voice cutting through the explosion of outraged comments.

Silence was immediate. It thundered in the room, louder than any sound. Lord Bucksden made a garbled sound and whirled to face his patroness.

"What nonsense is this, Your Grace?" he demanded.

"This nonsense," Eleanor snapped and tossed the two cards onto the table so they lay face upward. The eight and the seven of diamonds. "One seems to be missing, and that one happens to be the seven of spades. I know this because I watched you as you lifted it from your hand. You palmed the card."

Every eye was on Lord Bucksden. Colonel Egremont took a step toward the earl.

"I think I shall have to beg a little of your time after you finish with Percy, my lord," he said. Gone was the soft, plain young man who'd played charades with Eliza. A capable soldier stood in his place. "I suddenly find myself thinking that this might not be the first time you've done such a thing. Indeed, I find myself remembering that game we played, the one that cost me almost a thousand pounds."

"I fear I see a trend forming, Bucksden," Lucien said, his harsh voice filled with hints of vindication and triumph. "How many more challenges will follow, my lord, as men begin to ask what happened when you sat at their card table? Tens? At least fifty."

Lord Bucksden turned a sickly green beneath his bruises. Without a word, he left the table, starting for the door. Lord Ryecroft's guests moved aside, forming a corridor so he could pass. To a one they watched his departure, their faces filled with disgust.

"Good riddance to him," Eleanor sniffed. "His mother must have slept with the stable master. No true nobleman cheats."

Chapter 25

C assie sat frozen, capable of doing nothing more than staring at the card table's surface, at her losing hand. She had to force herself to breathe.

It was over. Eliza was safe and so was she. Lord Bucksden wouldn't dare strike out at her, not after what he'd done here.

Slowly she turned her head to look at Lucien. He stood with his arms crossed, his head bowed and his eyes closed. Relief radiated from him.

As Cassie read the message his body sent, the ice that held her captive melted. She came to her feet and grabbed Lucien by the arm, yanking on his sleeve until he turned. Grim satisfaction filled his eyes. Cassie's heart burst into flame as she read the rest of his message.

"You used me!" she cried out. "You and Lord Rye-croft tricked him into agreeing to this game, expecting him to cheat!"

The noise in the room died, except for Eliza's sniffling. Everyone turned to look at Cassie. The satisfaction on Lucien's face mellowed until he was again the man who'd greeted her in their bed that morning. He smiled, his expression radiating love for her. Cassie's anger gave way to confusion. If he still loved her, then why had he been so cold at his lodge, and at Ettrick House?

"We did," he agreed with a nod. "It was unfortunate but necessary, my love."

My love? That he used the endearment in front of all these people punctured Cassie's anger. It fizzled, taking with it the last of the tension that had sustained her over the past hours. Her knees weakened, done in by the enormity of her success.

He caught her by the arms. Emotions flicked through Lucien's gray eyes—compassion, gratitude, but behind it all was love. Love for her. Here, in front of everyone, he put his arm around her.

He looked at their audience. "If you will excuse us? We need a private moment."

The duchess made a disgusted sound, but a good number of the women smiled. A few men chuckled. Lucien led Cassie around the table and toward the french doors. Lord Ryecroft laughed.

"And the curtain falls," he called after them.

Cassie felt as if she walked on stilts, her pace jerky as they exited into the warm, windy day. He led her around a corner. It took her a moment to realize they were in the same alcove they'd used for their kiss. She balked, pulling away from him.

"No, I won't go there. You used me to avenge yourself on Lord Bucksden." Never mind that she would have played that game even if Lucien hadn't been involved at all.

Lucien caught her face in his hands. Cassie clamped her hands around his wrists, intending to force him to release her. His thumbs brushed her cheeks. All the strength left her hands. Sensations stirred, their intensity an all-too-potent reminder of the joy they'd shared.

His skin was warm against hers. As had happened from the moment they made their reacquaintance at the ball, his presence reached out to envelop her. His gray eyes softened.

"You're right," he said, his voice gentle, "I did use you. Tit for tat. Didn't you admit to using me?"

Cassie started to protest that it wasn't the same thing. He shook his head to stop her. "I would never have let Bucksden have your sister, although keeping Eliza from him would have meant airing the story of the wager. It wasn't something I wanted to do, nor would you have wanted that.

"Now, don't nag, Cassie. My little trick worked and he'll live out his life in exile on the Continent." His expression softened. "Instead, marry me."

It wasn't a request, but a command. Cassie's head swam. This was all too confusing.

"But I thought," she started, only to let her comment fade into silence. How could she have been so wrong about him?

He smiled. "You're not the only one who reads others. I know what you thought," he said, then lowered his mouth to brush his lips across hers in a brief caress.

Cassie shivered, then stepped back, still holding him by the wrists. She collided with the alcove's statue. "Why were you so cold when we left your lodge, and when you came to Ettrick House?"

Lucien laughed, closing the gap between them. "Shame on you for having so little trust in your husband," he said, and again brushed his mouth across hers in gentle caress.

Cassie lost herself to the sensation. Her mouth softened beneath his. He made a pleased sound and freed his hands to pull her closer.

That brought her to her senses. She braced her hands on his chest, holding him away from her. "But you weren't and aren't my husband," she told him. "How was I supposed to trust you?"

Lucien touched his lips to the spot beneath her ear. Cassie's reluctant defenses against him strained, sorely tested.

"Of course I am, was, will always be your husband," he murmured against her throat. "Didn't I tell you last night that we'd been married these past six years?"

Cassie couldn't stop her laugh at the reminder of their fantasy union. Her defenses melted, although she still craved an explanation for why he'd done what he had. That didn't stop her from tilting her head, exposing more neck for him to kiss.

"Six years, is it?" she asked.

He moved his mouth down to nuzzle at the place her throat and shoulder met. She shivered. He straightened.

"Marry me," he repeated, again commanding, not asking.

Even besieged by her emotions and her needs Cassie refused to give way. She had to understand all of it. "If you weren't disgusted by the tale of my father's wager, then why did you turn your back to me in"—she caught herself before she said *our bedroom*—"your lodge?"

He grimaced, chagrined. "Must I explain that?"

Cassie fought her smile, his reaction telling her more than words ever could. Her father's behavior wasn't his reason for turning from her. "Yes," she said. It was her turn to command.

"If I must," he sighed.

Turning her, he walked her backward until her back rested against the alcove wall. Cassie didn't resist, not when the memory of their kiss on the same spot was as potent as any aphrodisiac. Lucien almost leaned against her.

"I'm not a man who likes to make a show of anger," he said, his expression a little guarded. "I knew Bucksden surely planned to hurt you after what you'd done to him, and that left me wanting to howl in rage. I didn't know how to protect you. My only purpose in turning away from you was to regain my control. Before I could, your aunt came and took you away."

It was the explanation Cassie needed. Her heart filled with him, almost aching against the power of her joy. Then the longing to once again be at his lodge, in their bed, rushed over her. She slipped her hands into his coat, resting her palms against his chest. The thick silk of his waistcoat felt rough against her skin.

"Now, answer me," he demanded, once again touching kisses down the length of her neck.

She shook her head, once again refusing him. "Explain to me why you had to behave as if you didn't know me when you and Lord Ryecroft came to Ettrick House."

He straightened and caught her face in his hands. Amusement filled his gaze. "You intend to make me work for my answer."

Cassie gave a tiny nod, fighting her smile. She clasped her hands at his nape and pulled herself against him, teasing him. Heat flared in his eyes.

"Trust me. I have a very good reason for it," she whispered, touching her lips to his in playful kisses.

When he could bear it no longer, he kissed her with all the passion of that morning. His arms slipped around her. "I couldn't let Bucksden know there was a connection between us. If he'd known, he would never have accepted your challenge. Answer me," he insisted in a whisper.

She shook her head again, then touched tiny kisses along his jaw. "But you couldn't have known I would challenge him," she breathed against his skin, wanting Lucien as much as this morning.

"You're right, I didn't. I arrived too late to discuss it with you, which was my intent," he replied, his voice hoarse. "I don't know how Devanney managed to keep a straight face when you made your challenge. I had to bend behind Percy's horse so no one saw me grin. Why won't you answer me?"

Cassie shifted to touch a light kiss to his lips, withdrawing as he tried to make the meeting of their mouths more passionate. She did it again, then again, because it fed her need for him.

"Because," she said, punctuating her words with these tiny kisses, "the moment I tell you yes everything will change. You'll take me back inside and announce our engagement, then my aunt will take me home. We won't again be alone until we say our vows. There'll be no kissing, and only the briefest of touches, when I find myself desperate to know what it's like when you bear my weight."

Lucien groaned. He kissed her again, his arm tightening. This time she didn't suppress her desire. Glorious in its hunger, it consumed her. They were both panting when he broke their kiss.

Smiling, he leaned his brow against her forehead. "I cannot wait to show you," he murmured.

She shifted against him, earning his gasp of pleasure. "This is Scotland, not England. We don't need a license here. We can marry as we please," she whispered, praying he'd accept even if a hasty union would be unseemly. She was willing to do anything if it meant a swift return to their bed.

He slid a hand between them to trace the outline of her bodice against her skin. Cassie shivered, and cursed the conservative cut of her dress. He slipped his hand down onto her gown until it rested atop her breast, then slid his palm over its peak. Her corset and gown didn't allow much in the way of feeling, but just the suggestion of his caress was enough to make Cassie gasp.

"Not this time. No impoverished ceremony for us like that one we had six years ago," he said with a quiet laugh, again teasing her. "This time I think I want a grand ceremony."

"Ahem," Philana said from behind them. "Lord Graceton, this is twice today that I find you doing heavens knows what with my niece."

"Oh no," Cassie groaned, her arms tightening around Lucien, not ready to release him.

He gave a hoarse laugh. "I hope that wasn't your answer, love."

Epilogue

⟨⟩⟨⟩

"**T**hen, I now pronounce you man and wife," said the vicar of Ettrick Village's tiny church.

Wearing a new pale blue gown and fine bonnet decorated with brightly colored ribbons and orange blossoms, Cassie turned to face her husband. She boldly rested her hands on his chest. Lucien looked wondrous in his black attire, wearing a waistcoat that was the color of his eyes, his sun-streaked hair brushing his collar.

Her heart filled with love for him, the emotion so intense that she had to blink away tears. He smiled, the bend of his mouth as happy as she felt. Lucien didn't wait for the vicar to suggest a kiss. Catching her face in his hands, he took what he wanted.

There was nothing subtle about it. Her knees weakened. For four weeks, they'd been forced to behave like well-mannered members of society—no stolen kisses, no kidnapping, no pretense of marriage so they could satisfy their longing for each other. For Cassie, not having Lucien in her bed had been excruciating. His nights had been no less empty, or so his kiss told her. Indeed, they were both starving.

Only the barest of a kiss was needed to seal a marriage. That wasn't good enough for him. Theirs stretched far beyond that point.

Their witnesses began to chuckle. Lucien smiled against her lips. He retreated a bare inch.

"I need you. We go straight to my lodge," he breathed. "They can hold their celebration without us." It wasn't a question. Philana had insisted on hosting a celebration to lend a little glamour to the small ceremony.

"Yes," Cassie whispered in return. Then they turned to be presented to the guests they intended to abandon.

The tiny chapel was crowded with both guests and curious villagers. Philana, Eliza and Roland occupied the closest pew on the bride's side. Lord Ryecroft and his sister sat on the other. All of local gentry who'd attended Lord Ryecroft's house party had come, many of them applauding. The only one not participating in the joy was Lucien's sister. Lucien's elder by a number of years, Lady Milicent Waybourne shared her brother's raw-boned features and gray eyes. Where what Lucien called his Hollier features lent him a rugged handsomeness, they made his sister look formidable and austere. Neither she nor the better born members of the *ton* were particularly happy about her brother's choice of wife. Not that Cassie cared. All that mattered was that Lucien loved her.

As they left the altar step, Eliza bounded forward, the first to greet them, hugging Cassie and shaking Lucien's hand. Now that Lord Bucksden's threat was only a memory, she looked like the young miss she was. Eliza's return to carefree innocence was premier among the many things for which Cassie was grateful to Lucien.

Roland came up to them next. His arm was yet bound in a sling. He'd shed at least two stones over the past month. Although they'd had his clothing altered, his garments still seemed to hang on him.

Shame and gratitude filled his face as he shook Lucien's hand. "My lord, I cannot thank you enough for all you've done for us," he muttered.

Lucien had paid Roland's debts, something he said he was induced to do because Roland had tried to convince Lord Bucksden to murder him. However, Lucien had taken the title to both Roland's London town home and his country house, just in case Roland considered again using them for collateral. Roland had agreed without complaint, although he assured Lucien that it wasn't necessary. He insisted his gambling days were over, and that he'd be content to retire to the country, with only Eliza to bear him company.

Philana swiftly replaced Roland, hugging them

both. Tears stained her cheeks and reddened her nose. "I knew I was right about you two," she said, her trembling voice filled with vindication.

"So you were," Lucien agreed, putting his arm around Cassie. His fingers slid provocatively against her hip. She bit back a laugh.

Philana's eyes narrowed. "You will be at Ettrick House in a few moments, won't you?"

"But, of course," Lucien lied. Cassie gave her aunt her most innocent look.

Lord Ryecroft appeared next, pleasure radiating from him. He embraced his cousin. "Much better choice this time, Hollier," he said in approval, then he took Cassie's hands.

"There is but one thing certain between us, my lady. I will never, ever play cards with you," he said, his smile taunting. "Everything else is in question."

Lucien huffed. "Find your own interesting woman to kidnap, Devanney. Touch my wife at your peril." There was nothing but amusement in his tone.

"You win. She's yours," Lord Ryecroft said, backing away from them, his hands lifted in mock surrender.

After the register was signed and the cake distributed, Lucien and Cassie left the church, stepping out into a glorious September day. It was as if God Himself had wanted to honor their wedding. The breeze, bearing a hint of coolness in its warmth, the promise of winter's coming, made Cassie's ribbons flutter. Wood pigeons strutted across the church yard, pecking at the gravel. A corbie cawed from the tall tree beside the church. The horses harnessed to the flower-bedecked phaeton, borrowed from Lord Ryecroft, flicked their tails and stamped.

They paused on the step as Lucien donned his hat and gloves, then started between the ranks of their waiting guests. Mr. Percy, resplendent in his pink-and green-striped waistcoat shouted his congratulations. Squire Kerr and his wife threw rice along with Lady Ross and her mate. Maggie and Jamie Laidlaw applauded with all their might.

Ducking under the shower of grains, a laughing Cassie raced with Lucien to the phaeton. He helped her into the vehicle, then mounted beside her and took the reins. Eliza bounded up to the phaeton, a conspirator's expression on her face.

"Should you not reach the celebration in a timely manner, Maggie says she left you a cold dinner in the lodge." She winked and danced away, joining Philana for the jaunt to Ettrick House. Except for Lady Waybourne and Lord Ryecroft, the rest of the party meant to walk the short distance.

Lucien laughed. "Philana made a formidable enemy when she thwarted Maggie's plan to keep you captive at my lodge," he said.

"Thank God for all matchmakers," Cassie said, easing closer to Lucien, wrapping her hand around his arm as he flicked the reins and set the phaeton into motion.

Shifting the reins into one hand, he patted Cassie's abdomen. "You're safe now, my son. You'll have a father and a name," he said, speaking to the child Cassie believed she carried. She had all the signs, according to Philana.

"What if it's a girl?" Cassie asked.

"Then, we'll keep trying until we get a son," Lucien said with a happy shrug.

"And what if there is no child?" Cassie murmured, fighting her laughter. She already knew what Lucien's answer would be.

"Then I say that it's well past time that we get to the business of making one," he said, then kissed her. It was filled with shared awe and desire.

"How can I love you so much?" she asked him, leaning her head against his shoulder.

"I'm only glad you do. How could I have waited so long to recognize how much I loved you?" he asked with a quiet laugh, then sent her a taunting smile.

"Look at us, six years married and still newlyweds," he teased. "Now, if we don't reach my lodge in the next fifteen minutes, I vow I'll expire from wanting you."

With the snap of the reins he urged the horses to their fastest pace.

Start the New Year with these thrilling new romances coming in January from Avon Books

MARRIED TO THE VISCOUNT by Sabrina Jeffries
An Avon Romantic Treasure

Abigail Mercer had married Viscount Ravenswood by proxy, but when she arrives on his doorstep, the dashing rogue denies their union! Now, rather than risk a scandal, the Viscount has proposed a marriage in name only, but Abigail has other plans.

DO NOT DISTURB by Christie Ridgway
An Avon Contemporary Romance

Investigative reporter Angel Buchanan has just uncovered a whopper: her deadbeat dad is actually a man famous for his family values. But legendary lawyer C.J. Jones is determined to keep Angel quiet . . . and he'll gladly woo her into submission.

NO ORDINARY GROOM by Gayle Callen
An Avon Romance

Jane Whittington wants excitement and adventure, not marriage to a fop! But William Chadwick is more than he seems. And if excitement is what Jane seeks, then he'll give her what she desires . . . one kiss at a time.

SEEN BY MOONLIGHT by Kathleen Eschenburg
An Avon Romance

Annabelle Hallston will do anything to keep her younger brother safe—which is the only reason she agreed to marry Royce Kincaid. The notorious black sheep of an aristocratic family, Royce does not believe in love . . . until Anabelle unlocks his true passion and frees his wounded soul.

Discover Contemporary Romances at Their Sizzling Hot Best from Avon Books

Avon Romantic Treasures

Unforgettable, enthralling love stories,
sparkling with passion and adventure
from Romance's bestselling authors

Have you ever dreamed of writing a romance?

*And have you ever wanted
to get a romance published?*

Perhaps you have always wondered how to
become an Avon romance writer?
We are now seeking the best and brightest undiscovered
voices. We invite you to send us your query letter to
avonromance@harpercollins.com

What do you need to do?

Please send no more than two pages telling us
about your book. We'd like to know its setting—is it
contemporary or historical—and a bit about the hero,
heroine, and what happens to them.

Then, if it is right for Avon we'll ask to see part of the
manuscript. Remember, it's important that you have
material to send, in case we want to see your story quickly.

Of course, there are no guarantees of publication,
but you never know unless you try!

*We know there is new talent just waiting
to be found! Don't hesitate . . . send us
your query letter today.*

**The Editors
Avon Romance**

MSR 0302